Delores Fossen, a *USA TODAY* bestselling author, has sold over fifty novels, with millions of copies of her books in print worldwide. She's received a Booksellers' Best Award and an RT Reviewers' Choice Best Book Award. She was also a finalist for a prestigious RITA® Award. You can contact the author through her website at www.deloresfossen.com.

Julie Anne Lindsey is a multi-genre author who writes the stories that keep her up at night. She's a self-proclaimed nerd with a penchant for words and proclivity for fun. Julie lives in rural Ohio with her husband and three small children. Today, she hopes to make someone smile. One day she plans to change the world. Julie is a member of the International Thriller Writers (ITW) and Sisters in Crime (SinC). Learn more about Julie Anne Lindsey at www.julieannelindsey.com.

Also by Delores Fossen

Always a Lawman
Gunfire on the Ranch
Lawman from Her Past
Roughshod Justice
Grayson
Dade
Nate
Kade
Gage
Mason

Also by Julie Anne Lindsey

Federal Agent Under Fire

Discover more at millsandboon.co.uk

ROUGHSHOD JUSTICE

DELORES FOSSEN

FEDERAL AGENT UNDER FIRE

JULIE ANNE LINDSEY

MILLS & BOON

First Published in Great Britain 2018
by Mills & Boon, an imprint of HarperCollins*Publishers*
1 London Bridge Street, London, SE1 9GF

Roughshod Justice © 2018 Delores Fossen
Federal Agent Under Fire © 2018 Julie Anne Lindsey

ISBN: 978-0-263-26566-8

39-0418

MIX
Paper from
responsible sources
FSC™ C007454

This book is produced from independently certified FSC™ paper to ensure responsible forest management.

For more information visit: www.harpercollins.co.uk/green

Printed and bound in Spain
by CPI, Barcelona

ROUGHSHOD JUSTICE

DELORES FOSSEN

Chapter One

Texas Ranger Jameson Beckett felt his stomach twist into a hard knot. There was too much blood on the ground. Of course, a single drop was too much, but there was enough for there to be multiple dead bodies.

What the devil had happened here?

He stepped around the first pool of blood, around the CSI who was photographing it. There were cops. Medics. The medical examiner. Chaos. A flurry of adrenaline-laced movement, something that came with the territory of a crime scene like this.

The sun was already setting, but Jameson picked through the dusky light and the chaos, looking for his brother, Gabriel, who was the sheriff. Gabriel wasn't the biggest guy in the mix, but he had an air of authority that made him easy to spot. Jameson made his way to him.

"How bad is it?" Jameson asked.

Of course, he partly knew the answer to that. It had to be bad for his brother to call in the Rangers to assist. Gabriel only did that when it was too much for him and his deputies to handle. Those were situations that didn't happen very often in Blue River, the small ranching community they called home.

"We've got two dead bodies." Gabriel tipped his head to the pair just a few yards away.

They were both men, both sprawled out in the pasture as if they'd collapsed in those spots. There was a black SUV not far from them on the road, the doors open, the engine still running.

Since the blood was between the SUV and the men, they'd likely been shot in or near the vehicle and then had gone into the pasture. Maybe to escape their attacker or maybe in pursuit of the person who'd shot them. Then the men had either succumbed to their injuries or been shot again.

Jameson turned back to his brother. "Any idea what we're dealing with? A drug deal gone bad, maybe?"

"No drugs that we can find. But both men were heavily armed. So was she." Gabriel motioned toward the ambulance that was parked just behind his cruiser.

"She?" Jameson asked.

Since it was a simple question, Jameson was more than a little surprised that his brother didn't jump to answer. Instead, Gabriel started leading him in that direction. "I don't know who she is, she won't say, but she keeps asking for you. That's why I called you."

Hell. This could be connected to one of his investigations. He had a couple of female criminal informants helping him with a homicide, and Jameson hoped one of them hadn't been involved in this.

Gabriel stopped to talk to one of the CSIs, and Jameson went ahead to the back of the ambulance, where he immediately saw someone else he knew. Cameron Doran, a deputy in the Blue River sheriff's office. Cameron was also about to be Jameson's brother-in-law since he was engaged to Jameson's kid sister Lauren. Cameron had his hand on his holstered weapon, and he was clearly standing guard.

"Has the woman told you who she is or what happened?" Jameson wanted to know.

"No. She hasn't given us much of anything. She just keeps repeating your name."

Jameson braced himself for the worst, because if his CI was in an ambulance, then she'd clearly been hurt.

And she had been.

The first thing he saw was more blood. It was on her clothes, in her pale blond hair and all over her face, making it hard for him to tell who the heck she was.

"It's not as bad as it looks," one of the medics volunteered. According to his name tag, he was Chip Reynolds. "Head wounds just bleed a lot. It appears she got clubbed, so she needs stitches. She also probably has a concussion, but the doc will need to confirm that. Can we go ahead and take her to the hospital?"

"Not just yet." Jameson wanted to know who and what he was dealing with, and he figured Gabriel would want to know that, as well.

Jameson moved closer, leaning down so he could make eye contact with the woman. Her head whipped up, their gazes connecting. He still didn't recognize her, but he wasn't seeing much of her, either, because of the blood.

"Who are you?" he demanded.

She opened her mouth, closed it and looked up at the EMT as if expecting him to know. He just lifted his shoulder. "She didn't have any ID on her," the medic explained.

"Are you Jameson Beckett?" she said to him.

"I asked first." But then he paused and replayed what he'd just heard.

Hell.

He didn't recognize her hair, her eyes or her face with all that blood, but Jameson sure as heck recognized the voice.

"Kelly?"

Jameson went even closer, and the medic helped by wiping off some of the blood. Yeah, it was Kelly Stockwell all right.

"I thought you were dead," Jameson grumbled.

She blew out a breath, and it sounded like one of relief. Though Jameson couldn't figure out what she was relieved about. She was injured, and there were two dead bodies just yards away from her.

"You know me," Kelly whispered after another of those breaths.

Clearly, this was some kind of sick joke. "Of course I know you."

He had the memories to prove it, too. Memories of Kelly being in his bed. Also memories of her disappearing without so much as a text. Jameson truly hadn't thought she was dead, though, only that she'd run out after she'd gotten what she wanted from him.

And it hadn't been sex that she'd wanted.

"Your sister thinks you're dead, too," he added, just to get his mind back on the right track.

"I have a sister?"

Jameson didn't roll his eyes, but it was close. "Mandy. Ring any bells?"

"No." But she seemed to latch right onto that. "Is she okay?"

"I have no idea. Mandy and I haven't talked in months."

They had in the beginning, though, after Kelly disappeared about two years ago. Jameson had spent several months looking for her without so much as a clue to her whereabouts. Mandy had helped with that. *Some.* Not nearly enough, considering her sister was missing, but Jameson figured not all siblings were as close as he was to his brother and sisters. After that initial search for Kelly had turned up empty, he'd put both the woman and his hunt for her on the back burner.

"Can you call Mandy and make sure she's all right?" Kelly asked. Except it was more than a plea for help. It was a demand.

Jameson huffed. "I thought you said you didn't remember her."

"I don't, but...please, just call or text her."

Jameson considered refusing, but since Mandy could indeed be connected to this, and even if she wasn't, she would want to know that Kelly was alive. He scrolled through his contacts, located Mandy's number and called her. No answer, but when it went to voice mail, Jameson asked her to get in touch with him ASAP.

Kelly thanked him under her breath. Paused. "You're...angry with me," she muttered. "Why?"

A burst of air left his mouth. Definitely not a laugh from humor. "You stole a file about an investigation from my office in my house," he snapped.

Yes, it seemed a bad time to bring that up, especially considering that Kelly obviously had much more serious problems on her hands, but hell in a handbasket, it stung that he'd been so wrong about her. Jameson had trusted her, and she'd pretended to like him so she could get her hands on the file.

The file itself wasn't one of Jameson's cases. Not

officially anyway. But it had been a compilation of everything that had to do with his parents' murders. It had statements of witnesses' accounts, court records and even notes from the investigations his father was working on when he'd been murdered.

She shook her head. "I don't remember anything."

"That's convenient." Jameson didn't bother taking out the sarcasm. "We'll get to that stolen file later. Right now, tell me about those dead men."

Kelly closed her eyes for a moment. Gave a heavy sigh. "Several people have already asked me that. I don't know what happened. I don't know who they are. I don't know who I am."

He didn't repeat the "convenient" comment, but that's exactly what Jameson was thinking.

Of course, it was possible she did have some memory loss. That was a nasty gash near her hairline, and the medic had said she might have a concussion. But pretending to have amnesia would be a quick way for Kelly not to have to answer any of his questions.

Jameson didn't get a chance to say anything else to her. That's because Gabriel finished his chat with the CSI and joined them.

"So who is she?" Gabriel immediately asked Jameson.

"Kelly Stockwell."

She repeated that as if trying to figure out if it was right or if she recognized it. Either she didn't or else was faking it, and tears sprang to her eyes.

A first.

Kelly wasn't the crying sort.

"She's not linked to the…other stuff going on, is she?" Gabriel asked.

Jameson didn't need him to clarify "the other stuff."

They were just two days away from the tenth anniversary of their parents' brutal murders. Murders that had been splattered over every newspaper in the state, and because of all that news coverage, it had brought out a couple of crazies. People who'd wanted to see the old crime scene. Others who'd talked of copycat killings.

At least his parents' killer, Travis Canton, was behind bars and was no longer a threat. Of course, there were some, and Kelly was one of them, who thought the wrong man had been convicted.

Jameson didn't see it that way. Travis and his father had had plenty of run-ins over the land boundaries they shared. Added to that, Travis was a drunk. A mean one. And Jameson believed it was in one of those mean rages that Travis had slipped into the Beckett home and knifed Jameson's dad. When his mother saw what was going on, Travis killed her, too.

And that was the theory the prosecution had used to give Travis a life sentence.

"She's connected in a way," Jameson verified. "She's a PI, and she and her sister, Mandy, owned an agency in San Antonio. A few years back, August hired them to find any evidence to clear Travis's name."

No need to clarify to Gabriel who August was. He was Travis's half brother and a pain because he was always pushing hard to come up with someone else who could have murdered the Becketts. That way, he could spring his brother from jail.

That wasn't going to happen.

At least not with anything August might have gotten from Kelly and Mandy. Even though there hadn't been any new evidence to find, that hadn't stopped Kelly from digging. And she'd done her digging by getting close to Jameson so she could steal that file.

"I didn't know what Kelly was up to when I met her about two years ago," Jameson went on. "I didn't know she was working for August. But when I found out, she disappeared, and her sister eventually closed the business."

Jameson didn't mention anything about his sleeping with Kelly. Didn't have to do that. Gabriel slid him a glance to let him know that he knew. It was that sixth sense that his big brother had.

"I take it there's some bad history…and more…between you two," Gabriel added, and he aimed a look at Kelly.

"You could say that. At best she's a liar and a thief. She stole everything I had about our parents' murder investigation, including files with info that hadn't been released to the public." Obviously, though, that was the least of her worries right now. "Who found her?" Jameson asked. "Who called this in?"

"A guy driving by saw the two men in the pasture, and Kelly was running away. Or rather trying to do that. She collapsed near the ditch. Since she was armed, the guy didn't get out of his truck, but he called it in. I had him go to the station to wait for me, and I'll question him later."

Good. Jameson wanted to hear what the man had to say. But more than that, he wanted to finish this conversation with Kelly.

"I can ride in the ambulance with her to the hospital," Jameson offered.

Gabriel didn't exactly jump to agree to that. Probably because he knew Jameson wasn't in the best of moods.

Still, Gabriel also knew that Jameson wouldn't do anything to disrespect the badge. It didn't mean, however, that he wouldn't grill Kelly. As much as he could grill an injured woman anyway.

"Watch your step with her," Gabriel warned him as Jameson got into the ambulance. "When I frisked her, she had two guns and a knife, and she would have hit me with a karate chop if I hadn't gotten out of the way in time."

"I thought you were going to try to kill me," Kelly said.

Jameson hadn't even been sure she was listening, but she obviously was. He also hadn't remembered Kelly having any martial arts skills. Of course, probably everything she'd told him about herself was a lie. As far as Jameson was concerned, he didn't really know the woman in front of him.

"Are you going to try to kill me?" she came out and asked, glancing first at Gabriel and Cameron. Then at Jameson.

Jameson tapped his badge. "I'm not the bad guy here."

Her gaze darted away from his, and she took another of those uneasy breaths. "Sometimes bad guys wear badges."

That didn't sound like a guess or a general observation. "Is your amnesia cured and you're remembering something specific?" Jameson pressed.

But he instantly regretted the snark. More tears came, and even though Kelly quickly brushed them away—cursed them, too—Jameson still saw the pain on her face. Not just physical pain, either. Whether or not the amnesia was real, she'd still been through some kind of ordeal.

"The CSI swabbed her hands for gunshot residue," Gabriel explained, "but she put up a real fight about being fingerprinted."

Jameson pulled back his shoulders. People who did that usually didn't want their identities known. Coupled with the dyed hair—Kelly had been a brunette when he'd met her—she was obviously trying to disguise her appearance. Even her eyes were different. She'd hidden her green eyes with brown contacts.

"Call me if she says anything we can use to figure this out," Gabriel added, shutting the ambulance door.

Jameson nodded and got seated just as the ambulance driver took off. The EMT continued to hold a compress to Kelly's head and probably would have to do that the entire time since it was still bleeding.

It wouldn't be a long ride to the hospital, only about ten minutes, and Jameson wanted to make the most of that time. He started by reading Kelly her rights. Gabriel had likely already done that, but Jameson didn't want there to be any unticked boxes if she did confess to everything.

Whatever "everything" was.

"Did you shoot those two men?" he asked. "And before you lie, just remember we'll know if you've fired a gun because there'll be gunshot residue on your hands. Your weapons will be tested, too."

She touched her fingers to her mouth, which was trembling a little. "I honestly don't know if I shot them or not. They're dead?"

He nodded, though the confirmation might not have

even been necessary. Because she might already know the answer. "Who were they?"

An immediate head shake that time. So fast that the medic told her to keep still. "I don't know that, either," Kelly answered. Her gaze came to Jameson's again. "Did you send them after me?"

There it was again—her distrust of him. Well, the feeling was mutual. "Let's get something straight. I didn't send thugs after you. I'm not here to kill you. Everything I've told you has been the truth, but you can't say the same, can you?"

She stared at him. "You're talking about that file you mentioned to the sheriff. I don't remember it. I need to remember," she added as she choked back a hoarse sob. "Because I have to know who you really arc and why this is happening."

He huffed again. "I'm really Jameson Beckett, Texas Ranger," he supplied. "Now, start from the beginning. Tell me everything you know, everything you remember."

"I remember them," she said, glancing at Chip and the other EMTs. "And the sheriff. Someone swabbed my hands."

That was a good start, but nowhere near what he wanted. "What do you recall before that?" Jameson pressed. "Before the sheriff and the EMTs arrived."

Kelly stayed quiet for several moments. "I remember the pain in my head. Being on the ground. It was damp. And I saw the blood." She stopped, her gaze going to his again. "What did the sheriff mean when he said there's a bad history *and more* between us?"

Well, there was nothing wrong with her short-term memory, that was for certain. Jameson didn't answer her, but he thought she understood what he wasn't saying because she muttered a simple response.

"Oh." Then she groaned. "Oh, God." The tears filled her eyes again. "But it doesn't make sense."

"I agree. Not much about this makes sense, but you mean something specific. What exactly?" When she didn't answer, Jameson added another question, one that was at the top of his list of things he wanted to know. "If you don't remember anything, why did you keep asking for me?"

"Because of this." She moved her hand to the front of her shirt. Then stopped. "I need to show you something, and I don't want you to shoot me."

"Is it another gun or knife?" he growled. Because he was pretty sure his brother would have found something like that when he frisked her.

"No. It's a message."

Everything inside Jameson went still. "What kind of message?"

Her hands were shaking when she unbuttoned her top. Some of the blood had soaked through to her chest, too, and that's why it took Jameson a moment to see the small piece of paper that she took from her bra. She unfolded it, the trembling in her hands getting even worse, and she showed it to him.

What the heck?

Jameson drew his gun. "Explain that," he demanded, tipping his head to the note.

Or rather the threat.

Kill Jameson Beckett or you'll never see her again.

Chapter Two

Kelly hadn't been sure what Jameson's reaction would be, but she'd known it wouldn't be good. And it wasn't.

The anger flared through those already-intense blue eyes.

Eyes that she wished she could remember.

There was something about him that tugged at her. Attraction, probably. He was a hot cowboy after all. But there seemed to be something else. Something that she wished would become clearer in her muddled mind. Clearer because the last thing she wanted to do was kill this man.

He was glaring at her now, but still she studied him. Hoping there was something about him that would trigger a memory. He was tall and lanky. Dark brown hair like his brother. The family resemblance was there as well, but it wasn't a resemblance that caused her to recall anything other than what'd happened to her in the past half hour or so.

"Who wrote that message?" Jameson snarled. He snapped a picture of it with his phone and sent the photo to someone. Probably the sheriff. Then, taking the note just by the edge, he snatched it from her and put it on the seat next to him.

Kelly buttoned up her top. She definitely didn't want to sit there with her bra exposed. "I don't know who wrote it or how I got it."

That was the truth. And it was something she figured she'd be saying a lot tonight. She prayed this memory loss was temporary. Prayed, too, that her injuries weren't so serious that she couldn't get the heck out of there ASAP. Other than the attraction she was feeling toward Jameson, she knew in her gut that it wasn't safe to be here.

Plus, there was the "her" in the message.

It was obvious someone—a woman—was in danger.

"I think it could mean my sister," she added. "That's why I had you try to call her. Could you try again, please?"

He glared at her, hesitated, but he did fire off a text to someone. Kelly had no memories of Mandy, but if those dead men had taken her, their comrades could be holding her somewhere.

Waiting for Kelly to do what they'd demanded and kill Jameson.

"If you really have amnesia," Jameson went on, still snarling, "how did you know that message was there?"

"I just knew." It was an answer that obviously didn't please him, because he cursed. "Why would someone want you dead?" she asked.

Jameson gave her another of those flat, scowled looks. "I'm a Texas Ranger, and I've put a lot of people in jail. One of them might not be happy about that."

Yes, it could be that. But she had the feeling there was more to it. Jameson confirmed that several seconds later.

"My family has been getting threatening emails and letters." His jaw clenched. "Threats connected to my parents, who were murdered ten years ago. The killer is in a maximum security prison, but someone has been sending out these sick messages to taunt us." He tipped his head to the note. "Messages like that one."

"Is there a *her* in any of those emails or letters?" she asked.

"No. But that doesn't mean it's not from the same person. Are you the one threatening us, Kelly?"

She tried to pick through the tornado in her head but couldn't latch onto anything. Other than the pain. "I don't think so. No," she amended. She didn't want to harm Jameson. Didn't want to harm anyone. She just wanted to figure out what the heck was going on. "Was I connected to your parents' murders, to their killer?"

Now it was his turn to shake his head. "Not to the murders but to August Canton. His brother is the one who was convicted of killing my folks. August somehow convinced you of his brother's innocence, so you were looking for anything to help with the appeals. You stole from me to do that."

Yes, she'd heard the conversation that he'd had with his brother about the stolen file. Again, no memory, and it didn't seem like something she would have done. Especially steal from a man who'd likely been her lover.

Kelly repeated August Canton's name, hoping it would trigger something. It didn't. "I don't remember him, either. Could any of this be linked to August or his brother?"

"Not Travis, because he's in jail." Then he paused. "But even if August or he managed to arrange something like this, I can't imagine either of them going about it this way. You're not a hired gun. Or at least you weren't two years ago."

And she wasn't now. Kelly was certain of that. However, she didn't get a chance to try to convince him because the ambulance pulled to a stop in front of the emergency room doors of the hospital. The EMTs used the gurney to take her inside.

There was a uniformed deputy waiting for them, and when they went in, Jameson immediately motioned toward the note that he'd left on the seat. "Bag that and show it to Gabriel. I'll need her clothes bagged, too."

Yes, because there might be some kind of evidence on them. She hoped so anyway. She needed answers.

"Who were those dead men in the pasture?" she asked. "Do you have ID's on them?"

Jameson seemed annoyed with her question. Of course, he probably was annoyed—and highly concerned—about all of this. Because of the note that had ordered her to kill him.

"We'll know more soon," he finally answered. "Especially when you remember what you should be remembering."

There it was again, the tone that indicated he didn't believe her. She couldn't blame him. There were two dead guys, a threatening note and an ex-lover who didn't have a clue what was going on.

The medics transferred her to an examining table in a room just off the ER, and Kelly immediately looked around to make sure someone wasn't there, ready to come after her. Every nerve in her body was on high alert, and she prayed if there was another attack, she could protect herself.

Jameson didn't immediately come into the room with her, but he stayed in the doorway while he made a call. However, he didn't take his attention off her. Too bad.

Because Kelly thought it might be a good idea for her to put some distance between Jameson and her.

While he was still on the phone, a nurse came in, took her vitals and made a quick check of her head wound. It was throbbing, but that was the least of her problems right now. Apparently the least of Jameson's, too, because whatever he was hearing on the phone caused his forehead to bunch up.

"What's wrong?" she asked the moment he ended the call.

The nurse mumbled something about the doctor seeing her soon and walked out, leaving them alone.

"Your sister's still not answering her phone, so I'm having the San Antonio cops go out and check on her," Jameson said.

"Good. Thank you." But that wasn't an explanation for the renewed tension in his face. "What else?"

"You have gunshot residue on your hands, and one of the guns you had matches the wounds on the dead guys. It's looking as if you're the one who killed them."

Kelly felt the tears again. Felt the icy slam of fear in her chest. "I don't think I had a choice. I think they were trying to kill me."

Jameson blew out a long breath. It sounded bad. *Was* bad, she mentally corrected. She'd been sent to kill him. Maybe those men had been sent to kill her. And whoever had orchestrated it was maybe still out there. Maybe that someone was also the reason her sister wasn't able to answer her phone.

Kelly tried to focus, tried to make sense of the whirl of memories that were in her throbbing head. But when she wasn't able to sort through it, she decided it was time to get as much info from Jameson as he would give her. Maybe then she could use that to piece together this puzzle.

"We were lovers?" she asked.

"No. Yes," he amended after he cursed. "We had sex, but it was all a ploy on your part to steal that file."

That. They kept going back to that file. "Why would I help someone like August Canton?"

"You tell me. In fact, I wanted to ask you that question about two years ago, but you disappeared."

Maybe Mandy would be able to help with that. She likely would have told her sister why she had disappeared. Well, maybe. If her sister and she had been close—since they'd owned a PI business together, maybe that meant they had been.

"Other than the Canton case, any idea what else I was working on around that same time?" she asked.

Kelly hadn't figured that Jameson would actually know. Especially if she had gotten involved with him because of the Cantons, and that's why she was surprised when he readily answered.

"You were investigating a guy named Frank Worley."

Finally, that sounded familiar. More than familiar. It sent another chill through her. "He's a money launderer."

Jameson stared at her and then moved closer. Too close. And he looked into her eyes. "That's what the San Antonio PD thought. So did one of his former employees. You remember that?"

"No." But she motioned for him to continue.

He did, after he huffed. "Worley's ex-girlfriend, Hadley Beecham, hired you to find their infant daughter, Amy, whom she claimed Worley had stolen and hidden.

Hadley was killed in a suspicious car accident, but that only made you dig deeper into the case."

She thought about that for a moment. "Maybe Worley's the reason I disappeared. Maybe he's the reason this is happening now?"

Jameson shrugged. "Worley's bad news, I have no doubts about that. But I was never able to link your disappearance to him."

"You searched for me," she said. But wished she hadn't. That comment only put more frustration back into his eyes.

"Because you stole that file," he grumbled.

So he'd been looking for her to arrest her. Maybe still would. But she instinctively knew that it wouldn't be safe to be locked up where someone could get to her. Everything inside her was screaming that she should get to a safe place, and behind bars wouldn't be that place. Plus, she wouldn't be able to look for that *her*.

A man stepped into the room. He was wearing jeans and a blue shirt, but he was in the process of putting on a white coat with a name tag stitched on it. According to the name tag, he was Dr. Timothy Halston.

"It's okay," Jameson said, taking hold of her arm. Until he did that, Kelly hadn't even been aware that she was trying to get off the table. "He's the local doc in Blue River."

Neither the doctor nor his name meant anything to her, but Blue River rang some bells. It was Jameson's hometown. She was sure of it. And she'd been on her way there when, well, when the incident with those men had happened.

"Jameson's right," the doctor added. "And I need to have a look at that gash on your head."

The doctor moved in to do that just as Jameson's phone rang. He stepped back into the doorway, moving away from her. Something that sent her heart racing. Even though she wasn't sure she could fully trust Jameson, right now Kelly trusted him more than she did anyone else.

"It's not that deep of a cut, but I guess you took a hard enough lick on the head to mess up your memory," the doctor continued, but Kelly tuned him out and tried to hear what the caller was telling Jameson. He didn't put his phone on speaker, but after a few seconds, he mumbled some profanity.

"When?" Jameson asked the caller.

She had to look around the doctor when he moved in front of her to continue the exam. Not that there was much to see or hear. Jameson was clearly in listening mode. And like before, he didn't like whatever it was he was hearing.

"When will I get my memory back?" Kelly asked the doctor.

"Can't say. Sometimes, these things only last an hour or so. Sometimes, longer. I'll order some tests," the doctor said, waving a penlight in front of her eyes. "How bad is the pain?"

"I'm okay," she lied. But there was no way she wanted pain meds. Her head was already too foggy as it was.

"All right. Then I'll get started on those tests." The doctor again. "A nurse will be in soon to take you where you need to go."

Jotting down some notes, the doctor left, but it took Jameson several more seconds to finish up his call. Even when he put his phone away and came back to her, he took his time saying anything.

"Is it Mandy?" she came out and asked.

Jameson nodded and didn't seem surprised that she'd guessed that. "The cops went to her apartment. She wasn't there, but it appeared there had been some kind of struggle."

Oh, mercy. So this probably was connected to her sister. Someone likely had her and was holding her hostage.

"They found blood in her apartment," Jameson added.

He had to take hold of her again or she would have bolted. Where, Kelly didn't know, but she had to find her sister.

"The cops are looking for her." Jameson's grip stayed firm on her arm until she quit moving. Then he waited until their gazes were connected before he continued. "A neighbor said she saw Mandy with two men about five hours ago. She didn't see any guns, but Mandy was walking in between the two."

Kelly had to press her hand to her chest to try to steady her heart and her breathing. "Why didn't the neighbor call the cops?"

"She didn't think anything was wrong and didn't see any signs of an injury. Apparently, she doesn't know Mandy that well so she thought they might be friends."

Definitely not friends. Not with that blood in the apartment. Even though the neighbor hadn't noticed any injuries, it didn't mean Mandy hadn't been hurt in some way. Now those goons had had her for five hours or more, and there was no telling what they could have done to her.

"They're holding her until I kill you." Kelly hadn't intended to say that aloud, but judging from the sound of agreement Jameson made, that was his theory, too.

"Please tell me you're remembering something. *Anything*," he added, "that'll help us with this."

Kelly tried again, but the jumble was still there. She tried to catch on to bits of it, but there was only one thing that was clear. "I'll never see her again if they find out you're still alive." And finally something fell from that jumble. Not a memory. But an idea of how to fix it. "Is there a way for you to fake your death?"

No sound of agreement, but he didn't jump to nix the idea, either. "But then what? Whoever has your sister might just decide to tie up loose ends and kill her. You're a loose end, too."

Yes. The worst kind. Because somewhere in that jumble of memories was perhaps the identity of the person responsible.

"I can't just sit here and wait," Kelly said. Her voice hardly had any sound, and the blasted tears came again. She cursed the tears because they wouldn't help. Heck, nothing might at this point. She could risk the men coming after her, but she couldn't take the chance that they would murder Mandy.

"There's more," Jameson said, sitting on the table beside her. "The neighbor gave the cops a description of the men who were with your sister." He paused. "It matches the description of the two dead guys."

Kelly snapped back her shoulders and shook her head. "I don't think Mandy was with me tonight. Was she?"

"There was no sign of her, but the CSI team will process the dead guys' SUV. We'll also show the neighbor their pictures to see if she can confirm that's really the people she saw."

And if they were the same men, then that could mean only one thing. Well, one thing if Mandy was still alive. "They wouldn't just kill Mandy if they plan to use her for leverage to get me to do…something." The "some-thing" in this case was to murder Jameson. "That means they must have her stashed somewhere."

He nodded. "Gabriel will check it out. There might be something on their GPS. The CSIs will also check their phones so that we can try to pinpoint where they'd been in the past five hours."

All of that was a good start, but it wasn't nearly enough. "I can search for her, too."

He gave her another of those flat looks. He was good at them, too. "You're staying here and having those tests. In fact, you'll probably have to spend the night here."

Now she was the one to give him a flat look. That wasn't going to happen even if she had to sneak out. Too bad she hadn't managed to hang on to at least one of those weapons the sheriff had confiscated. Of course, even if she had them, Kelly wasn't sure she'd remem-ber how to use them.

"So what can I do?" she came out and asked.

"You can stay put and let the cops and me do our jobs." He opened his mouth, no doubt to add more. Probably a warning for her not to try to escape. But movement in the doorway caught their attention. At first, Kelly thought maybe it was the nurse coming to take her to those tests, but it was a man. Jameson got to his feet, moved in front of her and drew his gun.

Kelly stood, too, and she peered over Jameson's

shoulder to get a better look at the man with the shaved head and bulky build. He was tall, at least six-four, and wearing a suit.

"Frank Worley," Jameson said like profanity. "What the hell are you doing here?"

Worley. The man she'd been investigating when she disappeared. He might also be the man who'd hired those thugs to take Mandy.

"No need for that gun," Worley insisted. "And I'm going to show you why. Don't shoot me when I pull back my jacket."

"Don't give me a reason to shoot you," Jameson countered. "But if you pull a gun, you're a dead man."

"What I'm going to show you isn't a gun, but I'm carrying one. And here's why." Worley eased open his jacket, and she immediately spotted something she hadn't expected to see.

A badge clipped to his belt.

"I'm a Justice Department agent," Worley added, his attention sliding from Jameson to her. "My real name is Lawrence Boyer. And I'm here to arrest Kelly for murder."

Chapter Three

Jameson didn't know who was more stunned with Worley's announcement—him or Kelly. But Kelly did look as if she was about to try to sprint out of there. Jameson wouldn't let her do that. Nor would he take anything Worley said, or what he was wearing, at face value.

Including that badge or his name.

"Federal agent, huh?" Jameson asked him, and he didn't bother to sound even marginally convinced.

Worley blew out a long breath as if annoyed with this. Well, Jameson was annoyed, too. He didn't have time for this clown, especially since Worley could be behind the attack and Mandy's disappearance. Jameson didn't want to examine why he was suddenly on Kelly's side. But when it came to Worley, he was.

"I figured you wouldn't believe me." Worley checked his watch. "But you should be getting a call any second now from someone you will believe. Your brother, the sheriff. He's verifying now that I'm an agent. Once that's done, you'll turn Kelly over to me."

"I won't go with him," Kelly said just as Jameson snarled, "Like hell I'll turn her over to you."

That caused Kelly to look at him, and he saw not tears this time but an unspoken thanks. But a thanks wasn't going to help right now. He needed some things cleared up.

"Who are you claiming Kelly murdered?" Jameson asked.

"Those two men your brother and his deputies are investigating."

Jameson certainly couldn't deny that she had been the one to shoot them. In fact, the evidence pointed to her doing it. But the evidence was equally clear that she'd also been attacked, probably by those two men. Unless...

He didn't like even thinking it, but Jameson had to at least consider it. Kelly could be playing him again. She might have had a beef with those guys. Could have even written the note herself. But none of that felt right, especially now that Mandy was missing.

"Who were those men?" Kelly asked Worley.

Worley just stared at her. "You tell me."

"She can't," Jameson volunteered. "See that cut on her head? Someone clubbed her, and she has amnesia."

Worley looked as skeptical about that as Jameson probably had when he'd first heard Kelly say that she couldn't remember. But some of that skepticism was fading. Worse, he suddenly felt the need to protect Kelly. Coupled with the remnants of the old attraction, that wasn't a good combination.

Jameson's phone rang, the sound slicing through the room. Slicing through him, too, because he saw Gabriel's name on the screen.

"Worley's here," Jameson answered, and he put the call on speaker so that Kelly could hear.

"Yeah. And if he told you he's a Justice Department

agent, he is," Gabriel said. "I just confirmed it. His real name is Lawrence Boyer."

Kelly hadn't had much color in her face, but that rid her of what she did have. "Impossible."

Normally, Jameson would have agreed with her, but he didn't doubt anything Gabriel told him.

"My source in the Justice Department is reliable," Gabriel continued, "and according to him, Boyer aka Worley is a joe, someone who spends months or even years in deep cover."

So Boyer had told the truth, about being an agent anyway. "Does he have a court order for Kelly's arrest?" Jameson asked.

"No. Why? Is that why Boyer says he's there? Because my source couldn't tell me."

"Yep, but without a court order, Boyer's not taking our witness to what could be a double homicide. You agree?"

"Agreed," Gabriel quickly said. "You need backup?"

"Not yet. I'll call you if I do." Jameson finished the call, slipped his phone back in his pocket and turned to Agent Boyer. "Tell me everything you know about those men," Jameson demanded. "In fact, tell me everything you know about Kelly."

Boyer volleyed several glances at Kelly and him. For a moment Jameson thought he was going to have to remind this agent that the Rangers and the sheriff had jurisdiction here and that meant Boyer had to cooperate. Even if it was obvious that was the last thing he wanted to do.

"You really don't remember anything?" Boyer pressed when his attention finally settled on Kelly.

"I remember a few things." It sounded as if Kelly was

carefully choosing her words. And lying. But maybe she didn't want this guy to know that she had no memory of her association with him. Perhaps it was her way of forcing Boyer to tell the truth.

"I met you and your sister about two years ago," Boyer finally started. "By then, I'd been on a deep cover assignment for well over a year, and I was posing as a money launderer so I could gather info on a cartel operating in the state. I didn't tell many people who I really was, but I told you, and I gained your trust."

"What?" Kelly snapped. She looked over the man from head to toe, and there wasn't a drop of trust in her eyes or expression.

Boyer nodded. "Mandy and you were working for my ex, Hadley." His mouth tightened when he said her name. "She was accusing me of stealing our newborn daughter, but you soon realized she was just doing that to get back at me because I'd broken things off with her. After that, you agreed to help me."

Jameson went through that info, but it only created more questions. "Hadley knew you were an agent?"

"No. And that should tell you something about her. She got involved with me while thinking I was a criminal."

Jameson lifted his shoulder. "It tells me something about you, too. It tells me you were lying to a woman pregnant with your child."

Boyer's mouth tightened even more, and his eyes were narrowed when he turned to Jameson. "The pregnancy was an accident. On my part anyway. I think Hadley planned it to trap me into marriage. When I didn't go for that and broke off the relationship, she retaliated by accusing me of kidnapping the child just days after she was born."

As much as Jameson hated to admit it, that could all be true. He didn't know Hadley, and in his line of work, he ran into plenty of people who didn't mind bedding down with criminals.

"So what happened to your daughter?" Jameson asked.

"I don't know." Boyer scrubbed his hand over his face. "I suspect Hadley had Amy hidden away from me and the cops, and when she was killed in the car accident, the location of that hidden place died with her. Don't get me wrong. I haven't given up finding my daughter, but at the moment I've run out of leads."

Kelly made a sound, sort of a muffled moan. Maybe because she realized this could turn out to be a similar situation for her sister. With a similar ending of them never finding her. But Jameson wanted to prevent that from happening, and maybe Boyer could help with that. He was about to ask Boyer to spill all about the two dead guys, but Kelly spoke to Boyer before he could do that.

"You said you got me to trust you. How exactly did you manage that?" Kelly asked. "Because I'm certainly not feeling any trust for you now."

Boyer made a sound of agreement. "Ditto. I don't trust you, either. But your misplaced mistrust is probably because you betrayed me. That's how you got into this mess you're in right now."

Jameson moved to Kelly's side so he could face Boyer. "Explain that," Jameson insisted.

"After I told Mandy and you I was an agent, you both said you'd back off so that my cover wouldn't be blown. A blown cover could have gotten me killed by the men I was doing business with. You also agreed to help me with my assignment." Boyer paused, gathered his breath. "I needed you to get a file from Jameson."

Jameson had anticipated what Boyer might say, but he certainly hadn't anticipated *that*. He looked at Kelly to see if she was remembering any of this, but she only shook her head.

"What file?" Jameson snapped. "And why the hell not just come to me for it?"

"I didn't go to you because I didn't want you to know I was an agent. I didn't want it leaked, and at the time there were rumors that there was a mole in the Rangers."

"There wasn't a mole," Jameson argued once he got his jaw unclenched. If so, he would have darn sure heard about it.

"I couldn't risk it. I'd already told Mandy and Kelly, but I only did that so I could get any information you had on your parents' murders."

Of course, he'd known the file that Kelly had stolen was about the murders, but he didn't care for a deep cover agent having an interest in the case. He made another circling motion for Boyer to continue.

But Boyer only said two words. "August Canton."

Now Jameson had to take a moment because the memories came. Of his parents' murders. Of the pain and grief over losing them.

"August was originally a murder suspect," Jameson said. "Several people were. But my father was also investigating a situation where a local widow, Hattie Osmond, had been milked out of lots of money. August was a suspect in that crime, too, but Hattie refused to name him. She passed away last year so there's no way to press her for the truth."

Boyer nodded. "I interviewed her. So did Kelly."

"Kelly?" Jameson repeated. She seemed just as surprised about that as he was.

"Yeah. She talked to Hattie about two years ago. And she questioned Marilyn Deavers, the woman who'd given August an alibi for the night of your parents' murders."

Jameson looked at Kelly, but she only shook her head. "I don't know why I did that. Or if I learned anything."

"Marilyn is dead now, too," Boyer went on. "She died in a car accident."

So if Marilyn had altered her story about August being with her, then there'd be no way to confirm it. Unless they found that file.

"I believe August did scam money from Hattie," Boyer continued a moment later. "Maybe others, as well. But that's not why I was investigating him. I believe August is involved in a money laundering scheme. I'd hoped there'd be something in your files that would help, something that hadn't been in any of the police and FBI reports. But there wasn't."

Kelly whispered a single word of profanity under her breath. "So I stole that file for nothing?"

"I obviously didn't know that at the time." Boyer didn't sound the least bit apologetic, either. "When I realized the file was useless, I pressed you to get more info from Jameson. You said you would, but then you disappeared."

"Why did I do that?" she asked.

"I have no idea. I didn't hear from you for two years,

and then this morning, I got a frantic phone call from you. You said you were in Houston and that someone was trying to kill you."

"Someone did try." She touched her fingers to her head. "Who?"

"I don't know that, and you didn't know, either. You said someone tried to run you off the road, and you needed my help."

Jameson considered maybe that was how she'd gotten the head injury, but he dismissed it. She'd been bleeding in the ambulance, and that didn't look like a wound that'd happened hours earlier. It still looked fresh.

Kelly looked at Jameson. She opened her mouth, closed it, and it seemed as if she changed her mind about what she was going to say.

Had she remembered something?

Something that would incriminate her?

"I told you to go to a hotel," Boyer continued, "and stay there until I could arrange security. I sent two men, both federal agents, and I believe those are the two men you killed tonight."

Kelly fumbled around behind her, located the table and sank back down on it. "Why would I have done that?"

"You tell me." Boyer glared at her. "That's why you're under arrest."

"She's not," Jameson argued. "Remember that part about you not having a court order. Plus, we don't even have ID's on the dead guys so we don't know if they're agents or not. They could be the same men who were trying to kill Kelly in Houston. Once the doc has released her, we'll all go to the sheriff's office and get this straightened out."

That didn't please Boyer, and he gave Jameson more of that glare. "Why are you protecting her?" Boyer growled. "Are you sleeping with her again?"

Jameson hadn't cared much for Boyer, and that question didn't help. "Before tonight, I hadn't seen her in two years, either."

He considered telling Boyer about the note that Kelly had tucked inside her shirt. But decided against it. Best to keep that close to the vest until they could figure out what was going on. That started with identifying those two men. And making sure Kelly got the medical attention she needed.

"We also have a witness," Jameson added just to test Boyer's reaction. "Someone saw part of the altercation between Kelly and the two dead men."

And it got a reaction all right. Boyer's eyes widened. "Who is it? I want to see the person right now."

"He's in protective custody."

Not exactly a lie. The guy was at the sheriff's office and had hopefully stayed there. Just in case he was thinking about leaving, Jameson stepped to the side and sent a text to Gabriel to tell him to keep an eye on the man and to keep him away from Boyer. Until Jameson was certain he could trust this agent, he didn't want him to be part of the investigation.

"Are you warning your brother that I'm on my way to the sheriff's office?" Boyer snapped.

"I sure am," Jameson admitted.

Boyer cursed and glanced around as if debating whether he should leave or stay there to watch the woman he intended to arrest. "Kelly's not to leave here unless I say so," Boyer said as if his order would be obeyed. "I'll come back after I've spoken to this witness."

"Good luck with that." And Jameson didn't bother to take the sarcasm out of his voice.

As much as Jameson hated to pawn Boyer off on Gabriel, he was relieved when the agent stormed out. But not nearly as relieved as Kelly was. She blew out a long breath, and while she didn't exactly relax, her muscles seemed to loosen up a bit.

"Please don't let him take me," she whispered.

He couldn't promise her that it wouldn't happen. If Boyer did manage to get that court order, then Jameson would have no choice, and that's why he needed to press the CSIs to get identities on those dead men. However, his phone rang before he could even start the call. Not Gabriel this time, but rather Cameron.

"Jameson, we got a problem," Cameron said the moment he answered. "The security guard at the hospital just called 911. He said there's a guy in the back parking lot, and that he's got a rifle."

Chapter Four

Kelly's breath froze. From the moment she'd been carried into the hospital, she'd had a bad feeling about this place. It just wasn't safe. And the gunman that the security guard had spotted proved it.

The gunman was after her.

She didn't need her memories to know that, but it certainly would have helped if she remembered why someone wanted her dead. Because if she knew the why, then maybe she could figure out who was behind this. And perhaps put an end to it. Of course, at the moment she wasn't in shape to stop much of anything. But she did need to get the heck out of there.

Kelly stood to do just that, but Jameson immediately made sure that didn't happen. "You're not going anywhere," he warned her. However, he did draw his gun from his holster and stepped in front of her.

Protecting her.

She figured that wasn't something he especially wanted to do, but he was a lawman, and he probably considered this to be part of his job.

"Get me some backup now and patch me through to the security guard," Jameson told Cameron. He now had the phone sandwiched between his shoulder and ear. It only took a few seconds for that to happen.

Seconds that the man in the parking lot could be using to make his way to the hospital. Kelly looked around for something, anything, she could use as a weapon, but other than some medical equipment, there wasn't much. Plus, she definitely wouldn't win a hand-to-hand fight with this guy. Not with the way her head was still spinning. She could barely stand up.

"Hank, do you still have eyes on the guy with the gun?" Jameson asked the security guard.

Jameson didn't put the call on speaker, but since Kelly was right behind him, she heard the guard answer. "Yeah, but he's on the move. He's darting from one car to another, using them for cover, but he's definitely heading this way."

Jameson growled out some profanity under his breath. "Some deputies are on the way, but if you have to, shoot this idiot. Don't go for a kill shot, though, because I'd like to take him alive." He paused. "Did another man just leave the building? Bulky build and bald?"

"No. Haven't seen anybody like that. Why? Is he dangerous, too?"

"Maybe," Jameson answered. "Just watch your back around him if he shows up. And lock down the hospital. There could be other gunmen at the front or sides of the building."

She hadn't needed anything else to rev up her heartbeat, but that did it. There could be any number of hired guns, and Kelly doubted that just locking up would keep them all out.

Jameson ended the call, putting the phone back in his

pocket, and he looked at her. "I need to go to the guard to make sure this gunman doesn't get out of the parking lot. I know the guard—Hank Winston—but I have no idea if he's a good enough shot to stop this person."

And even if he was a good shot, it was too big of a risk to take. The gunman could shoot an innocent bystander. Heck, if he got inside, he could shoot Hank as well before coming after her.

"I want to go, too," Kelly insisted. "Just give me a gun."

Jameson gave her a flat look. "No gun. But I don't think it's a good idea to leave you here alone since we don't know where Boyer is. That means I want you to come with me, but I don't want you to do anything stupid."

She nearly asked Jameson what he would consider stupid, but he didn't give her a chance to say anything. He got them moving out the door of the examining room. Fast. Too fast for Kelly to keep up with her wobbly legs, and Jameson cursed again when he glanced back at her. He looped his arm around her waist and started walking, slower this time.

"Once I take care of this," Jameson said, "you can finish up with the doctor and then I can get you to the sheriff's office. If you need protective custody, we can work it out there."

Kelly didn't miss the "if." He still didn't trust her— which was reasonable—since she couldn't remember what she'd done or why she was carrying that note ordering her to kill him.

"We need to find my sister, too," she reminded him, though Kelly was certain he remembered.

"Gabriel's looking," he assured her.

Yes, but that didn't mean she couldn't look, as well. And she would. But first she had to take care of a possible killer and then find a way to escape. Or at least find a way to get Jameson to believe her so he would help her.

No easy feat.

Apparently, they'd been lovers, but judging from the way Jameson glared at her nearly every time their eyes met, he didn't feel even a trace of affection for her. However, the attraction was still there, and perhaps that was one of the reasons he was glaring. He didn't need this heat between them any more than Kelly did.

They made their way down a wide corridor with shiny gray tile floors, and Jameson slowed when they neared the back exit. The guard was there, his gun drawn and pointed at the glass door.

"He's still out there," Hank said, sparing Jameson and her a glance. "What should I do?"

"Come over here and wait with her." Jameson tipped his head to the hall. He took up position by the side of the door so he could peer out into the parking lot. "But keep watch. I don't want anyone sneaking up on us."

Neither did Kelly, so she kept watch, as well. "Maybe if I could get a look at the gunman, I might recognize him?" she said.

Jameson spared her a glance. "Your memory's starting to come back?" There it was again. The skepticism that she'd never lost it in the first place.

"No. But seeing him might trigger something."

"Seeing him might get you killed," Jameson pointed out. "This glass is reinforced, but it's not bullet-resistant."

Which meant Jameson could be shot, too. Kelly had

already put him in enough danger, so she leaned out, trying to get a glimpse of the gunman.

And she got it all right.

The tall lanky man ran from the back of an SUV to a truck. But the new position didn't put him closer to the building. Nor did his next move when he darted behind a car. He was moving laterally. Maybe so he could have a better shot?

Or was this about something else?

"Hell," Jameson said. "I think this clown is just a decoy." Obviously, he'd reached the same conclusion Kelly just had. "A second gunman's probably already in the building."

Both Hank and Kelly shot glances around them. The hall wasn't empty. There were two people wearing green scrubs, a man holding the hand of a toddler and a woman carrying a vase of flowers. All seemed to be doing normal things that people would do in a hospital.

Seemed.

The flower-carrying woman was walking slow, staying behind the man and the little boy, but Kelly didn't think they were together. She got confirmation of that when the boy stumbled and the woman didn't even reach out to break his fall. It was the man who picked up the child. He kissed the boy on the cheek and started walking again, coming up the hall toward them.

Jameson took out his phone and texted someone. Gabriel, probably. To let his brother know what was going on.

"See anyone suspicious?" Jameson asked Hank and her when he'd finished.

Hank shook his head. Kelly didn't. "The woman with the flowers could be carrying a gun," she said.

Though it wasn't visible. Still, she was wearing jeans and could have a concealed weapon in a slide holster. Plus, there was something about the intense look on her face that set off alarms inside her. So intense that Kelly moved out of her line of sight and pulled Hank next to her.

Jameson hurried from the back door just long enough to glance down the hall, and he made a frustrated sound of agreement. "We can't risk her firing shots. Not with that kid and the other innocent people standing around."

Kelly could see and feel the debate going on inside Jameson. They didn't have time to wait for backup. Nor did they have a lot of options here. If whoever was behind this had indeed set up a decoy, then there could be more than one hired killer in the hospital.

"Come on," Jameson finally said. He motioned for them to follow him to the door, and he made brief eye contact with Hank. "Keep hold of Kelly, and when we get outside, get her down behind the first vehicle you reach."

The blood rushed to her head, and Kelly felt the kick of adrenaline. And fear. So many things could go wrong right now, and staying put could be the biggest mistake of all. Still, she hated to go out there without any way to defend herself.

Hank put his arm around Kelly's waist, and the moment Jameson unlocked the door, they started moving. So did the decoy. He lifted his head, and Kelly saw the surprise register in his eyes.

It didn't last.

Because the moment the man turned his rifle in their directions, Jameson took aim and shot him square in the chest. The guy dropped like a stone, and Kelly could tell he was dead. But she could no longer see him because Hank did as Jameson said, and he pulled her to the side of a minivan.

"Do you have a backup gun or knife?" she whispered to Hank. "I'm a PI. I know how to shoot." Or at least she thought she did. Now, if she could just remember the firearms training she would have almost certainly had in order to get a private investigator's license.

Hank glanced back at her, and even though Kelly could tell he was plenty uncertain about this, he lifted the leg of his pants and took a small handgun from his boot holster. Kelly didn't waste a second pivoting toward the door so she could keep watch for that woman who might be coming after them.

Jameson took cover as well—using the red truck on the other side of the door. And they waited.

The moments crawled by, and Kelly soon heard a welcome sound. Sirens. Backup had arrived, and maybe that meant these would-be killers would call off the attack. She wanted answers. Wanted to know who was responsible for this. But she didn't want those answers if it meant innocent people could die.

"Get down!" Jameson shouted just as a shot was fired.

Kelly expected the bullet to go in Jameson's direction. It didn't. It came in hers. The shot slammed into the minivan just inches from where Hank and she were crouching.

That sent Kelly and him scurrying to the side, but moving in any direction was a risk. Yes, Jameson had shot the decoy, but that didn't mean others weren't all over the parking lot.

But this shot had come from inside the hospital.

Kelly peered around the minivan and spotted the woman. She was no longer carrying flowers, but she had the back door open a couple of inches. Her gun was jutting out through the space.

And she fired again.

This time at Jameson.

From their new position, Kelly could no longer see Jameson, but he'd probably tried to shoot the woman. Judging from the sounds Kelly then heard, Jameson had been forced to take cover, as well.

Kelly figured Jameson wasn't going to like what she was doing, but she leaned out enough from the minivan so she could see if she had anything close to a clean shot. She did.

And she took it.

Kelly aimed, fired, and the bullet crashed through the glass and into the woman's chest. Like her decoy comrade, she fell, but that wasn't the only sound Kelly heard. Jameson cursed—the profanity aimed at her.

"I told you to stay down," Jameson snarled, and in the same breath, there was another shot.

Sweet heaven. Who was Jameson shooting at now?

Kelly scrambled around Hank and made her way to the rear of the minivan. There, she had a good angle to see Jameson. To see the glare that he tossed her, too. Obviously, he wasn't happy that she had changed her position or that she fired that shot. Kelly wasn't especially happy about it, either, but she saw it as a necessary choice.

"Put down your gun," someone shouted.

Gabriel. He had apparently arrived with backup. Good. Kelly hoped he had brought a lot of deputies with him so they could secure the hospital.

"He's there," Hank said, motioning in the direction of the far side of the building.

There was a man carrying a handgun in the spot where Hank had indicated. However, the man didn't drop his weapon as Gabriel had ordered. He turned and fired a shot, no doubt aiming for the sheriff.

Jameson took care of the guy. He double-tapped the trigger, but he hadn't gone for kill shots. The bullets went into the man's shoulder and shooting arm. He stayed on his feet, but his gun clattered to the ground.

Suddenly, there were the sounds of footsteps. Plenty of them. And they were all converging on the injured man. With his gaze still firing all around him, Jameson reached the guy first, but Gabriel and a deputy soon joined him. Another deputy stepped out from the back door where the gunwoman was still sprawled out. She was almost certainly dead. It gave Kelly a sick feeling in the pit of her stomach to know she'd killed someone, but if she hadn't, Jameson, Hank and she could have been murdered.

"Don't kill me," the gunman yelled, attempting to hold up his hands. Hard to do, though, with his injuries.

Kelly had been right about the gunshot wounds. They didn't appear life-threatening, but he was bleeding and needed medical attention. That wouldn't be difficult to get since they were in a hospital parking lot, but Gabriel likely wouldn't let any of the medical staff approach until he was certain it was safe.

Even though Kelly knew Jameson wasn't going to like it, she started to make her way toward them. She did keep low, though, crouching, and her pace wasn't exactly fast since she was still unsteady.

When Jameson spotted her, he didn't curse, but she

could tell that's what he wanted to do. "Stay behind cover," he warned her.

She did, but that didn't stop her from getting a better look at the gunman that the deputy was now cuffing. Just as everyone else she'd encountered, Kelly didn't recognize him, but when the man looked in her direction, he did something strange.

He smiled at her.

Jameson and Gabriel noticed that smile, too, because they both shifted their attention to her. "You know him?" Jameson asked her.

Kelly immediately shook her head. But the man just kept on smiling.

"I know you," the injured gunman growled, "because you're the woman who hired me."

Chapter Five

"I didn't hire that hit man," Kelly insisted.

Jameson had lost count of how many times Kelly had said a variation of that denial, but it had started immediately after the gunman's accusation. It had continued, too, even after the man had been hauled away to the ER and after she and Jameson arrived at the sheriff's office.

As with her other denials, no one responded. The two deputies who weren't at the hospital working the investigation were both busy at their desks. Gabriel was in the interview room with the driver who'd first seen Kelly and the two dead guys in the pasture. That left Jameson, and even though he, too, was on the phone, waiting for an update from Cameron, he wasn't there to give her any assurances but rather to make sure she didn't run.

Good thing, because she certainly looked like a woman on the verge of taking off.

She was pacing across the squad room. Well, her version of pacing anyway, considering she was still wobbly. She would occasionally catch on to desks and chairs to steady herself.

Thankfully, she hadn't been so shaky that she hadn't managed to take out the female shooter in the hospital door. If she hadn't, the woman could have done some serious damage. It was that shot that had Jameson believing that the injured gunmen had been lying.

He stopped, rethought that.

Actually, he hadn't believed it from the moment he'd heard it. And yeah, that made him stupid. It was this old fire that was between Kelly and him. She'd stolen the file from him, but it was a huge leap to go from that to murder.

Kelly glanced down at the burner cell phone she had gripped in her hand. One of the deputies had given it to her after she said she wanted to make some calls. Of course, the calls had been related to her sister. Kelly hadn't remembered any phone numbers—or so she'd claimed—so Jameson had given her a contact at SAPD. The detective had nothing new on Mandy but promised to call Kelly the moment he found anything.

Jameson hoped what they didn't find was a body.

Kill Jameson Beckett or you'll never see her again.

That wasn't exactly a reassurance that Kelly's kid sister was okay.

She went to the watercooler and had another drink. Her third in the past hour. Jameson had already had her doctor come to the sheriff's office to check her and finish his exam, but Kelly had practically dismissed the man. Too bad. Because Jameson was certain that head injury needed additional treatment. Probably even a night or two in the hospital. He doubted, though, that he was going to be able to convince Kelly to go back there after what'd happened.

They'd nearly been killed.

It'd been pure luck that both Kelly and he had managed to nail those shots. And they'd managed that before the thugs had gotten their own brand of luck and killed all three of them and anyone else who happened to get in the path of those bullets.

Jameson finished his call with Cameron and went closer to her. The doctor had told him to watch her for any signs of dizziness or fatigue. He didn't see either. However, Jameson did see the troubled look on her face.

"I didn't hire that man," she repeated. Except this time, there were tears in her eyes.

Hell. The tears were his Achilles' heel, and Jameson had to force himself not to pull her into his arms. That definitely wouldn't be a good idea.

She stared at him as if waiting for something. A response, maybe. Maybe that hug. But instead Jameson relayed what he'd just learned from Cameron.

"No ID's on either the dead man or woman," he explained. "But Cameron took their prints and will see if they're in the system. I called in the Rangers to assist on this. When I have the names, I'll definitely run them past you to see if they ring any bells."

Kelly nodded. "Good." She repeated both the one-word response and the nod, and she kept staring at him.

"What about the guy you shot?" she asked. "The one who lied and said he was working for me?" She hadn't needed to clarify that last part, but the renewed anger in her voice seemed to help with drying up those tears.

"He lawyered up, but we do have an ID on him. He gave his name to the doctor because apparently he has some allergies to certain meds and wanted the doc to access his records. His name is Coy McGill. Know him?"

"No." Kelly added a heavy sigh. "But he's trying to set me up. Please tell me you know that." She was clearly calling him on this.

"I do know that," he assured her. "The shot that woman fired could have killed you. If you'd been the one who hired them, she would have kept her gun aimed at me. After all, I'm the one that someone wants dead."

"Yes," she said after a long pause. Their eyes met again. "Why?"

For a simple question, it encompassed a lot. With everything going through his head, he hadn't exactly had much quiet time to think, but he kept coming back to two things.

"It could be connected to my parents' murders. The anniversary is just two days away." That would mean someone obsessed with the case. It could be someone who wanted revenge for Travis being behind bars.

"It's possibly connected to one of your cases," Kelly provided.

He had to nod again. As a Texas Ranger, he had made his share of enemies, and there were at least a half dozen guys behind bars who would want him dead. But this felt, well, personal.

"Why use you to do this?" Jameson was talking more to himself than her now.

She groaned softly, but it looked as if she wanted to curse. "I don't know, and that's why I need to remember."

"Then you should let the doctor examine you again. Maybe there's something he can give you—"

"He can't. I asked," she added. "He can rule out a brain injury with tests, but even if that is what's wrong with me, the only treatment is time."

Jameson had no idea if the doctor had actually told her that or if it was something Kelly had decided was true. Either way, he couldn't force her. But he could force her into custody.

"Until Coy McGill starts talking, I can't let you leave," Jameson spelled out for her.

"Because I'm a suspect," she readily supplied.

Great. That brought back the tears. They shimmered in her eyes along with tugging at his heart. And Jameson finally caved in and gave her arm a gentle rub. She noticed, too. She looked down at his hand. Then at him.

And there it came.

That old punch to the gut. Jameson had been with plenty of women, but none of them had ever made him feel the way Kelly had.

And that's why he took a huge step back from her.

She noticed what he'd done, and the corner of her mouth lifted. A smile, sort of, but it wasn't from humor.

"Plus, you can't let me leave because Boyer is still threatening that arrest warrant against me," Kelly added a moment later.

Bingo. There were a lot of pieces in this mess that didn't make sense, and Boyer was just one of them.

The door to the interview room finally opened, and Gabriel came out with the witness, a man named Merrill Stover. He wasn't a local but rather had been to a nearby ranch to look at some calves that were for sale. Jameson had run a background check on the man while Kelly was with the doctor, and Stover had a squeaky-clean record. No indications whatsoever that he'd had part in whatever the heck had gone on in that pasture.

Stover started for the door but stopped when he saw Kelly. "Ma'am, I'm real sorry for what happened to you."

Kelly pulled back her shoulders. "What *did* happen to me?"

Stover glanced back at Gabriel, but he waved off the question. "I'll fill her in. You're free to go," Gabriel assured him.

The man gave a suit-yourself shrug and left. Gabriel didn't say a word until he was out the door.

"I believe what he told me," Gabriel started. "But before you ask," he added to Kelly when she opened her mouth, "he didn't see the actual shooting. Only the aftermath of it."

She gave another of those weary sighs and scrubbed her hand over the back of her neck. "So I'm not cleared. Boyer can arrest me."

"No, he can't," Gabriel assured her. "Well, not without a court order, which I seriously doubt he'll get. That's because those two dead men aren't agents as he claimed. They both had long rap sheets."

Finally, Jameson saw some relief on her face. It was short-lived, though. "Why would Boyer claim they were agents?" she asked.

Gabriel lifted his shoulder. "I tried to call him, but he didn't answer. I left him a message."

Kelly leaned against the wall, and her eyelids fluttered a little. Jameson silently cursed. She was probably dizzy, something he was supposed to be watching for. Not that she'd ever admit it. However, she didn't balk when he took her by the arm and led her to a chair in Gabriel's office.

"Why would those men attack me?" She touched her fingers to her head.

"I don't know." Gabriel sounded as frustrated about that as Jameson was.

But Jameson had a theory. "Let's say someone wanted me dead and decided to use you to do that. You're not a thug or hired gun, but you've got the skill set to do the job since you're a PI. To force you to do this, they kidnap your sister."

That put some tears back in her eyes. Still, this was something Kelly needed to hear. It was something he needed to say aloud, too, to see if it made sense.

"They would keep your sister alive because that's the only leverage they have over you," Jameson reminded her. Now, here was the sticky part. "But something went wrong with their plan. You could have refused to do the hit on me, and the person behind this sent those two men after you. When they found you, you killed them in self-defense."

"Self-defense," she repeated in a whisper. Obviously, Kelly was trying to work this out, as well. She looked at Gabriel. "Did the two men have any kind of defensive wounds on them?"

"None. Only the gunshots that killed them. The shots came from your gun. We got the test results back on that," Gabriel added. "And you had gunshot residue on your hands."

Kelly stayed quiet a moment. "You think that's enough to convince Boyer to back off?"

"I hope so. Because I want you here in our custody at least until SAPD finds your sister."

Yeah, and it'd be a good idea to keep her until that head injury was healed enough so she could tell them what was going on. Whenever the heck that would be.

"We probably haven't seen the last of Boyer," Jameson said. "He could be trying to figure out another reason to arrest you. Do you remember if you trust him?"

"No specific memories," she answered without hesitation. "But I don't trust him." She didn't hesitate with that, either.

Kelly's lack of trust definitely put Gabriel and him between a rock and a hard place. They wanted to cooperate with fellow law enforcement, but things weren't right here. Maybe Kelly had done something to Boyer and now he wanted to get back at her?

Jameson didn't get a chance to speculate more about that because he heard a familiar voice in the squad room. "Where the hell is the sheriff?" the man snarled.

Kelly practically bolted from the chair. "Who is that?"

"It's August Canton," Gabriel answered. "I called him in for questioning. I figured since you'd worked for him, seeing him might trigger some memories. I also want to ask him about the attacks."

Gabriel and Jameson stepped out in the hall to face their visitor, and Kelly was right behind them.

It was August all right, but Jameson hadn't had any doubts about that. August made regular visits to the sheriff's office, and even though Jameson worked in San Antonio, he still managed to run into the man.

"That's August?" Kelly whispered. "When you said he was Travis's brother, I thought he'd be older. Thought he'd look different, too."

"He's Travis's half brother and only a few years older than Gabriel and me. As for the looks, well, he doesn't dress like most ranchers." More like a magazine version of a rancher in his designer clothes.

August was the offspring of his father's second marriage, and when his parents had been killed in a car crash when he was twelve, Travis had raised him. Jameson figured August always thought of Travis as more of a father than a half brother. That was probably why he was always fighting to get Travis out of jail.

And August had the money to keep up the fight, too. Jameson didn't know the man's net worth, but August had inherited a trust fund from his mother's family.

"You two really need to get another whipping boy," August snapped. "Because I'm damn tired of you hauling me in here every time something goes wrong in your lives. I can't help it if some folks just want you two in the grave."

It was the typical junk that August spouted, but there was some truth in it. Gabriel and he had plenty of criminals who wanted to do them harm. But August had motive, too, because he blamed them for Travis's being convicted of the murders.

August looked ready to launch into more of that tirade, but he stopped when his attention landed on Kelly. The anger and tension dissolved from his expression, and he went to her, pulling her into his arms. The tension definitely didn't dissolve from Kelly. She went board-stiff.

"Are you okay?" August asked, leaning back enough so he could make eye contact with her.

She shook her head. "Someone tried to kill me. *Us*," Kelly corrected, motioning toward Jameson.

"Yes, I heard, and I'm sorry." August sounded genuine about that. *Sounded*. "I heard you lost your memory, too? I saw a nurse at the gas station, and she was talking about it."

Kelly nodded and eased back farther from him. Her forehead bunched up. "I don't remember you, but Jameson said you hired me and my sister to find something to clear your brother's name."

"I did. You both looked very hard but didn't find anything." August glanced at Jameson. "You don't think that had anything to do with someone trying to kill Kelly?" But he didn't wait for an answer. "I've told you all along that the real killer is out there, that my brother is innocent. The real killer probably thinks Kelly found something and wants to silence her."

Jameson didn't know whose huff was louder, his or Gabriel's. "Kelly worked for you two years ago," Jameson reminded the man. "If there is a *real killer* and he truly thought Kelly was a threat, why wouldn't he have gone after her back then?"

"I don't know. But it's your job to find out." August cursed. "How many more people are going to have to die or be put in danger before you reopen my brother's case and find the truth? And that truth is he's an innocent man."

Jameson didn't even bother to groan that time. They'd rehashed this argument so often that it no longer got much of a rise out of him.

"Do you know where Mandy is?" Kelly asked August. "Have you heard from her?"

"No," August said, sounding surprised. "What happened to her?"

"I'm not sure, but there were signs of a struggle in her apartment. And blood." Kelly's voice cracked when she said that last word.

August patted her arm much the way Jameson had earlier. Jameson didn't want to feel that coil of jealousy go through him. But he did.

Hell.

He really needed to find a way past these unwanted feelings for Kelly. She wasn't his, and it needed to stay that way.

"I'll make some calls and see if I can find out anything about your sister," August told her.

"The cops are doing that," Jameson snapped.

It was a knee-jerk reaction whenever he was around August. It came from all those years Gabriel and he had had to deal with August's claim that they'd arrested, and convicted, the wrong man for their parents' murders.

"And we know the cops never drop the ball on things," August grumbled back. When he turned to Gabriel, there wasn't a trace of the pleasantness that he'd shown Kelly. "Now, why don't you tell me why you summoned me here this time, and should I have brought my lawyer with me?"

"Did you do something illegal that would warrant your attorney being here?" Gabriel fired back. "I want to know if you had anything to do with hiring the thugs who tried to kill Jameson and Kelly."

"No. Of course not." August's eyes narrowed. "I have no reason to hurt Kelly. And I resent you insinuating that I did. Kelly and I are friends."

"Really?" Jameson questioned, and he didn't bother to sound sincere. "When's the last time you spoke to your *friend*?"

August turned that nasty expression on Jameson. "I haven't seen Kelly in a couple of years, but that doesn't mean I don't still consider her a friend. I want to help her. I want to keep her safe."

"We all want that," Jameson said. And he glanced at Kelly to see how she was handling this intense conversation.

Not well.

She was looking shaky again, and Jameson took hold of her arm to steady her. August didn't miss the gesture, and his mouth tightened. Heck, maybe the man was jealous, but it was just as likely that he didn't want to see his *friend* with a Beckett.

"If I'd known someone was after her," August continued a moment later, "I would have gotten in touch with her. With Mandy, too." His voice drifted off, because he turned in the direction of the front door that'd just opened.

Jameson and Gabriel looked there, too. And both probably had a similar reaction—they didn't need this now. But apparently they were going to get another visit from Boyer.

The agent's gaze went directly to them, and he walked toward them, flashing his badge to the deputy who tried to stop him.

"Hell," August muttered. "Why is he here?"

"You know him?" Gabriel asked August, and Jameson realized that with everything else going on, he hadn't filled his brother in on this.

"Yeah, and Agent Boyer knows me." August definitely didn't sound happy about that.

Boyer lifted an eyebrow. "And I know you. I'm investigating you for money laundering."

"For bilking Hattie Osmond out of a lot of money, too," Jameson added.

"It's all bogus." August didn't take his glare off the agent. "Are you here to harass me?"

"No, he's here to harass me," Kelly volunteered. "He thinks I murdered two thugs, but the truth is they were criminals, and I shot them in self-defense."

Boyer's gaze slashed to Jameson and Gabriel as if the agent expected them to confirm that. Jameson just settled for a nod. In light of the latest attack, Jameson was almost certain that's what'd happened.

Almost.

"You sure spend a lot of time fiddling in other people's business, Agent Boyer," August went on. "Seems to me you should be focusing on getting your own kid back."

That was yet something else Jameson hadn't had time to explain to Gabriel. And it probably didn't have anything to do with this case anyway. August was just muddying the waters by tossing it out there. He was also riling Boyer, and it'd obviously hit a nerve. The veins on Boyer's neck were practically bulging.

"I'll deal with you later," Boyer told August, and it sounded like a threat. "For now, I need to deal with her." He tipped his head to Kelly.

"What do you mean by that?" Kelly asked before Jameson could speak. She sounded a lot stronger than he knew she was. After all, she was practically leaning on him. "I've told you I'm innocent."

"But you don't know that, do you? In fact, you don't know much of anything right now because of this so-called amnesia."

"I know you're not taking her without an arrest warrant," Jameson said, "and you're not going to get one because you don't have enough evidence against her."

"We'll see about that." Again, it sounded like a threat, and Jameson doubted the man would just give up.

Kelly let out a long breath after Boyer walked out, but she kept her eyes on him until he was no longer in sight. "I wish I could remember what I did to make him come after me like this."

"You don't know?" August asked, but it wasn't exactly a question. It was an isn't-it-obvious tone.

The three of them just stared at August, and Jameson motioned for him to continue.

August did after he huffed. "Boyer believes Kelly has his little girl stashed away somewhere. And he'll do anything to force Kelly to give him back the child."

Chapter Six

Kelly jolted herself out of the dream. Or rather the nightmare. Images of gunmen trying to kill her.

Other images, too.

Before she opened her eyes, she could see some of the images. Watery bits of colors. Faces. Some of those faces were of her attackers, but one of them belonged to Mandy. Even though Kelly still didn't have any real memories of Mandy, she was certain that it was her kid sister.

That brought on the ache that was already heavy in her heart. Her sister was missing, and she wasn't able to help her. Mandy could be hurt. Dying. And here she was safe. For the moment anyway. But Kelly didn't exactly feel welcome here.

That's because she was in the guest room at Jameson's house on his family's ranch.

Jameson didn't want her at his place. Actually, he didn't want to be with her at all. She knew that. However, they hadn't exactly had a lot of options, considering he wanted to keep her close in case she remembered something that could help them unravel the reason behind the two attacks.

She checked the time on the clock, nearly 6:00 a.m.,

so Kelly got up and used the shower in the en suite bath. Her muscles were sore and stiff, but the pain was minor compared to her head. She was tempted to take some of the meds the doctor had given her after the exam at the sheriff's office, but she was afraid the pills would dull her memories even more.

She dressed, changing into the clothes Jameson had left for her the night before. The jeans and shirt were loaners from his sister Ivy, and they were much needed, too, since Kelly's own clothes had been covered with blood. She wasn't sure she would have been able to put them back on.

When she was done with the clothes, she made the mistake of looking in the mirror, and the jolt of seeing herself was as bad as the nightmare. That's because it was a stranger staring back at her.

Kelly touched her fingers to the bandage on her head. Whoever had hit her had probably been trying to kill her. Not exactly a thought to settle her queasy stomach. But what the person had done was take away who she was. Her name was Kelly Stockwell, but there were just a few traces of herself now. That had to change.

But how?

That question was repeating in her mind when she heard the footsteps. Kelly automatically reached for her gun—which she didn't have. She'd had the security guard's backup weapon during the hospital attack, but Jameson had arranged for it to be returned to the man. Too bad. Because she might need it now.

Or not.

There was a knock at the door, and a moment later Jameson opened it. "I heard you up," he said.

Not exactly a warm greeting, but there was some

warmth when he looked her over. Unwanted warmth, no doubt. He stood with his forehead bunched up as if waiting for something. But that's when Kelly realized she hadn't buttoned the shirt. Her bare stomach and a skimpy white loaner bra were showing. She quickly fixed that and mumbled an apology.

"I don't have my memory back yet," Kelly volunteered just to get that out of the way.

He made a sound, a rumble deep in his chest that could have meant anything. "There's coffee."

Kelly didn't know if she drank it or not, but she followed him to the kitchen and poured herself a cup. She tried it black, winced and heard Jameson make another sound. Maybe amusement this time.

"I guess that proves you're not faking the memory loss." He slid a small bowl her way. "You'll want three or four spoons of sugar in that."

She added three, sipped, then dumped in the fourth. Yes, that tasted right. It didn't surprise her that they'd obviously had coffee together. However, she was a little surprised that Jameson remembered how she took it. Maybe he'd had trouble erasing her from his mind— something that Kelly was certain he would like to do.

"Anything on my sister?" she asked. She sat at the table. Jameson didn't, though. With his coffee in hand, he went to the window to look out.

"Sorry, no. But the cops and Rangers are looking." He had a sip of his coffee before he said anything else. "I found out that August hired a couple of PIs to investigate Boyer. Not just Boyer's professional life, but his missing daughter, as well."

She could have sworn her heart skipped a beat. "Please tell me I didn't really take his child." Because even though she didn't remember August, Kelly had hoped that the man was wrong about that.

Jameson lifted his shoulder. "Boyer might truly believe you had something to do with it, but there's no proof that you did."

Thank goodness. That was something, at least. Though if she had done something like that, at least it would have been motive for Boyer to come after her. But then she had to shake her head.

"If Boyer is behind the attacks, why would he have coerced me into killing you?" Kelly asked.

"Maybe to throw suspicion off himself." Jameson answered it so quickly that he'd almost certainly given it plenty of thought. "This way, it would look as if this were between you and me and not between you and him."

Yes, and if he blamed her for taking his child, he would want revenge. Well, maybe. "He couldn't risk killing me if he believes I know where the child is," she pointed out. "Yet those gunmen seemed to have orders to eliminate us."

The moment Kelly said that, something hit her. And it wasn't something good.

"If Mandy also knew the location of the child," she went on, "she could have told Boyer. Then he wouldn't need me around. Or Mandy."

It suddenly felt as if someone had clamped a fist around her heart and kept squeezing. Her sister was at the mercy of someone who wanted her dead.

"Don't," Jameson said. "Boyer isn't our only suspect. August could have forced you to kill me because he hates me for putting Travis behind bars. He could have used you to do that."

True. But even if this was just directed at Jameson, it didn't help. Obviously, someone was after both of them. Heck, maybe Jameson's entire family.

"I've been looking for a possible money trail for the person who hired those thugs," Jameson went on. "I managed to get court orders for both Boyer and August."

Jameson had been busy. And lucky. Kelly figured it wasn't easy to get a court order for a federal agent's financials. "What did you find?"

"Nothing on Boyer, but then he could have some offshore or hidden accounts. Also he could have cash stashed away. A lot of it. He got a lawsuit settlement a while back for a car accident involving a drunk driver."

Having cash wasn't a good thing in this case, because they'd never know if Boyer had used it to hire hit men. Or kidnap Mandy.

"August is a different story," he went on. "Because of the attacks and threats that have been going on for the past couple of months, we've been keeping an eye on his financials. He's rich, by the way. A huge trust fund that he taps into regularly to pay for attorneys and PIs to clear his brother's name."

Yes, and she'd apparently been one of those PIs.

"The money trail definitely leads to August, but it's almost too obvious," Jameson quickly added. "The funds came from an offshore account that was set up just last week. I'm sure August will say that it's bogus, and it'll be hard to prove that it's not."

Especially since someone with Boyer's federal connections could have easily done something like that. But that led Kelly to something else that she'd considered.

"Is it possible that when I was working for August

I uncovered something that would, well, incriminate August himself?" she asked.

"Maybe. The file you stole from me had plenty about him in it, including my personal notes."

She remembered Boyer and him talking about this. Jameson had considered August a suspect in his parents' murders because Jameson's father had been investigating August at the time. But maybe she had used whatever was in that file to lead her to something else.

Like August's guilt.

That could possibly explain why she'd disappeared two years ago. Of course, the obvious reason she'd left was because Jameson hated her for stealing that file. She hated herself for doing it, too. Kelly hoped when her memories returned that there was a better reason for her taking it other than her just doing her job.

And that brought her back to what was happening now.

If August was connected to the attacks, then the motive had to go back to the file. Or maybe to what'd happened ten years ago.

"Did Travis admit to killing your parents?" she asked. But Kelly wished she hadn't. Jameson's long, weary breath told her this was a topic that was still picking away at those old wounds he had.

"No. He was an alcoholic and had blackouts. Like you, he has memory issues."

That sounded a little like a dig, but she couldn't blame him. If Travis remembered what happened that night, then it might help them solve who was behind the attacks.

"Part of me wishes it weren't Travis," Jameson

continued a moment later. "Because Travis's son and daughter are involved with my brother and sister."

Yes, that did create some bad family dynamics. Of course, maybe Travis's children hated their father for what he'd done. The Beckett murders had certainly created a lot of pain and suffering for those who'd been left behind.

Heck, it was still creating it because of those threats Jameson had mentioned and the attacks.

"You have someone protecting your sisters?" Kelly asked.

He nodded. "Ivy's engaged to a DEA agent, Theo. He won't let anything happen to her. They're staying at Gabriel's for now with him and his wife, Jodi. My other sister, Lauren, is engaged to Cameron, the deputy who works here."

Kelly figured she'd met these people. Or at least had known about them. But that, too, was lost in the jumble of memories.

"Even if your sisters are being protected, it's too dangerous for me to stay here," she reminded him. "In fact, I probably shouldn't be anywhere near you."

He glanced at her, his eyebrow raised. Maybe he'd taken that the wrong way. As in she shouldn't be near him because of the attraction, but his eyebrow lowered just as quickly.

"Once I get an update from Gabriel, we'll weigh the options," he answered. "Plus, you should probably go back to the hospital and press the doctor to see if he can do anything about your amnesia."

"No. Not after what happened. Besides, the doctor ran tests." Of course, those test results hadn't told her what she needed to know—would her memory ever return? Or would she be like this forever?

Jameson kept his attention pinned out the window, which made her wonder just how long he'd been keeping watch. Hopefully, not all night. Though that might explain why he was drinking the coffee like water. He poured himself another cup and went right back to the window.

Kelly joined him so she could get a better look at the place. When they'd arrived the night before, it'd already been too dark for her to see much. However, she certainly saw it now. The ranch was huge.

"All of this is Beckett land?" she asked.

"Yeah. My great-grandfather originally bought it and passed it down the generations. When my folks died... Gabriel, Ivy, Lauren and I inherited it."

He paused over the word *died*, and she noticed the sudden tightness of his jaw. His parents' murders were obviously still a raw wound.

Kelly leaned closer to the window so she could see the road that led up from a large house. Gabriel's, probably. There was also a house on the other side of the property, but it clearly wasn't occupied and appeared to have some recent damage.

"We had a fire last month," Jameson said, following her gaze. "Someone tried to go after my sister and her fiancé."

So the Becketts weren't new to attacks. But that still didn't mean Kelly should be there to bring more danger to their doorsteps.

"We've been getting threats for a while now," he went on. "There's been some press about the anniversary of the murders, and that sometimes brings out the lunatics and copycats."

"It's a shame because, despite everything, this is still your home." She paused. "Did you bring me here when we, uh, were seeing each other?"

He nodded, then drank more of his coffee. "Remember anything about it?"

Kelly glanced around the large open kitchen and living room. There was nothing familiar. So she closed her eyes to try again. Some images came. Fast and blurry. As she'd done with the nightmare, she tried to pick through them. And she finally did.

"You have a tattoo," Kelly blurted out, and she looked at his shoulder. She couldn't see the tat, of course, because he was wearing a shirt, but if her memory was right, it was a dragon.

Another nod to verify the tat. But he didn't verify anything else about it. Especially the fact that he would have had to be partially undressed for her to have seen it.

Jameson finally turned to her, but it wasn't exactly a loving look he gave her. He checked her bandage. Frowned. And gave it a slight adjustment. Of course, for that to happen, he had to touch her. His fingertips brushed against her skin, and the shiver went through her.

Kelly stepped back. And Jameson noticed. He probably noticed her reaction to him, as well. He stared at her as if he was about to say something, but then his phone rang, the sound shooting through the room. He touched her again, moving her back from the window, before he set aside his coffee and took his phone from his pocket.

"It's Gabriel," he said. Jameson hit the answer button and put the call on speaker. "Kelly's next to me," he added to his brother.

She hoped that didn't cause Gabriel to hold back something he might have said, but the sheriff's long pause told her that he would probably at least try to soften any bad news.

"McGill, the gunman, is finally talking," Gabriel explained, "but he's still insisting it was Kelly who hired him."

"He's lying," she repeated.

Neither man had a reaction to that, and Gabriel just continued. "I offered him a plea deal. He'd have to give me proof that it was Kelly who hired him, and in exchange I'd ask the DA for lesser charges. McGill didn't go for it."

"Maybe because he figures he's a dead man if he says anything," Jameson quickly provided. "Or else there's no proof to be found."

Kelly groaned. She hated to think there was nothing out there that could clear her name. "Maybe someone made McGill believe I was the one behind it," she suggested. "Maybe someone posing as me through phone conversations and such." It couldn't have been a face-to-face pretense, though, because McGill had gotten a close look at her in the hospital parking lot.

"That's my guess, too," Gabriel agreed. "Of course, he could have a more personal stake in this. Perhaps someone kidnapped a family member or his boss could be a friend. We're looking into any connections between McGill, August and Boyer."

Good. Because if they could make a link like that, it would put a quicker end to this investigation.

"I did talk to a few of Boyer's fellow agents," Gabriel added, "and, yeah, he does believe Kelly assisted in taking his daughter. Apparently, Kelly knew Boyer's ex, Hadley, and Boyer believes Hadley convinced Kelly to help her take the child."

"But why? Was Boyer abusive?" Kelly asked.

"Not according to anyone I spoke with, but no one had anything good to say about Hadley. People agreed that she was controlling and manipulative. She could have maybe made you believe that the baby and she were in danger. That could explain why you would do something like that."

Yes, it could. However, Kelly still couldn't remember Hadley or this baby. She forced herself to think, to try to sort through those memory fragments again. This time, she got a too-clear image of Jameson.

Naked.

It was so clear that she made a sound of surprise. A sound that certainly got Jameson's attention. "What is it?" he demanded.

She waved him off and was about to lie and say it was nothing, but another image came. Not of Jameson this time.

But of a baby.

A little girl with dark hair, and she was smiling. The image came and went in a flash, but it was just as clear as the one of Jameson.

"Oh, God." Kelly touched her fingers to her mouth. Both her mouth and hand were trembling now. "I might have taken her."

Jameson stared at her. Gabriel cursed. "What do you remember?" Gabriel snapped.

"Nothing other than seeing her in my mind. I can't recall anything about kidnapping her."

"You might not have," Jameson said. "It's possible Hadley brought her to you."

True. But where was the child now? Hadley was dead, and Kelly instinctively knew there was no way she'd leave the child alone.

"Maybe you can put out an APB for the little girl," Kelly suggested.

"There's already an Amber Alert," Gabriel explained, "but the Rangers have stepped up efforts to find her." He paused, and she could hear him talking to someone else in the background. "The emergency dispatcher just called, and he said he has Mandy on the line."

Kelly's heart dropped. She put her coffee cup on the windowsill and practically snatched the phone from Jameson. "Where is she? Is she okay?" Kelly's words were so fast that they ran together.

"I'll have the call transferred here," Gabriel said, "but I have to put you on hold for a second to do that."

"Mandy's alive," Kelly whispered while she waited. That didn't mean her sister was okay, though.

The seconds suddenly seemed like hours, and Kelly's hand only shook harder. So hard that Jameson finally pried the phone from her but held it so that she wouldn't have any trouble hearing.

"Kelly?" someone finally said from the other end of the line.

She didn't recognize the voice, but Kelly looked at Jameson and he nodded. "It's your sister."

"Kelly," Mandy repeated. "I can't stay on the line or they'll find me. God, Kelly, you have to come and get me now. I'm bleeding, and I'm not sure how much longer I can run from those men. Please, just come right now."

Chapter Seven

Jameson wanted to curse. Because that wasn't a good thing to hear Kelly's sister say.

I'm bleeding, and I'm not sure how much longer I can run from those men.

But it was better than the alternative. He hadn't come out and said it to Kelly, but he'd figured Mandy was dead. And she soon might be if what she'd just said was true. Just in case it wasn't or if this was some kind of ploy to draw out Kelly, Jameson fired off a text to Gabriel so he could try to trace the call.

"Remember, the kidnappers could be forcing her to say whatever she's about to say to you," Jameson told Kelly.

She shook her head, maybe not believing that. Probably because she didn't want to believe it. "Are you okay?" she asked her sister.

"No. I told you, I'm bleeding. I've been shot."

There went the rest of the color in Kelly's face. "Oh, God. How bad?"

Jameson wanted to know that, but more important, he needed to find out where to send the cops and an ambulance. "This is Jameson Beckett," he said to Mandy. "Where are you?"

Silence. Several long moments of it. That silence put a knot in Jameson's stomach.

"I'm not sure," Mandy finally said. "A day ago, two armed thugs took me and have been holding me in some kind of warehouse. When they weren't watching, I managed to get out of the ropes they used to tie my hands. I stole one of their phones and started running. That's when one of them shot me."

Jameson would need to hear a lot more details about that, but it could wait. "Where are you?" he repeated.

"I, uh, think I'm just outside of San Antonio."

If she was, then Gabriel should be able to find her. Well, unless she was using a burner phone. "Look around you," he instructed just in case it was an untraceable prepaid phone. "Do you see any landmarks, anything familiar?"

There was a rattle of static from the other end of the line, but he could also hear Mandy's heavy gusts of breath. "There's a road. Not an interstate, but I can see some buildings in the distance. No cars, though. Please, just come and get me. It's not safe here. Those men could find me."

Yeah, they probably could. "I have someone tracing the call," he assured her. "Just stay put and if there's anywhere you can hide, do it. Also, how bad are you bleeding?"

"It's my arm. There's blood on my sleeve and shirt."

Jameson felt some relief. An arm wound wouldn't necessarily be fatal unless they couldn't find her in time. If they didn't, she might bleed out.

"Try to clamp your hand over the wound," he told her. "It should slow the bleeding."

"I just need you to come," Mandy begged. "Kelly,

please. You told me if anything went wrong that you'd help me."

"And I will help you," Kelly assured her. "But I've been hurt, too. A head injury. I have amnesia."

"What?" Mandy repeated that, the disbelief easy to hear in her voice. "When did this happen?"

"Last night. Maybe a few hours after you were kidnapped." Kelly's expression was already troubled, and it stayed that way. "While Gabriel's tracing your call, maybe you can tell me why I was carrying around a note that said for me to kill Jameson?"

Mandy made a sharp sound of surprise. "I don't know." The static crackled through the line. "Obviously, you didn't kill him if he's with you now."

"No. But some men came after us. I need to know why someone would have sent me after Jameson."

Mandy hesitated again. "Maybe the same reason those goons took me, but I don't know that reason." More static. "Where are Jameson and you right now?"

Jameson shook his head when Kelly started to answer. "Someone could be listening to Mandy's conversation to figure out where you are so he or she can send more gunmen," he whispered to Kelly.

Her eyes widened, and she nodded. Of course, there were people who already knew that he'd brought Kelly here, but Jameson didn't want to hand over that information to possible would-be killers.

"Look around you again," Kelly said to Mandy a moment later. "Try to figure out where you are."

No answer. Just static. "I have to go," Mandy finally answered, her words were whispered but rushed together. "I'll call you when I can."

"Wait—" But Kelly was talking to herself because

her sister had already ended the call. "Mandy!" she shouted into the phone.

A hoarse sob tore from Kelly's mouth, and she sagged against him. "We have to find her."

"Gabriel should have the phone trace done in a few minutes." Jameson hoped so anyway, and maybe his brother would be able to pinpoint Mandy's exact location.

"We should just start driving," Kelly insisted. "We could head toward San Antonio—"

"No." This wasn't going to be an easy thing to tell her, nor an easy thing for Kelly to hear, and he slipped his arm around her. "All of this could be a trap to get to you."

She dropped her head on his shoulder, but just as quickly, it came back up, and she stared at him. "You don't think my sister is the one after me?"

"No." He didn't know of any reason why Mandy would do that. Of course, there was plenty about this investigation that he didn't know. "But the kidnappers could have allowed her to escape so they could use her to draw you out."

"Why would they have shot her then?" she asked.

Good question, and Jameson had some bad answers. "Maybe she wasn't shot. They could have told her to say that."

Kelly was shaking her head before he even finished. "I might not remember Mandy, but she's my sister."

"Siblings do bad things to each other all the time." And Jameson wished he'd toned that down some. Still, it was true. "Think about it. Mandy called the Blue River emergency number. She must have known you were here. And how would she have known that if she didn't learn about it from the kidnappers?"

He watched as she processed that, and her mouth started to tremble. The tears came back to her eyes. Tears that tugged at him almost as much as this blasted attraction between them. Jameson didn't push her away, but it was something he should have done. Because he found himself brushing a kiss on her forehead. Definitely way too cozy and intimate, considering there was no way he wanted to go another emotional round with Kelly.

"It doesn't mean Mandy wants to hurt you," he added. He pulled back, meeting her eye to eye. "In those memory fragments, you're not remembering anything about how Mandy is involved in this, are you?"

"No." She blinked back tears and wiped away the one that had spilled down her cheek. "But you're wondering why she said what she did. *You told me if anything went wrong that you'd help me.*"

Bingo. "There must have been some kind of plan. One that clearly involved her. One that had the possibility for danger if there was something that could go wrong."

She nodded. "Maybe something to do with Boyer. Probably to do with his child." Kelly looked away from him. "I keep seeing glimpses of a baby, and if I took her... God, Jameson. She could be in danger, too."

Yeah, and that was only the tip of the iceberg. Kelly could be charged with kidnapping and sent to jail. But if Boyer wanted revenge, he could kill her long before she made it behind bars.

His phone rang, causing her to gasp and reach for it. Probably because Kelly thought it was her sister. But it was Gabriel's name on the screen. Jameson jabbed the answer button as fast as he could and put the call on speaker.

"No trace on Mandy's call," Gabriel said right away. "It was a burner."

Jameson tried not to let his expression show that it was a devastating blow. That's because it hit Kelly as hard as he figured it would. This time, though, she didn't lean on him. She groped behind her to find the chair and dropped down into it. She buried her face in her hands and was no doubt crying again.

"Mandy did tell the dispatcher that she'd put the phone on silent because she didn't want her kidnappers to hear the ringing. That way, if you do call her back, at least the men after her won't be able to hear it."

That was a good precaution to take. One he was surprised that Mandy would remember considering she was on the run.

"Mandy thought she was outside of San Antonio," Jameson explained to his brother. "She said two men had been holding her in a warehouse. She was near a road."

"I'll give all of this to SAPD so they can start using traffic cameras to try to locate her. Just hang tight for now," Gabriel added before he ended the call.

Hanging tight was easier said than done. The moment Jameson put his phone away, Kelly got up and started to pace. She groaned softly, pushed her hair away from her face. And winced again. This time, though, it wasn't from hearing her sister. It was almost certainly because she'd brushed her fingers over her injury, and she was in pain.

"You could take some meds," he reminded her.

Kelly waved that off and kept pacing. "I have to try to help her," she said. "I can't just wait around here while something bad happens to Mandy."

Apparently the bad had already happened, but Jameson kept that to himself. He also continued to keep watch out the window. He'd alerted the ranch hands that there could be some trouble, but Jameson wanted to make sure none of those hired guns got anywhere on Beckett land, much less close enough to his house to fire some shots.

"Mandy and I must've planned something." Kelly seemed to be talking to herself now. Probably trying to work it out of her head. "She didn't know anything about that note I was carrying, the one that said I should kill you."

"No," Jameson agreed. "But maybe your plan didn't involve me. Not directly anyway. But that could have changed when the kidnappers took Mandy. You were obviously heading either here or Blue River when those two men attacked you."

And that led him right back to August, not Boyer. Because as far as Jameson knew, Boyer didn't have a reason to want him dead. He couldn't say the same for August. He really did need to get the man back in for questioning, and he could use the financial paper trail to do that. Of course, he'd interrogated August plenty of times and had rarely learned anything useful.

Well, except for August handing over Boyer on a silver platter by connecting the agent's missing daughter to Kelly. In this case, though, August might not have been blowing smoke.

"Tell me about the baby you've been recalling," he said. He didn't expect much, but maybe if he got Kelly's mind on something else, it would keep her from bolting for the door—something she looked as if she wanted to do.

She gave a heavy sigh. "Dark hair. Definitely a little girl because she's wearing a dress and smiling. Not a newborn. She's sitting up, in my lap, I think. In someone's lap anyway." Kelly squinted as if trying to give him more, but then she shook her head. "Sorry. That's all."

Definitely not much, but it was a good start. "Just keep focusing on it. If you don't have your memory back soon, I can get a sketch artist. That way, we can maybe do an age progression of photos of Boyer's daughter and see if they match."

"There are photos?" she asked.

"Yes. Ones taken shortly after she was born." And he wanted to kick himself for not showing them to her sooner. "I found them last night when I was looking into Boyer's personal life and his recent investigations." He tipped his head to the laptop. "I'm pretty sure I left the tab with the photos open."

Kelly hurried there while he stayed at the window, and Jameson volleyed glances between her and the road. Even though he couldn't see the computer screen, he knew the exact moment Kelly spotted them because she held her breath and leaned in closer to study them.

Jameson realized he was holding his breath, too. A lot was riding on whether or not she recognized that baby.

"I don't know," Kelly said several moments later. "The baby in my memory is older so I can't tell if the features are the same or not."

Jameson took out his phone again to text a Ranger

friend about getting access to some age progression software, but before he could do that, he got a call from Gabriel. Kelly must have known it was important, and she went back to him.

"It's Mandy again," Gabriel explained. "She won't talk to me and is insisting on speaking to her sister. I'm transferring the call to you now."

As with the other call, it took Mandy several seconds to come onto the line. "I got away from them," she immediately said in a hoarse whisper. "But I don't know how soon they'll find me again."

"Where are you now?" Jameson asked.

"Put Kelly on the line," Mandy insisted.

"I'm here," Kelly assured her.

"Good. Because I doubt I'll have long to talk so listen carefully. I'm hiding in a warehouse. There's no one here, but there are some boxes that say Carswell Shipping. I think that's the name of the place. I need you to come and get me, but don't call the cops."

Jameson had been about to text Gabriel with that info, but he stopped. "Why no cops?"

"Because I think the kidnappers have cop friends. Or hell, they could be cops themselves. Definitely some kind of law enforcement connections. I can tell that from the snatches of their conversations I've been able to overhear."

Jameson wanted to know more about those conversations, wanted to know more about a lot of things, but he would trust Mandy on this. For now.

"Gabriel's not on any kidnapper's payroll. Nor are his deputies," Jameson told her. "They can come and get you."

"No. I want Kelly and you. Only the two of you. I don't trust anyone but my sister."

"That can't happen," Jameson said at the exact moment when Kelly said, "We'll get there as fast as we can."

"Good." He could hear the relief in Mandy's voice. "Please hurry."

There was no way Jameson was going to agree to what Kelly had just assured her sister. "Mandy, someone's trying to kill Kelly. It's not safe for her to be at some warehouse looking for you. Especially when that might not even be the name of the place."

"I know, and I'm sorry. So sorry," Mandy repeated. It sounded as if she was crying now. "But please, just come."

Jameson shook his head when Kelly opened her mouth. No doubt to assure her sister they were on the way. He even took hold of Kelly's arm to make certain she didn't grab his keys and make a run for it.

"I'll come to you," Jameson finally said to Mandy, "but I'm leaving Kelly where it's safe." Which in this case would be the sheriff's office. No way would Jameson tell Mandy that, though.

"No, bring Kelly. You have to bring her. I won't trust anyone unless she's with them. And if you don't bring her, I'll just keep running."

Then Jameson heard something he didn't want to hear.

"Oh, God, they found me," Mandy whispered.

And that whisper was followed by the sound of gunfire.

Chapter Eight

"This is a mistake," Jameson said. He'd been repeating a variation of that since Mandy's second phone call.

Kelly figured he was right. It was a mistake, but she didn't have a choice. Just as Jameson hadn't had a choice to bring her along. Of course, he hadn't done it willingly, but she'd finally convinced him that one way or another she was going to get to her sister.

Apparently, she'd promised her sister that she would help her if anything went wrong. And something had. Now it was up to Kelly to try to make that right.

If that was possible.

She would hear the sound of that gunshot for the rest of her life. It had cut her to the bone. Since just thinking about it nearly caused a panic attack, Kelly reminded herself that Mandy could have gotten away from the men. After all, she'd managed to escape from them once, so perhaps she had been able to do it again.

"Mandy wouldn't have met with you if I hadn't been with you," Kelly pointed out to Jameson.

It also was a repeat, and they'd been hashing out the same argument since leaving for the Carswell Shipping warehouse on the outskirts of San Antonio. Not a long trip. Less than forty-five minutes, but each mile seemed like an eternity.

They hadn't followed Mandy's orders to a T, though. Yes, Kelly was with Jameson in a cruiser. Not alone. Cameron was driving it, and behind them was Gabriel and another deputy, Susan Bowie, in an unmarked car.

But that wasn't the only precautions Jameson had taken.

They were all wearing Kevlar vests, and SAPD would be nearby when they approached the warehouse. Jameson had insisted on backup. Had also insisted on her staying in the vehicle at all times.

"The ambulance will be there, too?" she asked.

Jameson nodded. "There'll be one with the SAPD officers." He looked at her. Except it was more of a glare. "You do know that this is a stupid idea."

"Yes, but I'd do plenty of stupid things to save my sister."

"You don't even remember her," he spat out. "Do you?"

"No. So far, the bits and pieces I'm remembering are of you and that baby."

Boyer's baby. Once Mandy was safe, then Kelly could find out where the child was and make sure she was safe, too. Because if those thugs had come after Mandy and her, they might go after the child, as well.

"Do you know of anything Mandy has ever done to make you distrust her?" Kelly came out and asked.

Jameson stayed quiet for a moment and then shook his head. "I didn't know her that well, and you never mentioned any concerns you had about her."

Judging from the flicker of his jaw muscles, there

was something else he wanted to say. Something that Kelly wouldn't necessarily want to hear.

"I guess I'm troubled by the fact that Mandy would participate in a baby's kidnapping," he finally explained.

That meant he was troubled with her own participation in it, too. Well, welcome to the club. Kelly didn't even know who she was any longer, but it didn't sit well with her to have done something like that. Especially if she'd been duped into it by Hadley. Because if Boyer was right, Hadley had wanted the baby taken to get back at him.

"I'll try to call Mandy again," she said, taking the phone from Jameson. Kelly had lost count of how many times she'd done that. Had lost count of the prayers she'd been saying for her sister's safety. Not just from the kidnappers but also from the gunshot wound.

When she redialed the number, there was still no answer. That didn't mean her sister was dead, though. Mandy could have ditched or dropped the phone while she was running from her kidnappers. Plus, since Mandy's phone was on silent, she might not know about Kelly's repeated attempts to call her. Of course, Mandy had to know they would be trying to get in touch with her.

"When we get there, you won't leave this cruiser," Jameson reminded her. Since it was yet another bit of repeated info, she wasn't likely to forget it. Or find some way around it. Still, if Mandy could just see her from a distance, maybe that would be enough to draw her out.

First, though, Jameson, Gabriel and the deputies would have to make sure the kidnappers were no longer a threat.

"Keep trying to remember anything that will help

us with this," Jameson added when he took back his phone. He also continued to keep watch around them.

Kelly was doing the same and considered pressing Jameson again to give her a weapon. He'd refused the other times she'd asked, but maybe once they got closer to the warehouse, he'd reconsider.

She didn't want to close her eyes for fear she would miss something, like someone following them. But Kelly did do as Jameson had said, and she tried to force those images and fragments back into her mind. Since there were so many pieces that didn't make sense, she tried to focus on the baby.

And she saw her again.

Smiling, wearing a pink dress. She was reaching up her hands as if she wanted someone to take her. Kelly looked past the child, hoping to figure out where she was. A room with white walls. It could have been any room in any house, because there were no other details for her to latch onto. Like the other memories, it was gone in a flash.

Replaced by a much more recent memory.

"You kissed me," she said. Though she certainly hadn't meant to say it aloud.

Jameson frowned when he turned toward her. He didn't say a word, but there was a what-the-heck look in his eyes.

"When we were at the window at your house," she added. "You kissed my forehead." Since he was still frowning, Kelly waved that off. "Sorry."

The frown continued, added with some muttered profanity. "You caught me at a weak moment." He paused, said more of those under-the-breath curse words. "I have a history of weak moments when it comes to you."

For some stupid reason, that made her smile. Though it shouldn't have. It was obvious Jameson wanted things to be over between them. And they would be. As soon as they rescued her sister and caught the people responsible. Kelly desperately wanted those things to happen, but it gave her an empty feeling inside to realize that after this, she might never see Jameson again.

"Are you remembering something?" he asked. Maybe to change the subject or maybe because Kelly was certain her expression had changed. Definitely not a smile now.

She shook her head but didn't have to add more because Jameson's phone rang. Just like that, her heart was right back in her throat, but it wasn't her sister. Those calls had come through as Unknown Caller, but this one had the phone number. Jameson answered it, putting it on speaker, and Kelly immediately heard a familiar voice.

"What the hell's going on?" Boyer demanded.

"Plenty," Jameson snarled. "Did you have something specific you wanted to whine about?"

Even though Boyer didn't answer immediately, Kelly could practically feel the man seething with anger. "You know why I'm calling. It's Mandy. You found her."

Jameson's eyes narrowed, and she knew why. Someone had obviously leaked the info to Boyer. That shouldn't have surprised her since the SAPD cops were on scene. Kelly didn't remember how law enforcement communicated with each other, but it was possible Boyer had access to those communications' channels.

"Did we find her?" Jameson countered. "Because we're not sure exactly where she is."

"The warehouse," Boyer snapped.

"That's just a guess, and she's on the run from kidnappers. Mandy could be anywhere."

It was true. And that caused Kelly's chest to tighten even more.

"She's there," Boyer insisted. "And I soon will be, too. If you get to her first, find out if my daughter is with her."

Jameson didn't agree to that. "Just stay out of the way," he added, and Jameson ended the conversation when his phone dinged to indicate he had another call coming in.

This time Unknown Caller was on the screen.

"Please tell me you're coming after me," Mandy said the moment that Jameson answered.

"We are if you're at the Carswell warehouse."

"I'm not. I had to get away from there. I'm about a quarter of a mile from there at a truck stop. I'm hiding behind the building."

Cameron immediately relayed that info to Gabriel.

"Do you have eyes on the kidnappers?" Jameson asked her.

"No, but they have to be nearby." Mandy made a sound that he thought might have been a muffled sob. "Please hurry."

"We will, but if you can, stay on the line in case you have to go on the move again."

"I'll try. Is Kelly with you?"

"Yes," Kelly answered, causing Jameson to give her another of those nasty glares.

She listened carefully for her sister's reaction, but there wasn't one. Not one that Kelly could hear anyway.

"Why did I tell you I'd help you if something went

wrong?" Kelly pressed. "What exactly were we doing that had the potential to turn bad?"

"You honestly don't remember?"

"No. Just bits and pieces that don't make sense. Who's trying to kill me and why? And who kidnapped you?"

"I don't know." Her sister didn't hesitate that time. "But I think it all goes back to that file you took from Jameson. Do you remember someone trying to kill you after that?"

Heavens. She definitely hadn't remembered that. "No. Who?"

"I figured it was Jameson. Or someone in his family. That's why I didn't want to trust him or his brother."

Jameson cursed. "I didn't try to kill her. Neither did Gabriel."

"Well, someone did, and that's why you went on the run." Mandy made that low moan again. "I figured there was something in that file that someone wanted to keep secret."

Kelly thought that could be true, but if so, she still didn't believe Jameson was behind it. "Do you have the file?" Kelly asked her.

"No. You do."

Kelly's stomach sank. That was not what she wanted to hear. Because she had no idea where it was.

"How far out are you?" Mandy asked, the urgency in her voice going up even more.

"Less than five minutes," Cameron provided.

"Well, hurry, because I just spotted the thugs again. I have to go." And with that, her sister ended the call.

Cameron was already driving as fast as it was safe to go, but he pushed even harder on the accelerator.

"Your sister is smart," Jameson reminded Kelly. "She'll stay hidden until we're there. You're smart, too," he added without even hesitating. "That's why you'll stay put in this cruiser. Agreed?"

Kelly nodded. It was the smart and safe thing to do. She only hoped they didn't arrive to her sister being caught in the middle of a gunfight. Or worse. Mandy could be hurt even more than she already was.

"Once we've had a chance to question Mandy," Jameson went on, "she might be able to fill in some of your memory gaps."

He put away his phone, and because they were getting closer to the truck stop, he drew his weapon. Kelly hadn't needed a reminder of the danger, but that gave her another jolt anyway.

Another jolt of memory, too.

This time it wasn't the bits and pieces but a fullfledged image. Of her running. It was so vivid she could feel her pulse throbbing, could hear her own ragged breath. There was a taste in her mouth, too, and it took her a moment to realize it was blood. She had blood in her mouth as well as on her face because she could feel it running down the side of her head.

"Are you okay?" Jameson asked. She heard the alarm in his voice, and he touched her arm.

Kelly tried to answer, but she was caught up in the images. So real. So painful. And the images kept coming. She stumbled, her body pitching forward, and she fell, landing on some damp grass. That's when she realized she was in a pasture.

No. *The* pasture.

The place where those men had attacked her and robbed her of her memory.

"It's not real," she said, repeating it so that it wouldn't cause her to have a panic attack. She had survived, more or less, and the memories and those men couldn't hurt her now.

But the reminder didn't work. More memories hit her. She saw the gun in her hand, felt the grass beneath her as she rolled over and came up ready to fire. If she didn't shoot, they would kill her. Kelly could see that cold, flat look on their faces. She was a job to them.

The one on the right took aim at her, but Kelly pulled the trigger first. Her shot slammed into his chest. Before he even dropped to the ground, she put two bullets in the other one.

"I remember killing those men," Kelly managed to say. "I did it. I killed them."

Judging from the sound Jameson made, that hadn't surprised him. However, he kept staring at her, clearly waiting for more. But there wasn't more. The images faded just as quickly as they'd come.

"It's a start," he added. "For now, though, I need you to get down on the seat."

She snapped toward the window, and that's when Kelly saw the truck stop just ahead. Or at least she saw the trucks. There were five semis parked around the one-story building, and four men were milling near the front door.

No sign of Mandy, though.

She slid lower in the seat but kept her head high enough so she could hopefully glance out the front window, but Jameson pushed her down.

Then he cursed.

"I see Mandy," Jameson said, "and she's got a gun."

Kelly shook her head, certain he was wrong. Her sister hadn't said anything about a gun when she'd called them. "Maybe she took it from one of the kidnappers."

Of course, there could be another explanation. One that Kelly prayed wasn't true. That this was a trap and her sister had betrayed her.

"She's bleeding all right," Cameron added a moment later.

That got Kelly sitting up, and it didn't take her long to spot the woman peering around the back edge of the building. She had dark brown hair that was cut short and choppy. There was nothing familiar about her face. Nothing familiar about her. But there was indeed blood on the sleeve of her light blue shirt.

Her sister lifted her head, her attention going straight to the cruiser. She didn't move, though. Instead, she looked around, maybe for those goons who'd taken and injured her.

Cameron pulled the cruiser closer and stopped at the side of the building. He couldn't go any farther because of a Dumpster and several parked cars. Mandy was still a good ten feet away.

"If you get out of the cruiser, I'll arrest you," Jameson warned Kelly.

She didn't think he was bluffing, either. However, he got out. Before Kelly could tell him that it was too dangerous, he had the door open. He didn't go to her sister, though. He kept cover behind the door of the cruiser.

"Jameson," Mandy said. "Where's my sister?"

"Inside the car."

It was hard to tell from Mandy's expression if she was relieved about that. "And you're positive you can trust the cops you brought with you?"

"I trust them with my life," Jameson assured her. "And Kelly's."

Mandy hesitated as if deciding if that was true or not, but she finally did start toward them.

"You're not getting in the cruiser unless you give me that gun," Jameson ordered. And it was indeed an order. It stopped Mandy in her tracks. "When you come closer, hold the gun down by your side and don't make any sudden moves."

Mandy glanced at the gun as if debating that. Not good, because it was probably way too dangerous for her to be out there. Too dangerous for all of them. Even with Gabriel behind them and the San Antonio cops nearby, Mandy and Jameson could be cut down in a gunfight.

"If this is a trick, I'll make you pay," Mandy spat out like profanity. She followed it with some real profanity before she finally walked to Jameson.

He took the gun from her, tucking it in the back waist of his jeans. In the same motion, he opened the front door of the cruiser and put her inside. "Search her," he told Cameron.

The deputy did. He patted her down and then shook his head. "No other weapons."

Mandy mumbled more of those curse words. "The only reason I had that gun was because I took it from the men who kidnapped me."

Kelly prayed that was true. Actually, she hoped everything her sister had said and done wasn't part of some scheme that Kelly didn't understand or couldn't remember.

"There's an ambulance nearby," Jameson told Mandy. "We can take you to it now."

But Mandy didn't even react to that. Instead, she looked over the seat, her eyes meeting Kelly's. Kelly thought maybe she saw some relief there. Relief that didn't last long.

"The ambulance can wait," Mandy insisted. "We have to get out of here now." She tipped her head to the car behind them. "Is that your brother, Gabriel?" she asked Jameson. "The one you said you'd trust with your life?"

Jameson paused so long that for a couple of seconds Kelly didn't think he would answer. Finally, though, he nodded.

"Good. Because we might need him. But not any SAPD guys. I don't know if any of them are working for the kidnappers or not. Come on," Mandy quickly added before Jameson could argue with that. "We have to get to the baby before those men find her."

Chapter Nine

Jameson hadn't liked anything about this plan to meet Mandy, and he was liking it even less now.

"What baby?" he snapped.

"Just go. I'll explain everything once we're there. Those kidnappers will go after her."

Her. Maybe as in Boyer's daughter.

"Please," Mandy said, looking at Kelly. "If they take her, we might never find her. They could hurt her to get back at you."

Hell. That wasn't what he wanted to hear. Of course, Jameson hadn't wanted to hear that Kelly had had any part in taking the child. Because there was no way Boyer was just going to let this slide. He would put Kelly behind bars. And then there was the issue of the child. Boyer would almost certainly get custody of his own daughter—unless Jameson could come up with some kind of dirt to stop him. At the moment, though, he had more urgent problems.

"Where's the baby?" Jameson demanded.

"Just drive," Mandy insisted. "I'll tell you once we're on the highway. Make sure your brother follows us."

Oh, he would. Jameson also hoped like the devil

that he wouldn't regret this. Still, if there was indeed a baby in danger, he needed to do something to save her.

"Go," Jameson told Cameron, and he made a quick call to Gabriel to let him know what was going on. He kept watch of Mandy, though, during the handful of seconds that he spoke to his brother. She didn't have a weapon and was hurt, but that didn't mean she wasn't a possible threat.

"Remember, no SAPD," Mandy said to Jameson once he was finished with the call. "It's too big of a risk to take to include them on this. If just one of them is on the take, it could cost a child her life."

Jameson wasn't immune to that threat. Especially since Kelly had indeed remembered the images of the little girl. It was a risk to go anywhere with Mandy, but he figured the biggest risk would be to stay put. After all, someone had caused that injury on Mandy's arm, and that someone could still be around.

"Take a right," Mandy instructed Cameron when he reached the end of the road.

Once the deputy had done that, Kelly made eye contact with her sister. "Start talking," Kelly said.

Mandy huffed. "I was about to tell you to do the same thing." She didn't keep her attention on her sister, though. Her gaze was firing all around, no doubt looking for those men. "Well, this is a mess. Do you know how close I came to dying?"

"Probably as close as Kelly did," Jameson countered, and he made a circling motion with his finger to prompt her to keep explaining.

Mandy opened her mouth, closed it and opened it again. "I'm not even sure where to start."

Jameson hoped this wasn't some kind of stall tactic. Just in case it was, he kept watch, as well. There wasn't much traffic on this particular road, but it only took one vehicle carrying those men to make this situation go from bad to worse.

"Start from the beginning," Jameson instructed. "And give me lots more details about where we're going and this baby that could be in harm's way."

Mandy nodded, then took a deep breath. "You mean the beginning two years ago when Kelly left?" But she didn't wait for him to confirm that. "Someone tried to kill her. That's why she ran away. And don't ask who did that because we don't know. Like I said, I thought it might be you. Guess not," she quickly added when Jameson's glare intensified.

"Where did I go?" Kelly asked. "And what happened? Why are you taking us to a baby? Whose baby is it?"

Judging from the way Mandy's eyes widened, one or more of those questions confused her. "Get on the I-35 north. Then take the second exit and turn right," Mandy said to Cameron before turning back to Kelly. "At first you went to Austin, but then there was another attack, and you moved again. I don't know where. You said it was best if no one knew."

Probably because she hadn't wanted to put her sister or anyone else in danger. But why had someone wanted her dead then? Or now, for that matter? It was too bad those memories didn't come back to her the way the other pieces had, because they desperately needed some answers.

Cameron took the ramp to the interstate, and there was plenty of traffic here, including Gabriel who was right behind them. Jameson only hoped those kidnappers hadn't managed to follow them.

"I hadn't heard from you in months," Mandy went on, talking to her sister, "and then you called me about a week ago. You asked me to meet you because you said something was wrong, that someone was following you. You thought it was August."

"August?" Kelly and Jameson repeated in unison. Jameson certainly hadn't been expecting Mandy to say that. Apparently neither had Kelly, because she made a sharp sound of surprise.

"Yeah. You told me that you believed August had turned stalker again."

Jameson looked at Kelly to see if she knew anything about this, but she only shook her head. "When did August stalk Kelly?" he asked.

"Two years ago. August had a thing for Kelly, and they even went out a few times. He was furious when he found out you'd slept with Jameson."

"That doesn't feel right," Kelly said, touching her fingers to her head. "Well, not the part about me dating August anyway. He gave me the creeps when I saw him at the sheriff's office, but he certainly didn't say a word about us going out."

"Nor has he ever said anything about it to me," Jameson added. "And I've had a lot of 'conversations' with him in the past two years."

Maybe that meant Mandy was lying. But why would she do that—especially since it was something he could verify with August? Of course, August might not tell him the truth.

"How did August know that Kelly had slept with me?" Jameson pressed.

Mandy lifted her shoulder, then winced. A reminder that she still needed medical attention for that gunshot wound. "Beats me. But the man was always hiring PIs to help get his brother out of jail. He could have had a PI watching Kelly."

"I didn't know," Kelly whispered, and she repeated it to Jameson.

"Well, you need to be careful around him," Mandy insisted. "The man is bad news, and I wouldn't put it past him to have set those kidnappers on me. He could be responsible for the attacks on you, too."

Jameson glanced at Kelly to see how she was handling that. Not well. She hadn't exactly been steady at the start of this trip, but she was obviously learning things that were hard for her to swallow.

Things hard for Jameson to swallow, too.

Hell. That's because he was jealous. Of August, of all people. Feeling the attraction for Kelly was bad enough, and now this was eating away at him. It was also something else he had to add to a growing to-do list. But if Kelly had indeed gone out with August, Jameson needed to find out why. Because it could be connected to the nightmare that was going on right now.

Cameron took the exit, and Jameson turned away from Kelly so he could make sure there were no suspicious vehicles around them. At least the traffic was thinner here, but there were plenty of buildings.

"Later, I'm going to want to hear a whole lot more about August," Jameson clarified to Mandy. "For now, let's get back to where we're going and the baby we're going to save from these thugs."

"We're going to a safe house. Of sorts," Mandy added in a mumble. "It's something Kelly set up last week. I'm just hoping it's as safe as we need it to be. As for Boyer's daughter, Hadley came to us, begging for help..."

Jameson followed Mandy's gaze and soon saw what had snagged her attention. It was a black SUV that came out from a side road and was now right behind Gabriel. Even though the driver didn't do anything suspicious like gun the engine and try to get closer to the cruiser, it still put Jameson on edge.

"The kidnappers used a vehicle like that." Mandy's voice was suddenly a hoarse whisper. "I'd like to have that gun back now."

Jameson didn't give it to her, but like the rest of them, they continued to watch the SUV. Apparently, Gabriel was doing the same thing because he got a text from his brother.

"Bad news?" Gabriel asked.

"Possibly," Jameson texted back.

A moment later, Mandy took her phone from her pocket, and she cursed when she looked at the screen. "Two missed calls. I'm betting this is the kidnappers. It's says Unknown Caller, but that's how their calls have been coming through."

Probably because they were using another burner cell. "You spoke to them after you escaped?"

She quickly shook her head. "No. I didn't answer. I didn't want them to hear me talking and use that to pinpoint my location."

Wise move. But Jameson very much wanted to talk to them now. He took the phone from Mandy. She reached for it as if to snatch it back from his hand, but he gave her a look that Jameson was certain could have melted ice.

"I just don't want them to find us," Mandy said. It was not only stating the obvious, but it was also an insult to him.

"I'm a Texas Ranger," he reminded her. "And I want you to stay quiet if they answer."

With that warning, Jameson hit the callback button. Even though he put it on speaker, Kelly still moved closer to him. Until they were shoulder to shoulder.

"Didn't you learn your lesson the first time you ran, Mandy?" a man said when he answered. "You want another bullet in you?"

That meshed with what Mandy had told them, but Jameson decided to stay silent to see what the kidnapper would say. It didn't take long for the guy to continue.

"I know the cat hasn't got your tongue," the goon taunted. "And I saw you get in the cop car. I know exactly where you are."

Mandy flinched, her attention shooting right back to that SUV. Kelly didn't fare much better. She clamped her teeth over her bottom lip, but that didn't stop it from trembling.

"Yeah, you're a special kind of stupid all right," the kidnapper went on. "This isn't much of a guess, but the cop is probably listening right now. So speak up, cop. If not, I plan to open the window and just start shooting. Might not hit the cruiser or the cop behind him, but I'll sure as hell hit something."

Jameson wanted to curse, but instead he handed Kelly his own phone. "Text Gabriel and tell him what's happening," he mouthed. He didn't want his brother blindsided by shots this idiot might fire. Once she'd started that, Jameson turned his attention back to the caller.

"Why'd you take Mandy?" Jameson came out and asked him.

The guy didn't jump to answer that, but Jameson

could hear him having a muffled conversation. Probably with his partner. Or rather his partners. Mandy had said two men had taken her, but that didn't mean there weren't more than that following them.

"I was following orders," the guy finally said. "Just like now. Either you and the other cop pull off the side of the road and hand over Kelly to us, or we start shooting."

"Kelly?" Jameson questioned. "I thought you were after Mandy."

"Not now that we have Kelly in our sights. And she is in our sights, cop."

Jameson wasn't sure how Kelly managed to finish the text to Gabriel because her hand was suddenly trembling as much as her mouth. She handed him back his phone.

"I can't put all of you in danger again," Kelly said. Her voice was barely audible, but Jameson heard it loud and clear.

He hoped Kelly didn't have trouble hearing him, either. "No. You're not surrendering to these nutjobs. You'll be dead within minutes if you step out of this cruiser." Just in case she had plans to jump out, Jameson took hold of her arm.

"He's right," Mandy assured her. "They want you dead."

Jameson hadn't been certain that Mandy would be willing to put herself in the path of those kidnappers, but it sounded as if she was bracing herself for a fight.

And that fight came.

"Time's up," the kidnapper snarled.

The guy ended the call, and within seconds a shot blasted through the air. That put Jameson's heart right in his throat, and he fired glances around, trying to figure out if the shooter had hit anything.

He had.

The back window of Gabriel's car had been cracked. It was bullet-resistant, but if the shots continued, eventually they'd be able to make it through.

The gunman fired again, and this time Jameson spotted the guy's hand when he stuck it out the window. It was impossible to see his face, though, because of the heavy tint on the windshield.

"Speed up," Jameson told Cameron. "Get us out of here." That way, Gabriel wouldn't be trapped between the cruiser and the SUV.

"Give me the gun, and I'll try to return fire," Mandy insisted.

Jameson couldn't say "no" fast enough. For one thing, he didn't want the window down to make it easier for shots to get into the vehicle. There could be other gunmen stashed along the road who could do that. For another thing, he didn't want Mandy firing a shot that could hit an innocent bystander.

Cameron sped up. Behind them, Gabriel did the same. But the shooter in the SUV didn't give up. It went faster as well, and the shots continued. These bullets didn't seem to be going into Gabriel's car, either. The snake was firing random shots, trying to kill someone.

In the distance, Jameson heard the sound of sirens. Gabriel had likely called for backup for them to already be that close to the scene. That didn't mean Jameson had plans for them to slow down or stop.

"Take the next left," Mandy told Cameron.

Cameron's eyes met Jameson's in the rearview mirror, and Jameson nodded. "Where are we going?" Jameson asked her.

"That safe house." Mandy's breath was gusting now, and she had her attention pinned to the SUV. Despite the sirens, the thugs were staying right behind them and were continuing to shoot.

One of those bullets slammed into the back glass of the cruiser.

Jameson cursed, shoving Kelly down onto the seat. "You get down, too," he told Mandy, but he didn't wait to see if she'd do that. He turned in the seat, positioning his body above Kelly and making himself ready to return fire if those shots did indeed take out the glass.

Cameron took the left turn, the tires squealing on the asphalt, and the deputy had to fight with the steering wheel to keep them from going into a skid. Beneath him, he could feel Kelly's tense muscles, and he knew she was scared. She looked up at him, their gazes connecting for just a second, but in that glimpse, Jameson also saw something else.

The determination to put an end to this.

Good. He preferred her riled than on the verge of losing it. That said, he didn't want her to do anything stupid. He'd already filled their stupid quota for the day by bringing Kelly with him and putting her in yet another life-and-death situation.

"Take another left at the stop sign," Mandy told Cameron.

Another shot smacked into the back window of the cruiser, but despite the webbed glass, Jameson was still able to see that Gabriel made the turn with them. So did the SUV. His brother stayed right behind the cruiser while the hail of gunfire continued. The only saving grace was that there wasn't much traffic on this road. No buildings, either, so it minimized the gunman's targets.

Of course, that meant the goon continued to send shots into the cruiser.

"I see the cops," Mandy said, volleying glances all around.

So did Jameson. There were two SAPD cruisers, their blue lights flashing and the sirens blaring. They were still a good distance behind them, but at least now the SUV would be sandwiched between them.

"Hold on," Cameron warned them a split second before he reached the stop sign. The deputy slowed just enough to make the left turn and then sped up again.

Jameson watched Gabriel take the same turn. But the SUV didn't. The driver went straight through the intersection and kept going.

Getting away.

"You want me to go after him?" Cameron asked.

It was tempting, especially since these goons had endangered so many people, but Kelly and Mandy had already had enough risks for the day. For a lifetime, really.

"No. Keep going," Jameson answered. Behind them, the SAPD cops went in pursuit of the SUV. Good. Maybe they'd catch the SOBs.

Kelly got up from the seat, glancing back at the messed-up glass before turning to her sister. "How far is this safe house?"

"Not far." Mandy paused. Stared at her. "You really don't remember?"

"No. How far?" Kelly repeated.

Mandy looked at the road, which was leading them to a rural area. In fact, there were no visible houses, just pastures. "About two miles. But we need to keep watch to make sure those men aren't following us."

Jameson was already doing that. There was no one behind Gabriel, and they hadn't yet passed any immediate side roads, where a gunman could park and wait. That was about to change, though.

"Take a right at the stop sign just ahead," Mandy instructed Cameron. Unlike Jameson, she kept her attention nailed to Kelly while Cameron took the turn. "Kelly, you're sure you want to go here?"

That spiked Jameson's concern a significant notch. "Why wouldn't she?" he snapped. "You said we needed to go here to make sure the men didn't get to the baby."

Mandy nodded without even looking at him. "Are you sure?"

"If it can save a child, then yes, I'm sure," Kelly said. But she didn't sound certain at all. Neither was Jameson.

There was also plenty of wariness in Cameron's eyes when he looked back at Jameson, silently asking him what to do.

Jameson leaned forward and got right in Mandy's face. "If this is a trap, you'll pay and pay hard. Understand?"

"No trap," she assured him in a ragged whisper. "Pull into the driveway just ahead," she added to Cameron.

Jameson got his gun ready again, and he handed Kelly the weapon he'd taken from Mandy. He prayed she didn't have to use it, but he needed her to be ready for anything.

"Anything" definitely wasn't what Jameson had expected.

The moment that Cameron turned into the driveway, Jameson saw the one-story white house. Not a fortress or a trap. It looked like, well, a home. There was a picket fence surrounding the yard, which was dotted with shrubs and flowers. And the place wasn't empty. There was a blond-haired woman sitting on the porch in a rocking chair.

The woman wasn't alone. Beside her on the porch was a little girl. A toddler. She was wearing pink shorts and a white top, and the vehicles got both their attention. The woman stood, scooping up the little girl, her motions jerky and fast as if she was ready to bolt with her. She might have done just that, too, but she stopped when Mandy stepped from the cruiser.

Even though Jameson was about ten yards from the woman, he saw the relief on her face. It didn't last, though, because she spotted the blood on Mandy's sleeve.

"You're hurt," the woman called out. "What happened? Do we need to leave? Has there been more trouble?"

Mandy waved it off and went closer. "Kelly's with me." She added something else to the woman, something that Jameson couldn't hear.

That put him on full alert, and he stepped from the cruiser in case Mandy had just given this woman the order to attack. But no attack. The woman carried the baby off the porch and stood her in the yard. The little girl grinned and toddled her way toward Mandy. The kid obviously wasn't very good at walking, because she teetered a few times as if she might fall.

Jameson was so focused on what was playing out in front of him that he didn't notice Kelly opening the door until it was too late. She got out, and since she was on the other side of the car, he couldn't get to her before she started going closer to the house.

As the woman had done with Mandy, she smiled at Kelly. So did the little girl. The baby immediately changed directions, no longer headed toward Mandy but straight to Kelly.

Jameson hurried to them, his gaze slashing all around in case they were about to be ambushed. But there didn't seem to be a threat. The woman certainly didn't seem alarmed.

When Kelly reached the baby, the little girl out-stretched her arms for Kelly to pick her up. And Jameson had no trouble hearing the one word that the child babbled.

"Mama."

Chapter Ten

Mama?

Kelly glanced at her sister to see if she had an explanation, but Mandy kept walking. "We shouldn't be out here," Mandy finally said when she reached the porch. "Bring Gracelyn inside with you."

Gracelyn. That apparently was the child's name. And her sister was right. They shouldn't be out there. Jameson must have thought so, too, because he scooped up the little girl, shifting her to his hip, and he hooked his arm around Kelly to get her moving. Gabriel, Cameron and Susan, the other deputy, were right behind them.

"Mama," the little girl repeated, and she tried to wiggle out of Jameson's arms to get to Kelly.

Kelly knew what all of this meant. She'd been the one to raise Boyer's daughter. She'd been the child's mother.

She tucked Mandy's gun in the back of her jeans and took Gracelyn from Jameson when the girl just kept squirming. The child immediately kissed Kelly's cheek. It was as if someone had warmed her from head to toe, and Kelly was positive what she was feeling was love. A mother's love.

"Pat, pat," Gracelyn said.

"She learned to play patty-cake," the woman on the

porch supplied. Kelly had no idea who she was, but the moment they reached her, she pulled Kelly into a short hug. "I'm glad you made it back." Her attention drifted to Kelly's bandage. "Are you okay?"

"No." Kelly could say that with complete certainty. Every inch of her was still spinning from the adrenaline, and she was getting more of those fragments of memories.

Fragments that didn't make sense.

"Pat, pat," Gracelyn repeated.

Jameson gave the little girl a long glance. Frowned. And he kept them moving. Once they were all inside, he shut the door and locked it.

"First things first," Jameson said. "Mandy, make sure you don't have a tracking device on you."

She groaned and looked ready to curse, but she stopped when her gaze landed on Gracelyn. Mandy began to look over her clothes and shoes. Kelly helped, too. Balancing the baby on her hip, she checked Mandy's hair and the back of her shirt.

"I don't see anything," Kelly relayed to Jameson when she'd finished.

"Want to tell me what the heck is going on?" Gabriel growled. "And who she is?" He tipped his head to the woman before going to the window to keep watch. The two deputies went to other windows to do the same.

The sheriff was obviously riled, maybe about this latest attack, maybe because they'd been brought here with such little information. But despite that, things suddenly started to feel, well, right. It must have felt right for Gracelyn, too, because she dropped her head onto Kelly's shoulder as if it belonged there.

"This is Erica Welker," Mandy said, looking at Kelly.

Mandy went to the adjacent kitchen and came back with a first-aid kit.

The name meant nothing to her, and Erica must have seen the surprise on Kelly's face, because she made a slight gasp. "What's wrong?"

Kelly decided to keep the answer short, especially since Mandy had so much explaining to do. "I have amnesia and don't remember a lot of things. I'm sorry, but I don't know who you are."

Erica stood there, her mouth not open exactly, but she did have a gobsmacked expression on her face. "But you remember Gracelyn?"

"I have some memories of her." Kelly shifted her attention back to her sister, who was now in the process of ripping off her shirtsleeve, no doubt so she could examine her wound. Kelly didn't come out and ask Mandy to start talking. However, Jameson's and Gabriel's glares must have prompted her sister to do that.

Mandy looked at Erica. "Could you take Gracelyn to her room to play?"

Erica volleyed uneasy glances at all of them before she nodded and took the little girl. Gracelyn started to protest, babbling "Mama," but she stopped when Erica said she would read to her. Kelly kept her eyes on them as they walked away, and the moment Gracelyn was out of sight, she felt the loss. Or something. It caused her chest to tighten when she could no longer see the child.

"FYI, there's a whole lot about what I'm going to say that none of you will like," Mandy began. When she started to clean away the blood from her arm, Kelly went to her and took over the task. It appeared the wound was shallow, but it was still bleeding.

"I haven't liked much of anything since this whole

mess started," Jameson assured her. "But I want to hear it anyway."

Mandy took a deep breath. "I've already told you that Kelly called me about a week ago. She said she was worried that someone, maybe August, was stalking her. She asked me to help her protect Gracelyn."

"Why would August want to harm a kid?" Jameson snapped.

"Kelly thought he might try to take her to use her for leverage in something he was planning. Maybe like a last-ditch effort to get his brother out of jail. I didn't think August would do anything like that," Mandy quickly added, "but then someone did try to kidnap Kelly and Gracelyn. They escaped, and Kelly brought Gracelyn and Erica here."

"Erica's a nanny?" Kelly asked.

Mandy nodded. "She used to be a PI, though. She worked for us when we still had the agency."

So more of a bodyguard than a mere nanny. Of course, that didn't surprise Kelly that they would need that. After all, she'd probably been in hiding with the child since she was born, and she probably trusted Erica.

"Anyway," Mandy went on, "we were here for a few days, and nothing happened. No more attacks. So I decided to go back to my place and get some supplies. That's when those two thugs kidnapped me. They were going to hold me and force Kelly to do whatever it was they wanted her to do."

"Kill Jameson," Kelly quickly provided. "I had a note telling me to do that. But why Jameson?"

Mandy huffed and then winced when Kelly dabbed the wound with antiseptic. "Again, I'm sure you think it's August trying to get back at the Becketts for putting his brother in jail. But I believe Boyer's behind what's happening."

"You mean because of his daughter," Kelly said under her breath.

"No. Because he's dirty. August thinks so, too, because he asked us to look into some money laundering rumors. Rumors that Boyer was stealing federally confiscated funds and then funneling them into his own private offshore bank account."

Now it was Jameson who huffed. "Why the hell would August care a rat about Boyer doing something like that?"

"August thought Boyer was going to set him up for it," Mandy answered without hesitation. "You must know that Boyer was investigating August?"

They did know that because Boyer had told them at the sheriff's office. Still, there was something that didn't make sense. "Did we find anything to incriminate either Boyer or August?" Kelly asked.

"Yeah." And that's all Mandy said for several long moments. "You apparently found a money trail, and when this recent trouble started, you were trying to figure out who owned the account because it seemed to be connected to the money laundering that August thought Boyer was doing."

Well, that would certainly make someone want to stop her. But it made Kelly wonder—how had August or Boyer known about her investigation into that money trail? Had someone tipped them off?

Jameson cursed. "You should have gone to the cops with this." He aimed that snarl at Kelly.

And she deserved it. But Kelly knew why she hadn't

done that, why it was critical for her to find something that would put Boyer behind bars.

"I didn't go to the cops because I couldn't," Kelly reminded him. "Because I'd stolen Boyer's daughter."

Since Kelly still had her fingers on her sister's arm, she felt Mandy's muscles go stiff. Mandy looked up at her, and Kelly didn't understand what she was seeing in her sister's eyes.

"You'll want to sit down for this," Mandy said before shifting her attention to Jameson. "You, too."

Jameson cursed again. "I'm not sitting down. Just tell us…" His words trailed off, and he glanced in the direction of where they'd last seen Erica and the baby. "How old is Gracelyn?"

Mandy's arm muscles tightened even more, and she pulled Kelly into the chair next to her. "She's fourteen months."

The room went still and silent. But that didn't apply to what was going on inside Kelly. Or Jameson, for that matter. He groaned. It was hoarse and raw and came deep from within his chest.

"She's not Boyer's daughter," Jameson somehow managed to say. He took the words right out of Kelly's mouth, and she had no trouble taking this one step further. Gracelyn wasn't Boyer's.

That's when Kelly knew Gracelyn was her and Jameson's child.

Jameson turned a very nasty glare in Kelly's direction, and it had a dangerous edge to it. He looked ready to explode. Kelly wanted to tell him that she hadn't remembered giving birth to the child, much less keeping her from him, but the words froze in her throat.

Because she did remember.

It all came flooding back. The night she'd landed in bed with Jameson. Running and hiding after someone had attacked her. There were even bits and pieces of the pregnancy. What wasn't a bit or piece, though, was what she felt for her daughter. She loved her more than life itself.

"Why?" Jameson said, and his tone matched that tight, lethal expression on his face.

"Someone was trying to kill her," Mandy supplied.

That wouldn't be enough to appease Jameson. No. Because he was a Ranger, and he would have expected her to go to him instead of running. Except she'd just stolen that file and hadn't even known if she could trust him.

"I need to see Gracelyn," Kelly insisted.

Jameson clearly didn't like that, but Kelly didn't take the time to say anything else. Everything inside her was urging her to get to her baby. To make sure she was okay. Later, she could hash things out with Jameson.

And it wouldn't be pretty.

Kelly hurried to the room where she'd seen Erica take the baby, and she threw open the door. Erica was sitting on the floor, Gracelyn in her lap, but the little girl had fallen asleep.

"She was tired from playing outside," Erica mouthed. She brushed a kiss on Gracelyn's head, and then did a double take of Kelly when she looked at her. "What's wrong? Did those kidnappers find us?"

Heavens, she hoped not. Now that she knew this precious baby was hers, Kelly had to do everything to protect her.

She went closer, sitting down on the bed next to Erica, and the nanny stood, easing Gracelyn into her arms. Kelly felt that same punch of love that she'd felt in the yard.

"Should I give you some time alone?" Erica asked.

The nanny didn't mean that offer for only Kelly and Gracelyn. That's because Jameson was in the doorway. He had anchored his hands on the jamb as if holding himself back.

"Yes, please," Kelly answered. Erica didn't jump to leave. She glanced at them, maybe trying to make sure it was safe to leave them alone with this cowboy cop. "It's okay," she added to Erica. "Jameson is Gracelyn's father."

The words hadn't stuck in her throat, and even though she'd just spelled out what Jameson already knew, he flinched a little. He stepped to the side to let Erica out, and then he came to them, sitting on the bed next to her.

"I should have told you," Kelly volunteered. "And there's nothing I can say to make this right. 'I'm sorry' certainly isn't going to do it."

A sound left his mouth. Almost a laugh, but it definitely wasn't from humor. He didn't say anything. Jameson just sat there, staring at their daughter.

Their daughter.

Kelly wondered how long it was going to take for that to sink in. Not just for Jameson, but also for her.

She studied Gracelyn's face and saw some parts of herself there. The shape of her mouth and eyes. But the coloring was all Jameson. Dark hair and olive skin. Kelly wondered why she hadn't noticed it the moment she laid eyes on the child.

"Do you doubt she's yours?" Kelly asked.

"No." Jameson didn't hesitate for even a second.

Kelly wasn't sure if that was good or bad. On the one hand, if Jameson didn't believe this was his child, he could just walk away and hand over their protective custody to someone else. But now that he knew Gracelyn was his, Kelly figured that meant he was going to work extra hard to make sure nothing bad happened to her.

He groaned, scrubbed his hand over his face and then turned to her. "I want to hate you for this."

She mentally repeated each word. "I hate myself for it."

"That doesn't make us even. It doesn't make it right."

Kelly was in total agreement with that. This was a mess, and it was all her own doing. "I must have thought I couldn't trust you."

That wasn't a good thing to say. It put more of that angry fire in Jameson's eyes. "You could have, but instead you kept her from me for over a year." He groaned again, and she could see this was eating away at him.

It was eating away at her, too. She touched her fingers to his arm, but he only jerked away from her. "I'm not going to give you a free pass on this," he said like a warning. "I'm not going to let you cut me out of her life again."

That stung as much as if he'd slapped her. Not just the words, but the raw anger in his voice. Anger that she'd need to face. It didn't matter that she only had pieces of her memories; she somehow had to make this right. And that was a reminder that making things right started with Gracelyn's safety.

"We can't stay here," Kelly said.

"No," he agreed. "I need to get started on that. But just know that this conversation isn't over."

She hadn't thought for a moment that it was. As if

it were the most natural thing in the world, Jameson brushed a kiss on the baby's forehead, and he stood. However, he'd barely made it a step when Gabriel appeared in the doorway. The sheriff was still scowling, and he had his phone pressed to his ear. He motioned for Jameson to follow him.

Kelly's stomach sank, because she figured this wasn't good news. She got up, cradling the baby in her arms so she could follow him. By the time she made it back to the living room, Gabriel had finished his phone conversation and had turned to Jameson.

"That was SAPD," Gabriel said. "Those men in the SUV got away."

It felt as if someone had punched her, and it caused Kelly's head to throb even more. Not good. It was already too hard to think, and the pain was only making it worse.

Mandy bit off some of the profanity she was mumbling. "How did that happen?" she asked Gabriel.

"The men turned on a side road and ditched the SUV. The cops believe they had another vehicle stashed there and used it to escape." Gabriel paused, stared at her. "Any chance those men know where this place is?"

"No," her sister answered. "If they'd known the location, they would have already come here. For the baby," Mandy added in a whisper.

Yes, because if they had Gracelyn, then they knew Kelly would do anything to get her back.

Mandy's attention went to the baby for a moment. "The only way for those goons to find this place would be by putting a tracking device on me, and you've already searched me."

The moment her sister finished saying that, Jameson

cursed, and he yanked the phone from his pocket. Not his phone but the one Mandy had stolen from the kidnappers. He immediately started taking it apart.

Oh, God. Kelly prayed there was nothing to find.

"Check the gun, too," Jameson said, aiming a glance at Kelly.

That spiked her heart rate even more, and since Kelly didn't want to handle the gun while she was holding the baby, she turned so that Gabriel could take it from the back of her jeans. Like Jameson, he immediately started to inspect it. But his inspection didn't last long because Jameson dumped the pieces of the phone onto the coffee table.

Kelly saw it then. The white disk that was about the size of a quarter. Even though she still didn't have many memories of being a PI, she knew exactly what it was. And what it meant. The kidnappers had planted it there and intentionally let Mandy take it so she would lead them here to the baby.

"We have to leave now," Jameson insisted. He snapped toward the deputies. "Pull the cruisers right up to the porch."

That sent Erica and Mandy scurrying, and Kelly realized they were gathering up the baby's things. Obviously, they had been prepared for something like this. But Kelly certainly wasn't. The other attacks had terrified her, but this was a whole new level of terror.

Because Gracelyn could be hurt.

Cameron drew his gun, opened the door, but just as quickly, he slammed it shut. "Are you expecting company?" he asked Mandy.

Mandy shook her head, and she hurried to the window along with Gabriel and Jameson. Kelly could tell from their body language that this wasn't good.

The gunmen had found them.

Chapter Eleven

They had already dodged bullets from Mandy's kidnappers, but Jameson should have known it wasn't over. He'd let the news of the baby—*his* baby—distract him, and that could turn out to be a fatal mistake.

He needed to push aside that baby news and the emotions that came with it and focus on getting them out of this.

"Go to the back door," Jameson told Susan. "Make sure it's locked and that these guys don't try to sneak up on us." There weren't any houses back there. Not that Jameson had seen anyway, but it was possible there were trees and shrubs that one of these hired guns could use.

"Check all the windows. Look for any vulnerable points of attack," Gabriel added to Cameron, and the deputies hurried off to do those tasks.

"Is there a bathroom without windows?" Jameson asked Mandy.

She nodded. "There's one just off the hall."

Good. That was a start, though it wasn't ideal since bullets could go through walls and still reach them. "Take Erica and Gracelyn there, now," he told Kelly.

Jameson could see the stark fear in Kelly's eyes, but

he couldn't assure her that this was going to turn out well. It could end up in a gunfight, though that wasn't what Jameson wanted. Not with his daughter in the house.

Gabriel took out his phone, no doubt to call for backup, and while Jameson kept watch, he quickly reassembled the phone Mandy had taken. Right now, it was the only way he had to communicate with these snakes other than opening the door and going out there to face them down.

"One of them is getting out of the first SUV," Gabriel relayed.

Yeah, Jameson saw the gun. He got out from the driver's side, which meant the SUV was in between him and them. Jameson doubted that was a coincidence. The guy was using it for cover, and he was no doubt armed to the hilt.

Kelly's gaze connected with his as she started moving. "Be careful," she said, but she frowned as if that weren't nearly enough.

She was right. Words alone weren't going to fix this, or their personal situation for that matter, but if the thugs heard backup arriving, they might run again. Of course, they might be a good fifteen or twenty minutes from that happening.

Jameson waited until Erica, Gracelyn and Kelly had gone into the bathroom, and he shot a look at Mandy to prompt her to go, too. "I'm staying," she insisted. "But I need a gun."

He debated it, because Jameson still had a strange feeling about her, but he finally handed her the gun she'd taken from the kidnappers. Maybe she wouldn't have to use it.

Jameson moved back into position at the window, and while keeping watch, he pressed the button to call the kidnappers. He wasn't certain they would answer, but they did on the first ring. He put the call on speaker so that Gabriel would be able to hear.

"You probably thought you'd gotten away," a man immediately growled. "Now it's time to pay."

Jameson didn't even bother to address that threat. "Backup is on the way."

"We figured it was. That's why this'll have to be fast. Give us Kelly, and the kid and everybody else will be okay."

Even if Jameson had believed that, he wouldn't have handed over Kelly. But he soon realized Kelly might have a different notion about that. He heard the movement behind him and saw that Kelly was in the doorway of the bathroom. She no longer had Gracelyn in her arms, but she'd clearly heard what the thug had said.

"Why do you want me?" she demanded, and she charged forward toward Jameson and the phone.

"You know why," the man answered. "So just step outside, and there won't be a shot fired. You gotta know that's best for the kid and everybody else in the house. That includes your cop boyfriend."

The hired gun had done his homework. Or else his boss had filled him in. It made Jameson wonder if these thugs knew that Gracelyn was his daughter. Or maybe they believed she was Boyer's, just as Jameson had before Mandy dropped the bombshell.

Jameson gave Kelly the meanest scowl he could manage, and he motioned for her to go back in the bathroom. "If you go out there, they'll kill you and then try to shoot everyone in this house. They aren't going to leave witnesses."

"Now, now," the thug taunted, but he didn't deny it. He couldn't. The guy wasn't wearing a mask, and even though Jameson hadn't gotten a good look at his face, there was no way these goons would want to leave alive four officers and a PI.

Jameson kept the scowl on Kelly until she huffed and went back to the bathroom. Once she was inside, he returned his full attention to the caller.

"I don't know what you're being paid," Jameson told him, "but it's not nearly enough. Because you're going to die if you stay here."

He figured that would prompt the guy to give him another taunt. It didn't. The man lifted his hand over the hood of the SUV and pointed his gun at the house.

And he fired.

The shot slammed into the house, right next to the window where Jameson was standing. It wasn't the only shot, either. Several more came, and one of them crashed through the window and sent glass spewing over the room.

"There's one in the backyard!" Susan called out.

Hell. That wasn't what Jameson wanted to hear. Neither did Gabriel, because he cursed.

"If you have a shot, take it," Gabriel shouted back. "Just don't let him get in the house."

Jameson hit the end call button so the goons wouldn't be able to hear what they were saying. There were more shots, not coming from the guy by the SUV this time. Jameson quickly realized they also weren't coming from the back. They had slammed into the side of the house.

"I got a shooter," Cameron let them know.

That caused the skin to crawl on the back of his neck, and Jameson's thoughts jerked to a really bad place. If these thugs had the house surrounded, they could keep shooting until they ripped it apart, and backup might not arrive in time to stop them.

Gabriel didn't repeat his warning to Cameron about not letting the guy in the house. His brother knocked out the glass on the side window where he was positioned, and he started shooting.

Jameson did the same.

That sent the guy behind the SUV dropping out of sight, but the gunfire continued on the side of the house. Worse, he heard shots at the back, too. "See if Susan or Cameron need help," Jameson told Mandy. "But stay close to the bathroom door."

He didn't need to spell out why he wanted her to do that, but if these thugs did make it inside, Jameson wanted someone standing guard to stop them from getting to Gracelyn and Kelly.

"There's one at your three o'clock," Gabriel said.

Because of his angle, Jameson didn't spot the guy at first, but then he saw him crawling toward the picket fence. Jameson took aim and put two bullets in him. The guy quit crawling. Whether he was dead or not was anyone's guess, but maybe he was at least out of commission.

"How much ammo do you have?" Jameson asked his brother.

"A lot. So do Cameron and Susan. You?"

"Plenty." He'd stocked up before they'd left to go find Mandy. "I'm thinking of trying to shoot out the SUV engine. They might get worried if they realize I can disable their ride. It could cause them to run."

Of course, part of him didn't want them to run. Jameson wanted to face them down and arrest the SOBs. But that was too big of a risk to take with the others in the house.

"Go for it," Gabriel agreed. "As long as you're shooting at the engine, it might keep thug number one pinned down."

That was a good side benefit. An even better one would be if he managed to shoot the idiot in the head.

Jameson aimed his gun and started firing. His shot slammed into the SUV's engine, and it got the reaction he wanted. The engine started to spew steam, which meant he'd hit the radiator. He caught a glimpse of thug number one scrambling to get back inside. He drove off, but it wouldn't get far. Nor did the second SUV go with him. It stayed put, making Jameson wonder if the hired guns who'd been inside were now the ones at the sides and back of the house.

More shots blasted through the air, all coming from the back of the house, and then Jameson heard a sound that he definitely didn't want to hear.

Breaking glass.

Not from the back or from where Cameron was, either. No. This had come from the other side. He didn't know the layout of the house, but it sounded as if it'd come from the window in the room next to the bathroom.

"Go!" Gabriel ordered him.

But Jameson had already started running. However, before he even made it to the hall, there was a different sound. A welcome one. Sirens. That meant backup had arrived. It would probably send the men outside running, but it was the one inside who was the immediate

threat. He could start shooting before the backup officers even got out of their vehicles.

The bathroom door was shut, thank God, and it was
hopefully locked, but the door adjacent to it was slightly
ajar. With his gun ready, Jameson peered around the
corner.

No gunman. However, he did see the broken glass
on the floor. That twisted his gut into a knot.

Jameson couldn't risk the idiot firing into the bathroom, so he couldn't wait to see what this guy was planning. He dragged in a deep breath and gave the door
a hard kick.

He got lucky.

Because the door smacked right into the thug who'd
just started to move toward him. The guy froze, and that
gave Jameson enough time to take aim at him.

"Move," Jameson warned him, "and you're a dead
man."

KELLY HAD SO many emotions running through her that
it felt as if there were a F5 tornado in her head. Too bad,
because she needed to think. Needed to figure out what
was happening so she could stop it.

It was almost a cliché, but this was one of the worst
and best times of her life. She had her baby, a baby she
hadn't even remembered existed, and that was an incredible feeling. On the other side of the coin, though,
her precious little girl was in danger.

"Pat, pat," Gracelyn said, drawing Kelly's attention
back to her. Not that it had strayed far. She hadn't let
her baby out of her sight on the trip from the house to
the sheriff's office.

And wouldn't.

But this wasn't an ideal situation for any of them. Gracelyn was on a quilt in the break room at the back of the building. It would be night soon, and she didn't like the idea of her little girl having to sleep here. Thankfully, Gracelyn didn't seem to mind and was having fun alternating her play sessions among Erica, Mandy and Kelly.

Jameson, too.

He was working the investigation from Gabriel's office, but he kept popping in every ten minutes or so. Each time he came in, he zoomed right in on Gracelyn and once had even taken her picture with his phone. The glances he spared Kelly weren't exactly of a friendly nature, and she couldn't blame him. He would probably never forgive her for this.

After she finished off another cup of coffee, Mandy sank down on the floor next to them, and Kelly didn't miss her sister wincing when her arm brushed against the sofa.

"The doctor left you some pain meds," Kelly reminded her.

He'd done that when he had come to the sheriff's office to stitch up Mandy and examine both Kelly and the baby. Gracelyn didn't have a bruise or scratch on her. That was something, at least. If she'd been hurt in all of this, Kelly wouldn't have been able to stomach it.

"The doc left you some pain meds, too," Mandy pointed out just as quickly.

He had. But Kelly shook her head. "They might make me woozy."

"Ditto," Mandy agreed. "I'm thinking this isn't a good time to be out of it."

No. They might have to move again at a moment's

notice. The sheriff's office was safe. Probably. But it was only temporary.

"Maybe Jameson will get some info from the gunman he captured," Erica suggested. Despite the serious conversation, the nanny smiled at Gracelyn when she babbled something.

Kelly made a sound of agreement to Erica's comment. She was hoping that would happen, too, but so far the yet-to-be-identified man wasn't giving them much. Like his comrade, McGill, who was still in custody. Both men had lawyered up. At least the most recent captive wasn't claiming that Kelly was the one behind this.

"FYI, I didn't know about Gracelyn until long after she was born," Mandy said a moment later.

Kelly tried to work through the clutter in her head to figure out why she wouldn't have told her. "Maybe I thought it would put you in danger if you knew."

Mandy shrugged, winced again. "If you'd told me sooner, though, I could have helped you. Like with that file from Jameson's office, for instance. As soon as you got your hands on it, you didn't tell me squat about what any of the notes and such meant to you. But that file could be the reason these snakes are after all of us now."

That immediately troubled Kelly. Why wouldn't she have shared that with Mandy? They were business partners. Fellow PIs. Again, it was possible she realized the info was lethal and she hadn't wanted to involve Mandy. For all the good it'd done. Obviously, Mandy had gotten involved when those kidnappers took her.

"I feel like an idiot," Mandy continued, groaning softly. "I should have known it was too easy for me to steal that phone and gun. Those men wanted me to lead them straight to you and Gracelyn. And that's exactly what I did."

"You didn't know." Kelly slipped her hand over her sister's.

But they certainly knew now, and it was proof of just how far these monsters would go to get to her.

She was about to ask if Mandy could fill her in on the months she'd been hiding. Those after Gracelyn had been born. But before she could say anything, Jameson opened the door. As with his other visits, he looked at Gracelyn first. Smiled. Gracelyn returned the smile and babbled something again.

"Is she okay?" Jameson asked.

Kelly nodded, and Gracelyn got up and started toddling toward her. She clearly hadn't been walking that long because she was still a little unsteady, but Jameson met her part of the way, and he scooped her up in his arms.

"I'm working on a place for us to go," Jameson explained to them. "It shouldn't be much longer."

He didn't add any other details, and Kelly didn't ask. She trusted that Jameson would do what was best. Unfortunately, even his best might not be enough.

"Pat, pat," Gracelyn said, clearly wanting him to play the game.

Jameson glanced around as if trying to figure out what to do, but his hesitation didn't last long. He sank down on the sofa, positioning Gracelyn so she was facing him, and he did something that stunned Kelly.

He played patty-cake.

It was a sight that got Mandy's and Erica's attention, too. A hot cowboy with a baby on his lap. Kelly hadn't even known he knew how to play patty-cake. The sight of them warmed her. And put a lump in her throat.

When he finished two rounds of the game, Jameson kissed Gracelyn's cheek and sat her back on the quilt. In the same motion, he looked at Kelly. "We need to talk. In Gabriel's office," he added.

Kelly didn't like the sound of that. This was either bad news about the investigation or Jameson was ready to rake her over the coals for keeping Gracelyn from him.

She gave Gracelyn a kiss, too, before she followed Jameson out of the room and to Gabriel's office just up the hall. Kelly expected to find other cops there, but it was empty. Jameson had obviously been working, though, because there was a laptop on the desk, which was cluttered with open files and paper.

"When did you learn to play patty-cake?" she asked at the same moment that Jameson said, "The second gunman is Weldon Rosa. His name might sound familiar to you because he was a former client of yours."

Both stopped, maybe surprised by what the other had said. Kelly was certainly surprised anyway. She shook her head. "I don't recognize him."

"Maybe because you never actually met him." Jameson blew out a long breath and scrubbed his hand over the back of his neck. "According to your computer records, you had an appointment scheduled with him around the time you disappeared. It's possible you never showed for that appointment."

"Or maybe he's the reason I went on the run. Mandy did say someone had tried to kill me."

He nodded and made a sound that caused her to think he'd already come to that conclusion. "I learned to play patty-cake with Cameron's nephew. Cameron lives on the ranch with him, and he brings him to my house sometimes."

Kelly couldn't help it. She smiled at the thought of that. It didn't last. And just as quickly, she felt the tears burning her eyes. Tears that she cursed.

"I like kids," he added. "I always wanted one or two of my own."

She hadn't known that about him. Of course, they hadn't dated that long before things had gone to Hades in a handbasket. Kelly could blame herself for that.

"I'm so sorry," she said. "Not just about Gracelyn—"

"Stop," he snapped. His tone was as lethal as those glares he'd been giving her. But like her smile, the glare didn't last, either. Maybe because she hadn't been successful in fighting back those blasted tears.

Jameson cursed under his breath, touched her arm. "It's a rough time for all of us." The corner of his mouth lifted a little. Almost a smile. "That's the mother of all understatements."

That helped with the tears. Some. But she really did want him to know how sorry she was.

"How can I make this right?" she asked.

His eyes came to hers, and he stared at her as if waiting for something. Maybe for the answer to come to him. Judging from the way he bunched up his forehead, it wasn't coming. Maybe because there was no way for her to fix things between them.

She wiped away a tear that made it onto her cheek. But Jameson wiped away the second one. His touch was a surprise. A welcome one. His fingers were warm on her skin. Strange that a simple touch from Jameson could suddenly make her feel a whole lot better.

Kelly expected him to move away. That's what he usually did whenever they got close. But he didn't. On a heavy sigh, Jameson slipped his arm around her waist and inched her to him. The touch had been a drop in the bucket compared to having her body against his again. There was more warmth. The attraction.

And memories.

More of those fragments came. Of another time he'd held her. Also when he'd kissed her.

She stood there, so close to him, and her body picked up the rhythm of his breathing. Her pulse was already thick and throbbing, and it only got worse when he pulled back just a fraction. That's because Kelly thought this was all going to end.

It didn't.

He studied her, easing her hair from her face. She could see the debate in his eyes, and he was trying to make himself put an end to this. Because she was a complication that he didn't want or need. He cursed again, and that was the only warning Kelly got before his mouth came to hers.

There. That's what she wanted. And she didn't need her full memory back to know that. The kiss suddenly made the heat ripple through her. It didn't stay a ripple, either. When Jameson kept kissing her, her body responded. So did his. She could feel him against the zipper of her jeans.

Kelly slipped her arms around his neck, pulling him down to her. Not that they could get any closer, but Jameson didn't fight it. In fact, he added to the complication by turning her and pressing her back against the wall. She hadn't thought they could get any closer, but Kelly had been wrong.

The kiss didn't stop, and Jameson deepened it when he took hold of the back of her neck. The fire was already too hot, but that created an urgency. A bad one. Because there was only one fix for it.

A fix they couldn't have.

Even if her body was suggesting otherwise.

Jameson finally stepped back, probably because he needed air. Time to regroup, too. And she saw the moment he realized just what a stupid mistake this was. Not only had it caused them to lose focus, but this intimacy also added to the complications. They had enough of those without acting on the attraction.

Dragging in some breaths and cursing himself, Jameson stepped back even farther from her. Not a second too soon, either. Because Gabriel appeared in the doorway. He opened his mouth and looked at them. As if he knew exactly what had happened between them, he shook his head.

"We have a visitor," Gabriel said.

"Yeah, and you need to see me," someone added.

August.

Despite the scowl Gabriel gave him, August came to the door, as well. His mouth tightened when his attention landed on them. Like Gabriel, he seemed to know they'd just kissed. Apparently, Jameson and she looked guilty as sin.

"I'm glad you're here," Jameson said to August. "I have some questions for you."

August's eyes went wide. "What are you talking about?" But he quickly waved that off. "Save your allegations and slander for later. Right now, you have a much bigger problem on your hands."

It took Kelly a moment to realize that August was talking to her. "What do you mean?"

"I mean Boyer." August huffed. "Now he's claiming that I helped you steal his daughter. And he's headed over here with some kind of paperwork. My lawyers think it might be arrest warrants for both of us."

Chapter Twelve

Jameson didn't need a complication like this. Not with so many other things going on. And especially since he hadn't found any proof that Kelly had taken Boyer's child. Those baby memories she'd had were of their own child.

Kelly shook her head, her gaze slashing to Jameson's. "I can't go with Boyer," she insisted. "You can't let him take me."

Agreed. If it was an arrest warrant, though, Jameson wasn't sure how to handle it. His first instinct was to get both Kelly and Gracelyn out of there, but that could be what Boyer or the goon behind the attacks wanted them to do. That way, they'd have another chance to kill Kelly.

But staying put meant Jameson would somehow have to stall the agent. Or defy a court order. He would do either or both. In fact, he'd do whatever it took to keep them safe, but it could land him in jail, too. No way could he let that happen.

Gabriel was right behind August, and his brother had obviously heard the conversation. That was no doubt what had put the fresh troubled look on his face. "I'll talk to Boyer," Gabriel offered.

"Yes, and tell him to back off," August snapped. "This witch hunt of his is getting old."

Probably not in Boyer's mind. Now that Jameson was a father, he understood why the agent couldn't let go of the search for his child. Jameson wouldn't have given up, either, and he would have gone after anyone who could give him answers. Unfortunately, they couldn't give that to Boyer.

But maybe August could.

"Talk to me about you stalking Kelly," Jameson threw out there while he stared at the man.

August pulled back his shoulders. Obviously, Jameson had managed to shock him, and August shifted his attention to Kelly. "You told him that? Because it's not true. You're mixing up the memories."

"Mandy told me," Kelly quietly added.

Now August's mouth tightened. "Your sister is wrong. *You* were wrong. I had feelings for you once, and you misinterpreted my concern as stalking."

Jameson groaned. "That sounds like something a stalker would say."

August's glare was scalpel-sharp. "I was worried about Kelly. Mandy, too. Obviously, I was right to feel that way, because someone wants them dead."

Not *them*.

Only Kelly.

Those gunmen had intentionally let Mandy go. Of course, that didn't mean they wouldn't come after her later, but they'd had ample opportunity to kill her and they hadn't.

Gabriel held up his phone, letting Jameson know he had a call coming in, and he stepped away, heading back to the squad room. Probably so he would be able to stop Boyer when the agent arrived. His brother likely wouldn't be able to stop him for long, though, and that's why they needed to get rid of August so Jameson could talk to Kelly about their limited options of dealing with this.

"Mandy said we dated once or twice," Kelly relayed to August. There was some disgust in her voice.

Disgust that Jameson felt, and he knew why. It was jealousy, plain and simple. Yeah, that kiss had thrown off his perspective. So had learning about Gracelyn. And it wasn't a good time to lose his objectivity.

"We dated, briefly. It didn't work out between us." He paused. "You wanted information from me, and I'm pretty sure that's the only reason you agreed to go out with me. Heck, you never even let me kiss you."

That grabbed Jameson's attention. Not the kiss. But the other part. "What kind of information?" he immediately asked.

"Same old stuff that everyone wants from me. Even though I was the one who hired Kelly, I think she accepted the job only so she could find out if I knew anything about your parents' murders. And the answer to that is what it's always been—I don't know anything about them, and I believe my brother is innocent. That means someone else killed them. The problem with that is you and your brother never did your jobs to find that other person."

Oh, they'd done their jobs all right. So had dozens of other cops and FBI agents. "All the evidence pointed to Travis."

"*Circumstantial* evidence," August spat out. "I believe Kelly was onto the real killer when she took that file from you."

This was an old argument, one that Jameson was tired of hearing. "That was *my* file she took, and there was nothing in there about someone else other than your brother killing my folks."

That wasn't entirely true. Jameson did have plenty of info on his father's active and past cases.

"Kelly used your file to make notes. Her own notes," August added.

She shook her head. "You read it?"

August suddenly got very quiet. "No, but you mentioned some of the things that were in it."

That sounded like a lie, and Jameson was about to press him on it when he heard the footsteps. So did August, and he turned in that direction.

"Mandy," August said on a rise of breath. "I didn't know you were in town."

Yeah, and Mandy was in a place Jameson didn't want her to be. He had intended for her to stay with Gracelyn and Erica, and Jameson stepped into the hall so he could watch the break room door. He definitely didn't want Erica bringing his daughter out here.

"You're hurt," August added, tipping his head to the bandage.

"I'm okay. You're here because of what's going on with Kelly and these hired guns?"

"In part. Boyer's on his way over with what I believe are warrants for my and Kelly's arrest." He paused again. "Do you know where his daughter is?"

"No." Mandy didn't hesitate. "And if Kelly knows, she doesn't remember."

"Yes," August said, glancing at Kelly. "Has your memory been returning? Can you recall anything about that file or Boyer's child?"

"Nothing about either of them," she assured him. "In fact, my memory might never return."

Jameson knew why she'd said that. If August was behind the attacks, she might believe that would get him to back off. It wouldn't. If there was anything in that file that could incriminate him, he would continue to go after it. Even if it meant killing Kelly. Or kidnapping Gracelyn to use her.

August's eyebrow lifted, and he stared at Kelly as if he expected her to say something different. Maybe the truth. That she was remembering and that it wouldn't be long before she figured out where she'd put that file.

And what was in it.

Finally, August gave up waiting and blew out a frustrated breath. "I heard there was another attack. Just a few hours ago."

"How did you hear that?" Kelly asked.

August lifted his shoulder. "I have friends at SAPD. I was at the prison visiting my brother when I heard, and I got here as fast as I could."

"You got here because Gabriel called you in to answer questions about stalking Kelly," Jameson corrected.

The man's glare sharpened a bit more. "I would have come anyway. Whether they appreciate it or not, I care about what happens to Kelly and her sister. When they worked for me, they did everything they could to find evidence to free Travis. That's more than anyone else has done."

Clearly, that was meant as a dig at Jameson, but he didn't care. He took hold of Kelly's hand so he could lead her back to the break room. Mandy, too. That way, if they did have to leave, Jameson would be able to get her out of there, as well.

"Tomorrow is the anniversary of your parents' murders," August added when Jameson and Kelly started moving. Jameson motioned for Mandy to follow them. "If the real killer is out there, then he or she will almost certainly strike soon."

That stopped Jameson in his tracks. "You personally know something about that?"

"No. But I've been getting threatening letters and emails, too. Just like you and your family. Someone's out there and wants to finish what he or she started ten years ago, and for whatever reason, they've included me in this."

Jameson prayed that wasn't true, but August was right about the threats. They were all getting them, and it was clear the violence was escalating. But August was right to question why he had been getting the threats. Unless it was to throw suspicion off himself.

Jameson got Kelly and Mandy walking toward the break room again, but this obviously wasn't his day for a quick exit. The front door opened, and Boyer stormed in. Or rather that's what he tried to do, but Gabriel was right there to block the agent's path by stepping in front of him. However, Jameson caught sight of something before his brother did that.

Boyer did indeed have some papers in his hand.

"Is it true?" Boyer asked. He wasn't looking at Gabriel, though. Instead, he was aiming his attention at Mandy.

Since Boyer looked ready to implode, Jameson moved in front of Kelly and her sister. "A lot of things are true," Jameson snarled, matching Boyer's tone. "Did you have something particular in mind?"

If looks could have killed, Jameson would be dead. "You know exactly what I'm talking about. You found a baby."

Jameson still had his hand on Kelly, and he felt her tense. He was certain he was doing some tensing, too. "Who told you that?" Jameson countered, and he hoped that Mandy or Kelly didn't blurt out anything. Best to fish for information rather than verify something he didn't want Boyer to know anyway.

"I heard," was all Boyer said. He didn't wait for Jameson to respond. "It's true." He groaned. "God, it's true. Where is she? I want to see her right now."

"We don't have your child." Jameson tipped his head to the papers Boyer was holding. "And if you're here to try to arrest Kelly and August, then you're wasting your time."

Boyer looked down at the papers, too, but his expression was odd. It was as if he'd forgotten they were there. He handed them to Gabriel.

"They're not arrest warrants," Boyer said. "Not yet anyway. The paperwork is for the transfer of a prisoner. McGill. I'm taking him into my custody."

"Why?" Jameson asked. He wanted to have a look at the papers, but he didn't want to leave Kelly in the hall with August. Plus, he didn't plan to get too far away from the break room.

"Justice Department business. I'm not at liberty to say."

"You mean you won't say." And Jameson could think of a bad reason for the agent's silence. "If McGill works for you—"

"He doesn't," Boyer interrupted. "But I'm taking him to headquarters to be interviewed."

By federal agents. Something was up, and Jameson hoped that didn't include Boyer trying to cover his tracks.

After reading through the papers, Gabriel looked back at Jameson. "Everything appears to be in order."

So either Boyer had bought off a judge or else there was a compelling reason for the feds to take McGill. Unfortunately, that meant the man wouldn't be around so Gabriel and the deputies could continue to press him for information. Information that could help them figure out who was orchestrating the attacks.

"Two marshals are on the way to transport the prisoner," Boyer added, and he looked at Mandy again. "Now tell me about the baby you found."

Gabriel got another call and stepped away to take it. Despite the fact that no one was now in his path, Boyer thankfully didn't come any closer. Maybe because all four of them—Jameson, Kelly, Mandy and August— were giving him looks from hell.

"She's not your daughter," Jameson settled for saying. No sense denying there was a child, since someone had obviously leaked details about not only the attack but the fact that Jameson and the others had left the crime scene with an infant.

"I don't believe you," Boyer snapped. "I want to see her *now*."

"No." Jameson had a quick debate with himself as to how to continue, and he just went with the truth. "She's my daughter. Mine and Kelly's."

"You had his child?" August asked.

Either August was genuinely surprised or else he

was doing a good job of faking it. However, there was one emotion that August wasn't able to hide.

Jealousy.

Since Jameson had had a recent bout of it himself, he recognized it in August. The man's mouth stretched into a straight line.

Kelly nodded. "Jameson didn't know. I kept her from him because I was in hiding."

She hadn't added that it was also because she hadn't trusted him. But apparently she hadn't trusted August or Boyer, either.

Boyer took a couple steps toward them. Unlike August, there was no jealousy on his face, but there was emotion. And disbelief. The agent obviously thought they were lying.

"I want to see the baby," Boyer repeated. "If she's mine, I'll know it."

No way was he going to allow Boyer in the break room or anywhere near Gracelyn for that matter. However, Jameson did take out his phone, and he quickly located the picture he'd taken of the baby a couple of hours earlier. He held it up so that Boyer could see.

Boyer eased the phone from Jameson's hand, his attention fixed to the smiling little girl on the screen. The moments crawled by before Boyer whispered "no" under his breath.

"You could have switched pictures of her." He thrust the phone back at Jameson. "That's why I have to see her for myself."

"You don't need to see her," Mandy verified. "Because I swear she's not yours."

Boyer groaned. The sound of a man in pain. Obviously, it was sinking in that they didn't have his child after all. "I can't give up hope," Boyer mumbled. "I have to find her."

The words had barely left his mouth when Gabriel walked back into the hall with them. "I just got a call from a criminal informant named Buddy Wells," Gabriel said. "He had something very interesting to tell me. Want to explain why we didn't hear it from you first?"

His brother hadn't directed that to Boyer or August. But rather to Mandy. Jameson expected her to be surprised by Gabriel's question.

She wasn't.

Mandy glanced away, dodging both Gabriel's and his gaze, and she muttered some profanity that Jameson silently repeated.

"What is he talking about?" Kelly asked. When her sister didn't answer, she took hold of Mandy's chin, forcing eye contact. "What is it?" she demanded.

Mandy didn't answer, but Gabriel did. "Mandy is working for Boyer. Not only is she on his payroll, but Boyer and she are lovers."

Chapter Thirteen

Kelly waited for her sister to deny everything that Gabriel had just said. But Mandy didn't. Instead, she said something Kelly didn't want to hear.

"I'm sorry."

That felt like a punch to Kelly's gut. It didn't matter that her memories of Mandy were spotty at best; her sister hadn't been honest with her. And it instantly made Kelly wonder—what else had Mandy not told her?

Kelly looked at Boyer to see if he would have some kind of excuse. But even he wasn't denying it.

Oh, mercy.

What was really going on here?

Jameson stepped in front of Mandy, and he put his hands on his hips. "I'll want to hear more than an apology. I want a full explanation."

"So will I," August said.

All of them looked at the man, and they were likely wondering the same thing. Why would he care if Mandy and Boyer were lovers or not?

"I've been getting threats, and I believe at least some of them are coming from Boyer. Because I have PIs looking into what I believe are his dirty dealings. Mandy could have helped him cover up his crimes."

It was a stretch, especially since they didn't know any of the details of this bizarre relationship, but August could hope to try to use this—or anything else for that matter—to find something that would help clear his brother. After all, August believed that Boyer had something to do with setting up Travis.

"One of you had better start talking." Jameson shot warning glances at both Mandy and Boyer.

"It's true," Mandy finally said. She huffed. "After Kelly disappeared, Boyer hired me to find her."

For only a single sentence, it certainly packed a wallop. Kelly's breath became so thin that she got dizzy. She must have wobbled, because Jameson took hold of her arm to steady her.

"I didn't have anything to do with the attacks," Mandy quickly added.

Boyer stared at Mandy as if waiting for her to declare his innocence along with hers. But she didn't. "Nor did I," he said, his words clipped and tight. "And we were lovers. For a short time anyway."

So the affair was over. That didn't make Kelly feel any better, and judging from her sister's expression, she wasn't especially pleased about it, either.

Mandy huffed again. "Look, I know what you're thinking. Can you trust me? Well, you can. I'm not behind the attacks." She pointed to her bandaged arm. "I was shot, remember?"

"It was a flesh wound," Jameson said, taking the words right out of Kelly's mouth.

Her sister's gaze flew back to hers, and Mandy hissed out a breath when Kelly didn't jump to defend her. She couldn't. Maybe if she had her full memory back, she would know things that would convince her of Mandy's innocence. But for now, Kelly had to consider that her sister might have contributed to this dangerous situation they were in.

"Great." Mandy cursed. "You think I faked my kidnapping. I guess you believe I led those men to Gracelyn, too. I didn't."

Kelly knew this wasn't a debate they could decide here. Not with August seemingly lapping all of this up. He was probably trying to figure out a way to use it against Boyer. At the moment, though, Kelly didn't care about any of that. She had to get out of there.

"I need a drink of water," she lied, and she headed up the hall.

Jameson was right behind her, of course. They went into the break room, closed the door and immediately checked on Gracelyn. She was asleep in Erica's arms.

"We're leaving now," Jameson insisted before Kelly could say anything. He took out his phone and sent two texts. "I'd already started the arrangements for us to move, but I just had those plans stepped up a little. I'll have Cameron pull a cruiser to the back of the building. The four of us will go with him."

"Four?" Kelly repeated. "What about Mandy?"

His forehead bunched up, and he looked ready to launch into an argument as to why it wasn't a good idea to have Mandy go with them. But it wasn't an argument she needed.

"I don't want her to go with us, either," Kelly quickly added. "Not until we know what's going on." And that might not be for a while. "If my sister is completely innocent, then I'll owe her an apology."

Erica stood, cradling the baby in her arms. "Is something wrong with Mandy?"

Jameson and Kelly exchanged glances before he answered her question with one of his own. "Did you know that Mandy was working for a federal agent?"

"No." She shook her head and repeated it. "I had no idea."

Too bad. Because Erica could have maybe filled in some memory gaps so that Kelly would know if she could trust her sister or not.

The door to the break room opened, and Kelly figured it was too much to hope that it was Gabriel or Cameron. It wasn't. It was Mandy, and she stepped in, shutting it behind her.

"I planned to tell you about Boyer," Mandy said right off. "But the timing wasn't right."

A soft burst of air left Kelly's mouth. "The timing was perfect for you to tell me that you work for one of our suspects."

"Worked," Mandy corrected. "I don't any longer." But she waved that off. "Fine. It's obvious I'm not going to be able to make you believe that my prior relationship with Boyer isn't playing into anything that's happening now."

"You're right. You won't be able to convince us, not now anyway," Jameson assured her. "I need to get Gracelyn and Kelly someplace safe, and then you can convince me you're innocent."

"I am innocent!" Mandy's voice was so loud that it woke up Gracelyn. The baby immediately started to fuss, so Kelly pulled Gracelyn into her arms. "Sorry," Mandy grumbled. "It's just that I'm in danger, too. I also need to be protected so the kidnappers can't have another go at me."

Mandy was right about that. If she had no part in the

attacks, she could be taken again to try to force Kelly to cooperate. And cooperation probably meant handing over that blasted file.

Jameson nodded. "You will leave. Just not with Kelly, Erica and me. Susan will be here soon, and she and a reserve deputy will take you to a hotel. They'll stay with you until we can figure out what's going on."

Mandy opened her mouth, and Kelly didn't think it was her imagination that her sister was about to insist she go with them. But then Jameson's phone dinged with a text message, and he cut off anything she might have said.

"Cameron's in place. Let's go." Jameson looked at Mandy. "Just stay here and Susan will arrive soon." He didn't wait for Mandy to object. He hurried them out of there.

"Erica, get in the front," he instructed. Probably because there was a child seat in the middle of the back one.

Erica did get in, but it wasn't just Cameron in the front seat. There was another man, and he had Erica sit between them.

"That's Deputy Edwin Clary," Jameson said to Kelly. Maybe because he felt her tense. "We can trust him."

Good. But the fact that there were now three lawmen in the car let her know this could be a dangerous ride. She prayed they weren't attacked again.

The moment Kelly had the baby strapped in, Cameron took off, and Kelly saw the second cruiser pull to a stop behind the sheriff's office. That was no doubt Susan ready to whisk Mandy away. Maybe Mandy would cooperate.

Cameron sped up as soon as he was out of the parking lot. Blue River wasn't a big town by anyone's standards, so it only took them a couple minutes before they were away from the buildings. After he took a turn, there weren't any other vehicles in sight. It made it easier for Kelly to see if anyone was following them, but that didn't mean they were safe. This was a rural road, where gunmen could lie in wait.

A road she recognized.

"This leads to your family's ranch," she said.

Jameson's gaze had been firing all around them, but he glanced at her now. "Are you remembering that?"

She took another look at the scenery. Then nodded. "I didn't see much of it when you brought me here, but I remember it, too. From the other time I came here." It wasn't exactly a peaceful feeling, though, that went through her. "Won't our attackers expect you to take me there?"

"Maybe." That's all he said for several moments. "There are hands at the ranch who can help protect you. And it's only temporary. In the morning, we'll be going to a safe house."

The ranch would be more comfortable for Gracelyn than staying at the sheriff's office, but still she hated to bring the danger to Jameson's home.

"She'll be hungry soon," Erica said, turning in the seat so she could look at the baby. "I have some food for her in the diaper bag, but I'm not sure it's enough for more than a day or two."

"I'll arrange to have supplies brought in," Jameson assured her. "Just write down what you need. Not just for Gracelyn but for yourself, too."

Erica muttered a thanks, but she looked as worried about this as Kelly was. "At least once Gracelyn's eaten and had her bath," Erica went on, "she'll sleep through the night. Well, she usually does anyway. After Kelly left she had some fussy moments asking for her mama."

That ate away at Kelly, and it didn't matter that she couldn't remember leaving or much about her little girl. She just hated that she'd put Gracelyn and even Erica through that.

The drive seemed to take an eternity, but Kelly figured it was less than twenty minutes. She got more of those memory fragments the moment Cameron turned onto the ranch road.

"This is a different way we went from last night, but I've been this way before. Two years ago," she added.

Jameson nodded. He followed her gaze to the large house that was just up the road. Not someplace where anyone lived. Not anymore. But she knew that it was his parents' house. She had seen it earlier from a distance that morning after the first attack when Jameson had brought her to his house.

"There was a fire a while back," Jameson added.

Yes. And once they were closer, she could see the burned streaks on the wood on one side of the place. Even without the damage, it didn't look habitable. Maybe she felt that way, though, because two people had been murdered inside.

"We're finally tearing it down," he went on a moment later.

That was probably a wise move, but it made her wonder why the Becketts hadn't done it sooner. It was still their childhood home, so perhaps there were more good memories than bad.

Cameron pulled to a stop in front of another large house. But this one looked a little more like a fortress than a home. There were shutters that were all closed, and what appeared to be three armed ranch hands were standing guard.

"This is your house?" Erica asked.

Like Kelly, she was taking in the sprawling place surrounded by equally sprawling pastures. The Beckett Ranch was huge. Not a good thing right now. Because it might be hard to keep watch over every part of it to stop gunmen from getting onto the grounds.

"No. It's Gabriel's," Jameson answered. "My place is about a quarter of a mile past his."

"A log cabin," Kelly provided. Except *cabin* wasn't the right word. Like Gabriel's, it was huge, as well.

She suddenly had plenty of memories of it. Specifically of Jameson's bedroom. And his bed. It's where they'd had sex, and that might explain why he'd brought them here instead of there. It likely had memories for him, too.

"FYI, my sister Ivy is here," Jameson explained when Cameron pulled to a stop in front of the house. "My other sister, Lauren, is out of town on business, and she has two Texas Rangers with her as bodyguards. I told her it was best if she stayed away for a while."

It was. That would mean one less member of his family in danger.

Jameson smiled at Gracelyn when she opened her eyes and grinned at him. "And Gabriel's wife, Jodi, is here, too. Once we're inside, you might not get your hands on Gracelyn for a while. They'll want to get to know her."

"This isn't a good idea," Kelly said. She took the baby from the car seat.

Jameson didn't reassure her—probably because he

wasn't so certain of this idea, either. But that didn't stop him from rushing them into the house. Cameron left the cruiser out front, and both Cameron and Edwin followed them in.

"We're staying," Cameron told her. "Gabriel's orders."

Gabriel was almost certainly stretched thin with his deputies, but Kelly was thankful there'd be three people guarding the baby. Apparently, there'd be a fourth, too, because the blond-haired woman who was in the foyer was wearing a shoulder holster.

"This is Jodi," Jameson said, making the introductions all the way around. "Jodi was in private security for years."

"Jodi Canton?" The name just came to Kelly, like one of those memory fragments. But this came with more than just a few pieces.

Jodi had been attacked the night Jameson's parents were murdered. Attacked and left for dead. She'd survived, but her father was none other than Travis Canton, who was in prison for a double murder.

"Yes," Jodi commented as if she knew exactly what Kelly had been thinking.

"You remember her?" Jameson asked.

Kelly shook her head. "No, I don't think we've ever met. But I saw pictures of her and read the articles." For some reason that was clearer in her mind than giving birth to her daughter.

Jodi didn't reach for the baby, but the woman who came from the adjacent living room did. The brunette made a beeline to Kelly and Gracelyn, and she gave them both a hug before she scooped up Gracelyn. This had to be Jameson's sister.

"She's a Beckett all right," Ivy said. "She resembles my son, Nathan. He's not here," she went on. "He's away at camp. His dad's there with him now just to make sure…well, just to make sure."

Again, that was smart. Because the person after her could use anyone to get to her.

"We don't have a crib here," Jodi explained. "It's at Cameron's house, where Lauren lives now. They have two kids so they needed it. Anyway, we can have someone bring it up or maybe we could use a lot of quilts and make Gracelyn a bed on the floor."

Since Jodi knew the baby's name, that meant Jameson or Gabriel had filled her in on what was going on. Had probably told her about the memory loss, too, since both Jodi and Ivy eyed the bandage and gave her sympathetic looks.

"I'm sure the quilts will work fine," Kelly answered. "Plus, we're only here for one night."

"Where will you go after that?" Ivy asked her brother.

"A safe house. Not just for Gracelyn, Erica, Kelly and me. You and Jodi will be coming, too."

"Gabriel's orders," Cameron repeated while he kept watch at the front window.

Apparently, Kelly wasn't the only one who hadn't heard about this, because both Ivy and Jodi looked surprised.

"It's just a precaution," Jameson assured them. "And it'll give you some time to be with your niece."

"With Kelly, too." Ivy smiled and gave Kelly's hand a gentle squeeze. Her attention shifted to her brother, gauging his reaction to that, but Jameson glanced away. Perhaps that was his way of telling his sister that there was no reason to get to know Kelly because she wouldn't be around much.

The foyer suddenly got very quiet. Too quiet.

"Why don't I go ahead and feed the baby?" Erica suggested, obviously picking up on the uneasiness. She took Gracelyn from Ivy.

"I'll show you the kitchen," Jodi offered. "It's this way." She led Erica out of the foyer.

Kelly followed them, but Ivy caught up with her in the living room and caught on to her hand again. "Stay. You need to hear this, too."

Judging from Jameson's frown, he wasn't so sure of that. Neither was Kelly, but he joined them in the living room.

"I love you, and even though I just met her, I love my niece, too," Ivy started. She kept her voice at a whisper probably because Cameron still was in the foyer and Edwin was at the front window only yards away.

"But?" Jameson challenged.

"You can be pigheaded about some things, and my advice is don't let that get in the way of forgiving Kelly for not telling you about Gracelyn. I'm sure she had what she thought were solid reasons for not telling you."

Kelly wasn't sure how to respond to that. Ivy had really put her brother on the spot, and that's why she decided to stay quiet.

Jameson didn't, though.

"I have forgiven her," Jameson said. And he didn't say it in a whisper.

Kelly had been hit with a lot of emotional punches in the past two days, but that seemed one of the strongest. It didn't tighten her stomach, didn't cause her adrenaline to soar. However, it sent a new warmth through her.

Memories, too.

Of the feelings that had caused her to land in bed with Jameson. Of course, he probably still thought she'd done that to get her hands on the file. She hadn't. Nor had it been solely the attraction. It had been because she had deep feelings for him.

She still did.

"Well, maybe you're not as pigheaded as I thought you were," Ivy told him. "Oh, wait. You still are. You're just not being pigheaded about this." She poked him with her elbow and grinned in a way that only a sister could. "All right, let me have some playtime with my niece."

Ivy kissed Jameson's cheek. Then she did the same to Kelly before she headed off to the kitchen.

Jameson stared at her, maybe seeing how she was going to respond to what he'd said. And Kelly did. Despite the fact that Edwin and Cameron were nearby, she caught on to Jameson's arm, drew him closer and kissed him. Not on the cheek, either. She went for broke. Because if this was a mistake, she wanted it to be one worth making.

The taste of him roared through her. Now, here was another of those punches, but it was a good one, too. That taste mixed with the now-familiar heat. All of it slid right through her. And though things were far from perfect, it all suddenly felt right.

She pulled back to gauge his reaction. The corner of his mouth lifted in what looked to be a smile. Good. Well, almost. That ghost of a smile vanished as quickly as it'd come. He was already regretting the kiss. Maybe regretting, too, that he had forgiven her.

He opened his mouth to say something, and then it

seemed as if he changed his mind. Jameson slid a glance at Edwin. The deputy had his attention focused on looking out the window, but he was also making occasional glances over his shoulder at them. In other words, this wasn't the time for a heartfelt private conversation. Or a kiss, for that matter.

"Let's check on Gracelyn," Jameson finally said.

That made Kelly smile. The thought of her baby could do that to her. Jameson and she started for the kitchen just as his phone buzzed, and she saw Gabriel's name on the screen. Jameson stopped and took the call, putting it on speaker.

"We got a problem," Gabriel greeted.

Kelly groaned, because they'd already had way too many problems today. She prayed it wasn't news of gunmen on the way to the ranch.

"Mandy was furious after you left," Gabriel continued a moment later. "At first she refused to go with the deputies, but I finally told her if she didn't, I'd have to lock her up. She's a witness after all."

Mandy was indeed that, but Kelly figured her sister probably hadn't cared much for the lockup threat. "What did Mandy do?" Kelly came out and asked.

"She escaped."

Kelly's next groan wasn't of frustration but concern. It wasn't safe for her sister to be out there. Judging from Jameson's profanity, he felt the same way.

"We have someone looking for her," Gabriel went on, "but I don't have a lot of manpower to search for long."

"You need Cameron or Edwin to go back to the station?" Jameson asked.

"No," Gabriel answered without hesitation. "They need to stay put and keep watch. All of you do." He paused. "Before Mandy escaped, she said she needed to find Kelly and settle some things with her."

That sent a chill through Kelly. Because it sounded like a threat.

"Oh, and be careful," Gabriel added a moment later. "There's a gun missing from my desk, and I'm pretty sure Mandy took it. She's armed, and I'm betting the first place she'll go is the ranch."

Chapter Fourteen

Jameson glanced at the clock on the nightstand before turning his attention back to the window. It was just past midnight. That meant it was officially the anniversary of his parents' murders.

Since he could see the old house where they'd died from the window, that wasn't exactly a calming thought, or sight, to settle his nerves, which were already on edge.

Neither was the fact that Jameson was second- and third-guessing himself about coming here. It wasn't just the danger—that would be a factor no matter where they'd gone. But having Kelly here was reminding him of old feelings for her that he'd thought were long gone.

They weren't.

And now she was under the same roof he was. In fact, she was just next door. Mere steps away. Steps that he forced himself not to take. For one thing, he wanted to keep watch a while longer. There'd been no sign of Mandy, or anyone else for that matter, but Jameson figured it would help to have an extra pair of eyes on the grounds just in case someone did try to come after them.

However, there were other reasons for him to stay

put. Any time Kelly and he were within ten feet of each other, the heat kicked in, and Jameson found himself making questionable choices.

Like kissing her.

And wanting much more than just a kiss from her.

He felt his body tighten and respond to that thought, and a certain part of him was urging him to go see her. Jameson told that part to take a hike. After all, Kelly wasn't alone in the room, and she might even be sleeping. Even if she wasn't, he could still wake up Erica or the baby.

Gabriel's house was huge, six bedrooms, but with all the "guests," it'd practically taken a flowchart to work out the sleeping situations. Jodi was in the master, where Gabriel would join her whenever he happened to make it home from work. Ivy and Jameson were in two of the guest rooms. Cameron was in another guest room, where he was resting to take the surveillance shift over from Edwin. Erica and Kelly had decided to share a room with the baby since Kelly wasn't exactly confident of her mothering skills just yet.

His phone buzzed, and Jameson answered it right away when he saw Gabriel's name on the screen. "Mandy hasn't shown," Jameson volunteered.

"Good. Maybe she'll stay away. Are you okay?"

There'd been enough of a hesitation before his brother's question to let Jameson know what that was really about. Their parents. Gabriel had no doubt been watching the clock, too.

"That old house needs to come down," Jameson settled for saying.

"Agreed." Another hesitation. "Do you ever think August could be right, that Travis could be innocent?"

Obviously, the anniversary of the murders had put his brother in a contemplative mood.

"All the time," Jameson admitted. "I wish Travis could just remember what happened that night. Gaps in memories, especially those kind of memories, aren't a good thing."

"Are you talking about Kelly now?" Gabriel asked.

"Yeah." Now it was Jameson who hesitated. "I have feelings for her."

It sounded as if Gabriel laughed. "And you're just now figuring that out. You're slower than I thought you were. Still, I get what you're saying. Feelings don't always make things easier."

No, and Gabriel was a living example of that. After all, he'd fallen in love with Travis Canton's daughter. And Ivy had fallen in love with Travis's son and had a child with him. In the grand scheme of things, Jameson's relationship with Kelly was far less complicated than theirs. Or at least it would be if she had her full memory.

"I had another reason for calling," Gabriel said a moment later. "I'm sending you a picture. I think this might be Boyer's daughter, Amy."

Of all the things Jameson had thought his brother might say, that wasn't one of them. With everything else going on, Boyer's child wasn't even on Jameson's radar. He waited a few seconds for the photo to come through, and he saw the blond-haired little girl. She was obviously a little older than Gracelyn and looked healthy.

"I pressed the CI who told me about Mandy and Boyer," Gabriel continued, "and he's the one who came up with the picture."

Jameson had a lot of questions, but he started with

the obvious. "Where has the baby been this whole time? And who took her?" Before Gabriel could answer, there was a knock at the door. "Hold on a second."

He hurried to answer the knock just in case it was one of the deputies with bad news. But it was Kelly. She was standing there, not looking at all certain that she should be there. She glanced around, rubbing her hands along the sides of her jeans. Clearly nervous.

Jameson figured he seemed uncertain, too. But only because he was surprised. His body certainly liked the idea of her paying him a late-night visit.

"Gabriel's on the phone," he explained to her. Jameson motioned for her to come in so he could shut the door. That way, their conversation wouldn't disturb the others. "He just sent me a picture of a child who could be Boyer's. He got it from the CI." He showed it to her, and Kelly's eyes widened.

"As for where the child has been for two years," Gabriel went on, "the CI didn't know that. He got the picture from the baby's nanny. A woman he knows only as Sissy. But as to who had her, well, the CI claims it was Mandy."

Hell. This was not a twist that Jameson wanted to hear. Neither did Kelly, and she groaned and shook her head.

"The CI is certain?" Kelly asked. She joined Jameson at the window.

"He says he is, but he's a criminal informant. Emphasis on the *criminal*. But he was right about Mandy and Boyer being lovers."

Yeah, he was. But that only led Jameson to another question. "Why would Mandy take Boyer's child?"

"Don't know, but it's something I intend to ask her

when we find her. I'll ask Boyer, too, but I'm going to wait until morning to do that. Get some sleep," Gabriel added.

"You should do the same," Jameson said right back to him. "When will you be home?"

"In a couple of hours. Be safe," Gabriel tacked on before he ended the call.

Jameson took another look at the picture before he put his phone away. "I'm sorry," he said in case she was upset about what she'd just heard.

Kelly lifted her shoulder. "I don't remember a lot about my sister, so I don't know if she's capable of taking the baby. Especially considering she had a relationship with Boyer."

It sounded as if she had plenty of distrust for Mandy. Even if it turned out to be unwarranted, in their case it was better to be safe than sorry. That's why he didn't want Mandy to get near Kelly or the baby.

"I wanted to check on you. To make sure you were okay." Her gaze drifted to the old house before Jameson moved her back away from the glass. The odds were the ranch hands or deputies would spot a gunman before he could strike, but like having Mandy around, it was an unnecessary risk.

"Gabriel wanted to know the same thing. Yeah, I'm fine," he repeated to her.

She stared at him. "You're lying."

He hated that she could see through him so easily. Most would have bought that lie. "Once the anniversary has passed, maybe the threats will stop."

Of course, the threats could get a whole lot worse before they ended, but Jameson didn't spell that out for her. She knew.

"Is Gracelyn okay?" he asked.

She nodded. "Erica says she'll likely sleep through the night. I was on the pallet on the floor with her, but she never even opened an eye or stirred around."

Good. Though she was probably the only one in the house who would get much sleep.

It suddenly got too quiet, and Jameson could think of plenty of things they could talk about. The investigation. The safe house where they'd soon be going. Or how they were going to work out custody arrangements for Gracelyn. But before he could say anything, Kelly fluttered her fingers to the door.

"I should leave," she said, her voice showing some strain. She dragged in a long breath. "But if I do, I'll just want to come back over here."

He knew exactly what she meant. "It's because I kissed you. It brought back a lot of old stuff to the surface." And it brought it back with a vengeance.

Cursing himself, Jameson slipped his arm around her neck, pulled her to him and kissed her again.

Even though he'd been the one to start this, it still gave him a jolt. The feel of her in his arms. The need she created inside him. He kissed her too hard. Too long. And yet it didn't feel like nearly long enough when they broke apart for air. Jameson would have gone right back for another kiss, too, if his phone hadn't buzzed again.

He glanced at the screen, expecting it to be Gabriel again, but the caller had blocked the number.

Hell.

"The gunmen," Kelly said, her breathing already too fast.

It probably was one of them, and that's why Jameson moved her even farther away from the window. "If things get bad, take Gracelyn into the bathroom and get in the tub with her."

Kelly gave a shaky nod, and he hit the answer button. However, it was a familiar voice.

It was Mandy.

"I need to talk to Kelly," the woman immediately said.

"I'm here," Kelly answered before Jameson could consider if that was a good idea or not. Of course, Mandy would have known Kelly would be with him.

"Where are you?" Jameson demanded.

"As if I'd tell you that. You two obviously don't trust me, and that's why I'm calling. I'm not responsible for what's going on. I didn't do anything wrong."

Jameson wasn't so sure of that at all. "What about taking Boyer's daughter?"

Silence. For too long of a time. "That was a mistake."

"A mistake?" Kelly repeated. "You took a man's child. A man who's a federal agent. And don't say you didn't know he was one because Boyer insisted that he told us."

"He did," Mandy reluctantly admitted. He heard her give a heavy sigh. "But Hadley convinced me that he was bad news, that he wasn't fit to raise the child. She said he was a dangerous man."

"Hadley might have been right," Jameson said. "But you committed a felony."

This time Mandy groaned. "I know, and that's why I haven't given her back. Because I'll go to jail."

Jameson wanted to point out that she deserved to be locked up, but if Boyer truly was dangerous, then maybe Mandy had done the right thing.

Maybe.

And if so, he would help her work her way through the legalities of this. But only after he was certain she wasn't the one who was after Kelly.

"Tell me what happened between Boyer and you," Kelly insisted.

"Nothing much to tell. It was just sex."

Jameson had to mentally shake his head. "But you just said you didn't know if he was a dirty agent."

"Not at the beginning. Not after his daughter was born. Later, though, things just sort of happened between us, and before you say it shouldn't have—I already know that. That's why I broke it off." Mandy paused. "I think Boyer was using me anyway. He was always pressing me for info about Kelly and that damn file she stole."

Yeah, that. Jameson certainly hadn't forgotten about it. "Were you telling the truth when you said you didn't know where it was?"

"Yes," Mandy answered without hesitation. "Kelly vanished without so much as a word. She didn't trust me to help her."

Jameson heard the hurt—and the bitterness—and he had to wonder if there was enough hurt to give Mandy a motive for coming after Kelly. Or maybe all of this was just a ploy to get her hands on the file so she could give it to Boyer.

"Mandy, you need to tell us where you are," Kelly said. "That way, we can get you some protection."

"No." She sounded adamant about it, too. "I've got to look into some things."

Kelly shook her head, clearly not liking the sound of that. "What things?"

"Just some things I have to do. I'm sorry, Kelly, but

what I'm about to do might make it more dangerous for you. For others, too. I might be handing you over to a killer."

And with that warning hanging in the air, Mandy ended the call.

KELLY COULD ONLY stand there and stare at the phone. Oh, God. What had her sister done? Worse, what was she going to do to stop whatever it was Mandy was planning?

"I won't let Mandy hand you over to anyone," Jameson assured her. He sounded exactly like the tough lawman that he was. But maybe no one was tough enough to save her.

She felt the tears burn her eyes and blinked them back. Or rather she tried. "You could die trying to protect me. I don't want that to happen."

"I don't have any plans to die." He blew out a weary breath, and maybe because he'd spotted those stupid tears, Jameson slipped his arm around her waist and pulled her back to him.

Not for a kiss this time. He just stood there and hugged her. All in all, it was an effective way to comfort her. Some anyway. There'd be no real comfort until the person responsible for the attacks was in jail.

Even if that meant putting her sister in prison.

"I'll bet you're regretting I came back into your life," she muttered.

He didn't answer right away, but he did ease back so that he was looking her in the eyes. "I'm not regretting it nearly enough."

It was a puzzling answer, but Kelly didn't even have time to process it before his mouth came to hers. Unlike the kiss that'd happened minutes earlier, this one was gentle. Like a whisper. So soft that there was no urgency in it. No demands. Just one incredible kiss. Of course, all of Jameson's kisses fell into the incredible category.

"If you leave now, we won't do something we might regret," he said with his mouth still against hers.

It sounded as if he was having the same debate with himself that she was. True, if she left, they wouldn't have sex. That might help them stay focused on the investigation. But leaving didn't exactly feel like an option.

And that's why Kelly pulled him back to her for another kiss.

She knew the kiss wasn't going to make this decision easier. Just the opposite. But she was tired of having this panic rising inside her. Tired of wanting Jameson more than her next breath. Sex wouldn't fix that. However, it could give them a reprieve from the relentless pressure. This heat, too.

He made a sound. Almost a protesting grumble. That didn't stop him, though, from snapping her even closer to him. Until her body was right against his. Kelly could already feel him hard and ready behind his zipper, and while she hadn't needed anything else to fire up every inch of her, that did it.

She had been the one to start the kiss, but Jameson seemed to be on a mission to finish it. He turned her, pinning her against the wall so he could lower those kisses to her neck. Then, lower. He kissed her breasts, first through her top, and then he shucked it off. Her bra, too.

The pleasure spiked through her when his mouth landed on her bare skin. The memories spiked as well, and she recalled another time they'd done this. It all came flooding back, the new images filling in the gaps, and she remembered in perfect detail the last time they'd been together. That didn't cool the fire. Just the opposite. Because she remembered what Jameson was capable of doing to her.

With the need building and building inside her, Kelly reached between them to unbutton his shirt. Jameson helped by taking off his shoulder holster, but it still took some more fumbling on her part to get the shirt off him.

He immediately came back for another kiss, and she got the pleasure of feeling his bare chest against hers. Yes, that was another pleasant memory, too, and they were making more of those memories right now.

The kiss made things better. And worse. Better because it was so good but worse because it made her realize she had to have him now. Thankfully, Jameson was on the same page, and the battle started to get them undressed. They managed the jeans before Kelly froze.

"Please tell me you have a condom," she said.

Jameson cursed, and for a moment she thought that meant he didn't. But he stooped down, fumbling with his jeans, and finally came up with one from his wallet. The relief came, briefly, but the pressure-cooker heat quickly took over again.

Kissing her, Jameson pulled her to the floor, moving on top of her. It seemed to take forever for him to get on the condom, but even a few seconds seemed like way too long. Not with this need she had eating away at her.

She got another slam of memories when he pushed inside her. Yes, she definitely remembered this, and it didn't take her long to slide right into the rhythm of his movements. Of course, this would all end too soon. No way could it last with them starved for each other.

Jameson upped the pace, moving inside her until Kelly could take no more. Even though she wanted to hang on to this as long as possible, she had no choice. She had to let go. She felt herself shatter. Felt the pleasure ripple through her. It rippled through Jameson as well, because he gathered her into his arms and surrendered right along with her.

It was perfect. The slack feeling in her body. Jameson's taste in her mouth. His scent on her body. But in that moment, Kelly had a stark realization. This wasn't going to satisfy that fire inside her.

Not for long anyway.

The need would return, but that didn't mean she wouldn't have Jameson again. No. It wouldn't take long for the regret to take hold of him. Kelly was certain that's what was already happening when he moved off her and landed on his back on the floor.

"We should check on Gracelyn," he said. He turned toward her, hauled her back to him and kissed her. "Give me a minute, and we can do that."

So maybe not regret after all. He gathered up his clothes and headed to the en suite bathroom. Since Kelly really didn't want to be lying around on the floor naked, she dressed, too. She braced herself for some awkwardness when Jameson came back into the room, but there wasn't any.

Probably because he kissed her again. His kisses had a way of tamping down everything but the attraction. Not only was it still there, but it was stronger than ever.

"I remembered some things," she said while she put on her shoes.

That got his attention. "What?" he asked, hesitation in his voice.

"Us being together." Which probably wasn't much of a surprise since she'd had plenty of visual reminders what with seeing Jameson naked.

But that wasn't all.

It didn't come to her in a flash as the last pieces had, but it came, and she had to shake her head. "I didn't steal that file for Boyer. In fact, I wasn't the one who took it at all. Mandy did. She's the one who brought it to me."

"What?" He pulled his eyebrows together. "But she said you stole it." He paused. "No, wait. Mandy didn't say that. When she was talking to you, she said *as soon as you got your hands on it*. I guess that means she gave it to you?"

Yes, her sister had used some clever wording, but with each passing second the memories of that were getting clearer.

"I took it from her," Kelly corrected. "Mandy had sneaked into your house the night we were together and she took the file back to her apartment. The following morning, I dropped by her apartment and saw her reading it. I was furious and took it from her." Now it was her turn to pause. "I wonder if she shared any of what was inside it with Boyer?"

Judging from the frustrated sound he made, the answer to that was yes. But that led Kelly to one very big question.

Why was that file so important?

"I went through all the data you'd collected," Kelly went on, "and I added some files and notes of my own. I'd also talked with some possible witnesses and such.

I had even interviewed one of the people involved in the money laundering operation that both Boyer and your father were investigating. I'd intended to take everything to you, but then someone attacked me when I went out to my car and I ran."

Jameson took a moment, clearly processing all of that. "Someone must have thought you learned something pretty damn important to try to kill you. Did you?"

She had to shake her head. "But I had the feeling that something was there. Some kind of…inconsistency."

"I know what you mean. I had the same feeling. That's why I kept digging." He paused again. "Tell me about that chat you had with the money launderer."

Kelly blew out a frustrated breath. "The guy's name was Lionel Rouse."

"Yeah, I tried to talk to him, too, but he wouldn't see me. My father had been investigating him."

"Yes, that was in your notes. I'm not sure why Lionel agreed to see me. Maybe because he thought I would help him get out of jail. Anyway, he said the wrong man was behind bars. I asked him who should be, and he said it was the head honcho. He wouldn't say more so I started looking for a money trail, something that would tell me who'd paid off this guy. Nothing."

"But the man or woman who paid him could have believed you found something."

His phone rang, cutting off anything else he might have added to that, and Jameson frowned, then cursed, when he saw the unfamiliar number on the screen. He answered it but didn't say anything. However, it didn't take long for the caller to speak.

"I'm so sorry." It was Mandy, and her words were

rushed together. "I really screwed up, and you have to help me."

"What's wrong?" Jameson snapped.

"Some men took Amy. They have Boyer's daughter, and they took her to your family's ranch. God, Jameson, you have to save her."

Chapter Fifteen

Kelly stared at Jameson's phone, praying that she had misheard what her sister said. But Mandy's earlier words came back to her.

What I'm about to do might make things more dangerous for you. For others, too.

Had Mandy been talking about Boyer's child then? If so, if those kidnappers had actually gotten their hands on her and brought her to the ranch, then yes, a lot of people were suddenly in danger.

Not just Amy, either, but Gracelyn and everyone else in Gabriel's house.

Her sister was sobbing. Kelly had no trouble hearing that. But she also knew that sobs could be faked. She hated to distrust Mandy, but there were too many unanswered questions about her sister's relationship with one of their top suspects. Now that suspect's child had supposedly been taken.

"Mandy, what happened?" Jameson demanded. He hurried to the window to look out. "How'd kidnappers get to the baby?"

There was another sob. "I had her in a safe place, and I managed to borrow a car and drive out there. But there was a tracking device on my shoe. The men who kidnapped me must have put it there when they knocked me out, and I must have missed it when we checked yesterday. They followed me there and took her. Please, just get her from them. They'll hurt her to get to Kelly."

Kelly couldn't help but react to that. Those monsters could have a precious baby. It didn't matter that it was someone else's child; the emotion hit Kelly as hard as if the little girl were her own.

"What do you think I can do to get her back?" Jameson asked, the frustration and concern in his voice.

"I don't know." Mandy was sobbing so hard now that it was difficult to understand her. "But you have to do something. You have to get to her before they hurt her."

Jameson kept his attention on the grounds outside the window. "I don't see anyone other than a couple of my ranch hands. Stay on the line while I text one of the deputies. I can have everyone keep an eye out for anything suspicious. You're sure the men will bring the baby here?"

"That's what they said. They hit me with a stun gun, tied me up and took her, but I could still hear what they were saying. As soon as I was able to move and get out of the ropes, I started driving to the ranch. But they're a good hour ahead of me. In fact, they could be there by now."

Kelly tried to see all possible angles of this, but it was hard to think. Not with this new round of panic coursing through her. "Was there a nanny or someone with Amy?"

"A nanny. They used a stun gun on her, too. I didn't bring her with me," Mandy added. "This is going to be dangerous, and there was no need to put her in the middle of it."

Kelly didn't like the sound of that. "The middle of it? What are you going to do?"

"Get back the baby," Mandy insisted. "I'll be there as fast as I can."

Jameson cursed again when Mandy hung up, but he didn't try to call her back. Instead, he called Cameron and filled him in on what was happening.

"Go ahead and tell Gabriel so he can get out here. You and Edwin should stay put for now, but I might need you to get Gracelyn and the others out of here in the cruiser."

She couldn't hear what Cameron said in response to that because Kelly's heartbeat was drumming in her ears. She did want her baby far from here, but that came with huge risks. Just getting in the cruiser meant they'd have to be outside. Even a few seconds in the open could give a gunman a chance to shoot them.

"I can't be with Gracelyn in the cruiser," Kelly said the moment Jameson finished his call with Cameron. "I can't do anything that will make her a target." And that's exactly what anyone with her would be.

The muscles stirred in Jameson's jaw. He was probably trying to think of an argument to counter that. There wasn't one. It was true the men might try to get to Gracelyn to get Kelly to cooperate, but she believed the men wouldn't go after the baby if Kelly was still on the ranch where they could get to her.

"It might not even come to that," Jameson assured her. He brushed a kiss on her cheek. "Go tell Erica, Jodi and Ivy what's going on. Jodi can get guns for all of you. I'm sure there's a stash in the house. Then the four of you should take Gracelyn into the bathroom and wait for me there. I won't be long. I just need to talk with some of the ranch hands."

Part of her hated being tucked away while Jameson and the deputies were in possible harm's way, but the bathroom would be the safest place for Gracelyn.

She turned to hurry out, but Kelly gave Jameson one last look. There was already a sinking feeling in the pit of her stomach, and she hoped this wasn't the last time they would see each other. Pushing that thought aside, she went to the bedrooms and alerted the others.

Jodi was already up and on the phone. "Gabriel's on the way," she relayed, tucking a gun into the back waist of her jeans. "Any sign of the kidnappers?"

Kelly had to shake her head, and she took another gun that Jodi grabbed for her from the nightstand. Jodi got Ivy while Kelly went to the bedroom to get Erica and the baby moving. Like Jodi, Erica was awake as well and had already scooped up Gracelyn in her arms. The nanny reached to turn on the light, but Kelly stopped her.

"It's just a precaution," Kelly told Erica when she saw that the woman was shaking, and Kelly prayed that was true.

Erica got in the bathtub with Gracelyn, but Kelly went to the only window in the room. Like the ones in Jameson's room, this one faced the old house. It was dark, though, with only a watery moon, and it was hard to see much of anything. Though she did spot a rifle-toting ranch hand just below them.

There were footsteps in the hall, and Jodi automatically pivoted in that direction. But it was only Ivy and Jameson. Ivy went to the tub after Jameson motioned for her to do that, and he went to the window with Jodi and her.

"The hands are in place," Jameson explained. "There are six guarding the house and the rest are walking the perimeter, and they've had eyes on the cruiser the entire time we've been here. No one could have tampered with it."

Good. Because if they had to use it to escape, Kelly didn't want there to be a tracking device on it.

Jameson moved both Jodi and her to the side of the window just as his phone buzzed. It wasn't Mandy, though. This time there was a name on the screen.

Boyer.

"Is it true?" Boyer asked the moment Jameson answered. Unlike his call to Cameron, he put this one on speaker and continued to keep watch. "Do the men who are after Kelly really have my daughter?"

Boyer certainly sounded like a frantic father in fear for his child. But like Mandy's sobs, those emotions could be faked.

"I can't say for sure," Jameson answered, "but we're looking out for them. How did you find out?"

"The kidnappers called me."

Kelly had been certain Mandy had gotten in touch with him. And again, she might have. She reminded herself that this could all be a ruse. At the moment, Kelly couldn't trust either of them.

"What did the kidnappers say?" Jameson asked.

"That they were at your ranch, in the house where your parents were murdered. Are they?"

Because she was close enough to Jameson, she could feel the muscles in his arm tense. "I don't see them. That doesn't mean they aren't there."

Sweet heaven. He was right. There were thick woods behind the house, and the kidnappers could have gotten in that way.

"I'm on my way there now," Boyer added. "If you see my daughter, get her away from those SOBs."

Jameson didn't argue with the man. Probably because he knew there was nothing he could say to stop him. If Boyer was truly a father terrified for his child's life, then he would come no matter what. If he was the person behind the attacks, then he could already be on the grounds. Added to that, Jameson's phone dinged, indicating he had another call coming in.

"I've got to go," Jameson told Boyer, and Kelly saw Unknown Caller on the screen. Probably Mandy. Jameson must have thought so, too, because he quickly answered it.

But it wasn't Mandy.

"I'm gonna make this real short and sweet," the man said. "I got a kid here at your folks' place. A cute little girl."

No. It was the kidnapper. Kelly automatically looked at the old house again, but she still didn't see anyone.

"How do we know for sure that you actually have her?" Jameson asked. "I'll want some kind of proof, something more than just the sounds of her crying."

There was a pause, some chatter, and several moments later, Jameson's phone dinged. "Just sent you a picture. Told you she was cute."

Kelly looked at the screen when the picture loaded. It did indeed seem to be the same little girl in the photo Gabriel had sent them. "Is that your parents' house in the background?" she whispered to Jameson.

He nodded. "That's the family room," he mouthed.

She hadn't exactly doubted the men when they'd told them their location, but it seemed to be true. The kidnappers were just up the path from them.

"What do you want?" Jameson snarled to them.

"Well, I want your lady friend, Kelly. You see, that's the only way you're gonna get back this cute little girl."

Even with the dim light, Kelly saw Jameson's eyes narrow and his jaw go stiff. "You're not getting Kelly."

"I figured you'd say that, and that's why I want her to make the decision. Put her on the phone."

Jameson shook his head, obviously not wanting her to say anything, but the kidnappers would have known she would be with him. "I'm here," she said.

"Good. Now we can have a real heart-to-heart." The kidnapper's tone had a sickening sweetness to it. "Are you the kind of woman who can live with herself if you caused an innocent little girl to be hurt or worse? I doubt you are. And that's why you'll do the right thing."

"And what is the *right* thing?" No sweetness to Jameson's voice. It had that lethal lawman's edge now.

"Start walking to the house, and it's okay if Kelly brings you with her. But only you. One cowboy is more than enough for this little adventure. Talk it out with each other and make your decision. But make it quick. I'll call back in five minutes, and I'll expect an answer. Oh, and I'm expecting that answer to be yes, or you'll hear a lot more of this."

The sound shot through Kelly as if a bullet had slammed into her.

Because the sound she heard was a baby's cry.

JAMESON HAD HOPED that all of this was a hoax. But he was pretty sure those cries were real. Of course, the kidnappers could be using a recording of Boyer's baby—or any baby for that matter—but he had to assume they did indeed have the child.

And the child was now in grave danger.

"Five minutes," the kidnapper repeated, and he ended the call.

He looked at Kelly, and Jameson knew what she was going to say even before she said it. "I have to go out there," she insisted.

She probably knew what he was going to say, too. "They'll kill you."

There were no doubts in his mind that's exactly what would happen. Well, it would after they tortured her to tell them the location of that file. After they had that, they would have no more need for her.

The thought of that twisted away at him. Hell. He had to figure out a way to stop this from happening. He considered calling Gabriel, but that would only waste those precious seconds that were already ticking away. He could fill in his brother after he set some things in motion. Instead, Jameson called Cameron.

"Have four of the hands go to the old house," Jameson explained. "The kidnappers say they're holding Boyer's baby there. A baby they want to exchange for Kelly."

Cameron cursed. "I'll have the hands start moving now."

"I want them to keep out of sight if possible." Jameson doubted it was. Those goons probably had the whole ranch under surveillance. "And tell them to be careful. I don't want any of them shot."

Cameron assured him he would, and Jameson hung up so that the deputy could get started on that.

"Will the hands make it there before our time is up?" Kelly asked.

"No." He hated the look that came on her face. Because it was a look of surrender. "But I want them in place to back us up if all else fails."

He hoped like the devil that it didn't come to that, though.

"You're not going out there," Ivy said. Jameson hadn't even known she'd heard the conversation, but she obviously had.

"We won't go out there on the kidnappers' terms," Jameson assured her. "When they call back, I'll negotiate it so that I go instead of Kelly. I'll tell them that she told me the location of the file." He glanced at her. "Do you know where it is?"

She must have remembered something because she nodded. "A safe-deposit box in San Antonio. We could just tell them that, and it might put an end to things."

It wouldn't. "Whoever hired those men won't want you alive. Because you know what's in the files."

"It's the same for you," Kelly quickly pointed out.

"No. I've only seen the portion of the file I created. I don't know the other things you added to it."

That part was true. But that didn't mean the kidnappers would believe him and keep him alive. Still, he was a lawman, trained in self-defense, and he might be able to overpower them and escape with the baby.

Jameson didn't want to think of all the things that could go wrong with a plan like that.

Even though Kelly had known the kidnappers would call back, the sound of his phone buzzing shot through the room, causing her to gasp. It certainly didn't ease the knot in his gut, but he answered it, praying he would be able to pull this off.

"Well?" the kidnapper said. The guy still had that smug tone that made Jameson want to punch him until he could no longer taunt them.

"I'll come to the house. Once we have the baby and we verify that she's okay, I'll give you the location of the file."

Silence, and the moments crawled by. Jameson could hear the kidnapper have a muffled conversation with someone, but he couldn't tell if that person was also in the house or if he or she was on another phone line.

"No can do," the kidnapper finally said. "We need Kelly to come to us. Oh, and if I were you, I wouldn't risk any deputies or those men who work for you. That's because we've set up explosives around the perimeter of the house. One wrong step, and they go kaboom."

That kicked up Jameson's pulse a significant notch. Kelly's, too. He heard the sharp intake of her breath and saw her hands begin to tremble.

"You're lying," Jameson told the man. "When would you have had time to set up explosives?"

"Oh, we've had them there for nearly two days now. We sneaked in when you were all tied up at the hospital with Kelly, tending her boo-boos. We had everything in place, and a *friend* just brought in the baby from one of the back trails."

With all the insanity that'd been going on for the past two days, it wouldn't have been that hard for someone to come onto the ranch and get into the house. Still, he wanted to kick himself for letting that happen. He should have put guards on the house. Hell, on the entire ranch.

"So here's what we want," the kidnapper went on. "Kelly comes out of the front of the house and starts walking on the trail toward us. No guns. Of course, she'll probably have one hidden away somewhere, but if we see the gun, we start shooting. Not at her, either."

Jameson wanted to reach through the phone and tear this idiot to bits. Because that was a not-so-veiled threat to hurt the baby.

"Who knows, some of those shots could get into your brother's house, where you've got your own kid and family stashed away," the kidnapper added. "Wouldn't want that, would we?"

No. They wouldn't. It would take a long-range rifle for someone to fire into Gabriel's place, but it could be done.

The kidnapper continued a moment later. "Like I said earlier, you can come with her, cowboy. But if you're not at the old house in ten minutes, well, you know what will happen."

"The baby is their leverage," Jameson told Kelly the moment the thug ended the call. "They won't do anything to her."

Jameson hoped that was true anyway, but the main reason he'd said it was to get the stark look off Kelly's face. It didn't work. She was still terrified, still shaking, but that didn't stop her from moving. She hurried to the tub and kissed Gracelyn. Their daughter was still asleep, thank God. No way did Jameson want her to hear any of this.

Including her mother's goodbye.

Kelly didn't exactly say the words, but it was obvious that's what she was doing. Because she might not get out of this alive. Jameson kissed the baby, as well. However, he didn't intend for this to be a farewell. Somehow he was going to make sure Kelly survived.

"You don't have to do this," Jameson told Kelly when she started out of the room. "I can go alone and negotiate with them once we're face-to-face." Of course, that was a serious long shot, and judging from the skeptical sound Kelly made, she knew that, as well.

"It's too big of a risk." She tucked her gun in the back waist of her jeans and headed down the stairs.

It was a huge risk, but Jameson had to try. He also needed to take a few more precautions and hope they would be enough. Nothing would be as safe as he wanted it to be, but at this point he didn't have time to figure out a better way to get close enough to those men to get back the baby.

He stopped by Gabriel's home office and found the Kevlar vests his brother had in a storage closet. He handed one to Kelly, and he put another on while he went to the front of the house to talk to Cameron. He also grabbed a pair of night-vision goggles. Maybe one of the hands could use them to pinpoint the location of the kidnappers before Kelly and he even reached the old house.

"I want Edwin and you to stay here," Jameson told Cameron. "Gabriel will be here any minute, but we can't wait. When he gets here, just fill him in on what's happening."

"What if he wants to go after you and Kelly?" Cameron asked.

"Then tell him to be careful and let him know about the explosives. Also, make sure everything is still locked up and rearm the security system when we leave." Jameson rattled off the code for him to do that.

"And keep watch. I don't want any of those thugs trying to sneak in."

"Please keep our baby safe," Kelly added.

"I'll protect her with my life," Cameron assured her.

Jameson hoped it didn't come down to that. Maybe he could defuse this dangerous situation without Gracelyn being in harm's way.

"Stay behind me," Jameson told Kelly the moment they stepped onto the porch. "And once we're on the trail, I want you to crouch down and use the shrubs and trees for cover."

"But you'll be out in the open," she pointed out.

"They don't want to kill me. They're after you." Not that she needed the reminder. He certainly didn't, either. Because each step they took could be their last.

There were two hands at the front of the house, two more at the back and one on each side. The one on the left side of the steps was Allen Colley, and he had both a sidearm and a rifle.

"Move onto the porch," Jameson told him. "If you see a gunman coming after Kelly and me, try to take him out."

Without hesitation, Allen nodded and did as Jameson said. It wasn't much backup, but it was better than nothing. Plus, maybe there were other hands already in position who could help out if things went from bad to worse.

He also passed Allen the goggles and told the hand to text him if he was able to figure out where the kidnappers were.

Jameson started for the path, and he made sure Kelly was squarely behind him. She was. He also spotted another ranch hand behind a tree just off the trail. Good. Maybe there were others scattered around the grounds.

As soon as they reached the area where the shrubs butted right up against the trail, Kelly ducked lower and went into them. Along with the Kevlar vest, it might protect her. Or at least make her a less visible target.

Jameson had walked this path many times because as a kid, it was the way he got between home and his grandparents' house, where Gabriel was now living. In those days, it had been a pleasant walk with the promise of ice cream or some other treat waiting for him. Definitely nothing pleasant about tonight, though.

"Once we get closer to the house, I want you to get all the way on the ground," Jameson told her. "I'll try one last time to negotiate with the men." But he wasn't holding out much hope for that.

His phone buzzed, and Jameson saw the now-familiar Unknown Caller on the screen.

"Time's up," the man growled when Jameson answered.

That was the only warning Kelly and he got before the shot blasted through the air.

Chapter Sixteen

Kelly wanted to scream for the kidnappers to quit shooting. But her breath froze in her throat. The fear came, too, not just for Boyer's baby but for Gracelyn. Because any shot fired could make it through the walls of Gabriel's house.

Jameson cursed into the phone. "We're coming to you," he snarled to the kidnapper. "But if that baby gets hurt, you've lost your bargaining power with Kelly, and you know it."

"The kid ain't hurt," the man answered. He still sounded arrogant and smug despite the fact that Kelly could also hear the baby crying in the background. "We just wanted to give you some incentive to go faster than you're going now. I'll pull the trigger again in one minute."

Oh, God. That got Kelly moving again. Jameson, too, but he kept the phone right next to them so she'd be able to hear.

"We were going slow because you said there were explosives," Jameson pointed out to the man. "If Kelly is blown up, you'll never get that file. Or whatever it is you want from her."

"The explosives aren't on the path between the two houses. Stay on it, and you'll be fine."

"Right." Jameson made a sound of skepticism. "And I'm to believe you? You just fired a shot with a baby in the room."

"Cowboy, you got no choice but to believe me," the man snapped, and he ended the call.

"Should you text Cameron so he can tell the hands there are no explosives on the path?" she asked. They definitely picked up the pace, but it was a pace and position that put them right out in the open.

Jameson shook his head. "He could have said that to lure them onto the path so he could kill them. Or there really could be explosives here."

That sent her pulse up a notch, something that Kelly hadn't thought possible. It already felt as if her heart were about to beat out of her chest. But what Jameson said was true. There could indeed be explosives, ones that the kidnappers could set off at any time. That thought didn't steady her any.

They continued to walk, probably not hurrying as much as the kidnapper would want, but Jameson and she were trying to keep watch. Not just at the ground but also their surroundings to make sure they weren't about to be ambushed.

Jameson's phone buzzed, and Kelly braced herself for another taunting call from the kidnapper, but it was the ranch hand, Allen. Jameson hit the answer button but then handed it to her. No doubt so it would keep his hands free since there were now very close to the house. As Jameson had done, Kelly held out the phone so they could both hear.

"I used the goggles," Allen said, "and I spotted someone in the side window of the second floor. It's the room at the front of the house. He's got a rifle."

Of course, Kelly had figured the guy would have a weapon like that, but hearing it gave her a new surge of adrenaline. And fear.

"Then there are probably at least two of them," Jameson answered. "Because the photo of the baby was taken downstairs in the family room."

True. The kidnapper could have moved her upstairs, but Kelly doubted he'd do that. It was more likely that he had a comrade or two.

"There are hands in the bushes just off the path," Allen went on, "but I told them to stay put for now."

"Good," Jameson answered. "Are they in position to return fire if it comes down to it?"

"Some should be," Allen assured him. "I got a glimpse of somebody else, too. It's not one of ours. Someone's in a cluster of oak trees in the backyard at the old house. From where you are, you might be able to see him or her."

Both Jameson and she immediately looked in that direction. Nothing. Not at first anyway. Then Kelly caught a blur of motion. A person moving to the back side of the house.

Mandy.

Her sister was right there, and she probably didn't know about the explosives. Well, Mandy didn't unless she'd been the one to hire these snakes who'd put them there.

"I need to try to text or call her so I can warn her," Kelly insisted. Because if her sister was truly innocent, she didn't want her killed. Nor did she want Mandy accidentally setting off a bomb that could hurt the baby.

"Let us know if you see anyone else," Jameson told the hand. "Go ahead and try Mandy," he added right after Kelly had hit the end call button.

Kelly cursed her fingers because they were shaking. Actually, all of her was shaking, but she finally texted the number that Mandy had used to call them earlier. She prayed her sister still had that particular phone with her.

Explosives might be near the house, Kelly texted.

Jameson and she kept walking, her heart pounding harder with each step. It pounded even harder when she got an answer to the text.

Haven't seen any explosives, Mandy responded. Going into the house now. Try to cover me if you can.

Jameson groaned when Kelly showed him the text. "Tell her to wait until we're there."

Kelly fired off that message but got no response. Worse, Mandy disappeared from sight. Kelly was about to send another text, but the phone buzzed. This time, it was Unknown Caller on the screen, and she immediately hit the answer button.

"We'll be there in under a minute," Jameson assured the caller.

"That's good to hear, but what I want to know is who's in the car that just pulled up on the road in front of the house."

Jameson craned his neck in that direction and shook his head. "I can't see the road. But it's not the cops, if that's what you're thinking."

"Oh, I know it's not them. Well, not your brother anyway. I see the sheriff just pulled up in front of his home sweet home. He used the back road and not the one that runs in front of your folks' place."

That gave Kelly a little relief. Now that Gabriel was there, that was one extra person to protect Gracelyn and the others. Of course, Gabriel would likely try to help Jameson and her, too.

"When you get into the front yard," the kidnapper continued, "leave Kelly by the porch, and you go to whoever's in that car and tell them to take a hike."

"You're sure it's not one of your fellow hired thugs?" Jameson asked him.

"Nope. I'm thinking this thug is one of yours. Just take care of the problem, or I'll have no use for you, cowboy."

It sickened Kelly to hear that, especially those final words before the kidnapper hung up. To know that no matter what Jameson did, the goons inside would try to kill him anyway. Plus, going up to that car could be just as dangerous as facing whoever was inside the house.

Jameson put his phone away as they reached the edge of the yard. There were still plenty of weeds and underbrush here, too, but they finally had a line of sight of the road.

And Kelly had no trouble seeing the black car.

The driver had stopped beside some thick trees. He'd probably done that with the hope the kidnappers wouldn't be able to spot him since it wasn't visible from the house itself. The fact that the thugs knew the car was there told her that they had some kind of surveillance—either equipment or men—on the road.

"You think it's Boyer?" she whispered.

"Maybe. Or it could be someone Mandy brought with her."

Yes, her sister hadn't said she was alone, but Kelly

hadn't seen anyone with Mandy before she'd ducked out of sight.

"Go to the car, cowboy!" someone shouted. It was one of the kidnappers, and he was in the upstairs window. The window was open a fraction, just enough for Kelly to see the barrel of the rifle sticking out. But the man carrying that rifle had stayed in the shadows.

Jameson glanced around as if trying to figure out what to do. The kidnapper had told him to leave her in the yard, but if he did that, they might just try to grab her. However, if Jameson took her with him to the car, the baby's captors might start shooting. But that mental debate came to a quick halt when they heard another shout.

Mandy this time.

"Watch out!" she yelled.

But there wasn't time for Kelly to try to figure out why her sister had given them that warning. That's because the black car on the road exploded into a fireball.

JAMESON AUTOMATICALLY PULLED Kelly to the ground and covered her with his body. Not a second too soon, either. That's because the flaming pieces of the car started raining down on the yard and smacking into the house. He heard glass shattering and something else.

The baby crying.

Hell. Jameson prayed that she hadn't been hurt and was just frightened from the noise.

"Mandy," Kelly said, her voice as ragged as her breathing. "She called out right before the explosion."

"I don't think she was near the car."

Jameson hadn't been able to pinpoint her voice, but he thought it might have come from the other side of the house. That's where the family room was located. And the baby if they hadn't moved her. If Mandy was indeed there, the line of trees should have protected the debris from getting to her.

"You would have been killed if you'd gone closer," Kelly said, her voice as ragged as her breathing.

Yeah. In fact, they still could have been killed if one of those metal chunks had hit them. There were huge pieces of what was left of the car scattered all around them. The question now was—had there been anyone in that car? If so, they were dead.

"Why would the kidnappers do this?" Kelly asked. "Why would they take a risk like that?"

"I'm not sure they did," Jameson mumbled.

From that second-floor window, the kidnapper was cursing. Clearly, he wasn't pleased with what had just happened, which meant either it was malfunctioning explosives or someone else had set it off.

Someone, maybe, like Boyer?

But that didn't feel right, either. Boyer seemed to love his little girl, and he wouldn't want to put her at risk. Of course, it was possible that Boyer had just gotten unlucky and parked on one of the explosive devices the thugs had set.

Jameson's phone dinged with a text message, but he passed it to Kelly because he didn't want to take his eyes off their surroundings.

"It's Gabriel," she relayed. "He's on the way down here."

Not exactly the best news, but Jameson doubted he could stop his big brother. "Tell him to watch for explosives."

While she was doing that, Jameson saw some movement on the far side of the house. Mandy. She was leaning out and looking in their direction. Kelly saw her, too, because she lifted her head, tracking her sister as Mandy moved to the front porch. Jameson wanted to throttle her for that. It was too big of a risk, and if she wasn't the one behind this, she was going to get herself killed.

"Cowboy," the kidnapper shouted. "You and Kelly can start moving again now."

"Is the baby okay?" Jameson demanded.

"For now. Keep it that way, and do as I say. You walk to the center of the front yard. Better find a spot that's not on fire from your little prank. I'm guessing that was your brother's doing."

Not a chance. But Jameson kept that to himself. "What about Kelly?"

"I want her on the front porch. And no more lollygagging around. Move fast."

Kelly started to stand up, but Jameson pulled her back down. "I can't stop this," he said, and that ate away at him. He could lose her, right here, right now. "But let me go out there first. That way, I can be in position to pick off anyone who tries to shoot. And when you get to the porch, drop down by the steps. They're stone, and they'll give you some cover."

She nodded, staring at him, and even in the moonlight, he could see the fear in her eyes. "What about you?"

"I'll take cover, too." Though he wasn't exactly sure where that would be yet. Nor did he have time to work it out now. Jameson just had to pray that the kidnappers didn't gun them down the moment they stepped into the yard.

"I love you," she said, dropping a kiss on his mouth.

It wasn't a good time to be stunned, but that's exactly what those words did to Jameson. They probably weren't even true. This could just be Kelly's way of saying goodbye. Well, it wasn't goodbye for him. One way or another, he was going to save her and get them out of this.

"Move it now!" the kidnapper shouted. "And remember, no guns."

Jameson did. He got up, tucking his gun in the back waist of his jeans. He walked out into the yard. Fast. He fired glances all around them, especially at the house and Kelly. But he saw Mandy, too. She was crawling her way to the door. He shook his head, but Jameson doubted it would do any good.

Behind him, he heard a strange sound. A gasp. And he whirled around in that direction to see something he damn sure didn't want to see.

Kelly.

She was on her feet, but she wasn't alone. There was a man behind her, and he had a gun. Jameson got just a glimpse of him before the guy fired a shot. Not at Kelly. But at Jameson.

It slammed into his chest.

He heard Kelly scream. There was nothing he could do about it, though. The pain exploded inside him, and Jameson had no choice but to drop to his knees. The bullet had hit the Kevlar, but it had knocked the breath out of him. Had maybe cracked some ribs, too, and the hot metal was burning a hole in him. But the worst part was, he couldn't get to Kelly.

And the man who'd shot him had now put the gun to Kelly's head.

Jameson got a better look at him then. Saw the man whispering something in Kelly's ear.

That man was August Canton.

KELLY TRIED TO call out to Jameson, but her throat had clamped shut. Oh, God. He'd been shot. And it didn't matter that she couldn't see any blood. He was down on the ground, writhing in pain and clutching his chest. He needed help.

Help that she couldn't give him because the man had her in a choke hold.

Too bad she couldn't use her gun; her captor had stripped that from her the moment he'd grabbed her.

That didn't stop her from fighting, though. She tried to slam her elbow into his stomach so she could break free from him, but she failed. He dodged her blow, tightened his grip on her and dug the barrel of his gun against her temple.

"Move and I shoot Jameson again," he growled right in her ear. "And this time, the bullet goes in his head."

As sickening as that threat was, what twisted at her even more was that she recognized that voice. She hadn't managed to see the man before he'd grabbed her, but she knew who their attacker was now. August.

"Why?" she managed to ask. However, Kelly already knew the answer. This had to do with that blasted file.

A file that no doubt incriminated August in some way. Or so he thought. But Kelly honestly didn't remember if there was anything in there that would do that.

"Now, let's go into the house and wait for Gabriel." August started pushing her in that direction. "Then we can really settle some things."

"What about Jameson?" The grip he had on her throat made it hard for her to speak. Hard to breathe, too.

"Oh, he'll be coming, too. This plan wouldn't be complete without him."

That sounded like the vile threat that it was, and she prayed Jameson would be able to move soon so he could scramble out of the way.

Kelly looked on the porch but didn't see her sister. Maybe that meant Mandy had slipped inside. Of course, that didn't mean Mandy was in there to help them out. No. She could be working for August and these thugs. Or for Boyer.

But where was the agent?

And where was Gabriel? She still had Jameson's phone, but there hadn't been a text message. It was possible, though, that Gabriel had already seen what was going on and was trying to figure out a way to stop it.

"This would be a bad time for cops to arrive," August warned her. "Anyone who comes near the house now will die."

She figured that applied to anyone who went inside the house, too, and that's exactly where August was taking her.

"I don't remember where the file is," she lied. She couldn't offer to give it to him, because once he had it, she had no bargaining power whatsoever.

"Then I'll torture Jameson and Gabriel until you do remember."

August kept dragging her across the yard, and when she got closer to Jameson, he looked at her. She could see the pain etched on his face, and he was fighting to get the vest off him. Probably because the bullet was burning like fire.

"If you try to get up, I'll shoot Kelly," August snarled to Jameson, and he kept on moving up the steps and onto the porch. When they went inside the house, though, August froze. "Randy," he called out.

There was some movement in the adjacent room, but apparently something was wrong. She could tell by the way August's arm tensed. Maybe the hired thug was supposed to swoop out and get her so that his boss could deal with Jameson.

Finally, a man staggered into the foyer. There was blood streaming down his face, and he was mumbling profanity. "That bitch sister of hers clubbed me on the head, grabbed the baby and climbed out the window with her."

Despite everything else that was going on, that caused relief to flood through Kelly. Mandy had gotten the child, and maybe her sister would be able to get the little girl safely away from all of this. It also meant that Mandy wasn't working for August.

"Have someone find her now," August growled. "She could have seen me."

That told Kelly plenty about this situation. August didn't intend on leaving any witnesses behind because he planned on getting away with this. And she soon saw how he'd intended to do that.

Someone had used what appeared to be red paint or maybe blood to write on the foyer walls.

Time for more Becketts to die.

Back to finish what I started ten years ago.

August was going to make it look as if the "real" killer had returned to the scene of the crime. And she doubted the timing was a coincidence, since it was the decade anniversary of the murders.

"You killed them," she said. "You murdered Jameson's parents."

August certainly didn't deny it. He turned her so that she was facing the door. That meant if anyone came charging in through there, he would use her as a human shield.

"Have someone bring in Jameson," August ordered his thug. The guy was still bleeding, still looked pretty shaky, but he was repeating August's order through a small communicator.

"That's why you want my file," Kelly pressed. Along with the fear, the anger roared through her. "You butchered two people, and you've let your brother rot in jail this whole time."

August cursed her and whacked his gun against the side of her head. It hurt—bad, but she'd obviously hit a nerve.

"My brother will be released once the law finds this new crime scene," August insisted.

"No. He won't be. Unless there's proof someone else did the killings. Planted proof…" She stopped, groaned. "You're going to set up Boyer. That's why you took his child, so that he would come out here. Where is he? Do you have him tied up somewhere?"

"He was in the car that exploded. Don't worry. There's enough evidence on his computer to convince the cops he did this."

A hoarse sob tore from her mouth. She certainly hadn't cared much for Boyer, but if August was telling the truth, then he'd just made Amy an orphan. Worse, August planned to get away with all of this death, pain and misery.

But Kelly didn't intend to let that happen.

Somehow, she had to stop him.

There was some movement by the front door, and Kelly steeled herself up for more thugs. However, it was Jameson. He still had that pained look on his face, was still having trouble moving, but one of the hired guns shoved him into the foyer, sending Jameson to the floor.

Without thinking, Kelly tried to break free and go to him. And she paid for that when August hit her with the gun again. The pain was the least of what she felt, though. She saw the rage that put in Jameson's eyes, and he came off the floor, ready to launch himself at August.

"Don't," August warned him, "because I'll kill her where she stands."

"I got his guns," the thug informed his boss. "And the sheriff is here. He's in those bushes off the trail where you were waiting."

August's arm muscles relaxed a little. "Good. Bring him here so I can finish this."

If looks could have killed, Jameson's glare would have blasted August to smithereens. "Why?" Jameson growled, his voice low and dangerous.

"Because I have to do something to get Travis out of jail. And that file that Kelly and you put together has too many pieces that can lead back to me. I'd hoped that you two wouldn't find so much, but I knew if you did that you'd be easier to take care of than the cops."

"What pieces?" Kelly asked. "Because I'd like to know the reason I'm about to die."

"It's the interviews with Hattie's friends," August said after a long pause. "Not the official ones. But the later ones that Jameson did. He talked to them, the other folks in the area."

She had to shake her head. "Hattie, the woman you milked out of her savings? The woman who died?"

"The woman who started Sheriff Sherman Beckett's investigation into me. Sherman was a little too good at his job, because he started poking around in other things I was involved in. Like money laundering."

"And that's why you murdered him," Kelly concluded. "I'm guessing, though, that his wife was just collateral damage. She probably walked in while you were killing her husband, and she tried to stop it."

August didn't deny any of that.

"This is all for nothing," Kelly assured him. "Because there wasn't anything in those secondary interviews to incriminate you."

"Yes, there was. If you dig hard, you'll see there's a problem with my alibi. When you talked to Marilyn, she got the times wrong. Stupid woman."

"We have the sheriff," the wounded thug said to August. "They're bringing him in now."

Kelly's stomach went to her knees. She'd hoped that Gabriel might be able to escape. Now this meant August would get all of the key players in the house. Where he would kill them.

"Tell them to hurry getting Gabriel here," August told the goon as he checked his watch. "Time is running out."

What did he have up his sleeve now? She didn't want to wait around and find out.

Her eyes locked with Jameson, and Kelly could sense he was about to do something. What exactly, she didn't know, but she didn't have to wait long to find out.

Jameson lunged forward, and in the same motion, he shoved the hired gun who'd brought him inside. The thug flew right into August and her, and it felt as if a Mack truck had hit her. But she instantly knew why Jameson had done that. That's because they all fell, and she heard at least one of the guns clattering to the floor.

August spewed out some vile profanity, and from the corner of her eye, Kelly saw the bleeding gunman about to join the fray. She put a stop to that by tripping him. He dropped down next to them, and she snatched up his gun.

But she didn't have a shot.

August, Jameson and now both thugs were in a fierce battle, and she couldn't fire for fear of hitting Jameson. Worse, the third gunman was probably about to come in at any moment, and since he had Gabriel, he would be able to stop this by threatening to kill Jameson's brother. That's why Kelly had to do something now.

She shifted the gun in her hand and bashed it against the wounded man's head. He howled in pain and rolled out of the heap.

And that's when Kelly took aim and shot him. Not to disable him, either. She went for a kill shot, and she made it.

With that one out of the way, she turned back to the fight. Jameson had August pinned to the floor, but her heart skipped a couple of beats when she saw the hired thug lift his gun toward Jameson. Since she couldn't risk firing, she kicked him as hard as she could. His muscles were rock-hard, and it didn't even seem to faze him, but it did cause the goon to look back at her.

Big mistake.

Because Jameson took advantage of that. Even though the man was much larger than he was, Jameson managed to take hold of him, and he shoved him at August.

Just as August fired off a shot.

A shot that went straight into his man.

Even in the darkness, Kelly saw the look of shock on August's face. For a split second anyway, before Jameson grabbed August and dragged him to his feet. Kelly quickly handed Jameson her gun, and he put it to the man's head.

She could feel the rage in Jameson. The need for him to avenge his parents' death. The muscles in his jaw were tight. His hands were shaking a little. And the moments crawled by with his finger tensing on the trigger.

Kelly also saw the exact moment Jameson remembered he was a lawman and not a killer. Nothing like the piece of slime he was holding.

"August Canton, you're under arrest," Jameson gutted out.

Behind her, Kelly heard the footsteps on the porch. This was no doubt Gabriel being led in by one of August's henchmen. She snatched up the dead thug's gun so she could use it to free Gabriel.

But there was no need for that.

Gabriel was alone. And unharmed. He came into the foyer, and he took in the scene with a sweeping glance. His eyes met Jameson's. Even though they didn't say anything, a dozen things passed between them. All the pain and loss. All the grief they'd suffered for the past ten years.

"The ranch hands have rounded up the hired guns," Gabriel said. His voice was a little unsteady, but that was a vicious glare he had nailed to August. "Let's get him locked up."

Gabriel used some plastic cuffs to restrain August, but when Kelly looked at the man, she saw something she didn't like.

August was smiling.

"Always have a backup plan," August taunted. He glanced at his watch again. His smile widened.

Just as the sound of the explosion ripped through the house.

Chapter Seventeen

One second Jameson was standing, and the next he was back on the floor. Somehow, he managed to catch on to Kelly and break her fall, and she landed in his arms. The pain shot through him again because that definitely hadn't helped with the ribs he was certain he'd cracked.

The pain was the least of his worries, though.

"Run!" Gabriel shouted. He, too, was on the floor next to August, and his brother hauled the man to his feet and headed for the front door.

Jameson did the same to Kelly. Not easily, but he got her moving. And that's when he realized the entire back half of the house was missing. There was a groaning sound, and the roof came swooshing down, the ceiling and boards clattering all around them.

Thankfully, Kelly seemed to be able to run, so maybe that meant she hadn't been hurt. Except he saw the blood on her forehead. It was possible they hadn't gotten so lucky after all.

With Gabriel gripping August, they ran down the porch steps and into the yard. Not a second too soon. Because the entire house fell right in front of them. Debris went everywhere, mixing with the burning car parts that were still all around them.

"Take my truck," Gabriel said, tossing Jameson the keys. "It's parked on the road just up from here. You and Kelly get back to the house, and Cameron and I will take this piece of scum to jail."

August sure as heck wasn't smiling now. He looked back at what was left of the house, and his nostrils flared. His face twisted into an enraged snarl. As arrogant as he was, the last thing he'd probably expected was to fail.

But he had.

Thank God, he had.

Even though Gabriel had said the hands had rounded up August's goons, Jameson didn't want to risk her being out in the open any longer. He hooked his arm around her waist and got her into Gabriel's truck. The moment he had her inside, he started the engine and got them moving. He also glanced at Kelly to see if that bleeding on her head had gotten any worse.

"It's just a scratch," she said, following his gaze and then touching her fingers to her forehead. "But you need to see a doctor. You wince in pain every time you move."

Yeah, he was wincing, but Jameson had hoped she hadn't noticed. "We'll both see the doctor in an hour or two. Once we're sure the scene has been cleared."

Her eyes widened, and she made a soft moan. "You think those men—"

"No. I just want to make sure all the explosives are gone." With August's sick mind, he could have planted others. Heck, he could have done it weeks or even months ago, since he'd apparently been planning this for years.

Kelly didn't exactly breathe any easier, but he hoped

once she saw that Gracelyn was all right, that it would help steady her nerves. Jameson did something that he figured definitely wouldn't calm her, but he couldn't help himself. He kissed her when he pulled to a stop in front of Gabriel's house.

He'd been wrong, though, about it not helping. Because he could feel some of the tension leave her body. It helped him, too, but he definitely didn't want to start a make-out session in the truck. Not with a deputy and his sister-in-law watching from the windows. Jameson got her moving, and they hurried up the steps into the house.

"Thank God, you're all right," Jodi immediately said. She gave them both hugs. "Gabriel?" He saw the worry in her eyes, too.

"He's fine. He arrested August."

"August?" someone repeated. Ivy. His sister was at the top of the stairs.

There was plenty he could tell her, but this wasn't the time for it. Not with their emotions still so raw. "August is the one who killed Mom and Dad."

Ivy shook her head, as if she might not believe that, but then a sob tore from her mouth. He pulled his sister into his arms. A hug wasn't much, but maybe knowing the truth would finally help them all heal.

"Where's Gracelyn?" Kelly asked, taking the question right out of Jameson's mouth.

"Still in the bathroom with Erica. They're both fine," Ivy added. She moved out of Jameson's embrace so he could head up the stairs.

But he came to a quick halt.

That's because there was someone in the family

room. Mandy. And she was holding a little girl. Boyer's daughter, no doubt.

"I started running and didn't know where else to go," Mandy said, her voice raw and broken. The baby seemed all right, though. In fact, she was sleeping in Mandy's arms. "Boyer's dead, isn't he?"

Kelly nodded. "August said he was in the car that exploded."

"He was." Tears shimmered in Mandy's eyes. "I saw him, but I figured if I didn't get to the baby, those men could hurt her."

"They could have," Jameson assured her. "You did the right thing getting her out. A dangerous thing," he tacked onto that. But it was hard to argue with something that had worked to save a child.

"I didn't have anything to do with August's plan or the attacks," Mandy insisted, her gaze shifting to her sister. "I love you and want you safe."

"I believe you," Kelly answered. "And I love you, too."

Kelly said the words as easily to Mandy as she had to him right before all hell had broken loose. She sounded sincere. Both now and then. But Jameson wasn't sure if the *I love you* she'd given him was because she had been afraid they were going to die.

"I'll have to go to jail, won't I?" Mandy asked. "Because I'm the one who took Amy. I'm the one who kept her from Boyer. But I swear I thought it was dangerous. I believed what Hadley told me about him."

Jameson would have liked to reassure her that all would be well. He couldn't. After all, Mandy had committed a felony, and that meant she almost certainly would do some jail time.

"What will happen to Amy if I'm arrested?" Mandy pressed.

Kelly went to her, and as Jodi had done to them, she hugged her sister. She also brushed a kiss on the baby's forehead. "I'll make sure Amy is taken care of while we look for her next of kin."

That was the right thing to say, and Jameson would indeed do just that. Heck, if they couldn't find any of her relatives, he could raise her himself.

That mentally stopped him.

He had obviously jumped right into daddy mode. But there was no way he was going to let Amy go into foster care, not after everything she'd been through.

"Should I, uh, go ahead and arrest Mandy?" Edwin asked.

"Not yet. Let her stay with the baby awhile longer." It was the best Jameson could offer her under the circumstances. "But if Mandy tries to run—"

"I won't," Mandy interrupted. "No way do I want her back out there with possible explosives." She cradled the baby closer and rocked her.

Later, he'd need to have a long chat with Mandy about all the details of the attacks that she might have witnessed, but it was just routine. Jameson didn't expect any more surprises. At least he hoped like the devil there wouldn't be. He'd had enough surprises to last him a lifetime.

Or so he thought.

But when Kelly and he went into the bathroom, and he saw his daughter, Jameson couldn't believe that he loved someone as much as he loved her. It was incredible and terrifying at the same time. And somehow perfect.

Gracelyn was asleep in Erica's arms, but the baby

opened her eyes and turned her head toward them. She gave them a sleepy smile before closing her eyes. Oh, man. There it was again. That punch of emotion. He went to her and eased Gracelyn from Erica.

"Is everything okay?" Erica whispered.

"It is now." Jameson brushed a kiss on Gracelyn's cheek and handed her to Kelly so she could do the same.

Erica made a sound of relief, and she must have sensed they needed some alone time because she excused herself and left.

Kelly gave the baby another kiss and looked up at him. There was still blood on her face, and he grabbed a tissue to wipe it away. The nicks and bruises were reminders of the hell they'd just gone through. But they would heal. In a week or so, there'd be no signs of all the bad stuff.

Plus, there was good, too.

Kelly smiled at him, and it gave him that same flood of warmth as Gracelyn's smile. She kept staring at him. Maybe waiting for him to say something. He had plenty to say all right, but he didn't even get a chance to start because his phone buzzed. Jameson answered it right away when he saw Gabriel's name on the screen.

"Please tell me August didn't escape," Jameson said. He walked into the adjacent bedroom so the conversation wouldn't wake up Gracelyn, but when Kelly followed him, he put the call on speaker.

"No. We just arrived at the station, and he's behind bars."

Jameson released the breath he'd been holding. August had evaded justice for a decade, and he didn't want the man getting away with anything else. "Has he said anything?"

"Yeah. Mostly curse words I won't repeat. He blames me and you for not finding someone other than Travis to convict for the murders."

That was warped logic, but then, August was a warped man. "If August was so torn up about his brother being behind bars, why didn't he just confess to the crime he committed?"

"I asked him that, and he put the blame on Dad for investigating him."

Yeah, August was definitely too far gone to see that he was the monster in all of this. And his arrogance and stupidity had caused a lot of pain and misery.

"In one of August's profanity tirades," Gabriel continued, "he did let it slip that he's the one who's been sending us threats."

Well, that was one thing cleared up. But once August had revealed himself as the killer, Jameson had just assumed he'd made the threats, too. And August had probably done that to try to make them think that either there was a copycat or they'd put the wrong man in jail.

Which they had.

"All the evidence pointed to Travis," Gabriel said as if reading his mind. "Since August insists he didn't set him up, I suspect Travis went by the house shortly after the murders, and that's how he got Dad's blood on his shirt."

That was possible, since Travis was their neighbor. Plus, the man had been drunk, so he wouldn't have even realized how incriminating it would have been to touch the body.

Jameson looked at Kelly to see how she was dealing with all of this. Her forehead was bunched up, and there was concern in her eyes. But he thought the worry was for him. For how he was handling all this discussion about his parents. He went to her and kissed her to let her know he was okay.

And he was.

His folks' deaths would always cut him to the bone, but there were new things in his life to help with the hurt. Mainly Kelly and Gracelyn.

"We'll go through everything that's in Kelly's file," Gabriel continued a moment later. "And I'll contact the warden of the prison to let him know that Travis will soon be getting out."

It wouldn't be easy, but Jameson planned to be there for the man's release. He wanted to look Travis in the eyes and tell him he was sorry for the conviction. After all, Travis's son and daughter were now part of the Beckett family, and Jameson wanted a fresh start for all of them. Well, everyone except August. The man would almost certainly end up on death row.

"Any idea who August planned to set up to take the fall for the murders?" Jameson asked his brother.

"I think Boyer."

Jameson made a sound of agreement. "When we were in the house, August mentioned putting something on Boyer's computer that would incriminate him." And now Boyer was dead. "Boyer's baby is here at your place," Jameson added.

"Edwin called and told me. After the CSI team and reserve deputies are in place, I'll have Edwin bring in Mandy. I can't make the charges against her go away, though."

"I know," Kelly said. "My sister has to pay for what she's done." She paused. "But maybe the baby can stay here and not be sent to foster care?"

"I'm pretty sure I can arrange that." Now it was Gabriel's turn to hesitate. "Are you two sure, though, that you can manage a second baby? I mean, you're going to be settling in with Gracelyn."

Settling in. That was an interesting choice of words. Was that what Kelly and he were doing?

"We can do this," Kelly assured his brother. "Well, with some help from the rest of you."

"Are we talking changing diapers?" Gabriel asked. There was a touch of humor in his voice.

"Definitely," Jameson answered. And he found himself smiling. Gabriel was going to be a good uncle, and one day a good father.

"All right," Gabriel agreed. "I'll change a diaper or two. Will even babysit some. What I want to know, though, is how soon will Kelly and Gracelyn be moving in with you?"

Good question, but Jameson didn't have the answer. "I'll get back to you on that. Let me know if anything else comes up."

"And you let me know when Kelly and you set a wedding date." Chuckling, Gabriel ended the call.

Jameson scowled at the phone and would give his brother a scowl in person later. Gabriel's comment had no doubt shocked Kelly. It was too soon for her to even be thinking about long-term plans...

Or not.

She slid her hand around the back of his neck, eased him closer and kissed him. Really kissed him. In fact, it was as hot and close as it could be considering that she was still holding Gracelyn. When she'd rid him of every trace of the scowl and made him pretty much mindless, she pulled back.

Smiled.

"I'm in love with you," she said. "That wasn't the fear or the adrenaline talking. I meant it. I fell in love with you two years ago, and the feelings are still as strong as ever."

Good. That was exactly what he wanted to hear.

Jameson pulled Kelly back into his arms and gave the words right back to her. "I'm in love with you, too."

He kissed her mouth. That smile. And then kissed her again.

Everything he'd ever wanted was right here in his arms—his precious little girl and the woman he loved.

* * * * *

FEDERAL
AGENT UNDER
FIRE

JULIE ANNE LINDSEY

Dedicated to double-shot espressos.

Chapter One

Marissa Lane knew something was wrong the minute she saw him. In the six months since she'd started her predawn ritual, she'd rarely seen anyone in the national park before sunup, save the occasional ranger, but there were no rangers today. Only *him*. A man nearly engulfed in shadows at the lookout where she watched the sunrise three days a week.

She slowed her pace before reaching the low wooden fence that separated hikers from a sharp plummet into fog-laced evergreens, angling her body to keep the man in her sights. Everything about the moment set her intuition on edge, but she forced the shaky feeling away. She'd met plenty of fellow hikers over the years, and they'd all been kind. Kindred spirits. Glad to be outdoors. It was the hour that threw her. She'd started to think of herself as the only one in town who enjoyed a good sunrise.

The rocky eastern face of the park's tallest mountain was the best place in Cade County to watch a sunrise, maybe the best in Kentucky. Marissa had yet to find a better one, though it was her job to try, and she did four mornings a week. Normally, she'd have finished her water and enjoyed her apple before walking back to her ride, parked nearly five miles down the trail, but today every cell in her body said that whatever had brought this man into her path wasn't good, and she didn't want any part of it.

"Mornin'." His voice was low and gravelly. The hood of his jacket was up, working in collaboration with the shadows to shield his face.

Marissa lifted her chin in acknowledgement. She moved her tired body another step away, feigning interest in the view closest to the trail. He'd probably come there to think and was feeling as intruded upon as she was. Courtesy said she should be on her way. Greedily, she dawdled for one more breathtaking look.

The fiery glow of daylight scorched a path across the sky, climbing the opposite mountain with vigor and bathing thousands of deciduous trees, already dressed in rich autumn colors, with luminous shades from amber to apricot and everything in between. These were her favorite seconds of the day; when an ordinary forest became an inferno, and the world was backlit by Mother Nature's glory.

The man broke free from the shadow and took a few casual steps in Marissa's direction, setting her intuition into overdrive. The light scent of cigarette smoke plumed from his clothes, tainting the crisp morning air. This man wasn't a hiker, wasn't a runner, and he was definitely not getting a second of Marissa's time.

She turned away with a frustrated sigh and headed down the mountain on tired, burning legs and a heart full of injustice. Anger churned in her gut with each forced step. She'd made the run in record time. She'd pushed her body for results and had gotten them. These few fleeting moments of sunrise were supposed to be her reward, but this man, whoever he was, was stealing those from her. She hated herself for letting him. For fearing him when she didn't know him. For denying herself the hard-earned prize because she was a woman and he was a stranger. All feminism aside, wrong or right, she'd promised her parents long ago to make safety paramount while she was on her adventures. It was her duty to hold to that, even now, when he had her sunrise and she had a long walk back to where she'd started.

The return trip was always a slower, more methodical process. A pleasurable cooldown, normally preceded by rest on the lookout. She massaged the warm muscles in her neck and shoulders as she moved, swinging her arms across her body for an added stretch. Her legs were rubbery beneath her, but the brisk autumn breeze was invigorating as it rushed over the sheen of sweat on her skin. If she could sell everything and live in the wild for a year, at one with nature, part of the beautiful multicolored kingdom around her, she'd do it in a heartbeat. But only for a year. Eventually she'd miss her crazy family, except for her little sister. Kara would probably be swinging in the hammock beside hers.

Back at the trailhead, the lot was empty except for her old Jeep, and Marissa couldn't bring herself to make the drive home without enjoying the moment of reflection she'd worked for. She checked the empty trail behind her, then hooked a left onto the short path toward Shadow Valley Lake. A hundred yards later, she slid onto the ground at the base of an ancient tree and pulled her knees to her chest. The lake was beautiful, peaceful and full of history.

Shadow Valley was one of Kentucky's lake towns. Someday Marissa planned to see for herself what remained of the underwater historic town. Records showed that residents were relocated up the mountain in the nineteen thirties before their town was permanently flooded. Hard to believe remnants of another time had stood silently beneath the surface for decades, disguised as part of the national park. Those were images she'd love to capture.

She sipped her water and wondered if she'd been irrational to change her daily routine for the sake of one man. Maybe, but what was he doing there? Where was his car, if not in the lot with hers? And who hiked five miles to have a cigarette? The scent had been strong and fresh.

She shook away the irrelevant thoughts and focused instead on the beauty before her. It was important that she start her days at peace, in harmony with her work. Marissa's adventure photos were fast becoming a lucrative business. The images she'd captured were used across the country in textbooks and at seminars on the preservation of wildlife. Her dreams were coming true and demand was rising. In the last year alone, she'd made more than enough to pay the bills and support her travels.

She ran a forearm over her brow before crunching into her morning apple. The sweet scent lifted a smile on her lips as she pressed her tired back against the supportive tree and breathed. Her eyelids dipped closed on the exhale. The moment was so perfectly Zen; she almost didn't turn around when the sound of snapping twigs forced her eyes open. Almost.

Marissa pushed slowly to her feet, listening hard for the next noise. Whatever had cracked the twigs was heavier than a rabbit and less stealthy than anything calling this area home. She opened her stance and braced her tired form. The sudden silence was astounding. She dared a peek around the large oak. There was nothing but the breeze and a pair of chasing squirrels, turning century-old trees into a playground. She puffed a sigh of relief.

The breeze lifted again, stronger this time and bringing a fresh rustling of leaves with it. This distinct scent of cigarette smoke stiffened her spine. Logically, she knew she wasn't in danger. She'd visited the national park three days a week and met dozens of people, all friendly. But her logic had already shut down. Marissa discarded her apple. She screwed the lid on her bottle and gripped it in both hands.

A jaunty whistle lifted slowly into the air and echoed off the trees. A strange, familiar tune she hadn't heard in years, and one that seemed wildly out of place in the forest.

She stepped silently around the tree and again, there was nothing.

Except the whistle.

Marissa turned in a small circle, seeking the source. Her accelerated heartbeat joined every other instinct telling her to go. She bounced forward, away from the sound, back toward the trail. To the safety of her Jeep. The normalcy of her life.

"Don't leave." A man's voice boomed in her ear, successfully ending the whistle and shattering the eerie silence left in its wake.

Something hard connected with the side of her head, sending her sideways into another large tree. Scents of earth and bark exploded in her senses as sharp pain tore through her face. Marissa cried out at the shock and agony. The sound was extinguished by a large pair of gloved hands, clamping firmly around her throat.

Softly then, the man began to sing.

Her eyes bulged. Searing pressure filled her lungs. She clawed uselessly at the massive hands until images of her sister and parents blurred in her mind. She was dying, and he was singing.

Suddenly her fight-or-flight instinct sharpened like a switchblade slicing through the fear. No longer able to flee, years of self-defense courses bubbled to the cloudy surface of her thoughts along with the voices of past instructors, her father, and every surviving woman whose story had served as a warning.

Marissa refused to be a victim.

She released his hands and balled her fingers into fists. She rammed her elbows into the soft torso behind her and drew strength from the gust of breath that swept out of him in response. She stomped one foot against her attacker's instep and followed with a kick to the shin. He swore violently and tightened the pressure on her throat, repositioning his fingers for a more effective grip. Black dots danced in her peripheral vision, but she wasn't done. *The human kneecap breaks with only eight pounds of pressure.* He was taller than her, but slower. She kicked again, raising her foot high behind her, this time earning a wild yelp. His grip faltered and sweet oxygen rushed into her burning lungs. She was small, but that was an advantage, not a curse. She bent her knees to lower her center of gravity and clutched his forearms with both hands. In one final heave, her body lurched forward, chucking the man over her back and soundly onto his. Air whooshed from his mouth, and Marissa's wobbly legs were in motion before he'd hit the ground.

FEDERAL AGENT BLAKE GARRETT stormed into the Shadow Point Sheriff's Department with a familiar mix of dread and adrenaline. "West." His voice echoed through the building as his long legs ate up the distance between the front desk and his brother West's office. He dipped his chin at the receptionist as he passed. If West was right about Nash Barclay, there was no time to waste on formalities.

"West." Blake strode past a set of deputies gearing up for their shift and down the narrow hall past West's empty office. The place never changed. Concrete floors. Metal desks. The constant aroma of black coffee in the air, and the words *Sheriff Garrett* painted on the big office door. The Garrett inside was once their father. Now, it was his younger brother. *Where the hell was he?*

Blake opened his mouth to call again, but stopped short.

Sheriff West Garrett popped his head through the open conference room door. "Hey." He met Blake with a hearty hug. "It's good to see you. Wish I could get you back to town this quick for fishing and birthdays, but I suppose a possible serial killer sighting is as good an invitation for you." West's hair was lighter than Blake's, bleached by hours in the sun. His face was tanned and his eyes were bright, mischievous for a reason Blake couldn't comprehend. They had business to discuss. Ugly, dirty business and no reason, as far as Blake could tell, for nonsense.

"How sure are you that this was Nash?" Blake asked. He owed Nash Barclay a bullet and he planned on making good on the debt. "He's been underground for nearly five years."

West furrowed his brows. "When was the last time you slept, man?"

Roughly? Five years ago. "I'm doing just fine, Mom.

Now, can we get down to business, or do you want to ask me if I'm getting enough to eat?" Blake forced a smile to smooth the sharp edge of his words. Yes, he'd been away more than around these last few years, but he'd had good reason. He didn't feel right showing his face in a town where he'd let a serial killer get away. Who would?

"All right." West nodded. "Cole and I agree the victim fits the profile. Blond hair, blue eyes, petite build." He circled a wrist, implying Blake knew the rest.

Four women had gone missing during Blake's rookie year at the bureau, and he'd worked long and hard to find a connection between them when no one else could. Beyond their appearances the women had nothing in common. On the surface. Once Blake had started pulling threads, he found the same toxic creature hidden in all their lives—Nash Barclay. Nash had worked as a maintenance man for the local library system, and each of his victims had frequented a branch where Nash made regular service calls. Blake went to pick him up for questioning, but Nash ran. He'd tried to lose Blake in the labyrinth of industrial park alleys and abandoned factories but Shadow Point was Blake's home turf, and Nash was soon confronted with the business end of Blake's department issued Glock. They'd stood ten feet apart on a sprawling asphalt roof at the old tire plant, daring one another to make a move. Nash had taunted him, screaming obscenities until he was redfaced, begged him to shoot or go home, but Blake had been determined to stick to protocols, obey procedures, wait for his partner. He wanted Nash in cuffs, not in the morgue. He'd relived the moment a thousand times, certain he'd done everything right *until Nash began to sing*.

Nash's mood had changed in an instant. The violence in his expression had morphed into an eerie smile, and he'd sang. The behavior had successfully fractured Blake's concentration, and in that splinter of a second, while Blake had pondered the mind of a psychopath, Nash dove headlong over the roof's edge. He'd landed on the shorter building next door with ease and disappeared behind a massive smokestack. For the last five years, he might as well have been the smoke.

The moment should have ended in an arrest. A victory for justice. It should have catapulted Blake's budding career. Instead, it had put him on a short list of screw-ups. Worse, his mistake had cost those missing women and their families the justice they deserved. That moment had changed his life and caused him to question everything, especially himself.

"And the song?" Blake asked. "She said he sang the song?"

"Yep." West leaned closer. "Why don't we go over things in my office?"

"First, I need coffee." Blake stepped forward.

West's arm bobbed up like a guard gate, blocking the conference room doorway. "We should talk first."

Blake stopped to look more closely at his brother. West never said no to coffee. "Why?"

"Well, I guess because Miss Lane's eager to meet you." He twisted his mouth into a knot.

"Great."

West grinned. "She'd like another crack at the man who attacked her. Thinks you can use her help."

Blake snorted. "I need a lot of things right now, but help from a little blonde woman isn't one of them. I need coffee and whatever information you gained from her interview, then I'll stop by the victim's place after you've debriefed me. See if she's thought of anything else that can help us."

West shook his head. "I'm trying to tell you she didn't go home."

"Parents' house?"

"Nope."

"Well, where'd she go?" Blake cocked a hip, resting a restless hand over the butt of his sidearm. "Boyfriend's place?" That'd be a first. Nash had specifically chosen single women in the past.

West dropped his arm and tilted his head toward the conference room. "She's waiting for you."

"What?" He craned his head for a better look through the doorway. "Why didn't you send her home?" He dropped his voice to a whisper and checked his watch. "Do you mean to tell me she's been sitting in there for more than two hours? You should've driven her home by now." He pushed West's arm out of his way and strode into the conference room. Blake stopped short at the sight of a clearly aggravated woman in running gear.

"I'm not a victim," she said. "Also, the sheriff tried to send me home, but I'm not one to be sent anywhere, especially when I can be useful. Someone's trolling the park for women, and I can help." Her disheveled ponytail was hanging on by threads, but her backbone was straight as an arrow.

Blake's cheek twitched. He cast an uneasy glance at his brother. "This is Miss Lane?"

West smiled. "I tried to get you to go with me to my office."

The woman was on her feet and moving in Blake's direction. "I'm Marissa Lane." She shoved a little hand his way. "It's nice to meet you, Agent Garrett. I wish it was under different circumstances."

Blake agreed. Marissa had managed to shock and impress him in under a minute. A task no one had ever accomplished, and Blake had met a lot of people.

"Miss Lane," he began in his most calming tone. "Thank you for your willingness to help. You've undergone an incredible trauma today, but I'd like to ask you a few more questions. Let me know if you need to stop at any point during the interview. We can take a break or pick up tomorrow. Whatever you'd like. I assume you've already told the sheriff everything you can recall."

"I have." She nodded. "If I understand correctly, you believe the man who attacked me is responsible for taking several women."

"It's a distinct possibility, yes. That's what I'm here to find out."

"Well, I have no intention of going home until I've told you everything I told your brother and accompanied you back to the park. I'd like to show you where it happened." She shot a pointed look at Blake's black dress shoes. "I hope you brought a change of clothes."

Blake dragged his gaze to the space behind him where West was retreating toward his office.

Blake unbuttoned his suit jacket and took a seat at the large oval table in the room's center, attempting to regain control of the situation. He cleared his throat and turned his face to the spitfire before him. She certainly looked like Nash's type. Obviously beautiful. Small features. Narrow frame. The clingy blue jogging pants and matching tank top left little to the imagination in terms of her shape. Blake's hands could easily cover the span of her waist. A very Southern-debutante appeal, but looks were deceiving. He fought a smile as he imagined the shock Nash must've had when this little woman kicked his ass.

"Agent?" Her voice drew him back like a slap in the face.

"Sorry." Blake shifted on his seat and gauged his words carefully. He also did his best to clear a few unprofessional thoughts from his mind. "The man I'm after is six feet tall, and he's probably got seventy-five pounds on you." Give or take the few that five years might have delivered.

Marissa crossed her arms. "And?"

Blake's cheek twitched again. Twice in ten minutes. She was funny. Did she know she was funny? "How'd you do it?"

"I fought." Marissa lifted a tuft of fallen hair off her cheek and hooked it over one ear, revealing a thick crimson line along her jawbone and faint purple bruising under the corresponding eye. "He grabbed me. Hit me. Choked me. I used my size against him. Would you like a demonstration?"

Somewhere in the next room, West coughed.

Blake gave the shared wall a dirty look before turning his attention back to Marissa Lane. "That won't be necessary." He opened a notebook and clicked his pen to life. "Has anyone evaluated your injuries?"

Marissa nodded. "Cole," she said.

"Good."

Cole was the youngest Garrett brother, a former army medic and a certified EMT. He was also a medical school dropout, but he hated when the family brought that up.

"West insisted I choose between Cole or a trip to the ER," Marissa added. "I figured, at least I know Cole."

Blake nodded, hoping the fact she had no bandages meant the injuries appeared worse than they actually were.

"Why don't you have a seat and start by telling me what you remember?"

She turned to pace the room. "I remember being grabbed from behind, hit across the face and nearly dragged into the forest. The assailant was your brother's height, West's, not Cole's." She waved a dismissive hand. "I went to high school with them. Never dreamed they'd become the town sheriff and deputy, but I guess I should have. Whatever happened to Ryder?"

"He's a US Marshal."

She cocked an eyebrow, as if to say more on the topic, but shook her head and stayed on task. "The lunatic was singing that old song. 'Going to the Chapel'."

Blake tapped his pen against the notepad. He'd have to ask how well she knew his brothers later. He'd left for college before they'd started high school. A curious sense of frustration knotted inside him.

Marissa dropped her arms to her sides. "Did you always want to work for the FBI?"

"No." The Garretts were a family of law enforcement and everyone in Cade County knew it, but Blake never wanted to be sheriff. Though there was a certain pressure for Blake to conform, he'd wanted to do something bigger than hand out traffic tickets and break up marital disputes. He'd gone as far as to finish his law degree, dreaming of a judgeship, before the allure of a shiny badge had caught up with him. Something about those coveted initials, FBI, had changed his life plan without warning.

Marissa leaned her slender backside against the table and crossed her ankles. Soft, distracting scents of coconut and pineapple lifted off her. "Whoever he was, I caught him off guard. I left him on his back by the lake and ran until I saw a car. I flagged the guy down and asked him to drop me off here. My car's still at the base camp parking lot. I had to run in the opposite direction, and I was afraid to double back. I can pick it up when we go see the crime scene."

THE SWOON-WORTHY AGENT stretched onto his feet and loomed over Marissa. His sharp blue eyes cut a line across her bruised face, lingering at her equally sore collarbone before returning to her eyes. "Fine. We can talk more on the way."

He patted a rhythm on the wall, and his brothers appeared. "Give me five minutes to change, then follow us up to the lake."

The men exchanged looks and broke off in three separate directions.

Several minutes later, Blake returned in a pair of low-slung jeans, military boots and a slate-gray T-shirt. He'd screwed a plain navy ball cap over his thick dark hair and covered his serious blue eyes with tinted aviators. An impressive FBI badge completed the look. "Time to saddle up."

Marissa followed a line of Garrett men to their cars. She smoothed her hair and straightened her shirt, uncertain if the bubbling of nerves in her core was caused by a return to the crime scene or something else entirely. Plenty of women's daydreams had begun like this in Shadow Point. Alone with multiple uniformed Garretts. Fortunately, Marissa had spent four years of high school learning about the inevitable heartbreak a lady could expect from any one of those unbelievably attractive packages. What she couldn't figure out was why Blake Garrett had thrown her off balance? The others didn't faze her, but they also didn't command a room with their presence the way Blake did. If she remembered correctly, he was just four years older than West. Five years older than her. He'd left town long before she'd thought about guys beyond their inability to beat her at anything at all.

The men stopped beside a big black pickup. The truck hadn't been in the lot when Marissa arrived. Blake pointed a fob in the truck's direction and the locks popped up. "Miss Lane?" He extended his hand. "Boost?"

Why not? She grabbed the open door frame in one hand and placed her opposite palm on Blake's. His warm, calloused skin sent a jolt of electricity through her. Blake closed strong fingers over hers and waited as she bounced into the cab.

The door snapped shut behind her, and the Garretts circled up, speaking too low for her to understand. The men seemed to take turns examining her through the closed window. Blake adjusted his ball cap a few times before breaking free from the group and swinging into the driver's seat.

"Everything okay?" she asked.

"No." He slid his eyes in her direction briefly, checked the rearview, and gunned the engine to life. "Someone attacked you today. That's a big problem, and I plan to fix it."

Chapter Two

Blake slowed his truck at the national park entrance where a line of cars blocked the gate. A park ranger moved car to car, waving his hands and pointing toward the exit.

"What the hell?" Blake powered his window down and shoved an elbow over the frame. He tipped his head through the open window. "Hey, what's going on?"

The ranger, still two cars away, shot him a dirty look and continued arguing with the driver of a rusted hatchback.

Blake shifted into Park and climbed down from the cab. He gave Marissa an authoritative stare. "Stay put."

She released her seat belt and twisted on the seat, scanning the scene outside. A big white van with a satellite on top came into view, along with a cluster of people and cameras. "This day keeps getting worse."

"What?" Blake peered over the crush of stalled vehicles. "The reporter?"

"I think the good Samaritan who drove me to the sheriff's department is being interviewed by that news crew."

"Sonofa—" Blake slammed his door and headed into the chaos. His FBI shield bounced against his chest on a beaded metal chain. "Hey," he called again, "what's this about?"

The ranger sagged in relief. He motioned to Blake's badge. "Sorry. I didn't know you were FBI. It's pandemonium up here."

"You want to fill me in?" Blake asked.

"Some guy showed up with a news crew an hour ago. He says a woman was attacked here this morning. They aired a live interview snippet, and people started pouring in to have a look at the crime scene. Campers are scared. Some are leaving. The phone won't stop ringing."

Blake could barely hear the phone inside the little guard booth. He climbed onto a massive tree stump painted with the park hours and strained for a better look at the crowd near the white van. A man in Dickies and flannel stood beside a woman Blake recognized from the Channel Six News team. If that man hadn't saved Marissa, Blake would've been tempted to escort him out of the park violently.

The ranger fixed Blake with an expectant look. "What should we do?"

As if on cue, the sheriff's cruiser rolled into view, bouncing through the grass alongside a line of waiting cars. Blake whistled and waved to his brothers as West angled between the guard gate and overcrowded lot. No other cars would get in until he moved.

Cole jumped out. "We've got this. You got her?" He flicked his gaze to Blake's truck.

Blake nodded and shook the ranger's hand, eager to get back to Marissa. "Sheriff and Deputy Garrett will take it from here." He jogged back to the truck and climbed inside. "You okay?"

"Fine."

"Good." He wrenched his truck free from the line and parked it in the grass beside the news van.

He pocketed the keys and turned for Marissa. "Ready?" The alarm in her eyes stunned him into silence. She'd put on a brave face at the station, but there was no confidence in her expression now. A distant part of him longed to comfort her somehow, but that wasn't his place. She probably had a long line of people waiting to fold her into their arms and ease her fear. Blake's job was to stop a madman.

She turned weary eyes on him. "Yes."

"Don't worry." The statement was out before he'd thought better of it. Then, already heading downhill, he made it worse. "I won't let him hurt you again." The words soured on his tongue. How could he promise to protect her? He'd let Nash get away once already. Wasn't it technically his fault that Nash had gotten ahold of her at all?

Marissa lifted her chin and rolled her shoulders back. "Thank you for saying so, but I'm not afraid." The lie was evident in the lines gathered across her forehead, but Blake didn't argue.

He climbed out and met Marissa on her side of the truck. "Why don't you take me to where you left him?"

"Sure." Marissa led the way down a gravel and mud path from Blake's makeshift parking spot to the trailhead. "I started here around five thirty."

"Miss?" A woman's voice carried over the drone of the crowd. "Miss? Excuse me." The Channel Six reporter hurried in Marissa's direction waving a microphone. Her pink dress suit and pearls were sorely out of place in the park. Her pointy heels sank into the ground with each hurried step. Worse, she wasn't alone. She was a mama duck, trailed by her cameraman, the guy who'd driven Marissa to the station and a row of nosy locals craning to get a look at the victim.

Marissa made a soft squeaky noise and Blake's hackles rose. He widened his stance and lifted a palm in the reporter's direction. "Stop right there."

"Absolutely." She fluffed her hair and straightened her jacket. "I'm Linda Somers, Channel Six News. And you are?" She eyeballed the badge around his neck. A sugary-sweet smile curved her lips.

The cameraman positioned himself near a tree and hoisted the camera onto one shoulder, arranging his shot. A little red light blinked at the side of his lens. He gave Linda a thumbs-up.

Her smile widened. "Are you here to investigate this morning's attack, Federal Agent…" She left the sentence hanging.

"That's Blake Garrett," someone called from the crowd. "He's the sheriff's brother."

Damn small towns. Blake ground his teeth. "Please direct your questions to Sheriff Garrett."

"Is this the victim?" she asked. Pencil-thin eyebrows rose behind her bangs.

The man who'd called this fiasco into action nodded. "Yeah. That's her. I found her running along the county road, crying."

"You're certain?" the reporter asked.

"Positive. I wouldn't forget picking up a lady dressed like that."

Marissa wrapped both arms around her middle and glared at the man. Her outfit might not be camera ready, but she was dressed appropriately for a run, which was likely the only thing she'd expected to do before her shower.

Blake groaned. "She has no comment." He moved between Marissa and the reporter.

The cameraman honed in on them.

"What's your name, Miss?" Linda asked. "Are you from Cade County? Do you come here often? How long have you known Federal Agent Garrett?"

Heat from Marissa's body warmed his side. Her fingers pressed against his back as she stepped into view of the mob forming along the trailhead. He should've guessed she'd refuse to stay behind him. Fire churned in his gut. The bigmouthed reporter had taken the only tactical advantage Blake had over Nash—surprise. Now, Nash would know Blake was there, and the games would begin again before Blake was ready.

Blake scanned the crowd for his enemy. What if seeing him with Marissa fueled Nash's need to get his hands on her again? What if Blake's presence put her in more danger? As if the fact she'd gotten away wasn't reason enough for him to come at her again.

West and Cole arrived a moment later, waving their badges and hollering instructions at the crowd.

"That's our cue." Blake wound his fingers around Marissa's wrist and tugged. "Let them take care of the crowd. Let's get back to what we came for."

MARISSA TOOK THE LEAD, but her stomach protested the trip, and her limbs strained against her. Instinct begged her never to return to the place where she'd nearly been abducted, but resolve pushed her forward. Whether she wanted to go or not was irrelevant. Who knew how many more women would be in danger if the man who grabbed her wasn't caught? Images of the awful moments flooded her mind, lifting the fine hairs along the back of her neck, and resurrecting another memory. A shiver rolled through her.

"What's wrong?" Blake's voice was low and cautious.

She scrubbed a hand over her lips. "I'm not sure. Maybe nothing."

"Let's hear it."

"There was a man who tossed bread crumbs into the lake this summer. He was always there when I came back from my morning runs. That guy had a black hoodie like the man I saw today at the lookout. I know it's not much, and everyone owns a black hoodie, but it could be something, right?"

"Anything could be something. You saw him more than once?"

She squinted against the brilliant sunlight, desperate for a more useful memory or detail. "He was there every morning for a while. Then, one day he just wasn't."

"Did he see you?"

"I think so. I'm hard to miss after five miles up and down a mountain." She heaved a sigh. "I probably looked a lot like this, except swinging my arms to cool down from the jog." Marissa plucked stringy bangs off her forehead and groaned inwardly. For the first time since she'd arrived at the station, she was fiercely self-conscious. Why hadn't she at least combed her hair or washed her face while she'd waited on Blake to arrive? It was bad enough she was bruised and dirty. She didn't have to be a disheveled nightmare, too. "I'm a mess."

"You've gone over ten miles on foot today and fought off a man twice your size. I think you get a pass."

So, he agreed. She was a mess. She pulled her pony-tail down and shook her hair out, raking fingers through the tangles. She stopped moving when the lake came into view.

Shadow Valley Lake was nearly eighteen square miles of water, much of it surrounded by tall grasses, angry geese and a well-beaten path courtesy of Cade County fishermen. Her apple, now covered in ants, lay in the grass near a massive oak tree. "I was there. Eating that apple." She regretted leaving the trash behind. "I'll take that with me when I leave this time."

Blake examined the ground near her apple. "The apple's evidence now. Look." He pushed the grass back and forth with his shoe, revealing two sets of imprints. Her Nikes and a pair of boots. He hovered his foot near the larger print. He fished his cell phone from one pocket and took pictures of the discovery.

Emotion coiled in Marissa's gut. Her eyes stung, and her bottom lip trembled. She sipped cool air and forced her mind away from the vivid memories clawing at her heart. "The man with the bread crumbs was always right there." She pointed to a crescent of mud and rock at the massive lake's edge.

They moved toward the spot. Boot imprints striped the soft earth, as if he'd been pacing. "Do you see those?" she asked.

"Yep." He snapped another picture. "Same tread pattern as the prints by your apple."

Marissa bit into her thumbnail. No one had been at the lake on her predawn trip up the mountain, and she hadn't seen anyone when she sat under the tree to enjoy her apple.

Blake scanned the area with sharp, trained eyes. He

mumbled something under his breath and raised his phone again, this time for a picture of the lake.

Marissa followed his icy stare to a sprinkling of white flecks on the glassy surface. "Is that bread?"

"No." Blake turned his phone over and tapped the screen. "Those are white rose petals."

Marissa wrinkled her nose. "There aren't any white roses in the park."

"Hey," Blake growled into the phone, now pressed to his ear. "Get me a cast kit. We've got pattern evidence at the lake." He disconnected and gripped the cell phone in his palm. "Any chance the man you saw here a few months ago could've been tossing these onto the water instead of bread crumbs?"

"Maybe. Why? What do they mean?" She tried to hide the fear settling in her bones.

Blake rubbed the back of his neck. "The fugitive I've been chasing left white rose petals on the doorstep of his victims' homes."

"I'm guessing you don't think these petals are a co-incidence." Marissa's stomach sank as she watched the little white boats skating across the serene water.

Blake snapped more pictures of the petals. "I don't believe in coincidence."

Well, they had that in common. She turned away and closed her eyes, engaging painful memories. "He was singing 'Going to the Chapel' and leaves roses. Does he have a fantasy about marrying his victims?"

"I don't know. He wasn't very forthcoming when I tried to haul him in, and we never found the women, but I assume this is all part of some sick fetish. He lost a girlfriend to suicide about a year before he took his first victim."

Marissa opened her eyes and headed back to her fallen apple. She worked methodically around the grass, parting the blades with her shoe like Blake had. Maybe she could find a clue, too. Something Blake could send to the crime lab where his science and tech people worked.

Something moved in the distance. A few seconds later, Cole appeared with a backpack.

"How well do you know Cole?" Blake asked. He stopped a few feet ahead of her and waved to his brother. "You went to school together. Anything else?"

"Not really." She tented her brows. Was she being accused of something? "We live in a small town and went to the same high school. We ran into each other from time to time. West and Ryder, too."

Blake turned at the waist and narrowed his eyes on her. She knew all three of his little brothers, but he hadn't met her until today? A nagging sense of injustice registered at the back of his mind.

"What?" She bounced her toe against something hard, and a little navy pouch flipped into view. "Hey, look at this." Marissa crouched over the object. Recognition swept through her like a hurricane, sucking air from her lungs and pushing her attention in a new direction. She stood on wooden legs and stared at the tranquil lake behind them.

"What is that?" Blake crouched where she had been a moment before.

Marissa pressed a palm to her roiling stomach. She owned several pouches just like that one. "It's a one-pound weight. They're used on scuba belts."

Cole settled in beside Blake and handed him the backpack.

Marissa pushed windblown hair from her eyes while the men bagged their evidence. Blades of ice seemed to wedge in her chest. "I know where he might've hidden those women's bodies. I'd planned to do a photo shoot there soon."

"Where?" the Garretts asked in near unison.

She lifted a finger toward the lake. *The rose petals. The creepy song.* "I think they're in Shadow Valley." Cade County's historic lake town, submerged long ago in the name of flood control.

BLAKE MADE THE necessary calls to rouse a dive crew and the remainder of his team from Louisville. The agents arrived in just over an hour. The divers were another story, being parceled together from approved volunteers across the state, policemen, game wardens, anyone trained and available to thoroughly explore the remnants of an entire underwater town, door by door if necessary, while preserving as much potential evidence as possible. He'd also called in a favor with a local private security firm for additional help clearing the park and tending the curious crowd, which had been pushed outside the gates.

The space around the normally tranquil lake bustled with speculation and activity. Once all the divers arrived, things would get worse, and if Marissa's hunch was right, more gruesome.

Her hunch. Not his.

Blake mentally kicked himself for never considering Shadow Valley Lake as a place to hide four bodies. If memory served, the Shadow Valley Chapel was one of the buildings swallowed by the lake. Finding victims in the underwater chapel would raise the stakes impossibly higher. That kind of discovery would suggest Nash was smarter and more resourceful than Blake had given him credit for. He'd always assumed Nash was the impulsive type, more likely to hide his crimes in a hurry than with careful planning and scuba gear. In fact, he'd considered Nash lucky for getting away at all. He'd blamed his own rookie hesitation.

Blake pressed the heels of his hands against closed eyes. What if Blake had been wrong all these years? What if the real mistake he'd made was underestimating Nash? The possibility came with all sorts of ugly thoughts. Blake had linked him to four missing women, but what if there were more? How many cases hadn't he connected? What had Nash been doing these last five years while Blake chased his tail? Blake had assumed Nash was hiding, but what if Nash was still killing and Blake had missed it?

He scrubbed open palms over his face and forehead. *How long had Nash been planning to take Marissa?*

His attention cut through the collection of lawmen to where she rested her head against an oak tree not far from the lake. Her swollen eyes were shut. Her cheeks were red. The bruises from her attack had grown more pronounced as the day wore on, making Blake angrier with each passing second. He couldn't seem to find it in himself to be thankful she was safe. He could only grow more infuriated that she'd been hurt.

She opened her eyes as he approached, a look of shock and panic on her face.

He lifted a hand and crouched beside her. "It's only me. How are you holding up?"

"Fine." Her knees bobbed with misplaced adrenaline. "Anything new?"

"The rest of the divers should be here soon, but it's a big lake. It's going to take them some time to search an entire town."

She sat forward, hugging bent knees to her chest. "I have street maps for the town under the lake at my place. I could go get them. I'd hoped to take photos for a magazine interested in doing a spread on lake towns. The maps could save the divers time."

Blake rested his forearms across his thighs, dangling both hands between his knees. "We have the town blueprint. Right now, the divers are fighting daylight to get here, and they haven't got much left." He stretched onto his feet and extended a hand to hoist her up. "How do you feel about taking a walk while we wait?"

She accepted his hand. "Where are we going?"

"You said you saw a man at the lookout. We should get up there while the park's closed to visitors." He motioned for her to lead the way.

Marissa stopped at the base of Sunrise Trail. She cocked a hip and stared up the dirt path. Uncertainty flashed in her eyes. "I didn't get a good look at the guy up there, but he smelled like cigarette smoke." She braced a hand to her forehead like a visor and squinted against the sun. "The man who attacked me also smelled like smoke, but I suppose that's hardly enough to conclude it was the same man."

"Do you think it was the same man?"

She cast her gaze to the ground. "I do."

Blake motioned her forward. "That's good enough for me."

She took a deep breath and began her second five-mile uphill hike of the day. At least this time she wasn't running. "I was a little spooked to see someone at the lookout before dawn. Confused, too. My car was the only one in the lot."

Blake turned an amused expression on her. "You hiked five miles before dawn." He shook his head in apparent awe. "You're making me regret the coffee and cruller breakfast I had on my way here from Louisville."

Marissa smiled. "Well, if it helps, I didn't hike. I ran."

He laughed. "Oh, yeah. That makes me feel much better. Thank you."

She fell into a comfortable stride and inhaled deeply, finding as much inner peace as possible on this horrific day. "I run every morning, but three days a week I do it here. I like the view, and I normally enjoy the solitude." She bit her lip against the tirade that had been swirling in her mind for the past few hours. "I knew something was wrong. I knew it, and I didn't leave."

Blake stopped moving and stared at her. "You couldn't have known. Even if you had, you weren't at fault here. Don't let that worm get into your head. From what I can tell, you did everything right, and if this man is who I think he is, you're the first to get away. You should be proud of yourself."

"Really? Because it was pride that kept me here when my instincts told me to go home. It was pride that took me to the lake for my reward."

"Reward?"

She groaned. "It's stupid, but I beat my best time getting to the lookout, and I'd planned to reward myself by watching the sunrise. I was mad that I'd let his presence keep me from enjoying the view." She dropped her head back and laughed. "So instead of getting in my car, I made a side trip to the lake. I was that close to leaving unharmed."

Blake's face darkened. "This wasn't your fault. I don't care if he shook your hand and said, 'I'm going to attack you unless you go home.' He's still the criminal. He's the one in the wrong. Not you."

Marissa stepped over a fallen branch. "Thanks, but it's hard not to think about what I could've done differently."

Patchy sunlight filtered through the lush forest canopy. A soft breeze kicked up, lifting scents of shampoo and sweat from Blake's body.

Marissa shook her thoughts back to the situation at hand. "Can you tell me more about Nash? That's his name, right?" Her hand moved instinctually to her throat. She blinked through the fresh sting of tears. "I've heard you and your brothers use it, but no one's filled me in on the specifics."

"I linked Nash to the disappearances of four women about five years ago. The missing women were never recovered, but I know he took them. I saw it in his eyes when I confronted him." His square jawline popped and clenched. Whatever he wasn't sharing was painful and Marissa's heart hurt for him, too.

"What does he look like?" Marissa asked.

Blake cast her a sidelong glance. "I'll show you a picture when we get back. I would've done that at the station but West said you didn't see the man who attacked you."

"I didn't. I thought a description might jar my memory about the man at the lake last summer."

Blake glanced over his shoulder. "Nash has brown hair and eyes. He's six foot. Average weight, but no definition. He wasn't much to look at. No distinguishing marks, scars or tattoos. Of course, that was a while back. A lot could have happened since then."

"Was he a smoker?"

"Yes."

Ice curled through Marissa's body. She'd been in the grips of a serial killer. The bruises on her face and throat throbbed at the thought. She pressed cool fingers against the aching pains.

"I'm going to find him." Blake's voice cracked the last ounce of composure Marissa had.

A hot, fat tear broke over her cheek and slid onto her jaw. Then another.

"Hey." Blake stopped climbing. "Miss Lane." He caught her trembling hand in his as she took another step without him. He squeezed gently before releasing her.

She swiped shaky fingertips across both eyelids before daring to look back. "I'm fine. Please call me Marissa."

"You're not fine, Marissa, but you're going to be. I'm going to find this guy. I won't let him get away again." He lifted a white handkerchief in her direction.

The sincerity in Blake's voice warmed her, and the sound of her name on his lips settled her fraying nerves. "I know." She accepted the handkerchief and pressed it to her eyes, thankful for his comforting presence. "Who carries a handkerchief?"

"Me. All of us." He fumbled for words, clearly uncomfortable telling her something so personal. "My brothers and I."

Apparently, even that legendary Garrett confidence wasn't bulletproof. Marissa smiled behind the soft cotton material, enjoying the aromatic blend of Blake's

soap and cologne caught in the wispy fabric. "I see."
She returned his quizzical glance. "Why?"

"You ask a lot of questions."

"It's a long hike."

Blake turned his face to her and smiled. Not another
lazy effort like he'd offered her before, but a true smile
that reached his eyes and scaled the years away.

She'd found Blake devastatingly handsome as a
straight-faced agent, but the smiling man beneath the
badge was so much more. His ability to show such
charm and compassion on a day as cursed as this was
enough to weaken her knees. "I'd love to know, and
honestly, I could use the distraction."

He paused to look her in the eye. "Our granddad gave
those to us when we were small. None of us used them
until his funeral a few years back, but we all carried
them to the service. That was the day I started bringing mine everywhere." He looked away, into the forest,
seemingly lost in the memory.

"You carry a piece of him," she mused. "That's
sweet."

He extended his hand. "Give me my hanky."

She set the cloth in his hand with a smile. "You aren't
what you seem, Federal Agent Garrett."

"Folks rarely are."

Chapter Three

There was nothing to see at the lookout. No clues. No boot prints. It was a five-mile walk for bust. Frustration churned in Blake's chest as he mentally replayed the morning's events. Every clue pointed directly to his nemesis, a maniac he'd dedicated years to finding. *Where are you, Nash?* Blake's muscles tensed as another terrible thought came to mind. "We need to go."

"What? Why?" Marissa followed him back down the trail at a clip. "What's happening? Did you find something?"

Blake slowed his pace by a fraction, adjusting for her shorter gait. "When was the last time you were home?"

"This morning. I left around five."

He furrowed his brow. "The rose petals."

"You want to see if he left them on my doorstep." She bobbed her head in understanding. "Well, that's completely terrifying."

Blake slowed further. "You should probably pack a bag while we're there and make plans to stay with family for a few nights."

"Do you really think he'd come for me again? He has to know you're on to him. It was broadcast on the news."

"He'll come."

"But you were standing right beside me on the air."

"Exactly."

Marissa marched silently for several paces. "Fine, but I'm not dragging my family into this. I'll stay somewhere else."

Blake's eyes widened. "Haven't you told them what's happening?"

"Of course." She'd called her parents the minute she'd arrived at the sheriff's department and again while Blake had organized his team. "I told them everything I knew this morning, which was that a lunatic nearly abducted me in the park. Then, I filled them in on the possibility of a fugitive at large and warned my sister to stay out of the park. Dad caught the news, so he knows I'm with you. My sister's been checking in by text every hour or so to make sure I'm still out here. Still safe."

Blake scowled. "So, stay with them."

"And paint a big red X on their door? No thank you. I'm not leading a psychopath straight to my family."

"Well, you can't stay at your place."

"Fine, but I won't stay with my parents or sister either. That'll have to be good enough." Five quiet miles later, she hooked a left at the trail's base and headed for the parking lot.

Blake fired up his truck and followed her older model mud-soaked Jeep down the county road through town at just over the speed limit until houses faded into farms and farms gave way to forest. She slowed at a partially hidden drive and turned onto a narrow gravel road. His truck bounced and rocked along behind her for several minutes before a small clearing came into view.

A log cabin was situated among the trees with a portion of somewhat flat land serving as her front and back yards. Flower baskets and wind chimes hung from the porch roof and a pair of rocking chairs stood sentinel beside the door.

He met her on the porch, gun drawn. No rose petals, but the front window was open, leaving her sheer white curtains to flutter.

"Do you normally leave this open?"

"No." Marissa's fearful gaze was latched to the parted window frame. "I always check the windows before bed, and I didn't open any this morning."

Blake ran cautious fingertips around the wooden trim, stopping at the first patch of splintering, a discreet but telltale sign of tampering. He sent a text to West. They needed a deputy for fingerprints. Normally, he'd suggest the deputy talk to Marissa's neighbors, but she didn't have any.

Marissa lifted her house key on trembling fingers, and he slid it into the still locked door. With any luck, Nash was hunkered down inside, feeling overly confident and about to be reunited with his maker.

He raised a flat palm between them. "Wait here."

Marissa followed him inside and pulled the door shut.

He gave her a warning look. "I told you to wait outside."

Her pale skin and flushed cheeks said what she wouldn't. Marissa was scared.

Blake's need for vengeance warred momentarily with his desire to erase the terrified expression from her face. "Stay close."

She crossed the floor on silent feet, thanking him with wide blue eyes. Her small pink lips were pressed tight. He cleared the front room and kitchen, then crept into the narrow hallway separating her living space from the rest of the home. So far, every window in the house was open.

"What was that?" Marissa pressed her fingers against his waist.

Blake froze as something moved in the next room. He set his hand on the doorknob and motioned Marissa to step back. Slowly, she uncurled her fingers from the fabric of his shirt and inched away. With the flick of Blake's wrist, the door flung open, and he rushed inside. "Clear." Blake was alone in a brightly colored utility room, surrounded by murals of birds in trees and yellow rays of sunshine.

Marissa poked her head into the room. "Nothing?"

The curtain ruffled, and she jumped. White eyelet lace rubbed the curled pages of a worn paperback on the sill.

Blake pushed the fabric aside for a look into the backyard. "How many more rooms?"

"Three. A bathroom next door and two bedrooms across the hall."

They moved in tandem through the next two rooms, both small, cheerfully decorated and void of Nash. The last door was several paces beyond the others and closed. Marissa gasped. "I didn't close that door."

Blake squared his shoulders, and Marissa fell back again. He shoved the final door open, and a slew of swear words lodged on his tongue.

Marissa padded into the room a moment later. "Oh, no."

A wedding veil was strewn across Marissa's bed and surrounded by hundreds of white rose petals. The soft scent raised bile in Blake's throat.

Marissa curved one hand over her mouth and pressed the other to her stomach, as if she might be sick.

Without thinking, he pulled her against his chest and wound protective arms around her back. She curled against him and buried her face into her palms. Warmth and resolve blew through him in a powerful gale. "You're going to be okay. I'm going to see to it."

His phone buzzed, and Marissa stepped aside. A text message from West confirmed that a deputy was on his way with a print kit for the window.

Blake snapped a photo of Marissa's bed, then texted it to his team and brothers. They were going to need more than a print kit.

"Can you tell me if anything else was altered, missing or left behind?" He moved methodically through the room in search of something that could lead him to Nash.

Marissa scrutinized the room, moving slowly from closet to night stand and dresser before creeping softly toward the bed. "Just this," she whispered, as if she might wake the sleeping veil. "Why would he do this?"

"I don't know. Maybe he hoped to meet you back here." He regretted the words immediately and hated Nash all the more for the truth behind them.

Her eyes widened in horror. "Meet me back here for what?"

Blake's tongue seemed to swell as a line of horrific ideas presented themselves. Too many years on the job and in the military had irrevocably polluted his thoughts. Now, he saw danger everywhere.

Marissa backed away from the bed and freed a duffel bag from her closet. "He came here after I got away."

"Yes." Blake swallowed a brick of regret. *If only he'd shot Nash when he'd had the chance.*

"We were looking for him at the park, and he was here."

The words, *I'm sorry*, filled Blake's heart and mind, trapped behind a much stronger will to stay focused and do the job this time. Apologies could come when Marissa was safe and Nash was behind bars or dead. Preferably the latter for what he'd put her through.

Marissa filled the bag with clothes, opening and closing drawers, shoving handfuls of random items into the canvas duffel without looking.

Scents of powder and vanilla surrounded them, distracting Blake in dangerous and unprofessional ways. "We can wait outside in my truck." He scooped a pair of white lace panties up as they hit the floor beneath her gaping bag. He passed the soft scrap of material to Marissa, doing his best not to picture her in only those. "You don't have to stay in here with this." He tipped his head toward her bed.

She stuffed the panties into her bag and opened another drawer. "Thanks." Her cheeks reddened as their gazes locked.

"I'm going to check the perimeter."

"No." Alarm changed her features. "Don't."

"It's okay." Blake infused the words with as much promise as possible. "You're safe with me, and I'll make sure to keep you that way."

She dipped her chin and went back to stuffing things blindly into her bag.

Blake circled the home's exterior and returned to Marissa several minutes later. A fresh text had arrived. "The team secured a room for us at the Blue Ridge

Lodge outside of town. We know now that you were targeted. That makes you safer with us until we find Nash, and we *will* find him."

She gnawed her bottom lip. "One room?"

"It'll be crowded but secure. My team and brothers will come and go as the investigation moves along. And don't worry, contrary to local legend, the Garrett men were raised to be gentlemen."

She pinned him with a fiercely ornery smile. "I was raised to be a princess. Look how that turned out. I'm about to spend the night with a man I just met."

He shot the ceiling another look and rearranged his ball cap. *If the job didn't kill him, protecting Marissa Lane might.*

MARISSA COULDN'T DROP the creepy sensation of being watched. Knowing a psychopath had been in her room had shaken her far worse than the attempted abduction. At least during the attack, she was aware of his presence, but he'd been inside her home. He'd been in her room. The contents of her overnight bag grew heavy on her lap. Had he looked inside her drawers? Touched her things? How long had he been planning to take her? How did he find her home? Endless questions ran rampant through her mind as she bounced on the passenger side of Blake's truck, feeling thoroughly violated.

Blake pulled into the parking spot beside a black town car at Blue Ridge Lodge and climbed out. He shook hands with a man in a gray suit standing outside the door to room one-eleven. They looked at Marissa through the windshield, mouths moving, eyes appraising.

She redirected her attention to the scenery. Blue

Ridge Lodge was gorgeous and nestled in the mountains where she'd practiced rock climbing and spelunking throughout high school. She'd long ago mastered the climbs and adventures the area had to offer, but back in the day, those hills were a great source of victory and self-confidence. If only she'd taken more photos of the excursions.

Blake lumbered toward the passenger door and pulled it open. "How are you holding up?"

She ducked her chin. "Okay."

Sympathy swam in his eyes. He moved away from the open door so she could climb down. "There's nothing we can do until the last of the divers arrive except keep you out of sight. The sheriff's department's on the lookout for Nash. My men are canvassing local hotels and campgrounds along with abandoned buildings and cabins. If Nash is still in Cade County, we'll find him."

Blake stole the duffel from her hand and hooked it over one broad shoulder. "Let's go inside. Neither of us have eaten since breakfast and that was one hell of a walk you took me on. Let me order dinner. We'll eat, and hopefully you can get a little rest while we're waiting on a new lead."

Marissa sank her teeth into the thick of her bottom lip and immediately released it. She was too late. Blake's gaze slid from her mouth to her eyes. He'd noticed her tell. He knew she was nervous. She could lie all day with her tongue, but she had no control over her face. "Okay. Dinner sounds good." As did a hot shower and fresh clothes. "Thank you."

She followed him inside the roomy junior suite. A small sitting area with a round table, chairs, couch and television were separated from the bedroom and en suite bath by a set of French doors. Marissa dragged her gaze away from the queen-size bed with notable effort. She told herself it was the fatigue in her bones that wanted her to head that way first, not the small tug in her belly that wondered if Blake preferred to be the big spoon or the little spoon.

He edged past her with the duffel and set it on the bed. "Burgers okay?"

She nodded too quickly, a sure sign of guilt. "Yeah. Good. Thank you. I'm going to shower." She snatched up the bag and hustled into the bathroom.

Safe behind the closed door, Marissa shed her dirty clothes and climbed into the steamy shower. Hot beads of water pounded against her tired, aching muscles, and she rubbed her eyes as the water ran over her face. The sensation did little to cleanse her mind of numerous inappropriate thoughts about Blake Garrett, the man who set her skin on fire with every smoldering look. She squeezed a dollop of shampoo onto her palm and worked her hair into a lather. Marissa was never plagued by so many inconceivable fantasies. The problem was obviously this awful day. Her emotions were too heightened to share a hotel room with that man. The excess adrenaline and fatigue were producing crazy thoughts. And why was there only one bed?

She rinsed the soap from her hair and body, clearing her skin and mind. There was no chemistry between she and Blake. She'd imagined his heated looks as a means of distraction, a psychological defense mechanism to deal with what had happened that morning. Clearly her subconscious assumed that if the hot FBI agent wanted her, then he'd protect her and she could feel safe.

She stepped onto the bath mat and wrapped a soft

terry-cloth towel around her torso. Even if the looks Blake gave her were real, they didn't mean anything other than he was in possession of a libido. It was practically what the Garretts were known for. And so what? She rubbed her arms and legs vigorously with a second towel. Blake might want her. Short-term, of course. His family was single-minded and the whole town knew it. Married to the endless pursuit of justice. Addicted to the chase. Which was likely the reason Blake hadn't settled down. He probably wondered where the fun was in pairing up for life. Marissa expected that was where the fun really began, but what did she know?

She wound her hair into the second towel and rubbed a clear spot on the steamed-up mirror. Tears welled in her eyes at the sight of her bruised face and throat. Her heart pounded with fresh panic, as if Nash were still with her, pawing at her and looking at her and plotting to kill her if she didn't keep fighting. She swallowed a sob and turned to sit on the floor, back pressed to the door as tears streamed over her cheeks. No, this wasn't a day for finding love. This was a day best forgotten.

Thirty minutes later, Marissa dragged herself from the bathroom, clean and dry. Her blond hair fell in soft piles over each shoulder, fluffy from the efforts of a complimentary dryer. She hadn't packed much makeup, but the lip gloss and mascara had helped her feel a little more human and less hideous despite the raging bruises along her jaw and throat.

Blake's body went rigid when he saw her.

The room was empty, save for a pair of white take-out bags on the little round table near the front window.

Marissa stared, unmoving. "What's wrong?"

Blake snapped into action, waving her closer to the

table "Nothing. The final divers arrived while you were in the shower. My team went to meet them, but the sun's setting soon and they've postponed until morning. My guys are filling the divers in on what to look for and anything else they need to know. West and Cole have promised to keep me updated on their end." He settled into a red cushioned chair. "Now, we wait."

"Will I get to talk to your team when they come back?" She shifted her weight foot to foot. "Not that I plan to badger them or get in the way. I just wonder if I'll be exiled to the bedroom while you talk shop."

"We won't say anything that you can't hear."

Meaning they'd wait until she wasn't around to talk about the classified details, not that they'd be open with her about everything. She mulled that over. "Okay." She didn't love being excluded from any information so closely affecting her, but she had to trust Blake to do his job.

"I ordered burgers, fries and malts." His brows furrowed. "Do you eat this stuff?"

"Comfort food? Absolutely."

He unpacked the bag and set her burger and fries in front of her.

One whiff was all her body needed to recall its desperation for sustenance. She unraveled the butcher paper and chomped into her sandwich like a ravenous animal.

Blake watched her intently. "I'm feeling less guilty for that cruller. I suppose running five miles uphill before dawn seven days a week earns you plenty of room for burgers."

She sucked her straw flat, working a taste of chocolate malt into her mouth. "I've got good genes."

"The running doesn't hurt," he added. "You hike, bike, swim and scuba?"

"I leaned to scuba dive in college. I did crazy things then. I even tried parasailing and rock climbing." She chuckled. "I learned that I prefer to be on the ground."

He pushed a fry between smiling lips. "I've never done any of those things, and I've always thought of myself as an outdoorsman. You're raising the bar."

"You'll get used to it," she teased. "Adventuring is my job."

"Nature photography, right?"

She wiped her mouth and examined Blake's odd expression. "You look confused."

"I assumed you took pictures of wildflowers and butterflies."

She rolled her eyes and went in for another bite of burger. "I get up close and personal with nature. My photos are used for education. Last summer I photographed an eagle's nest on the summit. It was amazing."

Blake dropped his napkin on the table. "The summit? That's one hell of a dangerous climb." He furrowed his brows. "You must really love what you do."

"I do." She smiled. Another thing they had in common. It was no secret Blake loved his job. The pride practically oozed from him when he wore that badge.

Marissa sat back in her chair, allowing her head to roll and her muscles to relax. Slowly, her eyelids drooped shut. Blake cleared his throat, and she jumped. "What happened?"

He stood over her looking inexplicably sad. "You fell asleep sitting up."

"Oh." She checked the corners of her mouth for drool. "Sorry. I should go to bed." She stretched onto her feet, wincing at the pinch of tender muscles in her shoulders and neck.

Blake matched her move. "May I?" He motioned to the place where her hand rested on her bruised neck.

He waited for her to nod before stepping near.

Marissa braced herself to be touched by another towering man today. "Do they put you through medical training at the FBI?"

His warm fingers touched the tender skin of her throat and chin, tipping her head gently for a better look at the wounds. "A little. I think I got more experience growing up a Garrett." He snorted quietly. "At least one of us boys were in constant need of a cast or stitches for about ten years. Nearly drove my poor mom to drink."

Marissa smiled, though he couldn't see her from his new position at her back. She and Kara had been the same way, though their parents were often right beside them.

He circled back to face her. "These bruises are going to look a lot worse before they look better. I can get some ice in here if you want. That might help with swelling." He widened his stance until his face was nearly level with hers and shined a light in her eyes.

She swatted it away on instinct. "Where'd you get that."

"Pocket. Hold still and let me look."

"I don't have a concussion. I was attacked hours ago. I'm fine. Cole already checked. Remember?"

"You need to clean these abrasions."

"I did."

Blake straightened and cocked a brow. "When?"

"Bathroom. I never leave home without a first aid

kit. The cuts are cleaned. They're already beginning to scab. I'm fine."

"That's what you keep saying. Did Cole offer to get a female medic to give you a more thorough evaluation?"

She sighed. "I'm. Fine. What happens to you now? Will someone come to relieve you so you can go home and sleep?"

"I don't sleep much." He walked her to the bedroom and made a slow circuit through the room, peeking into the bathroom before returning to the doorway. "I'll wake you if anything significant happens."

Marissa dawdled, frightened by the prospect of being alone.

Her phone buzzed with a text.

Blake nodded toward the sound. "Tell your family I said everything's going to be okay." He pulled the door shut behind him as he left.

Marissa climbed into the waiting arms of a comfortable queen-size bed and rolled onto her back. She lifted her cell phone into view and swiped the screen to life. She didn't recognize the number on her new text message, but she opened it anyway.

Panic swelled in her chest and throat as she stared at the image of herself enveloped in Blake's strong arms. The photograph was clearly taken from outside her bedroom window only hours earlier.

And the message read, Consider this Agent Garrett's invitation to the wedding.

Chapter Four

The chair toppled behind Blake as he lunged toward the freshly closed French doors, the only things standing between him, Marissa and whatever had elicited her bloodcurdling scream. The barrier sucked open before he reached it, whipping suddenly inward to reveal his trembling charge.

"Blake." She choked on his name, extending her cell phone in his direction.

His gaze darted through the silent room behind her. No signs of an intruder. The window was securely closed. The bathroom door was open. No one was inside.

"Blake," she pleaded, wiggling the phone. "Take it."

Slowly, he holstered his sidearm. "You're alone."

"Yes."

His muscles unclenched by a fraction. He dragged his attention from her stricken face to the offering in her white-knuckled grip. He hadn't left her alone for more than thirty seconds. He'd barely pressed the straw of his chocolate malt to his lips before she'd screamed. The fine hairs along the back of his neck rose to attention as he pried the small pink device from her hand. *That scream*. His guts twisted at the thought of what it could have meant. What he could've found behind the doors.

"It's him," she whispered.

The momentary relief he'd felt at the sight of her was quickly replaced by the image on her screen. Revenge boiled in his blood. "This was the text you received?"

She nodded quickly, her attention glued to the phone.

He powered the device off and used his own to dial West's number. "We've got a new problem. Nash has Marissa's number. He sent a text with a photo. I don't know if he's tracked her. I powered the phone down. I'm pulling the SIM card now, but we need someone to capture prints outside her house and match them to the ones at the site of her attack. Also, get me a burner phone so she can stay in touch with her family." He disconnected and returned his focus to Marissa, the statue in baggy white pajamas.

Her attention remained wholly fixed on the phone. "I can't have it back?"

"Not right now."

"I have pictures on there."

"We won't remove anything personal from the device. I promise. I'm just keeping the card separate so Nash can't track us here."

Marissa's gaze snapped up to meet his. "He can do that?"

Twelve hours ago, Blake would've said no, but his opinion of Nash Barclay was rapidly changing. "Better not to take any chances."

She wrapped her arms around her middle and lifted her chin. "Okay."

"Why don't you get back in bed? Cover up. Try to rest."

Marissa cast a woeful look at the bed she'd no sooner climbed into than leapt back out of. "I could sleep on the couch." Her voice lifted on the final word, bringing a hopeful expression to her pinched brow. "Then you won't have to patrol both rooms."

Blake rocked back on his heels. Having her in his line of sight would make his job a lot easier, but after the day she'd had, and whatever Nash still had planned, a good night's sleep was best for Marissa. There was no way she'd get any decent rest on the couch. Not with local and federal authorities swarming in and out all night, trading intel and updates.

He dropped his chin an inch and cocked his head. "I'll be just fine. You take the bed. I'll keep watch." If it meant Marissa could rest, he'd make the extra effort.

"Or," she said softly, "you could work in here."

Maybe it was her voice. Maybe it was the tenderness in the offer, but something stirred in Blake's chest, extinguishing a tiny portion of the fire in his belly. His contempt for Nash had driven him this far, and he needed it now. What he didn't need was to think of the kind of work he could do in a room like that with a woman like her. Marissa had earned his respect before they'd ever met. She'd done what he couldn't do. When challenged by Nash, she'd gotten the best of him.

Blake stepped carefully into the front room of their suite and wedged the door open. "How about I set up shop here? If we leave this open, I can see the bed and the front door. You'll be safe, and I won't have to leave my post to check on you."

Marissa turned on her socked feet and went back to the bed. Whatever she thought of the offer, she didn't say, but she didn't argue either.

He flipped the light switch, casting her room into shadows, and went to drag the chair and table to its new location.

MARISSA WOKE WITH a start. Her fingers curled deep into the soft fabric of hotel bedsheets. Her limbs were heavy with fatigue and her mind groggy with the effects of a restless night. She pried her stinging eyes open and squinted against the streams of poorly filtered sunlight sneaking through closed hotel blinds. Thank goodness the night was over. She hadn't remembered falling asleep, but the dreams had come quickly. The rose petals and the lake. Nash and his song. She hadn't stopped running through the dark forest since the moment she'd closed her eyes.

In the dream, she didn't get away.

Blake flashed brilliant blue eyes on her in that moment, as if he'd somehow sensed her waking. "Morning." His easy southern drawl pulled her back to reality. He'd repositioned the table and chairs from the front room, and by the looks of him, sat guard all night.

He swiped a travel mug off the table and pushed onto his feet. He stopped at the doorway. "May I?"

She nodded, pressing her lips together, certain she needed a toothbrush or chewing gum before speaking to anyone.

A few unfamiliar faces turned her way, then back, immediately disinterested. The vibration of quiet voices electrified the air beyond her bedroom door, buoyed by the scent of black coffee and the outdoors.

Blake handed the cup to Marissa. "How are you feeling this side of yesterday?"

She bobbed her head in positivity. "Awful."

His mouth ticked up on one side. "Coffee helps."

She pressed the cup to her lips and sucked the steaming hot liquid. The burn on her tongue and scald on her throat were a necessary evil. There was no time to waste on letting the liquid cool. "What have we learned?"

"Not much. We've got your phone at the lab, and my men are comparing the prints at the lake with those outside your bedroom window." His voice drifted slightly off.

Was he recalling the stolen image as she was? The photo of her in his embrace? She could still feel the strength of his arms around her.

Marissa scooted upright in the bed, suddenly guilty for the comfort he'd forgone to keep her safe. "Didn't you sleep?" The question was rhetorical, its answer evident. The stubble on Blake's cheeks had darkened, nearly as much as the circles beneath his eyes. He hadn't changed clothes, and the shiny FBI badge he'd worn proudly around his neck when they met was now missing.

"As much as ever."

"You don't normally sleep?"

He flicked his attention to the bustle in the front room. "No."

"Hazard of the job?" she guessed.

"Something like that."

"Are you always on a case like this?" she wondered. Surely he wasn't always on call. "Do you get time off when you're done? Can you sleep then?"

He pursed his lips and turned piercing blue eyes back on her. "The cases close, but the people stick with me."

"I see." A piece of her heart broke for his. She couldn't imagine the things Blake had seen or how he put them aside when it was time to move on. "Will someone relieve you soon so you can at least try to rest?"

"I'm fine. I'll step outside and pull the door while you…" he circled one wrist "…do whatever ladies do in the morning."

Marissa pushed back the comforter and swung her legs over the bed's edge. "Normally I run, but I guess that's out of the question."

"Yep."

"I use the adrenaline to wake me up. I like the endorphin rush."

Blake pinned her with a cheeky smile. "Coffee's going to have to do today."

Marissa had never had much interest in photographing people, but she wouldn't mind taking a crack at Blake. His square jawline and brooding brow were more than print-worthy. The slight imperfection of his nose and faded scar above his temple were interesting too, but it was the protective edge, the palpable energy, that fascinated her most. Too many people were out for themselves these days, but Blake spent his life watching over others.

"What?" he rumbled, scanning the room around her.

"I was thinking that what you do is noble," she said, "and I'm wondering if anyone ever tells you that."

He snorted. "That's not one I've heard before. No."

"That's too bad." Marissa stretched onto her feet and reached for the ceiling. Her bunched and exhausted muscles complained at the effort. "Well, if I can't run, what am I doing today?" She dropped her hands together at her waist. "Another trip to the lake? Maybe down to the station?"

"I'm headed to the station to see what the team's got down there," he said, pointing a finger at his chest. "You're going to stay here with your detail. I won't be long." He fished a small black cell phone from his pocket and set it on the nightstand. "This is ready for use. We'll get your personal device back to you as soon as tech's done with it. They're going to run a few more diagnostics first."

"Thank you." Marissa hurried into the attached bathroom and shut the door. "When are you leaving for the station?" she yelled.

She discarded her pajamas and shoved her legs into the soft jeans she'd set out the night before.

"Soon," he replied. "Take your time. If I'm not here when you get back…"

She pulled the door open with one hand and brushed her teeth with the other.

"Whoa." Blake stepped back. "What are you, Houdini?"

She'd dressed hastily in her chosen outfit and raked a brush through her hair, still slightly damp from last night's shower. Marissa lifted a finger into the air and turned to the sink to rinse her mouth. "You're not leaving without me."

"There's nothing you can do right now," he said, drifting closer to the open bathroom door. "My goal is to keep you safe and out of sight." His gaze slid over the multicolored bruising on her cheek, jaw and throat.

Her hand went to the aching spots on instinct. She'd tried not to look too long at her battered reflection when she'd driven a lip gloss wand along her bottom lip. The thick line across her cheekbone hurt, but it was nothing like the infernal sting where her face had collided with the tree, leaving heavy rows of scratches from the tree's bark.

"I'm coming." She grabbed a hooded sweatshirt from her bag on the floor and pulled the strings until welts left by Nash's fingers were no longer visible. The marks had raised and darkened overnight, leaving distinct imprints of his hands like shadows clasped around her throat. She didn't need everyone she saw today looking at her the way Blake was looking at her now.

Blake stepped into the doorway, blocking her view of the small crowd in the suite's front room. He searched her top to bottom with cautious eyes before lingering his gaze on her cheek. "You sure?"

"Yeah."

He stepped aside, opening one arm to direct her out. "We'll take my truck to the station. West says the sketch artist will be there soon. He was bringing her to you, but I'll let him know there's no need."

"A sketch artist?" Marissa grabbed the new phone from her nightstand. "I didn't see the face of the man who grabbed me."

"Anything you can tell her will help. I know this is Nash, but I need more than my gut to prove I'm right. Tell her what you remember, and whatever it is, it'll be enough."

"I don't see how."

Blake stopped to retrieve his badge and sidearm from the table. He signed his name to something, then whisked her out the door and into the cab of his truck.

"Last chance," he said, slipping the shifter into Reverse. "You can still stay if you'd like. There's lots of qualified personnel who could look out for you in there. West can still bring the sketch artist up here."

"No. It's good for me to get out. I feel like a sitting duck in there."

"Fair enough." Blake guided his truck away from

the hideout and down the winding country road back to town.

Warm autumn winds rattled the trees and speckled the pavement with brightly colored leaves. It was hard to believe something as ugly as Nash Barclay could exist in a place as beautiful and peaceful as this one. Harder still to believe Nash wanted her. What had she done to gain his attention? How close was he to finding her again?

Blake stared at Marissa as he took the next right. "You look ready to jump."

She loosened her grip on the seat's edge. "I usually run to blow off steam. Now, I've got more to worry about than I ever have and no way to work out the tension." Her cheeks heated as numerous ideas for burning energy with Blake came to mind. "How do you do it?" she asked, desperate to redirect the images in her mind. Another minute of those thoughts, and she'd need to crack a window for air.

Blake lifted and dropped one shoulder. "I run."

"You run?" A smile broke over her face. "Really?"

"Well, don't act so surprised. I don't do it in the wilderness or up a cliff at five a.m. like you, but yeah. I run."

Marissa faced forward, her smile set in place. She could feel his eyes on her cheek. There was no logical reason for the pleasure coursing through her, but the fact they shared a hobby made her happy.

"When you grow up with three younger brothers, like I did, you'll do anything for an hour alone."

What would life have been like for Marissa with two more little sisters?

"It was always just Kara and me. We did everything

with our folks. You think I'm outdoorsy. You should meet my family. Especially Kara. She's a leaf on the wind. She never stops moving, and she only comes inside when she has to."

"I'd love to meet them someday."

Marissa turned to face Blake. She'd like that, too, and she knew why. Dumb as it was, she liked Blake's company a little too much. But why would he want to meet her family? She examined the lines around his eyes and mouth for signs he was joking, or lying. Though, she had no idea how to tell the latter.

She turned her eyes back to the road with an internal groan. Blake was a nice guy and a good agent who was just doing his job. He probably said whatever he thought would make the people in his care feel most at ease.

She had to admit he was good. At his side, it was easy to forget they were in danger.

A little while later, Blake held the door as Marissa entered the bustling station. She recognized the members of her local sheriff's department. She'd grown up with most of them in one capacity or another. The FBI agents were easy enough to identify as well. Though she only knew Blake, the agents were dressed in slacks and jackets like the ones Blake had on when they'd met.

Small groups of official-looking men and women huddled around every desk, discussing the scattered contents of file folders or taking a call on speakerphone. Marissa's name was on the lips of a dozen local protectors at once.

Blake's warm palm slid against the small of her back and nudged her forward.

"Sorry." She hadn't realized she'd stopped moving.

West stood in the hallway, stirring a cup of coffee and frowning. His gaze locked on Marissa's throat.

She adjusted the hooded sweatshirt, but his eyes simply moved north and stuck to the abrasions on her cheek.

"Blake, Marissa." He nodded. "Can I get you anything?"

"No." She cleared her throat to sound more confident than she felt.

"All right, then let's get started."

BLAKE FOLLOWED WEST into the thick of the crowd where a half-dozen men and women handed him files and reports. He flipped through the slew of information looking for something to prove the man he was after was the same one who'd gotten away from him five years ago.

Marissa took a seat at the desk's edge and watched the group. Her head moved back and forth with each new voice, following every word. Blake could practically hear the line of questions compiling for their drive home. He grimaced. Not *home*. Back to the hotel where they were staying *because she was a victim in need of protection*.

"This is everything from the traffic cams?" he asked, turning a few grainy photos toward West.

"No. Those are everything we have from the surveillance camera outside the bank. We don't have traffic cams or face recognition software, hell, half the town still comes to the library to use the internet. We're lucky to have those shots."

"Right." Blake rubbed his burning eyes. "So, we think he drives a pickup."

A deputy nodded. "An unfamiliar pickup was spotted outside the northern forest gates around the same time Miss Lane flagged down the man who drove her here. We asked around about the truck, and when we learned it was seen on Main Street, we contacted the bank to review the footage."

"Thanks." Blake gave the picture a careful examination. The entire windshield was in shadow, probably the worst photo he'd ever seen. He couldn't even see the grill from that angle, let alone a license plate.

He clenched and released a frustrated fist at his side. Marissa lifted her gaze from his hand to his eyes. She didn't miss anything.

"Agent Garrett?" A woman in jeans and a *Doctor Who* T-shirt jogged up the aisle in his direction, bobbing between desks and around staring agents. "I'm Cora from tech. I came in as soon as they called. I've been here all night. Sorry about the…" she motioned to her outfit, then shook her head and continued. "I traced the text back to a burner phone. The phone was left on and dropped in a trash receptacle outside the national park. We recovered the phone. No prints, but it's a really basic phone."

"That's not a surprise," he said. "People don't buy basic phones for personal use. They want bells and whistles. Criminals buy basic so they can use them for something like this." He turned his attention back to the stack of useless intel gathered on the desk.

"Agent Garrett," Cora continued.

He dragged his most polite expression out and waited.

"I called every store in Cade County selling phones like the one we found. Most said they'd check their inventory against the stock and let me know. The guy at the truck stop diner on Deer Run Road said he sold a phone like this yesterday at three o'clock. He remembered the time because it was the end of his shift. The man paid with cash, but the truck stop has a camera watching the register."

Blake's spine went rigid. A spike of hope rammed through him. "Tell me he's sending a picture of the man who bought that phone."

"Yes, sir."

"How soon?"

"Anytime. He's looking through the footage now."

West leaned against the corner of the desk beside Blake. "Maybe take a load off until we hear something new," he suggested, spinning an unopened bottle of water in his palm like an Old West gunslinger. "You're so tired you can barely stand there without swaying."

"He didn't sleep," Marissa tattled.

"Wait," West said. "Why don't you put a pin in the nap and take a shower first. Isn't that what you had on yesterday?"

Blake snatched the bottle from West's hand and cracked the lid open. "Thanks, I'm fine." He took long deep pulls on the liquid, realizing then that he'd become dry as the desert.

West fanned a hand in front of his nose. "Feel free to splash some of that on you if you want to."

Blake finished the bottle and walked away from the crowd. West followed. Blake shot a look over his shoulder, where Marissa continued to watch from her seat. "He could've killed her."

"But he didn't," West said, not missing a beat. "She's tough, and she's smart, and he didn't get her."

Blake nodded. He'd give Marissa that. She was one of a kind. "If he had, it would've been on me."

West crossed his arms and locked Blake in his steady gaze. "He didn't, and it's not."

"Agent Garrett?" Cora's voice carried through the stream of white noise.

The Garretts moved instantly toward her. "What do you have?" Blake asked.

"I just heard from the truck stop, and it looks like we've got a match." She turned the large digital tablet in her hands to face them, and Marissa gasped.

"That's him," Marissa pointed, moving to join them in the room's center. "That's the man from the lake this summer."

Chapter Five

West marched forward, holding the digital image above his head to face the other officials. His voice boomed through the instantly silent room. "This is Nash Barclay. Get his name and face on every news channel this side of the Mississippi, and we need it done now. Right now. Talk to bus terminals and the highway patrol. He might be driving an old Ford pickup, plates unknown. We want sightings only, no civilian apprehension attempts. He's dangerous. Drive that point home."

The room scrambled into action.

Marissa caught Blake's sleeve in her fingertips. "It's him?"

"It's him," Blake answered.

An uncomfortable mix of fear and victory beat through her. She'd hoped Blake was wrong, that some other, less murderous man had grabbed her, but at least now Nash couldn't hide. Not with his face splashed across the nightly news and morning papers.

Blake's attention traveled to her hand on his sleeve before reconnecting with her eyes. "I guess you don't need to meet with the sketch artist."

"Right." She released him in favor of cradling her torso. "I didn't think I remembered his face, but that's definitely it." She tightened her arms around her middle, thankful to be at the sheriff's department when a known serial killer was running around. A sliver of guilt wiggled through her. Not everyone was as safe as she was, surrounded by federal agents and local law enforcement officials. Another woman could be next. There were plenty of twentysomething blondes to keep Nash entertained. In fact, she had a sister who looked a lot like her.

Marissa pulled her phone from her pocket and gave Blake an uneasy look. "I'm going to call Kara and tell her to stay in today." Hopefully Kara didn't need the advice. Maybe she'd taken the news of Marissa's attack to heart and planned a quiet day at home.

"Hello?" Kara's voice trilled through the speaker.

A whoosh of relief swept from Marissa's lungs. Kara was fine. "Hey, it's me. Thought I'd check in."

"Oh, hey!" The smile in her sister's voice was contagious. "Why didn't you call before bed last night? I was worried. Your phone was off. Where are you calling from? Did you get a new number?" Wind battered the speaker. Marissa's attention jumped to Blake's waiting face.

"No. Kara? Where are you?"

"Hiking. Why? Do you want to meet for breakfast? I packed a good one."

"I can't. I'm sorry. Listen, I need you to go home, or to Mom and Dad's. Stay there today, okay? They've identified my attacker."

"Is it him? The fugitive you said they were looking for?"

Marissa nodded, knowing Kara couldn't see, but finding the words impossible.

"Holy crap," Kara whispered. Marissa's silence must have been enough of an answer.

"He's still out there," Marissa warned.

She thought she saw Blake wince, but his blank agent face was in position when she gave him a closer look. "Please be safe," she continued to Kara. "I'll call again as soon as I know something. Tell Mom and Dad I'm safe. I'm staying with the authorities for now."

Kara swore. "I'll head straight there from here."

"Thank you." Marissa's eyes stung as she disconnected with her sister. "She's safe," she told Blake. "I sent her to our parents' house."

"Good. Why don't you let me take you back to the hotel now?"

"No," she blurted. "I'm okay here. I'm obviously safe, and you have things to do. I won't get in the way. I can wait in the break room again."

"Agent Garrett?" A man in a gray suit waved one hand overhead. His jacket parted in the front to reveal the FBI badge anchored to his sleek black belt. "We're needed at the lake."

"Take me." Marissa's hand snapped out to catch Blake's. "Please."

Blake ignored her. "What's going on?"

The man gave Marissa a long look. "They say they found something. We need to get up there."

Blake pulled his hand free from Marissa's grip. Before she could protest the rejection, he pressed those same warm fingers to the small of her back. "Let's go."

THE DRIVE TO the lake was a blur. Partially due to Marissa's hazy thoughts and morbid fears, partially as a result of Blake's speed. The silence was palpable in the warm cab. Blake stole looks at her from the corner of his eye, but kept whatever he was thinking to himself. She wished he'd just spit it out. The silence crawled all over her skin like a nest of baby spiders. He might be calm and focused under this kind of pressure, but the worry was eating her alive.

The vehicle slowed as a pair of rangers came into view near the park entrance. A line of reporters yammered into microphones along the roadside, just outside the gate, using a Cade County National Forest and Road Closed sign as the backdrop to their story.

Blake flashed his badge, and the rangers motioned him to pass. The looks on the uniformed men's faces suggested they knew more than Blake or Marissa, and it wasn't good.

The truck rocked to a stop in the grass between two black vans marked Cade County Coroner. Blake released his belt and turned on the seat to face Marissa. "I don't know what we're walking into, but I'm guessing it's going to be rough. I want to remind you that you don't have to be here. It's not too late to return to the hotel or go back to the station."

Marissa's tongue stuck to the roof of her mouth and sweat pooled in her palms. The coroner's vans weren't there by accident. She didn't want to see what the divers had found, but where else would she go? To a hotel room with a carousel of uniformed strangers all looking at her like she might break? Like she was a victim. No. She'd stay with Blake. At least with him, there was no judgement. He had other things on his mind, and she appreciated the room to feel however she wanted without those probing, curious looks.

"I'll stay," she said. She reached for her door, and

Blake followed suit, rushing around the truck's hood to meet her.

"You don't need to be brave." He moved into a broad shaft of sunlight with his jaw clenched, the expression flush with concern.

Marissa inhaled a steadying breath. She squared her shoulders, determined to be as honest as possible with a man whose mere presence seemed to put her at ease. "I'm not brave. I'm scared to death. I don't want to be here any more than you want me here, but this is just the way it is. I want to be with you."

Blake yanked his chin back. "What?"

She sank her teeth into the thick of her bottom lip. She hadn't meant the words the way they'd sounded, but could she deny them? He was rugged and handsome with a voice like molasses, and the man was nothing if not attentive. She blew out a slow breath as her mind began to wander.

Blake waited, hip cocked, gaze delving into hers, as if he could pull the thoughts from her head.

"Until this is over," she clarified, taking interest in a nearby tree and ignoring the warmth in her belly. She shored herself up and met his gaze once more. "The way I see it, this entire situation is horrible. There's no silver lining. No good angle. It's awful, and it's ugly, but I don't see how he can get to me again as long as I'm with you. So, I'm staying."

MARISSA'S POSTURE WAS RIGID, something she did to appear bigger, Blake assumed. Though, he hadn't thought of her as small since she'd first opened her mouth to tell him how he was going to handle her case. Being pocket-size required a person to apply themselves more assertively. He'd never thought much of that fact before meeting her. He'd passed six foot by junior year in high school. Being overlooked or underestimated had never been his problem.

Until Blake had met Nash, he hadn't had a lot of problems. Now, he had two major ones. Catching the sonofagun who'd eluded him for five years, and protecting the woman in front of him who was doing her best not to look nearly as frightened as she truly was. The second task would be a lot easier if she hadn't just announced her intent to stay under his thumb. Not only would her constant presence make it impossible for him to go hunting for his nemesis, it also made Blake vulnerable. Marissa was a distraction. She'd been slowly making mud of his clarity with those big blue eyes and endless bravado, and every minute he wasted worrying about her was time Nash gained on him.

Worse still, and ridiculous as it was, Blake wanted her with him. He'd promised to keep her safe, and he wasn't the kind of man who broke his word. "Fine." He set his hand against the small of her back once more, a frustrating habit he'd developed and couldn't seem to shake. Normally, he maintained a strict no-touching policy for those in his charge, but this was different. The added connection was a comfort to her. At least that was what he'd told himself when she didn't swat him away the first time he made the move. Not that he'd planned it. Reaching for her had come naturally, another thing that had surprised him. "You can stick with either of my brothers while I work. They'll keep you safe, and you can trust them."

"I know, and I do."

They moved toward the lake in unison, becoming

the center of attention as those already on scene noticed their arrival. A man in a wet suit leaned his backside against a tree, hands on knees, eyes closed. Blake's gut fisted. He knew that deep breathing technique. If the diver hadn't been sick yet, he was about to be.

"Blake." A familiar and commanding voice caught Blake's attention and turned him around. His father tromped through the tall grasses at the lake's edge wearing fatigues and waders.

Blake smiled, and led Marissa toward the grasses. He hadn't seen his dad in nearly a year, but it was eerily like looking in a mirror. One that told the future anyway.

"Here's another one you can trust," Blake told Marissa. "This is my dad, Martin Garrett. Dad, this is Marissa Lane."

Marissa raised her small hand to him. "Sheriff Garrett. It's nice to meet you."

His dad stepped free of the water and accepted her offer with a sad smile. "I'm sorry to hear about what happened to you yesterday."

"Thank you, sir."

"You're a brave woman."

She pursed her lips and looked away.

Blake's dad pinned him with a pointed look. "Did they tell you what they found down there?"

"Not yet, but I don't suppose they had to." The somber feel in the air, coupled with the coroner's vans, could mean little else.

"Probably not." His dad sighed the words. Twenty years as the local sheriff had worn him down. He'd spearheaded West's landslide campaign. It was time, he'd said, to get to know his family again. Let another Garrett take the reins for a while.

"Look," Marissa whispered.

Bubbles floated and burst on the lake's smooth surface, sending ripples through the reflections of Marissa, Blake and his father. A heartbeat later, two divers' heads broke free. Together, they towed a body to shore.

His father groaned.

Marissa stepped behind Blake. Her fingers pressed against his side, either for protection or balance, he couldn't be sure. When he'd moved between her and the reporter, she'd rejected the shielding. He didn't blame her now. No one should see what he was watching. It shouldn't be happening.

Her ragged breaths blew against his shirt. She was probably thinking the same thing he was. That body could have been her.

"Dad?" Blake said, turning for a look at his life-long hero.

"Yep." The town's former sheriff and eternal protector slid an arm around Marissa's shoulders. "Why don't we give these folks some room to work."

Blake waited as his father led Marissa several yards away, then headed for the divers as they arranged the exhumed body carefully on a sheet set out by the county coroner. Drops of water fell from their suits onto her pale, swollen face and tattered wedding gown.

Blake pulled his eyes away with a curse. "Was she alone?"

"No, sir." One diver answered as the other strode away on unsteady legs. "Five more," he added in the detached monotone of a man in shock.

"Five?" Blake cast his gaze over the bubbling water. That couldn't be right. "Nash had four victims in total. You're saying there were six bodies down there?"

A pair of men in blue windbreakers edged Blake and the diver away from the woman. "Excuse us." They stretched another sheet beside the first.

And another beside that.

With six sheets spread along the peaceful lake's edge, the men in windbreakers returned to the woman and went to work immediately, examining her eyes, nose and mouth, cleaning under her nails and probing her skin with blue medical gloves.

Blake rubbed a heavy hand through his hair and gripped the back of his neck.

Two new divers appeared on the water's surface, towing another woman dressed in white. The veil from her hair sank slowly in the water behind them.

The bodies kept coming, just as the first diver had said, delivered by the hands of men and women who'd undoubtedly retrieved many others from similar fates, but never, he guessed, had anyone there seen anything like this. The rescuers' faces were as white as the victims. They bumbled onto shore stricken, ill and rattled.

Blake watched with disbelieving eyes as the women were lined up and examined in the warm autumn sun. It was a juxtaposition that turned his stomach. Six women. *Six.* How had he missed two victims? He'd dedicated himself to knowing this case. He knew the victims. Had met with their families. Internalized their devastating losses. How could he have missed not one but two victims?

West's men met each diver as they finished their duty and led them aside. They'd need to give an account of what they'd seen down there.

Blake walked the space between five occupied sheets, studying the disfigured faces and patchy hair.

Years underwater had all but removed their identities. Aside from their families, and the animal who did this, Blake was probably the only one who'd recognize them. "Marcia Gold," he told the men working on the first body. "Angela Olmstead," he said to the next. "Jessica Snow. Monica Knisely."

He stopped beside the fifth body where a woman wearing an ID badge from the medical examiner's office tucked wads of loose hair into an evidence bag. "What happened to her?" he asked. The body was grotesquely misshapen, portions missing. Her gown was nearly torn to shreds by age and the lake's ecosystem.

The M.E. labeled the bag and set it into her case. "This one's been down there a while. Longer than the others. Maybe by as much as a year."

"A year." The words warbled off Blake's tongue. "Are you sure?"

She offered a patient smile. "It'll take longer to identify her, if we can. There's a lot of damage here, but we'll know more soon, and we'll get the facts to you the moment we have them." The woman stretched onto her feet and patted his shoulder.

A hush rolled over the crowd behind them, on the heels of splashing water. The sixth body had made it to the surface.

Blake hung his head as he turned to see what new atrocity awaited. Would it be another woman murdered *years* ago? Someone else who he had no clue existed? Would this have been Marissa's fate if she weren't so fierce and determined?

"Blake." Marissa's voice sounded nearby, closer than he'd expected, but he couldn't force his eyes from the lake.

The final two divers rushed forward with a woman

who couldn't have been underwater more than a few weeks. She was blonde and blue-eyed like the others, petite and dressed in a long-sleeved wedding gown.

Blake's chest tightened. The weight of too many sleepless nights and five years of self-loathing pressed the air from his lungs. Anger boiled in his gut. He could've stopped this five years ago and he didn't. Now someone else was dead. Another life taken. Because of him.

West strode into view, cell phone pressed to his ear. "I need the missing persons report on Annie Linz. Twenty-something jogger. Went missing near the county line early this month." He knelt beside the young woman and turned her face carefully toward him, then fell back on his haunches. He cast a look over one shoulder and dipped his chin at Blake.

The ground tilted beneath Blake. Nash had killed again and he'd had no idea. Everything he'd thought he knew about this case had gone out the window the moment he'd arrived home at the summons of a madman, which he realized was exactly what had happened. Nash could've killed anywhere, but he'd come back to Blake's hometown. It probably also wasn't a fluke that Marissa got away. Nash wanted to be hunted. He'd probably let her win that fight, and he'd used her to send the message right to Blake's ear.

"Blake." Marissa's voice was closer now, and more desperate. She fell against him with hands over her eyes. The impact sent him back a step. She buried herself against his side. "I was wrong. I can't be here. Please, take me away."

His chest ached as he pulled himself away from all those women he couldn't save and focused on the one he still could. In fact, he was slowly coming to realize that he'd do anything to protect Marissa from anyone who tried to hurt her again, and that truth had nothing to do with his job. "Okay. Let's go."

MARISSA FOLLOWED BLAKE through the crowd and away from the ghastly scene. She sucked lungfuls of air, desperate not to be sick. Whatever she'd expected to come out of the lake, that wasn't it. "I'd hoped they'd found some small piece of evidence," she said, choking back her fear. "I wanted the coroner vans to be a precaution, not a necessity. Did you see the last woman? She looked like me." She covered her mouth again to stop the rambling.

"They all did at one point," Blake said. He watched for her response. "Nash has a type, and you're it."

She did her best not to overreact. Was there an overreaction to what he'd just said? Blake probably thought so, and she didn't want to be labeled as baggage. He could exile her to the hotel room where she'd have no idea what was going on or if she was in danger again. She wasn't sure if that scenario was worse than playing witness to the things she'd seen today, but both were scary. Given the choice, she'd rather be afraid with Blake than without him.

He pinched the bridge of his nose.

"Are you okay?" she asked, recalling his expression at the sight of the women being extracted from the lake.

"I'm fine."

He wasn't. She could see it in his eyes. He'd aged in those last few minutes by the lake.

She'd watched him as a gauge. Was this normal to him? To the other officials? It wasn't. Everyone had looked the way she felt. Some of the divers were physically sick while being interviewed. This thing that was happening in her town was absolutely sinister, and she was caught in the center of it.

Marissa leaned against a tree to tie her shoe and pull herself together. "Maybe you should get some sleep when we get back to the hotel."

"I'm fine." The words were resolute, from the mouth of a man who'd clearly repeated them a thousand times.

"Your eyes are rimmed in red. I doubt you slept at all last night, and I know you haven't eaten today." West had made a similar assessment when Blake arrived at the sheriff's department yesterday. So his poor self-care wasn't just about the last twenty-four hours. It was something more. How long had he been this way?

He turned his suddenly heated gaze on her.

"Don't say you're fine," she warned.

"I am."

She snorted. "You're predictable. I'll give you that." She pushed off the tree and continued down the path toward the parking lot, in no hurry to get back to her new reality.

Blake fell into step, easily matching his long stride to her much shorter one. "I'm sorry you had to see that. No one should have."

"Do you think that he was dragging me toward the lake yesterday?" she asked. "That he had his gear ready to go? Was that why we found the scuba weights in the grass?"

"I don't know."

"Where do you think he gets the dresses?"

Blake didn't answer. "There's a lot I don't know these days."

The trail ended too soon, dumping them back at the crowded lot. Official vehicles peppered the space between those she presumed belonged to the divers.

Blake's truck was still sandwiched between coroner's vans. Marissa marched to the passenger door, careful not to think too long about what she'd seen at the lake.

Blake leaned over his hood and plucked a sheet of paper from beneath his windshield wiper. A slew of curses poured from his lips, and he pulled his phone from his pocket. "Get in." He unlocked the truck doors and pointed at Marissa. "West?" he barked into the phone. "I've got contact." He pressed the paper face-down on the window and turned in a small circle, examining the quiet forest around him. "There was a picture on my truck. Probably the next victim. We need a name and address. We've got to get to her before he does."

Marissa climbed inside and locked her door. Her gaze swept to the photo staring at her through the arching glass. A boulder of fear landed on her chest, obstructing her airways and aching in her throat. "Blake!"

The driver's door jerked open. "What?" He leaned over the seat, eyes wide. "What happened?"

She fumbled for her phone with weak, uncoordinated hands. Her tear-blurred gaze jumped to the photo on his windshield. "That's my sister."

Chapter Six

Marissa worked her fingers over the phone screen, dialing Kara as quickly as possible with shaking hands. Blake's voice boomed beside her in the truck cab as he contacted West and his team. His words were lost as Marissa counted the rings. Had they always been so long and far between? "Voice mail," she whispered.

The truck rumbled to life and reversed through the grass and gravel with a loud roar. Stones blew out behind them, clanging and rattling against the fenders and undercarriage as they spun for the gate.

Marissa's ears rang. "She didn't pick up." *Why* didn't she pick up? Marissa dialed again.

The truck jumped between a tree and the guard gate, not bothering to stick to the road or wait for the removal of the barricade. "There's a deputy en route to Kara's house," Blake said, tearing up the road at nearly double the posted thirty-five miles per hour speed limit. He pressed a button on his dash and a red glow flashed over his windshield, presumably from the unit on the truck's roof.

"Voice mail." Marissa hung up and dialed again.

A news van gave chase in Marissa's side view mirror. It was no wonder with the exit they'd made.

Blake cursed and jammed his finger against the touchscreen on his dash. "Dial West," he ordered.

Marissa's head swam and her tummy churned. Blake's voice became the backdrop to her fear as he explained the new situation to West and set plans to beat Nash to Kara. Assuming he didn't already have her.

Nash Barclay could have anything he wanted, except Kara. Marissa would trade anything she had for her sister. Including herself. The voice mail picked up again, and Marissa slammed the phone onto the bench beside her.

"Hey." Blake lowered a hand over hers, trapping her shaky fingers in his steel grip. "Breathe."

Marissa pulled in a long, shuddered breath and released it. Blake's presence was a tonic to her nerves, but his touch was so much more. She gripped his strong fingers, allowing them to syphon her fear and stall the erratic pounding in her chest. His broad palm engulfed her small hand, covering it with his protection and sending sparks of electricity over her skin. She refocused on the road. "Turn right on Main and head for Blue Grass Run. She's the yellow one-story at the top of the hill. There's a tree in the yard with a swing and window boxes on the sills." Marissa's voice cracked. Her sister was too sweet and kind to fall victim to a monster.

"Got it." He released her hand to jam the horn on his steering wheel before running a red light.

Cool air rushed over her fingers in the absence of his grip, and immediate disappointment set in. "I know Blue Grass Run," he said. "It's a nice neighborhood, and that's good news. There are probably people outside today. Kids playing. Dogs walking. Witnesses. Plus, if she's anything like you, then she's smart, and you've told her what's going on. She won't answer the door to a stranger or invite anyone inside."

That was all true, but Marissa hadn't invited Nash into her house either, and he'd been there just the same. Pawing through her things, lingering at the window. Photographing her with Blake.

She let out a ragged breath and dialed Kara again. *Voice mail.*

Blake drove onto the curb outside Kara's house a few minutes later. Marissa hit redial.

"Wait here." Blake locked her in the truck and walked through the yard to meet Cole and another agent at Kara's porch.

"Come on," Marissa whispered to her phone. When she hung up this time, she dialed her parents. Kara was probably already there. She'd probably just forgotten her phone in the car or left it on the couch while she helped their mom in the kitchen. Kara was sweet, but she was naive and a bit clueless, never really seeing the big picture. She was fun, but unintentionally reckless and as hopelessly self-absorbed as any twenty-one-year-old who'd never had a true reason to worry.

"Hello?" Her mother answered on the first ring.

"Mama?"

"Marissa? Where are you? Are you okay?"

"I'm fine. Is Kara with you?" she asked. "We're at her place now. She's not here, but I told her to wait with you and she said she would."

"She's on her way," her mom answered.

"Oh, thank goodness."

"Marissa," she whispered. "Have you seen the news?"

"Yes." The word floated from her lips like a ghost from her worst nightmare. She'd seen the news and much worse this morning. The last woman pulled from the lake could've easily been her or Kara. Blake hadn't even known Nash was back at it until Marissa had gotten away from him yesterday.

Her gaze drifted back to the men on Kara's porch, and the world spun. The trio of oversized lawmen had shifted their positions, revealing a previously shielded stack of old-fashioned suitcases beside Kara's door. The pile was topped with a wedding veil.

The luggage was posed as if waiting for a photograph.

Or a honeymoon.

Marissa said a hasty goodbye to her mother, and tried not to be sick. She gripped the door handle, debating whether or not to jump out and join the men. Questions flooded her mind, but Blake had told her to stay put. She chewed her thumbnail and watched as Blake moved methodically around the perimeter of her sister's home, running his fingers along the window and door frames, like he had at her place, while curious neighbors looked on. Cole and a member of Blake's team hauled the cases away with blue-gloved hands.

Tears of fear welled in her eyes. What did this mean?

The door locks popped and Blake swung himself in beside her. "Have you found her?" he asked.

Marissa nodded. "She's headed to my parents'. Can we go there? I need to see her."

"Yes, ma'am." He folded himself behind the wheel and started the truck, a measure of relief in his brow. "No signs of forced entry. You saw the cases?"

"Yes." She watched for his reaction, but his expression was painfully blank. "Nash delivered the luggage?"

"I think so, yes, but it only means that he's playing

with us, nothing more. Once we have Kara, we'll assign her a detail." He shot Marissa a pointed look. "This is going to be okay."

Marissa felt her brows grind together. "How can you say that?"

The news van that had attempted following them from the national park turned onto Kara's street and motored toward them.

"Because I won't accept any other outcome." Blake powered down his window as they drew near. He hung his elbow over the open window when the van stopped beside him in the street. "Deputy Garrett is patrolling this street with a federal agent. Someone reported a sighting of Nash Barclay. I'm headed back to the park to see if anything else has happened there."

The stunned news van driver bobbed his head. "Thank you."

Blake powered his window up and pressed gently on the gas pedal.

The van sat in the road for several long beats as Blake's truck rolled away. He snuck glances in his rearview mirror until the van sprang to life and headed for his brother and teammate.

Marissa turned on her seat for a better look out the back window. The fear of betrayal burned in her chest. Surely Blake wouldn't have given a reporter more information than he'd shared with her. Would he? "Was that true about Nash?"

"No. I lied about the Nash spotting to give the reporter a reason to stay here instead of following us to your parents' house. Cole has already bagged the evidence and put it out of sight. Let him deal with the reporter."

She swiveled back in relief. "What did you say Cole and the other agent are doing?"

"They're canvassing." Blake gave her a quick look. "It's due diligence to let her neighbors know he's out there. Educated civilians have stopped more than one killer. They'll be assets, keeping watch on her house and property. We'll broadcast the same message for vigilance on the nightly news, but one-on-one contact is better. People get desensitized. Knocking on their doors is a call to action. It makes them accountable."

Marissa nodded, eager now for her childhood home, and bubbling with the need to be with Kara and her parents. "I guess you get to meet my family after all."

Blake's lips curved slightly, and the small smile reached his eyes. "See, the day's looking up already."

She matched his easy expression. "Family's important to you." That made one more thing to like about Blake Garrett. Not that she was counting. Her dad would appreciate it, too. "Nothing trumps family" was practically her dad's motto.

Blake exhaled with an infinitesimal shake of his head. "Family's everything." He gave her a curious look before dropping the smile.

Marissa straightened in her seat and adjusted the belt, trying not to wonder too much about what that look had meant, or if Blake was making light of those suitcases when they were really something much worse. "Thank you."

"For what?"

"Everything. For keeping me safe and calm. For watching out for my sister."

He crawled to a stop at the red light before speaking. "My job is to protect people." The gravelly tone in his voice made her think there was more he wanted to say, but as usual, he didn't.

Marissa folded her hands in her lap and turned her face to the widow at her side. She'd almost forgotten the big picture. This wasn't about her. Blake's attentiveness and the things he was doing for her weren't personal. They were in his job description.

THE LANE HOME was bigger than Blake had expected, a stately affair with white columns and a long blacktop driveway. The expansive property was beautiful, but impossible to protect with his limited manpower. There was at least a quarter mile between neighbors.

He stopped at the end of the tree-lined drive, unsure where to park. "You grew up here?" A new Jeep with two bright orange kayaks on top sat outside an over-sized detached garage. "Is that Kara's car?"

"No. That's my mom's."

A moment later, Marissa's door closed behind her. She was halfway up the walk before he shifted into Park.

Marissa's arms stretched wide as an older version of herself launched off the porch and wrapped her in a rocking hug.

He ejected his key from the ignition and stretched onto his feet outside the cab.

The six-man sheriff's department in Shadow Point was already in over its head, and his team was working at capacity. There was no way he could properly pro-tect a property this size. He moved slowly up the walk, thinking of how to keep the Lanes safe. Maybe his dad could invite himself over for a while. One trained man inside with the family was a smarter move than five wandering the property anyway.

He turned his phone in his palm and sent his father a text.

"Mom, this is Blake Garrett," Marissa said, drawing his attention back to the women on the walk. "He's the federal agent heading up the case."

The apparent note of pride in her voice stirred something loose in his chest. "Hello." He struggled to ignore the emotion and concentrate on making a good impression. After all, he was there to deliver the heinous details of a madman's actions, and ask this woman to trust him with her daughter's life. "It's nice to meet you, Mrs. Lane." He shook the woman's hand. "Kara's not here yet?"

Marissa's mom dragged her gaze back to Marissa's beat-up face. Her expression teetered between horror and confusion. "Not yet. She's on her way. Why?"

Blake did the numbers mentally. If Kara had been anywhere in town, and spoken to her mom before Marissa had, then Kara should've beaten them there. Even if she'd stopped somewhere along the way, she should have arrived by now. "When was the last time you spoke with her?"

Mrs. Lane shook her head. "She just texts. I'm sure she'll be here any minute."

He forced a tight smile, hoping to break the unbearable tension and get down to business. Kara was late and that was bad. "We're having trouble reaching her by phone."

"I'll send her a text. I'm sure she's gotten distracted by a rare bird or pack of Boy Scouts, or anything really. Kara's like that." Mrs. Lane took her time looking Blake over. Her worn blue jeans and white thermal shirt looked nearly as casual as her bare feet and sagging ponytail. Marissa had clearly been cut from this cloth. "You know, I've lived in Shadow Point all my life, even raised two daughters here, but I believe you're the first Garrett to show up on my doorstep."

He rested his hands on his hips, unreasonably pleased to know none of his brothers had been here before him. "Is that so?"

"I've heard a lot of interesting things about your family."

Blake didn't love the way she'd said *interesting*. "Nothing too bad, I hope."

"Depends who's telling the stories."

Marissa blushed. "Mom."

"Ah." Blake had heard it all before. The Garretts were testosterone-driven cavemen, womanizers, married to the law and addicted to the chase. The last accusation wasn't limited to bad guys. "We're not so bad."

The front door opened with a snap, and a man Blake's father's age stepped onto the porch. His no-nonsense stance and heavy frown screamed military. No wonder Marissa had been able to fight Nash off. This man seemed the sort to require combat training before starting public kindergarten. "Well, don't just stand around in the open with a target on your backs," he demanded.

Marissa jogged up the wide front steps and wrapped her arms around his middle. "Hi, Daddy." She kissed his cheek with a relieved smile. His face went soft for a fleeting moment before turning sternly back to Blake.

"That lunatic's face is on every news station."

Marissa released him, and he gave her a closer look. "Good heavens." He skimmed a parental palm over her cheek, gently pushing the blond hair off her shoulder, revealing the evidence of Nash's fingers on her throat. "What the hell happened to you?"

"I told you yesterday. I was attacked. I fought him off," she said, flinging hair back over the marks on her neck. "Ran to the road and got a ride to the police station."

Her dad looked at her mom. "She got into a stranger's car after being attacked."

Getting into cars with strangers wasn't a move Blake personally recommended, but she was fleeing a crime scene. She needed help. "She's a fighter," Blake interjected with a ripple of misplaced pride.

"I know that," her father snapped. "Where were you while this was happening to my daughter?" He raised his hand to the bruising on her face.

"Louisville. I came as soon as I got the call from Sheriff Garrett. Thanks to Marissa, we were able to positively identify the man who did this. We put his name and face on the news hoping someone can help us find him."

Marissa motioned Blake to her side and gave the driveway a longing look, no doubt hoping for Kara's car to appear. "Come on," she said. "We can wait inside."

"That's what I said," her father grouched.

They were greeted by a soaring foyer with winding wooden stairs to the second floor. The floor plan was open. Walls were drenched in earth tones and family photos of the Lanes over the years. A fire roared in an exquisite stone fireplace at the head of their gathering room.

Blake took note of the expansive windows throughout and patio doors in both the dining and kitchen area.

Too many access points. "Do you have a home security system, Mr. Lane?"

Marissa's dad cast a look over his shoulder as they moved past the stairs toward the kitchen. "The wife and I have matching rifles and fifty years' experience knocking dust off tin cans. Does that count?"

Everything about him said he'd hit more than tin cans. "It helps," Blake admitted, "but a direct line to the authorities would be better. I'd like to station a man here until this blows over."

Mr. Lane stopped moving where wide-planked wooden floors turned to mosaic tile. "I'll accept help during the night shift. I can handle things during the day."

That was reasonable, but unacceptable. His dad would have to bring a rocker and sit on the porch then. "I'd also like to see Kara stay with you for a few days," Blake said.

"What about Marissa?" her father asked.

With enough men stationed here, Blake could probably keep her safe. He could take double shifts and bring additional people to protect the property. Hell, his cousin owned a private security firm, but something told Blake not to let her out of his sight. Whether it was professional instinct or plain personal interest, he couldn't say and didn't care. "I think she's safer with my team, sir."

Marissa squeezed between the men. "I smell coffee. Is there coffee?" She grabbed Blake's wrist and towed him to a granite-topped island. "Black?"

"Yes." He swung his attention to her mother who busily tapped her cell phone screen. "When did you get the last text from Kara?"

Marissa set a mug in front of him, then lined four more cups on the counter. She filled three to their rims and eagerly lifted one to her lips.

Her mom folded her arms, clearly uneasy. "Not long ago. Maybe forty minutes, but she was finishing a hike. Then, she needed to run home for some clean things to change into."

Marissa's shoulders collapsed. The coffee danced inside her mug from the slight trembles wracking her upper body.

Blake imagined folding her against his chest and telling her everything was going to be okay. Hell, if he could just put a hand over hers like he had in his truck, but she was flanked by her parents. A moment later, she leaned into her dad. "We were just at her house. She wasn't there."

Her mom paled. "Why were you at her house? Do you think something happened to her? What aren't you telling us?"

Blake ran his thumbs over the screen of his phone. "I'll check with Cole and see if she showed after we left, or if the neighbors remember seeing her before we got there."

He lifted his eyes to Marissa and her parents. "I'm truly sorry to be here under these circumstances. What does Kara drive and which direction would she have been coming? You said she'd planned to stop at her home before coming here?"

Marissa tapped her phone screen, presumably still trying to reach her sister. "She drives a Jeep like Mom and me. It's gunmetal gray. She bought it new last summer." She pressed the heel of one hand against her right eye. "She was hiking when I talked to her, too."

Her mother's jaw dropped. "You spoke to her? All I get are texts and little cartoon faces."

"I called her. She answered." Marissa set her phone on the counter. "I wish she'd just answer now."

Blake sent the make and model of Kara's car to his and West's teams. "Where was she hiking? We can contact gas stations between there and her home."

Marissa's face reddened. "I didn't ask."

Mrs. Lane let out a sharp breath and fixed Blake with a pointed stare. "She wouldn't be in the national park after what happened to Marissa, but there's no telling where she went. Now. Enough of this. Tell me what's going on and why my daughters are involved."

Mr. Lane crossed his arms and moved beside his wife.

Blake pushed his cup aside, shoring up the energy to lay it all out from the beginning. "It started for me about five years ago."

Forty-five minutes later, and seated around the living room with Marissa at his side, the story had been told, and the Lanes' questions had all been answered. Expect for the most important one. Where was Kara?

No one had seen her, and she hadn't answered her phone in two hours.

The realization that Kara wasn't coming arrived on the heels of a detailed description from Marissa about the last two days, including the strange luggage and ominous veil on Kara's porch.

Blake had let her take the lead on those events. They were hers to tell, personal in ways he wished they weren't. He'd filled in the larger aspects of the case and the role he'd played in it from the beginning.

Marissa pressed her hands to her face and stifled a

small sob, the first she'd allowed today, despite all she'd seen. To Blake's surprise, she leaned against his side and set her head against his shoulder.

Blake wrapped an arm around her and turned his mouth toward her hair. "We'll find her, I promise." He inhaled the soft scent of her shampoo and imagined idly waking up to it every morning. The notion took him off guard. Blake hadn't had thoughts like that in a very long time. Reasonably so. Still, he liked the idea of knowing Marissa long after this case was closed. He tipped his cheek to her head in wonder.

Her mother's eyebrows rose. Her father's eyes narrowed.

Blake was as shocked as they were by the bond forming between him and Marissa, but she needed his strength at the moment and he wasn't going to let her go for a few judgmental looks. He'd fix the mess he created five years ago and bring Kara home safely to the Lanes.

He wasn't the sort of man who broke promises.

BLAKE'S PHONE BUZZED for the thirtieth time in as many minutes. He'd received nearly nonstop texts and emails as they'd told her parents about Nash Barclay. Until now, Blake had shared the information. This time, though, he excused himself to take the call.

Marissa followed him through the house and watched from the front window as he paced the porch.

Her mom and dad moved in on her like bookends, each winding one arm across her back. "Do you trust him?" her mother asked. "Can he do the things he says? Bring Kara home? Catch this maniac?"

"Yes." Marissa felt the truth of the words in her core.

"We don't know where Kara is yet, but if we find out she's in trouble, then I trust Blake to bring her home."

Her dad harrumphed. "I think you'd be better off staying with us while he goes back into the field. You're our top priority. Let the sonofagun who's doing this be his. With you here, Agent Garrett can actively hunt this man."

Marissa's muscles bunched, the way they always seemed to at the thought of leaving Blake's side. Nash was probably watching them, even now, and staying together was smart. Besides, staying at her parents' home could put them in danger. She eased the sheer curtain aside with her fingertips and attempted to decode his muffled voice through the glass.

"He's too distracted," her dad continued. "Troubled. That's no way to lead an investigation."

Marissa gave her dad a sad smile. "You heard him. He blames himself for what happened to those women."

"And you," he said, frustration creeping into his voice. "This is happening to you, too, and your sister. This isn't about some strangers. My daughters are involved now." His voice cracked, and he turned away with a curse.

"I know," Marissa said. In fact, Nash was only after Kara because Marissa had gotten away. That was on her.

The front door opened, and Blake poked his head inside. "Time to go. They've got a lead on the truck."

Marissa drifted away from her parents. "And Kara?"

He shook his head infinitesimally. "Not yet."

"Don't go," her mom pleaded.

Marissa went back to squeeze her mom. "I'm going to be okay, and you can reach me anytime you want at the number I called from earlier, okay? I won't be alone. I've got Blake and his team, plus the sheriff and his deputies looking out for me."

Frustration burned in her dad's cheeks. His eyes were glossed with fear. "Anything happens to her, Garrett, and I'm holding you responsible."

Blake moved into their home, standing close and strong at Marissa's back. "Sir, you can rest assured that I will protect both your daughters at any cost."

Her dad's chin wobbled. "Do that."

Blake's hand was on Marissa's waist, turning her toward the waiting truck. "Time to go."

She took one last look at her parents, then let Blake lead her away. Frightened as she was for whatever lay ahead, Marissa was certain she could face it with Blake. She was also thankful for how shockingly natural it felt to lean on him for support. Yesterday, he'd been a stranger, and today he was her friend. More than that. Was there even a word to explain all Blake had become for her? The way he willingly shouldered her burdens? No one had ever done that, and Blake wasn't only strong when she was weak, but he was intuitive and kind. She trusted him to get her through whatever came next, and with a little luck that wouldn't involve any more bodies of Nash's victims.

Her baby sister's included.

Chapter Seven

Blake shifted into Drive and inched toward the road, discouraged by the Lanes' vast amount of land and lack of nosy neighbors. Hopefully his dad wouldn't be much longer. He'd responded affirmatively to Blake's text request for him to drop in on Marissa's family. Leaving the Lanes alone wasn't Blake's first choice, but he was needed at the station, and his dad was a solid stand-in. The town's former sheriff had training, experience and an innate compulsion to protect and serve. Exactly what the Lanes needed in a bodyguard.

Marissa turned weary eyes on Blake. "What happened? Where are we going?"

"Back to the sheriff's department. Cole says there's been an onslaught of sightings since the media picked up Nash's story, and they need help taking statements. He's pulled in a handful of volunteers meeting with folks in person, and West has Mom's quilting club manning the phones."

Marissa kneaded her hands on her lap. "You didn't get bad news about Kara then."

"No." Blake paused at the end of the Lanes' driveway. "I wouldn't keep news about your sister from you."

The street was quiet, no traffic, no vehicles parked

curbside. That was all good, but a jogger rounding the distant bend set off his internal radar. Blake added pressure to the brake, stopping to monitor the man. "You recognize him?"

"No." Marissa leaned forward. "He's too far away."

"All right." Blake freed his side arm and rested it against his thigh, then eased onto the road, moving them slowly in the man's direction.

His face was hidden beneath the shadow of a high-end hoodie. The brand symbol was printed in reflective silver across his chest. He had the posture of a runner. His strides were steady and evenly paced. He didn't appear to be out of breath or excessively distracted. No indication of unusual interest in the surrounding properties, specifically the Lanes'.

He looked into the truck's window and lifted a hand in greeting as they crawled past.

Marissa relaxed against the seatback. "It's not him."

Blake slid his trigger finger out of position, curling it back with the others. "Good." He reholstered his side-arm and tried to ignore the pinch of disappointment. If the jogger had been Nash, Blake could've watched his expression as he made him pay for everything he'd done.

Marissa twisted in her seat belt, straining to look through the back window. "Someone's turning onto my parents' drive." Panic raised her soft voice to a new octave. "I don't know that truck."

The small black Ford disappeared from sight in Blake's rearview as it motored toward the Lane home. "I asked my dad to stop by. See if there's anything he can do to curb their fears."

"You sent him to guard them?" Her voice quivered on the last word.

"Yeah." Blake took the next left and stole a look at her bruised face. His fingers tightened on the wheel. "It's precautionary. Nothing more."

Her shoulders relaxed by a small measure.

"How is it that you're so calm?" he asked. Most people he protected had at least one outburst by now, and their threats weren't always as immediate. He expected tears. Rage. Something. People in Marissa's position usually found someone in law enforcement to blame for their circumstance or a reason to complain about the way Blake handled the case. Instead, she'd been instrumental in every step of progress they'd made. "You were smart to think of the lake town." His stomach rolled at the memory of all those women being pulled ashore. "You did a mighty thing."

She pursed her lips and looked away, watching the view outside her window. "Lucky guess."

"And the calm front you're wearing?"

"A disguise." The inflection in her voice suggested she wasn't sure. "Maybe mind over matter. I don't know. I've always been pretty good at compartmentalizing in times of strife or challenge. I break big obstacles into smaller, more manageable tasks, then I handle the pieces one at a time. I use the same method to reach personal goals. It's how I got through college while working full-time, and pretty much how I learn to do anything. Horseback riding. Rock climbing. Nothing comes easily for me. I'm just a natural-born hardhead, and I guess I'm applying those strategies now. I hadn't really thought about it."

"Well, it's working."

"It's how I got away," she said, taking a look in his direction. "Now that you've mentioned it, focusing on the small picture is probably the only reason I'm not in the bathtub back at the hotel wound into the fetal position." She turned back to her window. "Besides, panic has never helped anyone accomplish anything, and Kara needs me to stay focused. I'll have a proper breakdown later. Privately."

Emotion welled in Blake's chest. He didn't like the thought of her alone and upset in a bathtub or anywhere else. "You can talk to me," he said, "if you want." He'd like that. Marissa was strong, maybe even the kind of woman who could handle life with someone like him, a man who spent his life in a perpetual state of danger. Most women either couldn't or wouldn't, but he suspected Marissa was fully capable of anything.

Truth be told, the Garrett boys' reputation for being a matched set of untamable playboys was deeply ironic. Even if they wanted to settle down, how would they find someone willing to endure life with a lawman? It was easier not to think past the third date than to haplessly search for someone who didn't exist.

"What?" Marissa asked.

Blake started. "What?"

"You shook your head. Was that because of what I said?"

"No."

Her gaze warmed the side of Blake's face.

He waited. Apparently, she had something to ask, and he knew firsthand how difficult it could be to put some things into words. Considering all that Marissa was going through, she deserved to take as long as she wanted. Personally, he found it easier to keep things to himself, speaking only when necessary and never longer than he had to. The practice had served him well as an agent. When he had something to say, his team knew it was worth hearing, and they listened.

Marissa lifted and dropped her hands against her thighs. "My dad thinks I should have stayed with him."

Blake's gaze jumped to hers, then back to the road. The uncertainty in her tone was a blow to his chest. Did she think her dad could keep her safer? Was that possible? Or was it something else? Maybe she wanted a break from Blake's constant presence and was too polite or overwhelmed to say so. He'd been enjoying their dynamic, but he hadn't considered how she might feel. Stifled. Smothered. Unhappy. He slowed the truck. "Nash is looking for you, so your presence will add to their risk. I won't stop you from going back, but I'm staying with you wherever you are." He could keep watch from outside if she needed a break from him.

Her blue eyes widened. "No. I want to stay with you."

His grip on the wheel loosened. "Okay." He turned back to the road with relief and nonsensical pride. "Then why'd you bring that up?"

She bit into the thick of her bottom lip and furrowed her brows. "My dad thinks I'm keeping you from playing a more active role in Nash's pursuit, and I think you should focus on the case and stop worrying so much about me. I don't want to be the thing that holds you back."

The sincerity in her eyes and voice sliced straight through him. He pulled the truck over and twisted on the seat to face her. "Your dad is wrong."

She wet her lips and waited, for what he wasn't sure, but the words from his head were piling on his tongue faster than he could sort them. "We're sticking together," he said. "If you're not with me, then I'll be worrying about you, and that's no good. My men can handle the field while I take point. We're doing it this way because it's the only way that makes sense, not because you're holding me back."

His shoulders sagged as he worked the truth over in his mind. He'd taken himself out of play on the most important case of his career. For years, he'd dreamed of tearing into Nash with his bare hands, and now he'd relegated himself to a desk. He'd done it so Marissa would be safer and feel less afraid.

Blake turned stiffly back to the wheel and angled the truck onto the road. The realization was a load of bricks dumped over him. Marissa's dad couldn't have been more wrong. Her presence wasn't compromising Blake's investigation. Meeting her had compromised *him*.

MARISSA GAWKED AT the line of people extended along the front of the sheriff's department.

Blake parked on the sidewalk outside the crowded lot. He circled the truck and opened the passenger door for her.

"Are these all volunteers?" she asked.

"Sadly, no." He offered her a hand out of the vehicle, then closed the door behind her. "Those are all witnesses." The sour look on his face said he didn't believe half of them had witnessed anything other than the morning newscast. "Excuse us," he said, escorting Marissa inside.

As promised, a gaggle of women her mom's age filled the seats at a row of newly erected tables near the far wall. Old-fashioned telephones with landlines had been set up in front of each seat like a telethon. "Is that your mom's quilting crew?"

He gave the group a peculiar look. "None other."

A pair of Shadow Point deputies conducted interviews at their desks, while an agent with a clipboard spoke to the next person in line.

Marissa looked to Blake. "Are all these people good news or bad?" It seemed the verdict could go either way.

Blake rubbed the stubble on his chin. "A little of both, I guess. Good news is that we know the newscast made an impression. Bad news is we have to sift through all the chaff to find the wheat, if there is any, and then hope we aren't too late to act on the intel."

Marissa's muscles tightened and her throat clogged at the implication. "I see."

Blake's hand found the small of her waist. He tipped his head downward, forming a private conversation space. "Hey. I didn't mean *too late for Kara*. I meant that if it takes us too long to learn Nash's whereabouts, and he moves on, then even the good information is still useless, and the efforts here are in vain. Timing's everything in cases like these."

Marissa smoothed sweat-slicked palms against her jeans. "Where should I sit?"

"Break room?" He lifted his brows in question.

Marissa cocked her head back. "If the local quilting crew can take calls, I can talk to the people in line. I know what he looks like. I'll know if someone really saw him."

Blake hunched lower into their private cocoon. His fingers relaxed, settling into the curve of her hip. "Listening to false reports can be infuriating. You don't have to put yourself through any unnecessary ordeals.

You've already done more than anyone expected." His voice was low and careful, evidently meant to protect her from potential trauma.

She formed her most pleading expression and matched his cautious tone. "You just said timing is everything, and I can help you get through this line of people waiting to be heard." Blake had made it clear that his job was to protect her, but her job was to protect Kara, and if listening to some cuckoo stories was the fastest way to get the facts, then that's what she would do.

Blake didn't answer. Instead, the two of them locked determined gazes.

"Hello." A woman's voice sounded nearby, and a shadow fell over them.

Blake turned his eyes on her without relaxing his stance. Mixed emotions flitted over his handsome face before he straightened. "Mama."

The woman's attention darted from her son's face to his hand on Marissa. "This must be Miss Lane." She squinted at the marks on Marissa's face before settling into a small smile. "I've heard a lot about you today. You're in good hands, now. I promise."

Blake dropped his hand away and rolled his shoulders back.

Marissa offered his mother a hand to shake. "It's nice to meet you. I hope Blake's said nice things."

"I haven't heard a thing from Blake." She gave him a curious look as she took Marissa's hand. "I've spoken to West, Cole and their father, but not Blake."

Marissa ignored the senseless tug of disappointment. Of course Blake hadn't rushed to call his mom and tell her all about her. This was business for him. Marissa, on the other hand, had too many emotions and not enough sleep.

Blake's chest expanded and fell in a silent sigh. "I've meant to call. I've had my hands full."

"Yes, I saw." She smiled warmly at Marissa. "Is there anything I can do to make you more comfortable?"

"I'm fine." She pushed her hand into her pocket hoping it wasn't too clammy during the shake. "I was just asking Blake where I should sit to help with witness statements."

A mix of surprise and pleasure flitted over his mother's face. She turned mischievous eyes on Blake. "Why don't I show her to the community bulletin table? No one's using that space." She started toward the far wall and motioned them to follow.

They stopped at a four-foot folding table. Blake stacked the piles of community event flyers in a heap and moved them to the center. He released a sharp whistle, and Marissa flinched.

A passing deputy stopped to look their way.

"Can I get two chairs over here?" Blake asked.

"Yes, sir."

Blake rested his fists on the wobbly structure. "This will work. I'll take one end and review reports while you talk to witnesses on the other."

Blake's mom shot him a look and returned to the table lined with middle-aged women and ringing phones.

"Great." Marissa fought a wave of nausea. She even needed a protective detail inside the sheriff's department. She was in so much danger that she was being escorted around town by a federal agent. Her breaths came short and hot.

"Marissa?" The warmth of Blake's body was back in her space. Scents of his cologne and aftershave were everywhere. "Are you okay? Remember. You don't have to do this."

She swallowed the lump of fear in her throat and nodded.

Did he really think someone might try to hurt her at the sheriff's department? Was Nash Barclay that bold?

The deputy arrived with a pair of folding chairs. "Anything else?" His gaze lingered on Marissa's swollen cheek.

She swept the length of her hair over one shoulder and let the thick strands form a veil over the marks on her fast-heating face.

"No." Blake took the chairs and opened them, setting one at each end of the table.

Her knees buckled easily as she fell onto the seat.

Blake watched with a heartbreaking expression.

She would've asked what he was thinking, but where would that get her? Blake wasn't exactly a sharer. If he wanted her to know something, he'd volunteer it. Besides, it wasn't as if that look had anything to do with her, and if it wasn't about her or her sister, then it wasn't any of Marissa's business.

She pulled her attention to the line at the door. "I'm going to collect my first witness." She had plenty of work to do and all night to speculate about the cause of Blake's troubled face.

"I'll be here if you need me."

If there was ever a Blake Garrett action figure, that would be the tagline.

Marissa faltered only steps from the double glass

doors. Her heart rate kicked up, and she felt the chill of fear roll down her spine. "Blake."

Amidst the white noise of traffic and soft rumble of the crowd, another sound trickled into her ears. "Blake?"

He was at her side in an instant. "What is it? What's wrong?" His hands were on her hips, his cautious blue eyes weighted with worry.

"I hear his song." She raised a finger to her lips. "Listen."

Blake jerked his head around to face the lot. "Stay here." His eyes widened, and he barreled outside with one hand on his sidearm.

Marissa clutched her chest and crept closer to the open door, torn between wanting the song to be in her imagination and not wanting to be crazy.

Silence fell over the witnesses as they moved against the building in an awkward wave, nudging one another and pointing as Blake rounded each car and surveyed their faces.

West and a pair of agents strode into the lot where Blake stood.

Nash's creepy chapel song blared from the pocket of a black hoodie.

A sheen of sweat formed on Marissa's brow. Nash's hot breath blew fresh on her face, as real and sickening as the day they'd met. She rubbed her heated cheeks and shuffled through the doors, desperate to know what would happen next.

Blake snaked an arm out and spun the person around.

The hood fell back to reveal a homeless-looking woman with ratty blond hair. "I saw him," she said with a grin.

Blake yanked an old CD player from the hoodie and jammed his finger against the power button, ending the awful tune.

Marissa's shoulders sagged with release.

"He gave me a coat, money, music and a sandwich," the woman said. "All I had to do was stand here until I got the chance to tell you." Her wide toothless smile sent tremors over Marissa's frame.

Didn't the woman understand her benefactor was a cold-blooded killer? Didn't she know? He could have hurt her. Drowned her.

A fat tear rolled over Marissa's cheek and she sucked in another ragged breath before turning back for the station. Surrounded by law enforcement, and Nash had still been right outside the glass double doors.

Marissa wasn't safe anywhere.

Chapter Eight

It was after four before Blake had a chance to check in with West again. He knocked on his brother's open office door and wedged himself in the threshold. "A line of witnesses around the building and no one saw anything."

West looked up from his file. "You mean no one except the nice homeless woman."

Blake rolled his back against the jamb and rested his head on the cool metal. "The one who spoke of Nash as if he were the Messiah, bringing her a warm jacket, music from her heyday and money?"

"That's the one."

Blake blew out a long breath. "What'd you do with her anyway?" The woman had been gone when he and two of his team members finished scouting the area for signs of Nash nearby.

"I took her statement then drove her to a shelter where she could get a hot meal and a warm bed for the night. I put the sweatshirt into evidence with the CD player and gave her a replacement with a little cash for her trouble."

"Great."

West hunched over his desk as Blake stepped into the hall. "Where are you going?"

"To find Marissa. I'm going to see if I can get her out of here. Get some food. Get some sleep." He'd tried to coax her away an hour ago, but she'd insisted on staying until the last witness was heard.

As if her day hadn't been bad enough, there wasn't any news about her sister, and Kara was still unaccounted for.

Blake returned to their table and slid copies of the most promising witness accounts into a manila envelope for later.

Marissa's head was on the desk, one cheek cradled in the crook of an arm. Her free hand dangled at her side. It would've been a peaceful scene, if the marks of a lunatic weren't displayed across her visible cheek and throat. She'd done her best to hide the evidence behind her hair as "witnesses" made their statements, but the fight was now lost to exhaustion.

"Ready?" he asked. Blake moved to her side, gut and jaw clenched as he imagined the terror and confusion when Nash attacked her. He'd come so close to losing her that day. Except that wasn't true. He hadn't known her then. So, how did a woman he'd met less than forty-eight hours ago feel like she'd been a part of his life forever?

"Marissa." He squatted beside her chair and used his most soothing voice so as not to startle her. "Marissa." His fingers ached to reach for hers, to twine them with his, or maybe just pull her into his arms. Blake let his lids fall shut for a quick internal curse. He could *admire* her without *touching* her. He needed to get thoughts of the latter out of his head.

He scanned the room for prying eyes and found plenty. His brother, West, was among the spectators.

Two members of his team turned away when they were caught staring, but West crossed his arms and rocked back on his heels, a distinct look of interest on his brow. Blake didn't like it. What did it mean? Surely it wasn't romantic interest in Marissa. He felt his scowl deepen. "Marissa," he repeated, slightly louder this time. "Hey." He lifted her hand in his and met West's gaze once more.

She stirred at his touch. "Hi." She blinked unwilling eyes. "I fell asleep." Her small hand turned against his, locking their palms.

A shock of victory blazed through him at her small acceptance. "Time to go back to the hotel. Can you walk or would you like me to carry you?" he teased, feeling much too light for the day they'd had.

"Both?" She squinted up at him with a lazy smile.

He tamped down a broad grin and stole another look around the room before leaning closer. "I wouldn't mind carrying you, but I think that might get some rumors started."

Across the room, West headed into his office with a smirk.

The haze of sleep fell from Marissa's face, and her smile went flat. "Sorry." She freed her hand from his and used it to straighten her hair and shirt, then to wipe the corners of her mouth and eyes.

Blake returned to his side of the desk, unsure what had happened in the moment between her dreamy hello and near-instant recoil. Had she initially mistaken him for someone else? Had he offended her by being overly playful on what must be the worst day of her life? He made a trip around the room while she got her bearings and gathered her things.

Once his team had their orders, he leaned against the doorjamb of West's office and waited for his brother to take notice. "We're headed out."

West dropped his pen onto the desk and stretched. "Sounds good. If I get anything substantial, I'll route it in your direction. You need anything else?"

Blake relaxed against the cool metal frame. "Besides Nash Barclay in cuffs or a pine box? Not really." And preferably neither. Nash didn't deserve the life sentence he'd get for his crimes. Hell, he didn't deserve a pine box. What he needed was to be kicked into the lake and assigned the same fate he'd given those poor women.

West interlocked his fingers behind his head, elbows pointed skyward. "We're going to get that done, brother."

Marissa appeared in Blake's periphery, emerging from the restroom and looking somewhat revived. Her hair was split into low pigtails and arranged over her shoulders, probably to mask the marks on her neck. Her cheeks were pale with exhaustion and a swath of loose hair fell over her bruised cheek. "Are we still leaving?" she asked, stopping inches from his side.

"Yeah." Blake shook the vengeful thoughts from his mind and refocused on the beauty before him. She needed words of hope and comfort, not a list of ways he wanted to see Nash punished. "West and I were just wrapping things up."

West rocked out of his office chair and moseyed to his filing cabinet. "I was just telling Blake that I'd pass along any information that seems solid. You guys both look like you could use some sleep." He opened the bottom drawer and tossed a duffel bag at Blake. "I got you something."

Blake pulled the zipper back. "What is it?"

"I brought you a couple changes of clothes and stopped for some basic bathroom stuff. I thought you could use it."

Blake had left Louisville the moment West called yesterday morning. He'd torn out of town with one thing on his mind, and it wasn't a change of clothes or toothpaste. "Thanks, man." Now, he wouldn't have to make a stop at the store for those things. He could stay on task.

Marissa fidgeted beside him, eyes fixed on West. "No word on my sister?"

West's gaze swept to Blake, then back to Marissa. He shifted his stance and seemed to weigh his words. "Nothing yet, but remember it's only been a few hours, and if not for the picture Blake found, a four-hour absence wouldn't be cause for concern. We're on guard because of it, but the truth is that photo wasn't taken today. Based on background structures and foliage, I'd say it's at least three months old and shot at a crowded event. The image could've been pulled off the internet. It could be nothing more than psychological warfare aimed at you or Blake. We just don't know."

Tears sprang to her eyes. "Of course."

Blake curved a protective arm over her shoulders and narrowed his eyes on West.

He shrugged. "What?"

Blake wasn't the only one in the family who was better off keeping his mouth shut. Psychological warfare? Way to make an already terrifying situation worse. He shook his head at West, and ushered Marissa toward the front door. Everything West had said was true, but Marissa wasn't a lawman. She hadn't signed up to live in this world, and she didn't need to hear all the ways a man like Nash Barclay was likely to taunt her.

He fought an unstoppable yawn. West was right about something else, too. Blake and Marissa both needed some sleep.

It was only a matter of time before Nash struck again.

THE DRIVE UP the mountain was beautiful. Blake took it slowly enough for Marissa to enjoy the gently swaying trees and familiar bends in the country road. The sky was a glorious mix of apricot and amber, bringing harmony and peace to her cluttered mind. She dragged a fingertip over the passenger window. "I appreciated what your brother said back there."

Blake slid his eyes her way, then back to the road. "Yeah?"

"It probably looked like he upset me, but that wasn't it. That was the first time anyone has reminded me that there are other alternatives to this for Kara. There's still a chance she's out there doing something completely normal with plans to go to Mom and Dad's place as soon as she finishes." Marissa just wished she could think of a few reasonable possibilities. "She's carefree to the extreme. Sometimes a little flighty, but she's smart. Just young. I said there was a fugitive in town. She wanted to hike, so she probably left town to do it. She's like that, and I like thinking that she'll still turn up today, happy and unscathed."

Wisps of feathery gray clouds flitted into view as the sun dipped lower on the horizon. Barely after five o'clock and the world was already tinted by night's approach. Whatever Kara was doing, she'd have to wrap it up soon. There was barely an hour of sunlight left.

Blake slowed for the turn at the resort entrance. "I used to ski here. The slopes are nice." He cruised between large stone columns marking the final leg to their room on the hill. "Do you ski?"

She made a show of rolling her eyes and gave a small smile. "Of course. I'm a little impressed that you do."

"I'm not any good."

Marissa doubted that. "Did you know there are some beautiful caves on this side of the mountain? I've actually spent a lot of time here spelunking. I've gotten some amazing photos for the effort."

"What kind of caves? Bear caves? Bats?"

"Probably both, but I didn't run into either. The caves' mouths are fairly well hidden by natural camouflage, jagged rocks, clay, that sort of thing. If you ever have time, you should see for yourself. The moss is gorgeous near the mouths, and the ecosystems inside are fascinating."

He squinted through the windshield, presumably trying to see a hidden cave from their position on the road. A moment later he passed the hotel without slowing.

"What are you doing?" Marissa twisted for a view of the lodge sign disappearing behind them.

"I'm buying you dinner." He pulled off at an old diner just outside of town. "Ever been here?"

"Not since I was young. We came here for ice cream after softball games."

Blake loped around the front of the truck and opened her door. "Us, too. Baseball, then peewee football. I think we were here every Friday night for a decade."

Marissa smiled, filled with nostalgia and renewed energy. "I bet we were here at the same time once or twice. I would've been in middle school during your last few visits." She liked knowing Blake was from her hometown. There was a certain camaraderie in loving the same beautiful place and sharing childhood memories of the same locations.

He escorted her inside with a hand on her back and chose a table against the far wall.

The place hadn't changed. It still smelled of stale black coffee and apple pie. Same brown tile flooring and cracked orange-vinyl seats. A bar ran the length of the narrow rectangular space.

Blake's gaze made a continuous circuit through the parking lot and across the front door as the waitress took their order. Chili and coffee for him, chicken noodle soup and water for Marissa. Though she doubted she could eat anything until she knew Kara was safe.

She checked the large oval clock above the counter. "Kara should be home anytime. There's nowhere to jog or hike after dark."

Blake shifted forward in his seat, sliding his arms over the table's cool surface, and clutched her trembling hands in his steady ones. He stroked the warm pads of his thumbs over her skin. "We'll find her." There was fierce promise in his eyes.

Marissa's worried mind began to settle, but her body was winding up once more.

Too soon, the waitress ferried drinks and meals to the table, effectively breaking Blake's spell. He pulled his hands back to his sides and dug into the chili with gusto.

Marissa rubbed her hands together beneath the table, wishing she could trade the noodle soup for more of Blake's confident touch.

He tapped a packet of crackers against the table, seemingly unaffected by the moment they'd shared.

"When we met, you asked me if I'd always wanted to be an agent. Have you always wanted to be a nature photographer?"

She dipped a spoon into her soup, dunking a thick homemade noodle and releasing rich buttery scents into the air. "No. I've always wanted to be a mom." Her cheeks heated immediately, wishing she hadn't been so transparent with a man who would probably never have the time or desire for a family of his own. Not that her life plans would matter to him. She stuffed the spoon into her mouth before she said anything else she'd regret.

"That so?" His cheek kicked up. "Would you just put the baby in one of those backpacks and hit the trails?"

"Probably." Marissa sighed. Leave it to him to make her feel completely normal about making family plans when she hadn't been on a date in over a year. "That's pretty much what my mom did with us. She never stopped moving, and neither have we. What about you? Did you always want to be a fed? You didn't answer me before."

Blake gave Marissa a long, careful look. "Nah. I wanted to be a judge. They have the real power to make things right. I can haul criminals in all day, but it's the judges who make the big decisions from there."

"But judges can't do any good if people like you don't risk everything to bring the bad guys in." She tipped her head, trying to understand how someone went from wanting a seat behind a bench to chasing murderers. "What happened?"

He shot a guilty glance her way. "I went as far as finishing law school before the allure of the badge pulled me in."

"Wow. That's a powerful pull."

"You have no idea."

She imagined doing all the work it must've taken to complete law school, only to drop it all and go another way. Maybe protect and serve really was in the Garrett DNA.

"Dumb, right? I gave up a comfortable future for half the pay and ten times the personal injury."

Marissa leveled him with her most sincere stare. "No. I think you're exactly where you're supposed to be, doing exactly what you were called to do. You can't put a price on that."

His lips parted and his brows raised. "You have no idea what that means coming from you."

She dipped her spoon into the steamy broth and smiled, enjoying the swell in her chest. Federal Agent Blake Garrett was nothing like any man she'd ever met. He had brains and brawn, as well as a little more of her heart every time they spoke.

MARISSA EXCUSED HERSELF to the ladies' room, and Blake angled in his seat, attempting to keep an eye on both the front door and rear hallway. Two bites of chili later, he gave up and headed for the ladies' room.

"Oh!" She started at the sight of him in the narrow hallway.

"Sorry." He dipped his head forward to rub the back of his neck. "I wasn't sure if there was a rear entrance, so I thought I should keep watch by the door."

Marissa looked strangely refreshed. She'd touched up her lip gloss and the baby hairs near her temple were speckled with tiny droplets of water.

She tucked a long blond strand behind one ear and

smiled shyly. "I splashed some water on my face." Her cheeks grew ruddy with the admission. "I looked awful."

Blake doubted that Marissa had ever looked awful in her life. He watched with rapt attention as a small drop followed the curve of her jaw and traveled the length of her slender neck. Whatever she'd said next was lost to the thrumming in his chest. Blake drank her in with greedy eyes, from the flush of her skin to the gentle sway of her back. Marissa was breath-taking.

She moved slowly forward in the cramped space, stopping only when the toes of her shoes bumped his. "Please quit looking at me like I'm going to break."

"I don't think you're going to break." He raised his hand carefully, never taking his eyes off hers, allowing her every opportunity to back away like she had at the station when she woke. He was tired of fighting the urge to be closer to her, and she needed to know what she was doing to him. Her rejection would set him straight. It would put these ridiculous feelings to rest so he could start thinking of ways to keep her safe instead of ways to keep her near.

Her lids fell shut as the backs of his fingertips reached her cheek. He stroked the tender curve of her jaw before cupping it in both his palms.

The ache in his belly grew as he struggled to understand this thing that had taken hold of him from the moment she'd walked into his life.

Her lips parted on an intake of breath, and he strained against the need to taste them. He fought the crackling electricity coursing over his skin from hers, and he forced himself to think of the *right* thing. *For Marissa.*

"Blake." Her eyes eased open. Were they heavy with desire? Or was he merely hoping?

She lifted her hands to his chest, sliding them gently upward to his shoulders.

The buzz of his phone nearly killed him.

She dropped her forehead against his chest and exhaled a gush of warm breath. "Sorry."

"No." Blake glared at the blasted phone, his heart beating like horses' hooves against his ribs. "Do not be sorry." He lifted a finger as he studied the phone's small screen, then raised apologetic eyes to hers. "The coroner has preliminary findings."

"Okay." She inhaled deeply and squared her shoulders. "Let's go."

THE TRIP TO the coroner's office was quiet. He couldn't say where Marissa's thoughts were, but his were back at the restaurant with her hands winding over his shoulders.

"Garrett." An elderly man in a white lab coat greeted him at the front desk. "Your dad and I used to do this." He motioned between them.

Blake tried to smile, but failed. What he needed now were facts. Niceties could come later when he knew all there was to know about Nash's victims. "What do you have?"

"We've confirmed the identities of five of the six victims." He handed Blake a file folder. "I've put copies of all our preliminary data in there for you."

Blake scanned the pages. Four women were the victims whose families Blake had gotten to know in the course of his investigation. West had correctly identified the fifth victim as a recently missing jogger at the county line. "What about the woman who'd been down there longest?"

"That will take a while longer. She was in…" the man cast his gaze to Marissa before reaffixing it to Blake, "worse shape."

Blake flipped between the listed causes of death. "The victims were all drowned."

"Yes, that's correct."

Ice slid through Blake's veins. He'd wrongly assumed that Nash had killed the women elsewhere and dragged them to their watery graves afterward. He winced at the memory of scuba weights near the tree where Nash and Marissa had fought. Nash would have drowned Marissa in the lake and dressed her there, along the bank or underwater. So, the veil left on her bed was strictly meant to antagonize her after she'd gotten away. Just like the suitcases left on her sister's porch. Nash wanted to keep her afraid. Break her focus. Make her easier prey.

A sudden cacophony blasted outside the building. Marissa jumped at Blake's side, curling against him for safety.

"It's my truck alarm." He smoothed a palm down the length of her hair and back before peeling her away. He pointed at the man. "Take her into your office and lock the door."

Blake eased into the dark lot, gun drawn. The night was clear, and his truck undamaged, but a large white envelope was seated on his windshield. The sight of it turned Blake's stomach. Five small words were formed in soaking red ink.

A gift for the bride.

Chapter Nine

Blake's team and West's deputies filled the small sitting room at the hotel. The contents of the mysterious envelope were spread throughout the room, some on the small table, others pinned to a corkboard borrowed from the sheriff's department. The rest moved hand to hand through the room for inspection.

Together the stack of glossy surveillance photos was a quarter-inch thick, and Marissa was centered in each frame.

West sat on the edge of the sleeper sofa, elbows pressed against his knees. "He left them on your windshield?"

"Yep." Blake paced the patterned commercial carpeting, struggling for focus, the dangerous heat of vengeance roiling in his gut. "Set off my truck's alarm to make sure I knew he was there."

Marissa sat with West on the sofa, feet tucked beneath her. "They're just like the photo that someone took of Kara."

Blake ground his teeth. "Not someone. Nash." He swore before turning back to his brother. "He's practically following me around and I can't find him."

West kneaded his hands where they hung between

his knees. "At least tell me there were surveillance cameras where you parked."

Blake stopped to glare. The fire in his belly was nearly painful. "He looked right into the camera while he made the delivery."

"So it's on tape," West said. "That's good."

Blake leaned against the wall and tipped forward at the waist. He'd spent years thinking he was after an unhinged psychopath, but that wasn't who Nash was. The dresses. The underwater chapel. Months of dedicated stalking. Blake had him all wrong. Nash was a sociopath. Cold and calculating. Biding his time. Planning his kills. Probably enjoying the hunt as much as the attack.

"I found something else after you left the station," West said. "I pulled the missing person report on the woman abducted earlier this month. It struck me as inconsistent that he'd taken months between the other kills, then after five years off, he made two back-to-back attacks." He danced his thumbs over the screen of his phone.

Blake's cell phone buzzed on the table. He flipped it around to face him and typed in the access code.

It was a photo of the last woman to be pulled from the lake. She looked like Marissa. Marissa had said so herself.

Marissa peered at West's phone and made a strange gurgling sound. "I think I'm going to be sick."

In the photo, the woman was wearing the same fitted running gear Marissa had worn the morning of her attack.

Blake swallowed a mouthful of bile. Nash had mistaken her for Marissa. "He'd been expecting Marissa on that towpath."

West nodded. "I think so. The fitness app on Marissa's phone showed a pattern of morning trips to that park. Typically, Tuesday mornings, the same day of the week that this woman went missing."

Marissa's face paled impossibly further. "Sometimes, I skip my morning jog to meet Kara for breakfast. It's kind of our thing. Very impromptu. I'm always busy, and she slows me down with an unexpected invitation. I never say no." Until today. A tear rolled onto her cheek and she quickly swiped it away. "That woman is dead because of me?"

"No." Blake and West growled the answer.

Marissa scoffed. "He came for me. I wasn't there, and this poor woman has my taste in clothes." A painful wedge formed in her throat. "She was just living her life."

West angled on the couch to face her. "So were you. You didn't know you were being watched. How could you? No one knew."

The truth was another hot poker to Blake's gut. He should've known. He'd become lax this year. Assuming Nash was either dead or out of the country after such a long hiatus. He'd slowly stopped wasting federal time and money chasing vapor.

Maybe that was why Nash got back into the game.

Could he have known that Blake had moved on? Would Nash start killing again to regain Blake's attention?

Had he been watching Blake all this time?

MARISSA LEANED ON her forearms, trying to remain calm. Her heart sprinted and her chest heaved, desperate for more air than her lungs could find. She concentrated on breathing. Slow and steady. *This is what Nash wants*, she chided internally. *He wants you in an emotional frenzy.* Hadn't West said as much at the station? *Psychological warfare.*

Well, it was working.

The jogger had been murdered because of her. Her sister had possibly been abducted because of her.

It had to stop. "Use me as bait."

The men fell silent. She hadn't kept up with their conversation, but their voices were suddenly still.

She released an uneasy breath and levered herself upright. "Nash wants me, so let him have me."

Blake's eyes bulged briefly before narrowing into slits. "Absolutely not."

West leaned slightly forward, catching her eye. "It's a noble thought, but we aren't in the business of putting people in danger."

"Or giving animals like Nash Barclay exactly what they want," Blake barked.

Marissa pushed onto shaky legs and moved toward him. "So, don't give him what he wants." She turned to West. "Protect me." That covered both their arguments. "Use me to save my sister."

West groaned. "We don't know if he—"

She waved her hand to stop him. "Then use me to save the next lady." She turned back to Blake's glaring eyes. "There will always be a next victim unless you stop him."

"No."

"Blake."

"I said no." His words sliced through her.

She wouldn't win this battle. "Then there must be another way," she pleaded. "So, what is it? Because it's certainly not to sit in this room and wait for his next move. His next move could be murder." She folded her arms, hoping to look resolute and hating the hint of whine in her voice.

Blake looked past her to his brother. "What do you make of the photos? What's the point? Why deliver them now?"

Marissa wrapped thin arms around her middle. "He's been watching me for months. Some of those photos were taken in the spring."

Blake ran a comforting palm down her back.

"Can we be sure I'm the only one under surveillance?" she asked. "Is there a chance it wasn't a case of mistaken identity with the other jogger?"

The more Blake learned about Nash, the less mistakes seemed like his thing, but anything was possible. "We'll know soon."

"How?" Her voice ratcheted up, drawing the attention of several men and women in quiet discussion. "When someone else is dead?"

"No." West shook his head. "We've got no evidence to suggest he's out randomly hunting women. He's taken six in total. He's practiced. Patient and methodical. Right now, I think he's acting out on his weird cops-and-robbers fantasy with Blake."

Marissa's gaze darted up to meet Blake's.

"Nash stopped killing while I was hunting him. I lost focus on him, and he started again. I think that's why."

Marissa's heart ached. Blaming himself wasn't helping anything, but she certainly understood the inclination for self-blame. After all, she was the crowned queen of that response.

"We found the other victims," West said. "That was a

huge move in the right direction, and the ME will have more details for us to go on soon." He cast a promising look at Marissa. "We're going to get Nash before he takes anyone else."

The room grunted in agreement around them.

She moved back to her place on the couch, stomach sinking further at the memory of the photos' invasive content. Marissa on a jog. Marissa at a stoplight. Buying groceries. Pumping gas. Hanging clothes on a line. She'd been so naive and vulnerable at home, rocking on the back porch while being spied on by a serial killer. Why hadn't he just taken her then? Why hadn't she sensed him there? Watching her. *Be aware. Know who's near. Look for danger.* Her dad had spent twenty-six years drilling those lessons into her head, but she'd learned nothing.

Images of the attack screamed to mind, as bright and vivid as the moments they'd happened. He'd stalked her for months, but he'd stood out like a grizzly bear that morning. He'd dressed in the wrong clothes. Smelled like cigarettes and even spoken to her. "He made sure I saw him." Her hands grew clammy with the thought. "He could've sneaked up on me, but he made me uncomfortable on purpose." He'd wanted her to be afraid. He'd probably even counted on her not going straight to her car. If he'd followed her all those months, he had to have known she wouldn't leave the forest without a moment of reflection. She was so predictable.

Moments later, the group seemed to stand in unison and the little room bustled to life as men and women sprang toward the door with purpose.

Blake headed for her room with the little black duffel West had given him. He returned several minutes later in a T-shirt announcing Property of Cade County Sheriff's Department across the chest.

West snickered. "Looking good, Garrett."

Blake dropped his beaded chain and FBI badge over his head and screwed a black ball cap over damp, mussed hair. "No sense in aiming for sheriff, that was always in your cards."

"What I heard was that you couldn't compete."

Blake smiled at his brother with warmth and pride. The quick shower had done him well.

Marissa's earlier shower had only reminded her how sore her muscles were from yesterday's fight.

Blake braced broad hands over narrow hips and locked sharp blue eyes on her. "Ready?"

"What?" She stood, unsure why. What had she missed?

Worry etched through his brow. "I want to make another pass by Kara's place. I'd actually like to have a look inside this time. I don't suppose you or your parents have a spare key?"

"I do. At home." Her tummy bottomed out at the thought of returning to her home at night.

Blake grabbed his truck keys from the table. "We'll pick up the key on our way to Kara's. West and Cole will talk to any of her neighbors who weren't home when Cole made his rounds earlier."

"Okay." Marissa forced her body forward, collecting her phone and a light jacket from the bedroom before heading for the door.

With any luck, they'd find Kara's home just as they left it. Safe and secure. No signs of invasion. With lots of luck, they'd find Kara asleep on the couch, wiped out after a long hike and hot shower. Marissa would be content to find her at the local hospital with a twisted ankle or some other non-life- threatening injury.

Marissa strode through the hotel door with renewed hope and purpose. Maybe this was all a misunderstanding with Kara. Maybe she'd lost her phone or the battery was dead. "Here." She placed her house key in Blake's hand. "I assume you plan to go in first."

"I do." He opened his passenger door and helped her inside.

"Kara's key is on the rack in the kitchen. It's the one with the four-leaf-clover chain." She tapped the dome on his ceiling with two fingers. "Your interior light's broken."

"Disabled." He shifted into Reverse and headed away from the hotel.

"Why?"

"Stealth. Vehicles are big and loud enough without flashing a light every time I climb in or out after nightfall."

Marissa pulled her attention back to the road, unsure if the explanation was frightening or genius, and hoping there would be no need for stealth tonight.

Chapter Ten

Things were profoundly quiet outside Marissa's home. The view was exactly as she'd expected, the same one she'd enjoyed most nights for many years. An owl cocked its head at the truck as Blake eased it onto the end of her driveway. Behind the owl, soft gray clouds raced past the harvest moon, driven by the gentle breeze that worked the trees along her property line. Her fingers stretched and curled on her lap, eager to capture the shot on film, and missing her camera more than ever. A rush of fallen leaves tumbled across her lawn and adhered themselves to the narrow trunk of a baby evergreen. This night was made for bonfires and friends with spiked apple cider. Anything other than hunting a killer.

Blake shifted into Park and snuffed the headlights.

"What's wrong?" she asked. Her home was another hundred feet up the driveway, and she longed to see that it was okay. A thousand warm memories filled those walls and the acres around them. She'd give just about anything to go inside, curl beneath her grandma's quilt by the fire and pretend the last two days were nothing more than a nightmare. Sadly, her old normal was her new fantasy. Mornings of scrambling eggs in the kitchen without feeling stalked were probably gone forever, but if that was all she lost to Nash, she'd count it as a win.

His posture was rigid at her side, eyes focused and square jaw clenched.

"I thought we were in a hurry to grab the key and get to Kara's?" she asked.

He pulled his phone from the cup holder and typed something against the screen. "Your porch light is out."

"So?" She eyeballed the shadows cast from her roof over the front yard. "I haven't been home. No one was here to turn it on."

He finished prodding his phone and set the device in his cup holder. "I turned it on when we left."

Marissa pulled her attention back to Blake. "You think Nash came back here?" The photo he'd taken of her and Blake came to mind. "He was here while we were. You think he stuck around and took the bulb after we left."

"Maybe, but why?" Blake narrowed his eyes on her home. "I don't know what to expect from him anymore, which, I suppose, is exactly what he wants." He scooped her house key from the cup holder and stuffed it into the pocket of his pants.

"Are you worried?" It was hard to get a read on him when he wore that blank agent expression.

"No." He flicked his gaze to the side-view mirror outside his door. "I'm pissed."

Right. She was the worrier. He was the warrior.

The sheriff's cruiser rolled into view beside them, the headlights flashing over her home.

A great gasp tore through Marissa's chest. A figure dressed in white swung from her porch rafters. She shut her eyes shut and prayed, shamelessly, that it wasn't her sister.

BLAKE CLIMBED OUT like a ghost and shut the door behind him. He gave her a sour look and pointed through the glass. As if she needed to be warned not to follow. As if she hadn't seen enough murder victims to last her ten lifetimes.

Cole opened the cruiser's passenger door and raised a massive black flashlight at the figure. Wind whipped the thing into a near horizontal position, and Marissa let out a cry of relief. Whatever was wearing the gown wasn't human. No one weighed so little that they would float like that, not even in the force of a brewing storm.

The Garretts met in the beams of the sheriff's headlights. Together they charged toward the gown and her mysteriously darkened home. West and Blake went inside, flipping the porch light on behind them.

Cole prodded the gown as it flipped and twisted in the wind, partially filled by what now appeared to be an inflatable doll in a long blond wig.

Marissa's home illuminated room-by-room. Living room. Kitchen, bedroom, bedroom, back porch. She winced with each new light, praying that Blake was safe and Nash wasn't waiting there to surprise him.

Cole stayed in near-constant motion, patrolling the perimeter, until the others returned to view. Their silhouettes were relaxed now, knees no longer locked, shoulders slack. They'd even removed their right palms from the butts of their weapons.

Marissa strained to hear them, but they were too far away, and the winds were gaining strength, getting louder by the gust.

A tornado of emotion built in Marissa's empty stomach. If the coast was all clear, and the woman in white was only a doll, then why was she still locked in the truck? Why hadn't she been invited to join them in whatever they were discussing?"

Clouds passed over the moon, casting the men into darkness. She could see them if she squinted, but only barely. Marissa craned her neck to curse the clouds.

The loaner phone buzzed in her pocket. She freed the tiny device and checked the caller ID. Her parents' home number glowed on the screen. "Hi, Mom," she answered.

"Hi." Her mother's voice was soft. Controlled. Marissa recognized the tone immediately. She was being brave. It was the same tone she used when anyone was sick or hurt. "I'm sorry to call again. I just wanted to know you're still okay."

Marissa smiled against the receiver, hoping her effort carried though the line. "I'm good. I promise. Very safe. I'm constantly surrounded by lawmen who are all about my well-being." She forced a nervous laugh. At the moment, at least three of them were intentionally leaving her out of their conversation, but she doubted that news would make her mom feel any better. It was certainly frustrating the daylights out of Marissa. "Any word from Kara?" she asked, redirecting her thoughts. She knew the answer already, of course. If her mom had any news about Kara, she would have led with that.

"No, but I missed a call earlier. I didn't recognize the number, and there was no message. I didn't call back. Do you think I should have?"

Marissa fiddled idly with her jacket's zipper. "Probably not. If it was Kara, I think she would've left a message or kept calling until you answered." Or called Marissa. "You should tell Mr. Garrett. See what he thinks."

"Okay. I will." Her mom's voice wavered. "I made up your old room today. In case you change your mind about staying with us."

"Mom."

"I know." She sniffled. "Our old Sheriff Garrett showed up after you left. He came out of retirement for this."

"Hey," Marissa interrupted. "We're going to get through this. We'll be stronger for it."

Her mom didn't respond.

Marissa imagined her mother pressing tear-soaked tissues to her eyes and sobbing silently behind a palm. "Where's Mr. Garrett now?"

"Outside. He's been patrolling the grounds with your father ever since."

Leaving her alone. She glared at the younger Garretts in her driveway, who were doing the same thing to her.

"I'm sorry you're alone," she told her mom. More than that, Marissa was sorry she couldn't be there to support and comfort her somehow. "I'd be with you if I could."

"I know." Her mom's careful composure was gone. "Where is your sister?" She choked the words out on a whisper. Her heartbreak split Marissa's chest in two.

"We'll find her."

Her mom's sobs flowed freely now.

Marissa would have given anything to hold her. To shoulder the burden. Her mother had lost hope, and she needed something to hold onto. "We're at my house, collecting the key to Kara's place. Blake says the house is all clear, and we're headed to Kara's next. I'm hoping she wrote her agenda on the calendar or made some other note about what she planned to do today. At least then Blake's team will know where to begin looking. I'll tell you what we find at Kara's as soon as we're finished there."

Marissa disconnected and tucked the phone back into her pocket. She'd thought yesterday was long, but today was officially worse. The hanging doll was just another attempt to scare and misdirect them, and frankly, Marissa was tired of Nash's games. It was time to get moving. Something at Kara's could be the clue they needed to bring her home.

Outside her window, growing winds bent the treetops and pushed little clouds faster through the sky. A storm was bad news, especially if Kara was still outside somewhere. Autumn rains meant plummeting temperatures, and Kara had probably dressed in a T-shirt and pants when she left home this morning.

She reached for the door handle and froze. A shadow passed over the rearview mirror, and Marissa's senses went on high alert. She spun on her seat, twisting for a better view of the entire scene outside. She found nothing but a sheriff's cruiser and the three men still engrossed in a private meeting on her lawn. Wind whipped and pulled the fabric of their pants and jackets. The Garretts took a few lazy steps in her direction before stopping again to look back at her house.

The hairs on Marissa's neck tingled and stood at attention. A sense of urgency squeezed her heart and propelled her to act. She gripped the handle on her door and shored up her nerve, suddenly preferring to be a lot closer to the guys with guns and badges. Gooseflesh crawled up her spine as she cracked open the door and planted her feet firmly in the gravel.

The air was instantly pressed from her lungs with

one powerful blow. A thick hairy arm wound over her rib cage and meaty fingers dug into the flesh of her side. A broad and calloused palm scraped against the cuts and bruises on her jaw and cheek, fingers clenching across her mouth. The stench of cigarettes overcame her.

Tears blurred her burning eyes as the unseen assailant dragged her into the shadows, her body crushed against his. Her feet twisted and flailed, unable to find purchase against her assailant's feet or shins. Her lungs burned with an increasing lack of oxygen as his palm flattened her nose and lips.

Not today, she screamed internally. *Not until I find my sister.*

Marissa's muscles tensed at the thought, and panic bled into purpose. She clutched his wrists in a powerful burst of adrenaline and bent them sharply into her abdomen and jaw until his hands shifted and his fingers loosened their grip. Marissa sucked in a fresh gulp of oxygen and screamed against his palm as he struggled to reposition his hold on her. She dug her toes into the gravel and kicked a cloud of stones at Blake's truck.

"Freeze!" Blake's strong voice bellowed through the night.

A trio of armed Garretts appeared in a flash of lightning, guns drawn. The brothers marched forward in a tight V formation. "Back away from her, Nash," Blake commanded. There was venom in his tone and vengeance in his eyes. "This is between you and me."

"And Miss Lane," Nash cooed, digging his fingers deeper into her skin.

The rebuttal from Blake's mouth was fierce and foul. He widened his stance just twenty feet away and lifted his gun higher. "You aren't getting away this time."

Marissa stopped fighting and tried to make herself smaller in case Blake planned to shoot him.

"That's a good girl," Nash whispered in her ear. A wave of stinky breath washed over her, souring her stomach and weakening her knees. "Make him fight for you," he said. "The agent thinks you're his, but he can't fight destiny forever." He pressed his hot mouth against the tender skin along the back of her neck before curling his fingers deep into her hair and sending her headfirst into Blake's tailgate.

The loud smack of her forehead on metal reverberated through her bones before the world went black.

Chapter Eleven

Blake's heart stopped.

Marissa's head snapped back, and her body went limp. She hit the ground in a heap.

Nash was already on the move, fleeing the scene, making his getaway.

"No!" Blake skidded in the gravel to her side. Nash could have broken her neck. She could already be gone. "Marissa!"

Footfalls pounded the earth behind him, arriving in the next heartbeat. "I've got her," Cole announced, falling onto his knees beside Blake. "Go on." His hands were already on her neck, counting her pulse.

West's silhouette raced into the woods across the street, gun drawn.

"Go," Cole insisted. "Cover West. I've got this."

Reality slapped back into focus and Blake was in motion. *Cover West.* Yeah, right. Nash was all Blake's and after what he'd done to Marissa, Blake would be damn sure he paid slowly.

He launched off the street and into the woods at a sprint, quickly catching and passing his brother.

Nash fled through the trees and underbrush ahead of them, cutting a wide path and leaving a trail impossible to miss. He was difficult to see in the darkness, dressed in black, a hoodie pulled over his head, but the sound of snapping twigs and kicked stones was a beacon guiding Blake straight to him. His ragged breathing was a bonus.

Nash was getting tired.

Blake, on the other hand, could run another half mile without slowing down, and ten miles after that before his legs grew spongy. He ran every day. Long distance. The time alone helped him think. It gave him a private place to plot Nash's demise. Now, his dreams were coming true.

Images of Marissa's bruised face challenged his concentration. The sound of her head against his tailgate. The fear in her eyes as Nash gripped her battered face in one palm and whispered into her ear. What had he said?

The overwhelming need to turn back and stand guard until the ambulance came nearly staunched his momentum. His mind and his gut were torn in two. The emotion. The confusion. These were unlike his drive to protect the public, this was like nothing he'd experienced before. It was ferocity. It was painful. And it was, he realized, a standoff between the need to stop Nash and the instinct to guard what was *his*.

For a moment, Blake had thought he'd won. He thought it was stupidity and brazen overconfidence that had brought Nash to him, but Blake was wrong. Nash came to show Blake that he could. He could get to Marissa anywhere and beat Blake anytime.

Blake slowed his pace, and his senses sharpened. Only two sets of footfalls remained. His and West's behind him. No Nash. Based on his earlier panting, Nash must've stopped to catch his breath and hide.

Blake raised a hand to alert West, and soon his footfalls ground to a halt beside Blake. He motioned his brother to the east, then Blake turned in the opposite direction. Together, they could silently cover more ground.

The night was dark, despite the harvest moon. Gathering clouds and evergreens blocked the starry sky. Incessant winds and the rushing branch of a nearby river easily masked the huffing of Nash's breath, but he was winded, and no doubt hiding, waiting for his chance to move.

Blake wouldn't give him that chance.

A lifetime of hunting and tracking in Cade County had made Blake an apparition in the woods. Nash wouldn't touch Marissa again. Right or wrong, Blake would kill that sonofabitch the moment he had a chance.

The snapping of a nearby limb reached his ears, and Blake spun to face the sound. A shadow sprinted toward the river, and Blake pounced after it, leaping easily over fallen logs and through piles of leaves. "Freeze!" he hollered.

The panting figure continued a bumbling path toward the rushing water just beyond the cliff's edge.

Blake gained on him by the second, hope and victory rising in his chest. Maybe he wouldn't have to kill him. Maybe he could haul Nash's sorry ass back to Marissa and let her even the score. *As soon as she wakes up.* He ground his teeth at the thought. No. This time it was Nash who would die. "Stop!" he boomed. "Or I will shoot you."

Nash skidded to a stop at the cliff's edge. There was nowhere to go but down, and if Blake remembered correctly, there was a sizeable drop on this side of the water.

Blake's eyes narrowed, moving in on Nash in small, silent strides, the way he had five years before. His trigger finger begged him to shoot and worry about the repercussions and paperwork later. Until West arrived, there were no witnesses.

Nash raised shadowy arms in surrender. "Please, don't shoot."

The plea stalled Blake's homicidal thoughts, reminding him Nash was the cold-blooded killer. Blake was the lawman. "Get on the ground. Put your hands behind your back," he barked. On his next step, Blake's boot caught on something hidden in the leaves and his heart seized. A booby-trap. The taut string pulled against his laces, and Blake launched himself away on instinct, hoping it was far enough to survive whatever came next. A ground-shaking boom blasted through the night air, rattling his teeth and jarring his bones. He crashed against the forest floor, sending shock waves of pain through his head and back. A mass of dirt and fallen limbs thundered down on him.

He wrangled his gun into position in case the attack wasn't over. The floating dust and debris complicated his newly blurred vision. The stench of tar burnt his nose.

Nash smiled. His lips moved, and he turned for the water.

Blake squeezed the trigger, getting off two shaky, half-blinded shots before the splash from Nash's plummet reached his ringing ears.

West skidded into view, giving the blast zone a wide berth. His normally tanned face was whiter than the wedding gown on Marissa's porch. "Blake!" Terror shredded his voice, raising it by octaves. "Are you hurt?" His words were garbled and hollow, but Blake raised his gun overhead and rolled back against the ground.

His brother appeared again, this time at his side peering down. "Don't move. Medics are on the way."

"Nah." He lowered his gun and reached for West's hand. "Help me up."

West hesitated before obliging his big brother. "What the hell happened?"

"The bastard set a trap. I tripped over the wire." He worked his aching joints to assess the damage. "I thought he was hiding, but he was leading me here. Now I can't decide if the strung-up doll was a setup for abducting Marissa, or if the attempted abduction was a setup to get me out here."

West dusted dirt and leaves from Blake's back and shoulders. "Did you hit him?"

"I don't know."

They inched toward the place where Nash had last stood and peered over the cliff into the dark waters below.

Sirens cried and wailed in the distance, turning Blake back in the direction he'd come. The cavalry had arrived.

"Go," West advised. "Get checked out. You're not bleeding, but that doesn't mean you aren't hurt. I've got this. My deputies are already on the way."

Blake hesitated, once again torn between his job and his heart. "There was C4 in that blast. I could smell it."

"You're lucky to be alive. Just go."

Blake swallowed painfully, and stretched his shaking limbs. "Well, watch your step."

West snorted. "I've got this. Take care of yourself and your girl."

Blake jerked into an uncomfortable jog, heart and mind racing along with his pace. It was Marissa's face he'd seen when the world blew up around him, and hers was the only one he wanted to see now. West was right. Blake couldn't be sure when it had happened or what Marissa would think of it, but the deal had been sealed in his mind. She was his girl. His to defend and protect, yes, but so much more if she'd let him.

Fierce determination powered his feet along faster. Toward the incoming sirens, the flashing lights, and Marissa. The thief who'd popped into his life, knocked him sideways and stolen his heart.

COLE'S FACE BLURRED into Marissa's view. The warmth of his body was everywhere, and the look on his face was wildly expectant.

"Ow," she groaned the first thing that came to mind. Her head and neck ached and throbbed as she struggled to recall why she was in Cole's arms instead of Blake's. And why they seemed to be sitting on the street outside her home.

He released her with one hand and raised two digits in the air like a peace sign. "How many fingers am I holding up?"

She swatted his hand away. "Why am I on your lap?" Why were they alone on the ground? Her mental wheels spun, getting nowhere.

A bright light beamed into her eyes, sending shards of pain through her skull.

She whacked blindly at the source. "What is wrong with you?"

Cole chuckled, bouncing her gently along with him. "Nothing's wrong with me. I'm trying to figure out what's wrong with you."

"What's wrong with me?" she asked.

His warm expression dimmed. "You hit your head."

"Oh." A groggy sensation crept through her bones. How had she hit her head?

"Stop fighting, and let me evaluate your injuries," Cole said, flipping the light into view again. "You could have a concussion."

She dropped her hands to her lap. "Why aren't you a doctor?" she asked. "I remember hearing you went to medical school. What happened?"

His brows furrowed, and he averted his gaze for a long beat, as if he didn't want to answer. "That's expensive," he said finally, "and a lot more people die. I like being the hero."

She rolled her eyes and winced. "Ow."

Cole pocketed the little light. "Any nausea?"

Marissa struggled upright, easing herself away from him. "No, but my ears are ringing."

"I think that's the ambulance."

Her body tensed. The sound of metal on bone echoed through her mind. "Nash." He'd gotten to her again. She covered her mouth. There was the nausea. "Blake!" She twisted in search of him, rocking onto her knees and forcing her shaky body upright. "Holy." She pressed a hand to her head and bent forward at the waist, fighting the sickness and pain coursing through her.

"He went after Nash." Cole rose to place a steadying hand on her back.

"Where?" She lifted her face and squinted into the dark woods.

"I think you'd better sit back down."

"Where are they?" she demanded.

Cole stepped into her view. He frowned, all pretense of congeniality gone. "You were injured, and Nash ran. My brothers gave chase. You need to stay still until the ambulance gets here."

An explosion rocked the world. Marissa sucked air and blinked through a painful bout of panic. "What was that?"

Two gunshots echoed through the night before Cole could answer.

Cole went rigid. His expression fell blank.

Marissa's stomach dropped and a whimper slipped from her lips. Tears streamed over her burning cheeks. She swallowed bile and forced five terrifying words from her mouth. "Did Nash have a gun?" She recalled his fingers mashed against her jaw. His arm around her ribs. But was he armed? Had there been a firearm under his coat? Pressed to her back?

Cole pulled her into his arms. "I don't know." The thread of worry in his voice betrayed his cool facade.

The wood line was silent, and the winds were picking up. No sounds of voices or footsteps. What was going on in there? How far had they gotten? Was Blake okay? Did he know about the cliff above the water? A knot of emotion clogged her throat and stung her eyes anew. What if she lost him? She'd only just found him.

Bright red-and-white flashes from an ambulance and several government vehicles arrived seconds later. The caravan stopped behind Blake's truck. At least two cruisers and as many black SUVs lined the space at the foot of her driveway. Multiple uniformed men and women rushed into the woods. Others paraded along the street, marking the wood line with flares and searching the ground from her driveway to the woods. Little flags were placed at boot prints in the mud. The flash of cameras and sirens mixed with a growing murmur of voices.

Cole peeled her off of him, then passed her to a man in an EMT shirt. "She has head and neck trauma. The facial abrasions are two days old. Bruising is a mix of then and now. Let's load her up. Get her out of sight while you take a look."

Marissa ran her hands over the marks on her face and neck. A flood of emotion overcame her. Fear, embarrassment, anger, humiliation. Hopefully Nash came across that cliff accidentally. "I'm not going to the hospital."

Cole snorted.

The EMT offered Marissa a concerned smile. "We don't need to go anywhere. Would you mind having a seat inside so I can make a proper evaluation?"

She eyeballed the open cargo doors. "Can we stay outside?" Her gaze ran the length of the street near the woods. "I'm fine. I don't need anything that's in there."

The man raised a stethoscope toward her in compliance, but Cole intervened.

He inched closer, nudging her toward the gaping ambulance doors. "You can barely stand up. Stop being a hero and get in so you can be checked out properly or Blake will have my ass."

She gave Cole a long appraisal. If Blake was okay, and she hoped that he was, she certainly didn't want to be another source of frustration for him. He had enough worries leading a team of federal agents and chasing a killer. "Fine, but you have to let me out as soon as you're done with your evaluation." She shuffled forward on noodle legs and struggled into the back of the ambulance. Her head swam, and she repositioned her feet for balance on the shiny metal step.

"She hasn't eaten," Cole tattled, boosting her the rest of the way inside. "The assailant threw her headfirst into Blake's tailgate. She was out for about two minutes, and woke with confusion, a headache and a few moments of memory loss, but I think that's all come back to her now. She's claiming no nausea, but…" He shrugged as if he didn't believe her. "She's under severe stress. Possible post-traumatic. Her sister's missing. She's attached herself to the agent on the case, who's currently in pursuit and we just heard two gunshots."

The EMT mouthed a slow "Wow," before speaking again. "Blake's the agent?"

"Yeah."

Embarrassment rolled through her. Was that what she'd done? *Attached herself* to Blake? Was that what everyone around them saw? A victim clinging superficially to her hero? She pressed a hand to her stomach, fighting another wave of nausea. Her cheeks burned with humiliation. They'd had a near kiss at the restaurant, and the moment had meant something to her, but maybe that sort of thing was an everyday occurrence for him. She could certainly understand why if it was.

The EMT flashed another light in Marissa's eyes, and she slapped it away. "Will everyone please stop doing that? It hurts."

He took her wrist in his fingers and checked his watch. "I'm Henry Garrett," he said. "I'm the uncle."

Marissa heaved a long breath. What was with these Garrett men? Was a hero complex in the DNA?

Cole climbed onboard and closed the doors behind him. "Uncle Henry taught me everything I needed to know about basic triage. He's the reason I pursued medical training in the army."

Henry strapped a blood pressure cuff on Marissa. "Our family requires a lot of first aid."

Marissa fixed Cole with a pleading stare. "Please find out why there were gunshots."

She fought to maintain her composure, no longer caring if everyone in Shadow Point thought she was a needy victim. All that mattered was that Blake was okay, and she needed to know that neither of those bullets had connected with him.

Cole swept his gaze to his uncle before slipping outside and shutting Marissa in.

THE AMBULANCE DOORS were shut when Blake arrived. Cole slid his phone into his pocket and lifted a palm. "I just called you."

"I didn't answer."

"I know. Why not?" He scowled.

Blake closed the distance between them in a determined stride. "Well?" he demanded, shooting a pointed look at the ambulance and fearing the worst. Why else would she be locked inside while his brother was forced out?

Cole's stance stiffened. He dropped his hand to his side. "Where's West?"

Blake reached past him for the ambulance doors. He thumped his palm against the metal. "Open up. This is Federal Agent Garrett."

Cole grabbed Blake's arm and jerked. "Where's West, Blake? Answer me." His no-nonsense tone implied there might be a fist coming if Blake didn't comply.

Blake reared to his full height and faced off with his baby brother. What the hell was wrong with him? "West's at the river. What's your problem?"

Cole stepped back, clearly relieved. "There were two gunshots and an explosion, man. What the hell do you think is my problem?"

Recognition dawned and Blake clapped a palm on his brother's shoulder. "West is fine. He's tracking Nash downstream." He dropped his hand and raised a humbled brow. "I got free of the blast, but Nash got away. Sorry man. I wasn't thinking."

Blake had been so focused on reaching Marissa that he hadn't considered what those gunshots might have sounded like to Cole. Any other day, Blake would've recognized the fear in his eyes and set the facts on the table immediately. He might've even given orders on what to do next, but at the moment all he could think about was whether or not Marissa was going to be okay.

Cole stared past Blake, confused. "You lost Nash?"

"Yeah, but I also shot him. I think. I don't know. He jumped into the river." Blake thumped the door again. "Open up."

"Jumped or fell because you shot him?" Cole asked.

The ambulance doors opened, and Blake hoisted himself inside on weakened limbs. "I don't know. Both, I hope."

"Me, too," Cole muttered, closing Blake inside.

Marissa sat on the gurney, an ice pack pressed to

her head. Another drooped over her shoulder. His uncle Henry monitored an IV attached to her arm.

"You're okay?" Blake asked, falling onto the bench against the wall. His knees bumped the gurney and Marissa flinched. "Sorry."

She batted teary eyes. Her face was splotched and puffy as if she'd been crying. "What happened?"

Blake's heart broke. He abandoned the bench for a seat beside Marissa on the gurney. He pulled her to her chest and stroked her hair. "I'm so sorry I left you."

Her arms wound around his middle and his heart swelled at the touch. She buried her face against the curve of his throat and the emotions she'd so carefully hidden from him before flowed freely now. "I thought you were shot," she cried. "I thought you were blown up. Gone."

"Shh," he whispered, cradling her in his arms. "I'm okay. So is West. Verdict is still out on Nash. That was my gun you heard. The explosion was poorly rigged. I got out of the way before I was hurt." He lifted his face to search for his uncle. "How is she?"

Uncle Henry tipped his head left and right, indicating it was a draw. "It doesn't look like a concussion and the bruises will fade." He slid his gaze to a sobbing Marissa, then back to Blake with a sad smile.

Blake understood. The wounds that would take longest to heal were the ones no one could see.

"Did you get him?" Uncle Henry asked. "What did you mean the verdict is still out?"

Blake grimaced. "I tried, but he jumped into the river. West's tracking him."

Uncle Henry scooted in Blake's direction. He opened and closed his hands in the universal sign for gimmee.

"Come on. Let me take your vitals and check on those cuts and burns."

Blake reluctantly stretched one arm in his uncle's direction for a pulse check and blood pressure cuff.

Someone pounded on the ambulance doors. "It's Sheriff Garrett, open up."

Blake jerked his head toward the door.

Uncle Henry waddled to the back, careful not to hit his head on the low ceiling. "All you kids with your titles. Just say, it's West. It's Blake. It's Cole. I know who you are." He pushed the doors open, and West stared inside.

"How is she?" West asked.

"She'll be okay," Uncle Henry answered. "How about the bad guy? Should I call for another bus?"

West shook his head.

"Coroner?"

"Nah. We didn't find him."

"So, I missed," Blake muttered, struggling not to upset Marissa again. Her sobs had finally fallen silent and her breathing returned to a slow and steady pace.

West raised an evidence baggie for Blake to see. There were leaves inside. "I found these on the banks near a patch of rocks and a little vomit."

Blake took the bag in one hand for closer inspection. "That's blood."

"Yep."

"I hit him."

Uncle Henry retook his seat beside the gurney and liberated a cell phone from one uniform pocket.

West cocked a hip and cast a goofy look at his uncle. "Did Blake tell you he tripped over a wire roped to some C4?"

Uncle Henry removed the blood pressure cuff and squirted something onto Blake's bloodied arm. "It's a wonder you boys haven't given your mother forty heart attacks by now. Ten for each of ya."

West rolled his eyes, then refocused on Blake. "The team's going strong. Your guys brought the lights and I've called in some of the best tracking dogs in the county. If the rain holds off, we'll have him by dawn. I'll get the leaves to the lab to confirm it's Nash's blood after the dogs get here. I'm going to stick around and direct the teams as they arrive. If you want to head back to the hotel with Marissa, we'll be okay. There's a lot of manpower in those woods chasing one injured man."

Uncle Henry shined a bright light in Blake's face.

Blake slapped it away. "Knock it off."

Marissa chuckled against his chest. Blake held her tighter, wishing he knew why she'd laughed and how to make it happen again.

"Did you check his head?" West asked. "He's talking really loudly."

Blake waved a hand over his ears. "Do not. My ears are ringing, but I can hear. My vision is fine. I'm fine. I hurt like hell, but I'll live."

Cole strode into place beside West, spotlight in hand. He tilted his head back and looked skyward. "Storm's coming. I'm heading out before it gets here. What we don't find tonight could be washed away by morning." He tipped his hat to his brothers, uncle and Marissa before jogging into the woods between flares.

Blake shifted Marissa in his arms and indicated that she should lie back on the gurney.

Shockingly, she complied.

He turned back to West. "We need to contact all the

local hospitals, clinics and facilities where Nash can either get patched up or work on himself. Veterinarians and dental offices included. He's resourceful, so put the word out. It's going to be a lot harder for him to blend in while he's bleeding."

Uncle Henry wiggled his phone in the air. "I'm ahead of you, young ones."

West watched Blake. His gaze lingered on the hand, now caressing Marissa as she tried to relax.

Blake lifted his chin in response to the questions on his brother's brow.

Yes, he'd fallen hard and fast for this woman, and no, there was nothing he wouldn't do to assure Nash Barclay never got anywhere near her again.

Chapter Twelve

The walkie-talkie on West's shoulder erupted in a short blast of white noise. "Sheriff Garrett, this is dispatch," a woman's voice announced.

Marissa's eyes popped open, her body on alert. Had they found Nash floating in the river? She chastised herself for wishing that he was facedown.

West depressed the button and turned his face toward the noisy device. "Go ahead."

"I know you've got the whole team with you, sir, but there's a call about some movement outside the Lane home on Blue Grass Run. Neighbor says there's no car, but the lights are all on."

Marissa shot upright, tugging her IV and ignoring the dull thud in her head.

"Whoa." Uncle Henry shoved one hand over the tape securing her IV. "Wait a minute. Settle down."

She wiggled free of his grip. "She's talking about my sister's house. I need to go." Had enough time passed for Nash to reach Kara's place? That was nearly a mile downriver from Marissa's. She squeezed her eyes shut and tried to gauge the possibility. In a kayak, yes. On foot? Maybe, but injured? That depended on where he was shot.

She gave Uncle Henry's hand a pointed stare.

"Let the drip do its work," he insisted.

"I feel better. My head's fine. I'm not going to puke." She grabbed Blake's arm with her free hand. "Take me with you."

West left the ambulance doors open as he walked away. A moment later, the lights on his cruiser flicked on, and he maneuvered through the crush of vehicles, heading downriver toward Kara's neighborhood.

Blake looked from Marissa to his uncle.

Uncle Henry puffed his cheeks in defeat and released her hand. "She should rest. I put something mild in her IV for pain. I'd say you could leave her with me, but you've got the gun."

Blake hesitated. "I can stay. Wait for West to report back."

"No." Marissa plucked the tape from her arm and slid the needle from her vein. "I'm going. My sister could be in danger, and we already know I am. You aren't leaving me alone in this ambulance."

Uncle Henry tugged his ear. "Call me if you need me. I'm on duty all night."

BLAKE LOADED MARISSA into the cab of his truck and cursed himself for having ever left her alone there. He'd never dreamed anyone, even Nash, would try to take her with three armed lawmen a hundred feet away. Still, he'd known Nash was out there, and he'd failed to keep her safe tonight. That was all him.

She didn't speak on the drive to Kara's, and Blake's gut fisted with the fear her injuries were worse than his uncle knew. What if he'd missed something critical in his evaluation? Or maybe she was just shutting Blake out. Blaming him, with good reason, for her fear and pain. Her head lolled and rocked against the seatback as they sped down winding roads toward her sister's home. She gazed out the passenger window, effectively keeping her eyes off of his no matter how he tried to catch her attention.

He hated the silence, but couldn't bring himself to break it. Knowing now how he felt about her and what she meant to him, her quietness felt like a wall keeping him out when all he wanted was in. He shook off the selfish urge to reach for her. Marissa would talk when she was ready, but she clearly wanted space. She'd never gone so long without speaking her mind or asking a question. He gripped the wheel until his knuckles whitened, determined to keep them there. He'd give her whatever she needed, even if what she wanted was away from him.

He sped along the dark winding road as lightning splintered across the night sky, ominous and threatening. The thunder was a wild animal giving warning before each attack. Soon, fat drops of rain exploded against his windshield, winding twisty paths through his view. He hit the wipers and said a silent prayer that this was the worst of it. Too much rain would ruin the trackers' chances of finding Nash. Even the dogs West had called in would lose the scent in a downpour.

He stole another look at Marissa, hoping she'd forgive him one day for the heartbreak he'd caused her by letting Nash live all those years ago.

A few more hills and one stop sign later, Blake pulled into Kara's driveway and parked behind West's cruiser. As promised, the porch light was on along with all the lights inside.

Marissa slid from the truck on wobbly legs. She'd been so quiet the last few moments that he thought she might've fallen asleep.

It wasn't hard to catch up with her on the path to Kara's door. "Hey, slow down." He caught her hand and pulled her back. There was no garage here, and only West's cruiser was in the driveway. Who knew what awaited them inside?

The front door swung open and another version of Marissa sprang toward them, arms open wide. The sleeves of her faded Kentucky University sweatshirt hung past her hands, and her worn-out blue jeans were torn across both knees.

Marissa shook Blake away and collided with, what could only have been, her sister hard enough to throw herself off balance.

"Whoa." He pressed a steadying palm between her shoulders.

The women rocked foot to foot as they hugged and laughed and sobbed. Wind whipped their hair and clothing. Rain pelted their cheeks.

"I'm so sorry," Kara cried. "Sheriff Garrett told me everything you've been through and I wasn't here for you. I hate myself." She pulled back to look at Marissa's face, tears streaming from her eyes. Wild wisps of damp blond hair clung to her cheeks and forehead, the rest was swept into a messy bun and quickly falling. "Look at you." She lifted gentle fingers to Marissa's bruised face, but stopped short of touching the multitude of marks. "Oh my gosh. You didn't tell me it was this bad. What is happening?" She hugged her again and cried louder. "You said someone tried to take you. You didn't tell me he hurt you!"

Blake could see where all the emotion went in this family. Kara seemed exuberant enough for the entire town. He pressed forward, corralling them toward the steps. "Can we take this inside, please?" Nash was still out there somewhere, and if he wasn't in the process of dying, then he was hurting, pissed and looking for revenge. Kara's house wasn't far enough from where Blake had last seen him to provide any comfort. The women needed to move their reunion inside. "Let's go. Come on."

Kara pulled back again. This time to glare at Blake. "Are you the one who's supposed to be keeping her safe? The sheriff told me about what just happened. He told me you were on the way, but he didn't say she'd show up looking like this."

Blake felt the blood drain from his face. What was it with Lane women? He pushed the two in front of him toward the door. "Inside. Now."

West sat at the island of a peppy eat-in kitchen stuffing his face with iced sugar cookies and drinking coffee. He'd hooked the heels of his boots in the rungs of a white padded bar stool and tossed his hat onto the broad laminate countertop. "So, Kara's fine," he said, munching his snack. "I got here as the coffee finished brewing." He hefted his bowl-shaped blue mug with a grin.

Marissa curled onto an overstuffed yellow couch in the adjacent sitting area and wiped her face with her palms. She pulled a furry white pillow into her arms. "Where have you been? Where's your car? Why haven't you called. Do Mom and Dad know you're okay?"

Blake stifled a smile. That was the Marissa he was used to.

Kara stretched her eyes wide. "You have no idea

what I've been through today." She grabbed two hand towels from the handle of her kitchen stove and threw one to Marissa. She rubbed the other over her face and neck.

Marissa dried her face and tossed the towel aside. "I'm sure your day was awful."

"Thank you."

Blake couldn't tell if Kara's response was the result of cluelessness or sarcasm.

"I barely got out of the shower and the sheriff was at my door." She motioned to West, then poured three more mugs of coffee. "Talk about scary."

Marissa leaned forward with narrowed eyes. "He's not scary. He's here to help. Why didn't you call us back? Or return our texts? Do you know how many times we've tried to reach you? We thought you were dead." She pressed her lips tight and shot Blake a horrified expression.

Kara stepped back as if she'd been slapped. "My phone died. I told you I had to walk home. I've been gone all day. I'd already talked to both you and to Mom. You knew I was fine, and I was trying to do what you asked." She motioned to the packed bag on her kitchen counter beside a Thermos and plastic container of cookies. "I plugged my phone in the minute I walked through the front door, then I got in the shower." Kara mimed her head exploding. "I've had the worst day ever. I've only been home for like five minutes, and I've been hustling since the moment I walked in. That's *after* I was forced to abandon my car and trek like thirty miles. Now, you're here yelling because I haven't made more phone calls? The phone was dead!"

"Thirty miles? Where were you?" Marissa asked.

Kara delivered a mug of coffee each to both Blake and her sister. "Blue Ridge Byway."

Marissa gasped. "What were you doing way out there?"

"Oh, I don't know. My only sister was attacked yesterday then taken into protective custody. I was a little upset. I wanted to think, but you said it wasn't safe here, so I figured I'd better choose someplace outside of town to hike. I planned to meet you at Mom and Dad's for dinner but when I got back into town this afternoon, my gas light was on, and I had to stop to fill up." She groaned. "Of course my money was in the coozie I wrap my water bottle in, and that was nowhere to be found, so I had to go back to the park and retrace my steps until I found it. When I got back to my car the second time it wouldn't start. I had to walk all the way back to town. It was getting dark. My phone was dead. It was awful."

"You could've called from the gas station," Marissa said.

Kara shot Blake a look. "Like I didn't think of that all by myself? I did. I called Mom and she didn't answer. I couldn't remember your new federal agent cell number and your old phone isn't on."

Blake joined Marissa on the couch, prepared to stop her from saying something she might regret. He blew casual ripples over the surface of his coffee and changed the subject. "And where's your car now?"

"In the main lot at Blue Ridge Byway."

Marissa dropped her head back against the couch cushion. "What were you even doing there? I tell you I was nearly abducted by a serial killer while hiking alone, and what do you do? Get up the next day and go hiking alone!"

Kara's jaw went slack. "You said fugitive. Not serial

killer, and I was trying to clear my head but you had me scared half to death, and everything was fine until I had to walk home." She made the same exasperated expression as Marissa. "Luckily, your friend's dad offered me a ride home for the last few miles."

Marissa froze, mug halfway to her mouth. "You got in a car with a stranger? Who?"

Blake fought the urge to remind Marissa that she'd done the same thing.

"I think he said you went to school with his daughter. Tammy something. He recognized me right away, thought I was you at first, actually."

Blake slid to the edge of the cushion and traded stares with West. "What'd Tammy's dad look like? What was he driving?"

"I don't know. He had a white truck. What's wrong now?" She looked to Marissa, stupefied. "I figured I was safer in a car than walking by myself straight through a town with a fugitive on the loose."

"Nash Barclay is a serial killer," Marissa growled, "and I didn't go to school with anyone named Tammy."

A powerful rumble of thunder seemed to underscore the revelation. Lightning flashed outside, illuminating the dark world for one long beat.

Blake and West were on their feet.

"How long ago did this man bring you home?" Blake asked.

Kara looked at the clock above her fireplace. "Not long. Maybe an hour? I barely had time to put cookies in the oven and jump in the shower before you guys started showing up." She rubbed her forehead and chewed her lip. "I came home. Started the coffee and cookies, packed my bag for Mom and Dad's then jumped into thc shower. I planned to call you for a ride to pick up my car, and use the cookies as a bribe."

Marissa grabbed the remote and turned the television on, then flipped to the evening news. Nash's face was anchored in the corner of the frame. A line of scrolling text detailed his past kills and recent attacks, followed by a warning that he should not be approached.

Kara watched, stunned. "That's the man who drove me home."

Blake tapped the revelation into his phone, informing his team of the development as West informed his. "Nash must've dropped her off and driven the mile over to Marissa's place from here. He probably had something in mind when he removed her porch light, but we showed up and offered him something more appealing." His chosen victim seated alone in a truck.

Kara made a gurgling sound, but didn't speak. She took the remote from Marissa and pumped up the volume on her television.

West dropped his mug in the sink and stuffed his phone back into his pocket. "Cole says it's a damn torrential downpour out there, and he's calling it a night on the river search. They can't track their own paths in this." He waved a hand toward Kara's picture window. "He's heading out to meet a tow truck at Blue Ridge Byway and collect Kara's car. I'll take her to her folks' house for the night and station a deputy there to relieve Dad." He grabbed her bag off the counter and hiked it over one shoulder. "I doubt Dad will leave, but I'll try. Is this everything you need, Kara?"

She stumbled back, dragging her eyes from a news clip time line of Nash's kills. She turned for her kitchen on shaky legs. "Let me grab the cookies."

Marissa heaved herself off the couch and met her sister at the island. "I'm sorry." She wrapped Kara in her arms and hooked her chin on her shoulder. "So. So. Sorry. And so glad you're okay. I should have led with that. I took this all out on you, and I was wrong. You couldn't have known." She hugged her sister tight.

Kara shook visibly in Marissa's embrace.

Blake ground his teeth and headed back outside to patrol the perimeter while the women said goodbye. If Nash was brave enough to have followed them here, it would be the last place he ever visited.

Chapter Thirteen

Marissa adjusted the vents in Blake's dash to dry her rain-soaked hair. Her heart was lighter, knowing Kara was safe, but having her back meant having her to lose, and she suspected that fear would never truly leave.

Rain pelted the windshield as they followed West's cruiser toward the stop sign at the end of the street. West turned right, taking Kara to their parents' home for safekeeping, and Blake idled his truck.

He glanced at Marissa before pressing the left turn signal. "She's going to be okay."

"How do you know?" Marissa watched as the cruiser's taillights faded into the night. The fear of never seeing Kara again knotted in her muscles. "How can you be sure Nash won't show up at my parents' house and hurt them?"

Blake made the turn, pointing them soundly away from Kara. "For one thing, I know he's hurt. For another, we both know he likes to abduct and overpower women when they're alone. Kara's not going to be alone again until he's caught. She has no reason to sneak away in a storm, and she'll be safe inside. He's not a home invader, and if he gets the notion to try, he'll find three armed men inside."

Marissa appreciated the logical explanation and the way Blake always took the time to fill her in instead of blowing off her concerns. He trusted her to handle the truth. As he should.

Wind whipped the trees along the road's edge, bending boughs fifty feet high. The storm had been in full force when they'd left Kara's house. Even the short run down her drive had been enough to soak them. Now, not only was she freezing, she was worried. The search for Nash had been called off due to weather.

She twisted a loose thread from her jacket cuff around her trembling fingers. There were too many questions and her eyelids were growing heavier by the second. Her adrenaline was long gone, and whatever was in her IV was starting to wear off.

"Hey." Blake stole a long look in her direction. "Why'd you quit fighting back there?"

"When?"

"Nash had you, and you were making headway toward freedom, but when we got to you, you froze. Was it the guns? None of us would have taken a shot with you there like that. Your safety is always number one."

She rolled her eyes in the dark cab. "I wanted you to shoot him. I was trying not to get in the way."

The truck slowed for several seconds before powering onward at the posted speed limit. Whatever Blake thought about her reasoning, he didn't say.

She forced her tired eyes open, and ran mentally through a growing list of concerns. Where was Nash now? How injured was he? Would he survive? Would he come for her again? For her sister? Someone else? Images of the women pulled from the lake came flashing back to mind, curling her fingers and knotting her empty stomach. He had to be stopped, but how? What could she do? Nothing. Nash proved that time and again. She was helpless, and he could reach her anywhere, even in her driveway with three armed men standing on her lawn.

Blake pulled into the parking space outside their hotel room and turned off the lights. How had they gotten there so fast? An agent exited the door to their room, just like before. This time, the man in the suit headed for Blake with a large umbrella overhead.

Marissa waited, too exhausted to get out, wishing she could just sleep where she was.

Blake took the umbrella and sent the agent away. He arrived at Marissa's door a moment later and reached for her hand.

"You know we're both already soaked, right?" She smiled and planted her hand in his.

He pulled her against him under the large black dome and shut the door behind them.

She shook her head, pushing away the bizarre fantasy that the small gesture meant something more than good manners. Cole's words to his uncle blared in her memory like a humiliating foghorn.

She'd attached herself to him. The connection she imagined wasn't real.

Marissa headed for the bathroom once they were safely inside. She pulled a dry towel off the rack and pressed it against the length of her hair, then patted her face.

Blake leaned against the doorjamb between her room and the sitting area, watching her through the open bathroom door.

She rubbed the towel against the gooseflesh rising on her arms. "I'll only be a minute."

"Take your time."

She closed the door and hurried through the process of washing Nash's touch from her skin. It was pointless work. Each time the washcloth passed over a part of her that had touched him, her stomach knotted, and the sound of his voice burned in her ear. His breath was on her cheek. The scent of cigarettes seemed to float on the steam around her.

A bone-jarring sob broke from her, and she turned the shower off with a snap. She dried and redressed quickly, barely removing the water from her hair and skin. She wrapped half-dry hair into a messy bun and let her clothing stick to still-damp skin. She just needed to see Blake was there, and she wasn't alone.

She reopened the door to find Blake in the same location, poised between rooms. His gaze kept a steady circuit from the front door to the bedroom and back.

"You're up," she said, tossing her duffel and wet things into the closet.

He tapped his phone screen, then gave her one stiff nod.

He disappeared into the bathroom, and Marissa exhaled long and slow. She hadn't been alone since her morning jog at the national park, but the suite felt safer somehow than the small bathroom had. She was less vulnerable. There was room to run. Lamps to throw. She circled the rooms checking the window and door locks. All secure. As she expected. Two agents stood outside the front window with giant umbrellas. "Well, that explains his last-minute text," she muttered, simultaneously thankful and concerned by the added protection.

Steam puffed beneath the bathroom door and scents of Blake's shampoo filtered into her troubled mind. She turned for the front room in search of the minifridge and a cold bottle of water. Anything to help clear her thoughts.

She climbed onto the small sofa with her drink and folded her legs beneath her. She dialed her mother's number and waited impatiently for an answer.

"Hello? Marissa?"

"Hey." She swiped a renegade tear from her cheek. "Did Kara get there okay?"

"Yes."

The joy and relief in her voice raised a smile on Marissa's lips. "Good." She nodded against the receiver. "And there's a deputy there now? Someone should be staying with you tonight."

"That's right." Her mother sniffled. "We have a full house. Mr. Garrett is staying and so is his youngest son and another deputy."

"Cole's staying?" Marissa asked.

"Mm-hmm." The background voices grew louder. "The sheriff dropped her off and waited for the deputies to arrive, then he had to go. I'm serving coffee now. I wish you were here."

"Me, too," Marissa admitted. It would be great to crawl into her childhood bed and sleep soundly knowing her parents were right down the hall, and that they were all the protection she needed. Maybe she could do that again one day, but this wasn't the night. Tonight, the whole family needed a team of guardians because one psychopath liked killing people who looked like the Lane women.

"Are you okay? Is there anything I can do?"

Marissa scanned the impersonal room before her, full of files, frequented by strangers and void of any personal touch. "No. I'm fine. I was just checking on you and Kara. I'm going to get some sleep."

Her mother sighed. "The last two days have been horrific for me. I can't imagine what they've been for you."

"I'm fine."

"You always are." Her voice was soft like a hug. "Tomorrow will be a better day. You and your sister are safe now, and that's all that matters. The whole sheriff's department can move into the guest room permanently for all I care, so long as I know my girls are okay."

The bathroom door opened, and Blake emerged in a black t-shirt and jogging pants. His hair was damp, and his skin red from the hot shower.

Marissa gripped the phone a little tighter. "Tell Dad and Kara I love them. I'll talk to you in the morning."

"You'd better. I love you, sweetie."

"I love you too." Marissa disconnected and set the phone aside, letting her mother's comforting words warm her bones.

Blake pulled an extra blanket from the closet and carried it to the couch. "May I?"

"Sure."

He fanned the blanket over her legs and took a seat beside her. "Checking in on your family?"

"Yeah. They're fine. Your dad, Cole and another deputy are all staying there tonight."

"Good. I don't think they need the coverage, but their presence should help your family sleep. They've all had a bad day." He bent to retrieve a fat stack of files, then balanced them on his lap.

Apparently, he had more work to do.

Marissa pulled the blanket up to her chin. "Why'd Nash drive Kara home tonight? Why didn't he take her or hurt her while he had the chance?"

Blake turned his heavily burdened gaze on her. "Nash doesn't want her. This isn't random for him. He's specific. Focused. Exact. He wanted to send us a message. He wants us to know he's done his research. He's watched you. He knows what's important to you, and he wants you to know he's in control. He may have even let you get away from him at the national park because that was the surest way to get me involved."

Marissa's jaw dropped. "You think he let me go?" She pressed her fingers to the pulse suddenly beating in her temple. "I fought like hell to get away from him."

Blake lifted a palm slightly off the folder. "It's just a theory."

She frowned. The storm rumbled outside the window, rattling the glass and whistling around the door. Sheets of rain streaked over the large pane of glass beside her as if they were slowly being submerged. "Anything else you want to share?"

Blake eased the top folder in her direction and flipped the cover open. "Yes."

He slid the open folder onto her lap and watched as she began to read.

Time moved more slowly as she pored over the pages, catching his eye from time to time when the messy scrawl on sticky notes became too much to decipher. She tapped her finger to the letters *BF* scribbled in a margin note.

Blake cleared his throat and began to explain the

context. "It was to remind me to find his birth father."
Nashville Levi Barclay was the child of a single, teen-
age mother. No father was named on his birth certifi-
cate. "I've always wondered about his true paternity.
One-night stand? Rape? Incest?"

Marissa's mouth turned down on both sides. "Do you
really think it could be one of the latter?"

"I never found out. I know he was raised in poverty
by his grandparents who weren't real thrilled by the burden. I had the significant displeasure of meeting with
them after he got away from me the first time. They
described him as an ungrateful child, and they believed
in corporal punishment. His mother was absent. I got a
good idea of why while I was there."

Marissa leaned back against the couch cushions.
"His life sounds terrible. No child should grow up feeling unloved or unwanted."

Blake twisted to face her. He'd decided in the shower
that he'd tell her as much as he could. She deserved to
know what he knew. "Nash had a relatively productive
life for a while. He finished high school. Got a job and
met a girl. They were engaged to be married, but she
died of a drug overdose before the wedding. She left a
vague suicide note. That was six years ago, and what I
see as his breaking point."

She stared at the pages. "He was going to have a family. He had someone who wanted him, but not enough
to keep living."

"I'd thought that Nash's first victim went missing
a year after his fiancée's death." Blake stopped to rub
the back of his neck and groan. "That's another thing I
was wrong about. One of the bodies from the lake was
a year older than that."

Marissa looked ill. "So, he'd actually started killing right away," she whispered.

"Maybe. I'll know more when I get the medical examiner's official report." Until then, everything he thought about what Nash had done to the victims was pure speculation, including the events on the day he killed them. Blake dropped his hands onto his lap and rubbed his palms together. "I think he attacked you and killed that jogger because I stopped trying to find him." Sickness coiled in his gut. He glanced at Marissa, wary of what he'd see in her expression. "I'd put his case aside and resolved to make myself useful on active criminal cases. Then, this happened. I don't think the timing is a coincidence."

Marissa raised an eyebrow. "You think he somehow knew you'd stopped looking for him?"

Blake watched her carefully as he answered. "I think so. Yes."

Someone knocked at the door. "Room service," a familiar voice called.

Blake hoisted himself upright and went to check the peephole. "While you were in the shower, I put in a request for some food." An agent with a bag of takeout and a giant umbrella stood at attention in the rain.

Blake thanked his teammate and accepted the meal before engaging the door chain and dead bolt once more.

Marissa pushed the files onto Blake's empty seat and rubbed her eyes.

"Any more questions?" he asked.

"Why do you do this?"

Blake set the bag on the couch and dropped the stack of files onto the floor. "I thought there should be food here if you got hungry. We know Kara's safe, so now maybe you can eat."

Marissa pulled the bag onto her lap and extracted a salad and cup of dressing. "I meant, isn't it hard to always be on the prowl for a monster? The people you go after are the worst of humanity, and I never gave them a second thought until yesterday. Not you, though. You chose this as your life." She popped the lid on her container, looking baffled. "You all do."

Blake moved the bag to the floor. He'd heard this before. "By all, I assume you mean my brothers and I."

"Well, yeah, and your dad. You've all chosen careers like this. Isn't it lonely and exhausting?"

"Tell me how you really feel," he joked. "Please don't hold back."

Marissa smiled. "I'm just trying to understand."

"Some families sing or sail or own horses. Garretts protect and serve."

"And you all enjoy it?"

Blake took his time answering. Marissa wanted to know him, and he didn't want to mess it up. "I think so. I do. I grew up in awe of my dad and uncles. They're all patriots and veterans, and I wanted to honor that by emulating it. So, I followed their paths to the military after high school graduation. All my brothers did, too."

"I think that's beautiful," she said. "Did you learn a lot in the service that helps you today?"

"I learned the importance of self-discipline, and I got a look at how bad life can be for some folks. Before that, I'd assumed my life in Shadow Point was the basic, standard issue stuff. I'd had no idea how great I had it here. I came home with a phenomenal appreciation for the freedom and profound safety in a rural American town. I knew I wanted to be a federal agent. I wanted to make more towns as secure as ours." He barked a humorless laugh. A lot of good he'd done.

Marissa worked through her salad, bite by greedy bite. "You wanted to make a difference," she said, pointing her fork in his direction.

He gripped the arm of the couch and tried to look less horrified at the amount of personal information he was unloading. "I know I'm not going to change the world. I don't have the tools or capacity to cure cancer or end wars, but I can do my part to protect the lives of my cases."

Marissa shifted her attention from her dinner to Blake's eyes. "I think what you're doing is noble. Most people wouldn't risk their lives to improve the lives of others."

He shifted in his seat, focusing wholly on Marissa. "I won't let him touch you again."

She pushed a hunk of lettuce with the plastic tines of her fork. "This isn't your fault. No matter how it feels to you."

Blake turned his face away. That was the kind of line he was supposed to give struggling victims and not the other way around. "Right."

"Do you ever miss normal?" she asked. "Ever wish you had a safe job counting beans or raising chickens or something?"

"I hate chickens."

She laughed. "No. Why?"

"Chickens are mean."

"Chickens are adorable." Marissa took another bite and chewed slowly. "Why do you think none of your brothers have ever married? Seems like having a family would be great for people like you." The color in her cheeks deepened. "You'd have people to care for twenty-four seven. Not cases or strangers, but *your* people."

She made it sound so simple. Blake teetered over the right way to answer a complicated question. "I shouldn't speak for my brothers, but I think we'd all like to have a family one day. Lord knows our mom would love to have some women around. She wanted one girl and got four boys."

Marissa set her fork aside and rested her hands in her lap, looking profoundly uncomfortable. "You all want families, but none of you date." Her eyebrows knitted together.

Blake had fielded these types of questions all his life, and they never got easier. The assumptions people made always seemed to reflect poorly on him or his character, and a few years back he stopped trying to explain himself, and started throwing snide responses to keep people from pushing. The remarks had gotten a lot of lip service and their impact had stained his brothers, too.

He worked his jaw. He wanted Marissa to understand him, even if she didn't like what she heard. "I've never been married because women don't respond well to being left alone for indefinite, sometimes frequent, periods of time where I care for other women." He motioned around them. "Alone in hotel rooms."

Her eyes widened. "I can't imagine being with someone I didn't trust completely, but even then, trusting strangers with the most important person in your life is a whole other problem. That must be hard." She wrinkled her nose in distaste. "You've been more than a comfort to me. Are you always this involved with the victims?"

Did he always hold their hands and embrace them as often as possible? Was that what she thought? He struggled to hold back a deeply frustrated groan. "No."

He rubbed his hands against his thighs. Discussing all the times he'd been dumped for choosing work over a personal life wasn't exactly easy, and the look on her face made it infinitely harder. "The women in my past have also taken issue with the number of secrets I have to keep and the injuries I regularly acquire. When I'm really unlucky, the secrets and injuries come in an inconvenient two-for-one package." He lifted cautious eyes to hers, and wondered again if Marissa was the kind of woman who could withstand life with a lawman. "I'm single because I stopped dating the minute I realized none of it would ever lead anywhere as long as I am who I am, and I like who I am."

Marissa's wide eyes grew inexplicably sad. "I like who you are, too." She set her half-eaten salad on the floor and tipped over, leaning her head against Blake's shoulder. She slid her arm under his and bent it to lock them together. "I think you're a brave and selfless man who risks his life to save others, and that's pretty amazing. I'm…" A long yawn interrupted her words. "I'm glad you're the one here with me tonight."

Blake's heart expanded until he thought it'd break his ribs. He wiggled free from Marissa's grip and wrapped his arm around her back, pulling her closer and repositioning her head on his chest where she'd be more comfortable. He twined the fingers of his free hand with hers and gently kissed the top of her head.

Maybe he was asking for heartbreak by hoping there could be a future with this woman, but damn it, a prize like that was worth the risk.

Chapter Fourteen

Marissa woke to the din of buzzing voices and scents of hot coffee, scrambled eggs and sausage. Someone had left a glass of orange juice on her nightstand beside a plate with an apple and enormous cinnamon muffin. Her tummy groaned at the sight of everything. She swung her feet over the bed's edge and arched her back in a gentle stretch.

This was the time of day when her limbs longed to run. She worked her neck carefully side to side, assessing the damage and lingering ache in her head after being knocked out by Nash. She winced as her muscles locked down in defense against the movement. Too far. Too soon. Maybe after she found out what all the commotion was about, she could locate an ice pack and some painkillers.

She gulped the juice and bit into the muffin before sliding bare feet onto the floor. An angel had also left a bottle of aspirin. She took a pair of those, too.

Beyond her bedroom, the sitting area buzzed with chatter. She padded closer and peered through the opening where Blake had left the door ajar. Two agents and a deputy took phone calls around the small table. Blake's palms were braced on either side of a topographical map. He was dressed in cargo pants, boots and a fitted long-sleeved black compression shirt. His badge swung over the image, as if it too was attempting to locate something.

Or someone.

"You found him," she said breathlessly.

Blake's head jerked up, and his gaze fell immediately upon her. He cut the distance between them with a look of excitement and purpose in his eyes. "Good morning," he said softly.

Her toes curled into the carpet. "Hi."

"How'd you sleep?"

"Okay, considering. Thank you for putting me in bed. I barely remember getting there." She'd fallen asleep on the couch with his strong arms around her and her head on his chest for a pillow. She hugged her middle, embarrassed by the happiness that memory brought her.

"I wouldn't have moved you, but your neck…" He trailed off. Blake moved slightly to one side, blocking her view of the sitting room, successfully erasing everything except Blake and his intoxicating energy. "How are you feeling this morning?"

She forced a tight smile. "I'm fine. My neck's a little stiff. Thank you for the breakfast and aspirin."

His lips curved into a prideful smile.

"I mostly feel lucky. I've had a lot of prayers answered these last two days."

"You're about to get one more."

"Why? What's going on?" She glanced past Blake toward the map and men in the next room. Something big must have brought them there and gotten Blake so wound up.

"Dispatch got a viable tip on Nash at dawn. Someone saw a man fitting his description at the national park. He said the man appeared sick or hurt." His eyes lit with the final report.

"You think it's really him?"

"West is there now. Park rangers checked it out first and found a pretty heavy blood trail on the forest side of the lake."

Marissa pondered the reasons Nash would return to the lake, but only found one. "He's dying. I bet he wanted to be with the women again." But they were gone now, no longer his sick trophies in an underwater tomb. Now, they would be laid to rest properly, given the peace and respect they deserved. "Would he drown himself to be with the women?" Wouldn't he know they were already gone?

Blake rubbed his palms against her arms, then curled long fingers around her biceps. Excitement pulsated off him. "I don't know, but I told West I'd meet him. I'm leaving a deputy with you. He'll be outside, so you can take your time having breakfast and getting ready to go home." He smiled at her. "I've been waiting a long time for this."

Marissa rocked onto her toes and wrapped her arms around his neck. She'd miss Blake terribly when he returned home to Louisville, but capturing Nash was all that really mattered now.

"Moving out," a man barked from the sitting room, and the area burst into a flurry of activity. Papers rustled and chairs bumped against the floor.

Marissa turned her mouth to Blake's ear. "Go get him," she whispered.

The front door opened and closed with a thud. "Let's

go, Garrett," the same deep voice from her sitting room, now bellowed outside.

Marissa rested her palms against his chest. "This is it, Agent. Your time to shine."

Blake was motionless. His grip on her tightened, and the look in his eyes nearly stole the breath from her body.

"Kiss for luck?" he asked. His gaze moved hotly from her eyes to her lips.

"Yes," she breathed.

He raised his warm hands to cradle the back of her head, and he lowered his lips over hers. "Yeah?" he whispered against her mouth.

"Yeah." The heat from his touch moved through her bones, electrifying her skin and pooling in her core. She curled her fingers into the fabric of his shirt and melded herself to him in confirmation. Blake deepened the kiss with a rumbling exhale, engulfing her in his strength and making delicious promises that he couldn't stay long enough to keep. She reveled in the taste and feel of him, trailing her hands over his shoulders and winding her fingers into his hair.

Blake ended the kiss far too soon, leaving her weak-kneed and woozy. A haze of desire lingered in his eyes. "We should probably talk about that when I get back."

She brushed careful fingertips over still tingling lips. "Then, hurry."

A broad smile spread over Blake's handsome face. "Yes, ma'am." He grabbed his black jacket, then Marissa once more. "I'm finally going to put this devil in handcuffs." He kissed her nose and forehead. "Don't go anywhere."

In the next moment, he was gone. Marissa watched

as he strode through the door and joined a caravan of waiting cruisers and black government vehicles in the parking lot.

As promised, one deputy remained outside her door.

Marissa collapsed on the bed, reliving the perfect moment. Her heart had pounded so hard, she was sure Blake could feel it in his own chest. She'd waited all her life to be kissed like that. It wasn't awkward, or polite and uncertain. It was passionate and comfortable and confident. Blake had kissed her with ease and familiarity, as if they'd kissed a hundred times before. As if he already knew what she wanted and how to give her exactly that.

She closed her eyes to savor the precious thought, but slowly, reality set in, raising her eyelids and putting her back on her feet. Nervous energy filled her mind with every form of worst-case scenario. She checked her phone for missed texts, then sent a few to her mom and sister letting them know that all was well. Nash was in the cross hairs, and she'd tell them more as soon as she knew something.

Both women responded within seconds, sending return texts of love and gratitude, complete with heart emoticons. Kara was clearly rubbing off on their mother.

With nothing to do but wait, Marissa finished her breakfast and helped herself to two cups of black coffee, then cleaned up. The clock seemed to stand still as she made the bed and returned the spare blanket from the couch to the closet. How long did it take to track a dying man through the forest in broad daylight? Blake and the team had been gone more than an hour already.

An ominous feeling crept over her, and she peeked

between the curtains to be sure her detail was still standing guard.

She was overthinking. Worrying. Confusing the awful things that she'd experienced over the past few days with what was happening now.

She carried her loaner phone into the bathroom and climbed into a raging hot shower hoping Blake would call before she finished getting ready. The pulsing water and thick steam slowly unknotted tension in her neck and shoulders, but the temporary escape from her thoughts didn't last.

She dug through her bag of hodgepodge clothing, smashed together and wrinkled beyond recognition. The day she'd hastily gathered those things seemed like something she'd seen in a movie rather than a moment she'd been part of. Of course, Blake had been right to insist she go into his protective custody. Nash had been watching her even then. Standing right outside her window, taking photos and stalking silently from the tree line.

She swept a dose of mascara over her eyelashes and dotted gloss on her lips. Blake and West knew what they were doing, and so did their teams. They would get Nash, and the worst part about today would be saying goodbye to Blake when the case was closed.

Marissa wandered to the couch and checked on the deputy again before turning on the television. Maybe the local newscasters had information that she didn't. Any form of update would go miles toward settling her worried heart.

A commercial for a local burger joint was cut short by the Breaking News logo. Marissa pulled her feet onto the couch and crossed her fingers for good news.

Maybe even an image of Blake and West hauling their bleeding nemesis from the forest.

Instead, fire trucks filled the screen and the news anchor bobbed into view outside an inferno. "I'm here at the Winchester Farm where a propane tank explosion has rocked several acres and a number of nearby homes. The tank exploded suddenly while the family worked in a neighboring field. First responders can be seen administering triage, but there's no official word on the number of injured or severity of their burns. The Winchesters' youngest child, Emma Grace, has gone missing in the chaos and local deputies are searching the area on foot for signs of the missing toddler."

The camera panned from the reporter's face to the mess behind her.

"Hey!" Marissa scolded the screen. She squinted at the line of deputies moving slowly through the tall grass field. Those guys were supposed to be at the national forest helping Blake. The idea that this timing was too poor to have not been choreographed niggled in her mind.

She swiped her phone off the couch, and dialed Kara. "Tell me you're okay," she demanded at the sound of her sister's voice.

"Mom's making me crazy," Kara scoffed. "I just showed her my driver's license to confirm my age is not ten."

Marissa turned on her knees for another look at the deputy outside. "Are you watching the news?"

"It's all we watch here."

Marissa's knee bobbed and her intuition spiked. "Do you think there's any way the fire could be related to Nash?"

"Which one? The Winchesters' or the Caswells'?"

"What?" Marissa scooted to the edge of her seat and increased the television volume. "What happened to the Caswells?"

"Barn fire."

Sure enough, the scrolling feed along the bottom of Marissa's screen covered a barn fire a mile or two from the propane explosion. If they were Nash's doing, at least the national forest and both fires were across town from the hotel where she was hiding. Blake and West were still close enough to get him.

"So, they just left," Kara finished.

Marissa had missed the rest. "What? Who left?"

"Weren't you listening? I said the Garretts left. The dad and the deputy. The Caswells are good friends of theirs and the wife was hurt. Then, the deputy who stayed behind left ten minutes later to go help look for the Winchesters' toddler."

Marissa's stomach knotted. There was no way this was a coincidence, not when Blake had just taken a team into the national park. "I wish they hadn't left you alone." She couldn't bring herself to be angry with the men who'd left her parents' house. What else could they do when lives were in immediate danger? They had to go.

"Maybe you should come here," Kara said. "Ask your detail to bring you over before he gets called away, too."

Marissa nodded. She should talk to the deputy. Make sure he would take her somewhere else if he was needed at the scene of another crime or tragedy. At the very least, he could check in with Blake and West about what to do. She certainly didn't want someone else to be denied the help they needed because she was monopolizing a deputy.

She hoisted herself upright and stuffed her feet into sneakers, then tossed a jacket over the crook of one arm. "Let me see what he says, and I'll call you back."

"You'd better," Kara said. "I love you."

"Love you." Marissa disconnected and steadied her nerves. If Nash had drawn all the lawmen away so he could come for her, would this deputy be able to handle him on his own? Nash had escaped Blake twice. He was smart enough to have possibly created this elaborate web of confusion for authorities. She peeked at the deputy once more. Maybe it would help if the deputy came inside instead of standing guard at the door like a neon sign announcing her whereabouts.

A worrisome chill filtered through her thoughts once more. Had Nash already come for Blake? Had he lured him into the forest to kill him?

Slowly, her world began to tilt and spin. Nash could be anywhere. He could be out there, hurting the people she loved, and there was nothing she could do about it. Except, come inside and barricade the door. There was still strength in numbers.

She unlocked the dead bolt and turned the knob.

The door snapped against her chest, knocking her into the wall and onto the floor.

Nash marched over the threshold with a sick, smug-looking smile. "Hello, lovely."

Chapter Fifteen

Blake stepped carefully through the fallen leaves of the national park, determined not to lose Nash's trail or destroy evidence with haste. He and West had parted ways with their teams, fanning out to cover more territory when the blood had seemed to disappear completely. Blake's agents had entered the forest two miles away, where the river behind Marissa's house met the national park. If the intel was good, covering the area in every direction was certain to result in Nash's capture.

Maybe Nash had stopped to suture himself when he'd gotten deep enough into the trees. Maybe the injury wasn't as bad as Blake had hoped, and the bleeding had simply stopped with enough continued pressure. Whatever had happened, Blake hadn't seen a drop of blood in twenty minutes despite his sweeping arch path and trained eye.

He'd moved on to looking for evidence another human had recently been this way. Footprints. Broken limbs. Dropped items. Thread caught in the brush. Following Nash through the woods to the river had made one thing abundantly clear. Nash was not a woodsman.

Blake stopped to zip his coat higher and unwrap a

stick of chewing gum. The temperature was dropping, and he needed to think. "Where are you?" he whispered.

A cluster of mismatched branches caught his eye. He squinted through the hazy mist of cold autumn rain. Even in the densest part of the forest, the configuration wouldn't occur naturally. The leaves were from different trees.

Hope rose in Blake's chest, and he scanned the area for West or a deputy, but found neither. He drew his gun and crept toward what appeared to be a hunting blind or makeshift shelter. Hunting was prohibited in the national park, so Blake's money was on the latter, likely crafted by a shifty fugitive whose face had been plastered over the local news.

"Nash Barclay," Blake announced, throwing his voice so that West and his deputies were certain to hear. He secured himself behind the width of an ancient oak, and positioned his weapon against the rough bark, lining up the best shot. "Show yourself."

Crunching leaves and heavy footfalls sounded in the distance.

Blake shored his aim and tried once more to coax the killer out. "This is Federal Agent Blake Garrett. You are under arrest. Come out with your hands where I can see them, then get down on the ground so I'm not tempted to shoot you again."

West appeared several moments later, gun drawn and moving stealthily toward the flimsy structure. A sharp whistle cut through the biting autumn air. West waved a hand overhead. "Empty." West kicked a line of evergreen branches loose, revealing the structure's interior.

Blake moved to his side, disgusted at another miss on the monster. He toed through the mess, previously hidden by the branches. A medical kit and food rations were visible among a pile of ratty blankets and gallon jugs of water.

"Back here," West called from outside the shanty.

Blake stepped over the items, certain to be covered in Nash's fingerprints and DNA.

A fallen deer lay behind the structure, gutted and carefully covered in leaves.

Gutted. Blake turned in a circle, debating whether or not to scream until the mountains fell or just lose his mind silently. "This is the trail of blood we've been following? A deer?" He cursed silently as the steady trickle of occasional raindrops grew into the steady patter of a budding shower.

West didn't bother answering the obvious. Instead, he moved in for a closer look at Nash's possessions, including a pile of papers under a blanket with foodstuffs. "We've got more photos of Marissa and Kara in here." He swore under his breath. "Newspaper clippings about the missing jogger he killed."

Blake fought to stay focused. They needed a new plan. Nash had led them to his little hideout? Why would a fugitive do that? He cast his gaze through the forest around them. None of his team or the other deputies had arrived yet. Were they all too far away to hear his voice like West had, or were they all in trouble? "Where is everyone?"

West cocked a hip and rubbed his forehead. "I had to send my guys to the Caswells'. Dispatch called in a barn fire. Mrs. Caswell's hurt. The barn's a loss. The fire's giving Shadow Point FD a mess of trouble."

"Caswells?" Blake repeated. "Mom and Dad will want to check on them."

West grimaced. "They do. Dad already sent the text. He and Cole headed that way about thirty minutes ago. Mom's meeting them there."

Blake stiffened. "Who's with the Lanes?"

"No one for now. My other man had to help at the Winchesters'. Their propane tank exploded, and their little girl's missing. I had to send everyone there who wasn't at the Caswells."

Blake turned on his heels and began the long run back to his truck. "Nash set those fires."

West fell into step beside him.

Blake called his team. "Get back to the hotel," he instructed. "This was a ploy to get us away from Marissa. What's your position?"

He hung up and dialed the deputy stationed outside her hotel room door. "No answer," he growled. "My men were halfway here, and now they're backtracking to their vehicles before they can get en route to the hotel. Your damn deputy isn't answering."

"We don't know this was Nash," West called.

Blake slowed to glare at his brother. "How long have you been the sheriff?"

"Four years."

"And when was the last time every one of your men were called out at once?"

West ran faster. "Never."

Blake's truck sprayed gravel through the parking lot before West reached his cruiser. He redialed Marissa's loaner phone a half dozen times. "Damn it!" He smacked the wheel. "Call Marissa."

Again, the call went to voice mail.

He crushed the gas pedal underfoot and gripped the steering wheel until his fingers ached from the effort.

His heart banged and flopped as wildly as his windshield wipers cutting through frigid rain.

Ten long minutes later, Blake arrived at the hotel, having broken every traffic law for the past seven miles. He rocked the truck to a stop outside the open hotel room door and jumped from the cab.

The deputy was down. Blake stayed low as he hustled to the fallen man's side and pressed two fingertips against the cold skin of his throat in search of a pulse. A rush of relief coursed through him at the feel of a steady beat beneath his fingertips. The deputy would live, but the group was in trouble. His walkie-talkie was missing, and Blake didn't have to guess where it had gone.

Blake stretched onto his feet and braced his back against the wall outside the partly open hotel room door, then kicked it wide. "FBI!"

He stormed the rooms, clearing them one by one. The place was empty but tossed. Someone had thrown all the lamps and broken one. Marissa hadn't left the room without a fight. Blake could only hope she wasn't out cold now, like the deputy.

Blake called the paramedics, then began a more calculated search of the room. "Where did you take her, Nash?" he whispered.

Her jacket and purse lay on the carpet near the door as if she'd planned to go somewhere. He said a silent prayer that she'd made it out on her own, that maybe she'd taken Nash down with the busted lamp and left him to lick his wounds like she had in the forest.

He dialed her phone again, a bubble of hope rising in his chest. They could trace her phone. Even if she wasn't answering, they could find her as long as the phone stayed on.

A phone rang several feet away. He kicked Marissa's jacket aside and watched the abandoned device pulse and vibrate on the floor, extinguishing the last of his hope.

The deputy moaned, drawing Blake's attention. He dialed West on his way back outside. "Your man's down, but alive. Looks like head trauma. Nash took his walkie-talkie. He'll be listening. Paramedics are on the way for this one."

"Marissa?" West asked, the engine of his cruiser growling in the background.

Blake swallowed a brick of emotion and rubbed the deep ache in his chest. "Gone." Of all the things he wanted to say, that seemed all that mattered. He rolled his eyes skyward, searching a soaring sea of evergreens. *Where are you, Marissa?*

A shrill and distant sound echoed through the trees. Blake's muscles tensed. He turned his head in search of the scream as it came again, louder this time. He moved into the lot and craned his neck for a better look at the towering mountains behind the hotel. Raindrops fell and burst over his forehead and shoulders. "One more time, baby," he whispered. "Where are you?"

"Blake?" West asked.

Blake's gaze darted over the hills. "I heard her scream." *Come on*, he willed her to yell again, to give him some indication of which direction to go. She could be anywhere. He didn't know how long she'd been gone or how much of a head start she had. He needed another scream.

"Do you still hear it?" West asked. "Did she yell again?"

The wail of an ambulance mucked up the silence.

"Damn it! She's somewhere in the hills behind the hotel, but the ambulance is coming. Now, I can't hear anything." He waved an arm to draw the EMTs in his direction. Maybe when the deputy had his wits back, he could tell Blake which way Marissa went.

"Behind the hotel?" West made the sound of a falling missile. "That can't be right. You must be getting the tail end of an echo from somewhere else. Those hills are mostly rock cliffs and—"

"Caves." Blake cut him off. "You're a genius, West." He shoved the phone into his pocket and ran straight for the trees.

Chapter Sixteen

The terrain behind the hotel was unexpectedly steep, slowing Blake within minutes. Thick craggy plants caught on his pant legs and tangled between his feet as he powered through the forest. Tiny mudslides seemed to sprout before his eyes, cutting slick paths between endless rocky snares. There were no trails. No well-trodden paths left by hikers or narrow byways formed by wildlife. There was only one obstacle after another, challenging his ability to stay upright and vigilant in the freezing rain.

He clipped his toe on the exposed roots of another towering tree and ground his teeth in frustration. This was nothing like the places he'd grown up hunting. Only black bears and bobcats would find this hellacious environment worth the trouble, and he had no interest in running into either.

Blake's phone vibrated in his pocket, and he pulled it free. "Garrett." He spoke in a hushed tone, eyes set to scan for any signs of Nash or Marissa.

"This is West. What do you have up there?"

Besides a broken toe and a growing ulcer, Blake didn't have much. "I think I'm going the wrong way. She hasn't called out again. Not since the ambulance finally shut up. I've got nothing." He wiped rain from his eyes and peered up the mountain. The clouds had darkened the day, and thanks to the recent time change, they'd be out of daylight in under two hours.

Where was the path Marissa had taken up here? He scanned the area more closely, begging an overlooked set of footprints to appear. *There should be a path.* A lump filled his throat as the memory of her scream replayed in his mind. What if the last scream he'd heard was the last she'd ever make? What if he'd been too slow? Struggling up the wrong part of the mountain, wasting time while Nash ended her life? Blake forced the thoughts aside and refocused on two things he knew were fact: Marissa's scream had come from this general direction, and he needed a better plan. "You know anything about the caves up here?" he asked West. "Marissa said she did some spelunking up here. She said the caves were naturally camouflaged, but I don't see anything that looks like a cave."

"I've been around the other side of the mountain, skiing, but I don't know anything about the caves."

Blake marched ahead, boots sliding in the soft earth. "If Nash doesn't have her, I think she'll hole up in one of the caves until we get there."

"I'll get a team together." West's words were followed by utter silence.

Blake examined the phone's screen. "I'm almost out of bars."

"…on our way."

He sure as hell hoped so. At the pace he was moving, he'd be lucky to find one cave before nightfall, let alone explore multiple ones in search of his girl.

The sharp peal of a woman's scream tore through

the air. An avalanche of leaves and branches blew into view along the eastern horizon where the sun had already dipped behind the mountain.

Blake moved doggedly eastward, toward the place where the leaves had rushed like a scarlet waterfall. Marissa's scream echoed in his heart and head. Why hadn't she made another sound? Was she unconscious? Was she dead? Did she fall or was she pushed? Rocks pressed against the soles of his boots, forcing gruesome images of Marissa into his mind. If she'd fallen as far as those leaves had tumbled, only to land on a pile of stones...

He forced himself to stop when the mound of earth and leaves came into view. Blake watched the perimeter for movement before inching forward to seek the pile's core.

Empty.

The setting sun cast shades of red and gold through the storm clouds giving the world a suddenly sinister appearance. He was thankful not to believe in omens. A small line in the earth caught his eye and he followed it steadily toward a rocky cliff ahead. The mark was consistent and deliberate, like someone dragging a broken limb or foot. He stepped cautiously over the leaf-covered ground, careful not to lose the trail or step headlong into Nash's trap.

Several feet farther, the mark stopped abruptly before a large oval stone. A thin sheet of moss drew him closer. Marissa had specifically mentioned the moss. *The moss is gorgeous near the caves' mouths.*

Blake moved stealthily toward the rock, senses peeled and muscles tensed to spring. The cave's mouth came into view seconds later, darkened by shadow and nearly invisible in the hillside. A mass of fallen rocks guarded the way.

He turned his back to the hill and eased forward, listening for footfalls, ragged breaths or any other sign that this was a trap. The hairs on the back of his neck stretched to attention as a long willowy shadow moved over the ground.

A feral grunt erupted, and Blake dropped back on instinct. Clay-scented wind rushed over his face. A thick, gnarled limb cut the air with a whoosh, missing his head by an inch.

He pressed off the ground in a flash, lunging for the shadow with his arms wide. His shoulder connected with the soft and narrow center of his attacker.

Marissa squeaked as air pushed from her core, and Blake's arms wound around her on instinct to cushion their collision with a cave wall. A massive branch clattered at their feet.

Joy filled his chest and lightened his heart. She wasn't dead, and Nash didn't have her. He cradled her to him as fat tears fell over her red cheeks. She sobbed into his shirt, and the moment of happiness was quickly replaced with fear. Her skin was like ice, covered in gooseflesh and red from the beating rain. "You're freezing." He stepped back and unzipped his jacket.

She teetered against the wall, balanced precariously on one foot.

"You're hurt." He squatted for a better look at her right leg. Blood had soaked through the material of her pants, down to her sock and into the top of her shoe.

Marissa gripped his shoulders and pulled him upright. "It's fine." Her teeth chattered. "Nothing's broken. My ankle is twisted. I can't put weight on it, and my shin is banged up from the fall. Something cut into my leg when I landed in the pile. My right calf is scratched pretty bad, but I'll live." She looked into his eyes with the saddest smile he'd ever seen. Another attempt to be strong and compartmentalize the horrors, he guessed. "Let's get out of here."

Blake helped her into his wet jacket and hugged her tight, willing his warmth over her. "It's not much, but it's dryer than you."

She zipped the offering up to her neck with trembling fingers. The chattering of her teeth increased, and her lips seemed to grow whiter. "I saw the fires on the news. Nash did that."

"I know." Blake rubbed his palms over her thin arms, hoping to create some heat from friction. "Smart girl."

"No," she sniffled. "No. I opened the door to invite the deputy inside, but Nash was already there. He forced his way inside. I fought back, but I had nowhere to go."

"It's okay. You got away again. That's all that matters." And getting her off this mountain. Blake assessed the cave for bats and bears. He couldn't see either, but he didn't want to stick around and press his luck. Marissa needed medical attention. "Is Nash hurt? Was he with you when you fell?"

"Yes, but I don't know if he was hurt." Marissa curled in on herself, measuring her breaths and breathing puffs of steam into the frigid air. "He's got a hunting jacket on. It's baggy and falls past his hips. I couldn't see any wounds. He might've been a little slower today." The inflection in her voice indicated further that she really wasn't sure. She was traumatized. Frightened and bleeding. "But he's mad," she whispered, "really mad."

"Okay." Time to go. "Help's on the way. We just

need to hold down the fort." A small smile formed on his mouth. "I told West you'd be hiding in a cave." This woman was so much more than he could ask for. He needed to get her home safely so he could tell her exactly how true that was.

She wobbled for balance on her good leg. "I was in the larger cave about fifty yards up but I blew it," Marissa said. "I heard West's voice coming from a radio, and I thought you were right outside. I ran straight into Nash."

Blake hugged her closer. "He took the deputy's radio."

Marissa nodded.

"That's when I fell over the hill," she said. "He got a hold on me, and I did everything I could to shake him loose. He tried to hang on, but I went over the mountain. I figured the fall was the lesser of two evils, so I took my chances with the hill."

"I saw you fall," Blake said. "Where's Nash now?"

"I haven't seen him again."

Blake struggled for the right plan of action. West was scrambling the troops, but thanks to the stolen walkie-talkie, Nash would know that. Unless West had somehow found time to instruct his men otherwise. Nash had had them all in a tailspin today. So, what was his grand plan?

Blake couldn't wait around to find out. He needed to get Marissa off the mountain. Now.

But how? She couldn't walk on a busted ankle, and he couldn't carry her and keep her safe. His reflexes would be staunched, and his attention divided. Not to mention, one swift shove could send them both down the mountain.

Marissa swayed in his arms.

"Hey." He pressed one palm to her icy cheek. "Marissa?"

Her knees buckled, and her head rolled back.

Panic beat through Blake's head. He lowered her to the ground and checked her vitals. What was happening? Another head injury? Something internal? Her tiny puffs of breath were barely visible in the dank cave. The rise and fall of her chest was small and shallow. He checked her pulse and prayed. The tiny thrum barely registered against the pad of his fingers, but it was there.

There was also a new pool of blood by her foot.

Blake rolled the cuff of her pants for a look at the wound on Marissa's leg. The cuts were bad, much worse than she'd let on, and the blood flow hadn't stopped.

He shredded the hem of his shirt and wrapped her calf below the knee to encourage a clot. "Stay with me," he told her.

Where was his team? Where was West?

The snapping of twigs brought his scattered thoughts into focus. He tied the bandage and moved Marissa more deeply into the shadows, before slipping through the cave's mouth once more.

Another snap pulled Blake westward. Senses on alert and gun drawn, he moved silently through the burgeoning storm. Icy drops pelted his bare arms and stung his skin as he followed the sounds upward. Every moment Marissa suffered was another knife to his chest.

He circled the cave, climbing carefully higher for the broadest view of his surroundings. A team of agents came into sight below, roughly halfway between Marissa's cave and the hotel, and all were headed in the wrong direction.

He hurried back to the cave's entrance, using the

limbs of reaching trees to keep himself upright. Once Marissa was safe, he could hunt Nash until they both died of old age if he had to. Right now, he needed to get her to those men. "I see the team," he announced, unsure if she'd woken in his absence. He scooped a baseball-sized stone from the cave floor, ready to throw it at the rescue squad marching away from him.

"No." Marissa's sweet voice warbled in fear.

He dropped the stone on instinct. Marissa was awake and frightened. The sudden realization that they weren't alone sent his right hand to his sidearm, flicking away the safety strap and blinking for focus in the dim cave light.

"Ah, ah, ah," the familiar voice taunted.

"Nash." Blake ground the word through clenched teeth.

The woman he loved moved slowly out of the shadows. A drip of her blood flowed over the hunting knife Nash had pressed securely to her jaw.

Chapter Seventeen

Marissa's heart hammered painfully, her breaths too short and swift to straighten her muddled thoughts. Her body ached and her teeth chattered, but the confusion was worst of all. She'd closed her eyes in comfort, tucked lovingly into Blake's arms, and a moment later, she'd awoken in the rough hands of a serial killer.

He'd yanked her carelessly upright, forcing a scream of pain from her lips. "Hello, darling," he'd snarled. "It's not nice of you to keep running away. You must know how hard I've worked for this reunion of ours. Setting fires. Distracting lawmen. Anything for you."

Marissa struggled to make sense of the change. Blake had been there, hadn't he? If he had, then where was he now? A new flash of panic coursed through her aching limbs. Her gaze dropped to the cave floor in search of him. Had Nash hurt Blake, or worse? "Where's Blake?" she cried. "What did you do to him?"

Nash gripped her harder, forcing her back against his chest like he had twice before. "Stop talking about him!" Unlike their previous encounters, Nash only needed his left arm to still her this time. Marissa was weak and hurt, and he knew it. He'd seen her fall, watched her crash, struggle upright and hobble away. The distance between them had bought her time, but not enough. She'd stopped running, and he'd found her. Again.

"Aren't you going to thank me?" he whispered hotly against her cheek. "For giving your baby sister a ride home last night? It's dangerous to walk alone these days, you know."

"Thank you." The nonsensical words arrived with deep sincerity. Despite everything Nash had done, Marissa was thankful he hadn't hurt Kara. That he'd chosen her instead of her little sister for his wicked game.

Nash petted her soggy hair, then wrapped ice cold fingers over her forehead, smashing her tighter to his chest. "First I had to siphon the gas from her car," he complained, "but in the end everything worked out as I'd planned. Things usually do."

Lightning flashed outside the cave, illuminating her world and glinting brightly off the stainless-steel blade of a four-inch hunting knife in Nash's right hand.

"We're going to be together now." He rested his chin against the top of her head. The scruff of his unshaven face caught in her tangled hair with each wag of his jaw. The stink of cigarettes filled her senses, reminding her of his other attempts to kill her. "You're mine. Not his. However, he and I have a game going, so I'm going to need you to do something for me." He raised the knife to her throat and used it to push wads of leaf-encrusted hair away from her neck and shoulder. He angled his mouth near the bare, frozen skin of her jaw. "Call for him," he whispered. His hot, rancid breath sent a flood of vomit into her mouth.

Marissa recoiled, squirming uselessly for fresh air and freedom. "No."

Nash lifted the silver hunting blade to eye level. He

twisted it inches away from her nose. "Call for him, or I'll cut you." His tongue darted out and licked the length of her jaw.

Her muscles knotted in disgust. She pressed her lips together and jerked her chin away. "No."

"Do it!" he growled. He released her head in favor of knotting calloused fingers in her hair. He shook until she lost her balance. "Don't be stupid." He pushed the tip of his blade into the soft flesh of her jaw. "You don't need to die for him. You die for me."

"Let her go, Nash." Blake's voice echoed through the cave. His hazy silhouette nearly filled the jagged opening. Rain sheeted behind him, forming puddles on the rocky floor.

Marissa's heart sputtered in a tide of mixed emotions. Blake had come to save her, but Nash only planned to let him watch her die.

Nash yanked upright, returning Marissa to her previous position, mashed against his chest by the pressure of one forearm. "There you are. The knight in shining armor. Come to steal my wife."

Blake moved slowly in their direction, eyes pinned on Nash and the knife. "She's not your wife. I've already taken all of those."

Marissa struggled for air as Nash clutched her tighter. She pried uselessly at his arm with weak and frozen fingers. She didn't want to die in a cave.

Blake raised his gun and pointed it over her head, presumably at Nash's. "You don't have to die today," he said in a tone that seemed to disagree, "but if you hurt her again, I promise you won't leave this cave without a body bag."

Nash laughed. He stepped back, opposing Blake's

advance and dragging Marissa with him. His grip loosened slightly, and Marissa sucked air, clinging to his arm now, for balance on her good foot. "Won't it be poetic for Miss Lane and I to die together? One final romantic gesture. A grand finale, if you will." He floated the knife near her throat. "Here's what I have in mind. I kill her, then you kill me, and then later you kill yourself because how could you live with that?" He exaggerated each word of the sick proposal. "It's the perfect show of our commitment to one another, really."

Marissa whimpered. Hopefully Blake had a plan because she had nothing left, and the finale Nash had in mind was the stuff of her nightmares.

Nash danced the knife closer to her face.

Blake's steady cop expression didn't waver. Nash's words had bounced uselessly off him.

"You don't mind?" Nash taunted. "No skin off your nose?" He tapped the tip of Marissa's nose with the blade for emphasis before lowering the blade to beneath her jaw, He slid it carefully along the length of her throat, and she flinched when the steel nicked her collarbone, just above the zipper of her borrowed jacket. "Oops," he said carelessly, no doubt enjoying the madness racing over Blake's face. "Still think you have the upper hand?" Nash asked, gloating over the response he'd driven from Blake. He dragged the blade's tip into the groove between Marissa's breasts, then stopped it above her heart.

Blake swung his hands up, palms forward. "Stop. Don't hurt her." He released his offensive stance and allowed the gun to hang from the crook of one thumb. His Adam's apple bobbed, and his gaze slid from Nash's eyes to Marissa's for the first time. "What do you want, Nash?"

"What do I want?" he parroted in a mocking whine. "Don't you recognize a cry for help when you see one? I want to finish our game."

"What game?" Venom and hatred coated Blake's words.

Nash rubbed his cheek against Marissa's. "Has he told you our story?"

She shook her head quickly. Tears formed in her eyes, and her shoulders crept nearer her ears, attempting to put space between herself and the madman.

"Why don't you tell it?" Nash asked Blake.

"Why don't you let her go and we can finish this alone."

Nash made a show of twisting the knife against her breastbone. "First, put your gun down."

Blake lowered his weapon to the cave floor and released it, then straightened slowly, palms in plain sight. "Your turn. Let her go."

Marissa's eyelids fell shut. Blake had given in to Nash's demand, and nothing good could come from that.

Nash lifted the knife from Marissa's heart, and her head went light with relief. "First," he said, "tell the story. I like our story."

BLAKE'S MIND QUAKED with five years of awful memories. Their story, as Nash called it, was Blake's personal hell. He could recite the lengthy list of leads he'd followed to their inevitable dead ends in detail, but what good would that do? He locked his jaw, refusing to entertain Nash or his whims any longer.

Blake had plenty of old failures engraved on his

heart, but he wouldn't add losing Marissa to them. He kept his chest carefully squared with Nash, concealing the spare firearm nestled in his waistband at the middle of his back. That gun was his last chance at fulfilling his promises. He'd vowed to keep Marissa safe, whatever the cost, and he would proudly fit Nash for a shiny new body bag.

"What are you waiting for?" Nash shifted Marissa in his grip, repositioning the knife at her side, just below her rib cage. "I'll get you started." He cleared his throat. "It's a tragic story of loves lost. Every time I find my perfect mate, she dies. First my mom, then my fiancée, then all the rest."

Blake forced himself not to lunge for the knife. It was a calculated risk he'd gladly take if it was only him who could get hurt. "You stalk innocent women. You attack them. Murder them. Which part of that sounds like love to you?"

"I marry them," Nash barked. "I give them the perfect gown, and the perfect ending. Then, I preserve them in the perfect moment. Forever." He ground his teeth and made a feral sound. "I created a legacy, and you ruined it!" A line of spittle landed on Marissa's soft cheek.

Blake winced. His stomach churned. Marissa was paler than before. She barely moved. The fight was gone from her, and that was scarier than anything Nash could say. Blake needed to speed this up and get her off this mountain. "The first one you took to the chapel was your fiancée."

"That's what I said."

Blake shook his head. The obvious finally clicked into place. "She's the one I didn't recognize." Nash hadn't begun killing immediately after her death, he'd taken her body to the chapel for her preservation in his "perfect moment." When that didn't satisfy him, he did it again, and again. "How did you do it? Steal her from the funeral home?"

"I made a donation to the grave digger's college fund."

Marissa's small mouth bowed down.

Blake inched closer, keeping the distraction going. Enticing Nash to stay focused on him instead of his captive. "Why are you doing this now? You'd stopped for so long."

Nash heaved an angry sigh. "First, you promised to kill me. Then, you chased me for five years. *Five. Years.* I couldn't stop moving. Couldn't settle in or make a place for myself anywhere, then one day you just quit. You moved on. What did you think would happen when you did that? Did you think I'd get a new hobby? Collect trains? Build ships in bottles?"

So, it was Blake's fault that Nash was at it again. He'd had a hand in the jogger's murder and Marissa's continued agony. His heart ached at the helplessness. At his utter inability to go back and change anything. He couldn't make those things right. But he could end this. "If this is between us, then let her go."

Nash shook his head. "No. You gave me time, and I got to know her. We fell in love." He spread his fingers wider across Marissa's ribs, skimming the pad of his thumb over her breast until Blake longed to break the digit off. "I knew the first moment I saw her that she had been worth waiting for," Nash said. "I got a little overzealous and took a subpar substitute last month when this one changed her routine." He made a droll face. "Plus, I was a little rusty, but again, that was your fault. Not mine."

Blake's fingers twitched with the need to pull his hidden weapon and fire. "You're not getting out of this alive, Nash. Backup is on the way. It's only a matter of time."

"I don't expect to get out alive," he said flatly. Nash lowered the knife and used dirty fingers to part his jacket at the zipper, freeing the material from between his body and Marissa's. A blood-soaked patch clung to his side. Nash raised his eyebrows.

"Looks like someone shot you," Blake deadpanned. "You should probably get that looked at."

"It's infected. That's a point for you. I can't go to a hospital. You've put my face and my truck all over the news. More points for you. You got ahead of me this time, but the game's not over." His brows furrowed and his mouth bent down in contempt. "I *am* taking this one before I go. I see how you look at her. I've seen you touch her. I know you want her, but she's mine."

Blake's gaze slid to Marissa. He hadn't had a chance to tell her how he truly felt about her. That he'd fallen in love with her. That he needed her in his life because she made him want to be a better man, a better agent, and generally *more* than he thought was possible without her. If he screwed up again, he'd never get that chance.

Marissa's fierce expression set him off balance. Where he'd expected to find fear and agony, there was resolute determination. She narrowed her eyes on Blake and lifted one finger from Nash's arm, where she clung for balance.

Blake flicked his gaze to the seething killer, and Nash repositioned the blade against her ribs, ready to cut.

"Say goodbye," Nash demanded.

Marissa lifted a second finger from his arm and began to suck and puff air in a wild show of panic.

Nash turned his attention to her as she lifted a third finger from his arm and buckled her knees. He struggled to catch her weight with both hands, but she was limp and falling. A beautiful, brilliant dead weight that had completely broken Nash's concentration.

A deafening roar blasted through the cave as Blake's finger connected with the trigger of his hidden gun. Nash's head thrust back, and the walls of the cave rattled. Nash landed on Marissa in a shower of rock and debris from above.

Blake dove to her side, tossing rubble and throwing Nash's body away from hers. He kicked the hunting blade through the cave's open door, and hoisted Marissa into his arms. "I've got you."

She tied her hands around his neck and pressed her lips to his cheek. "You did it," she whispered before resting her head against his swelling chest. "I knew you would."

A barrage of frantic voices beat against the wind, echoing and reverberating in the hills. The gunshot had surely drawn his team's attention. Blake strode carefully through the cave door and into the rain. His men and a mass of deputies jogged along a plateau several yards up. "Agent Garrett," someone called. "We heard gunfire."

"We need a medic," Blake called back. He adjusted Marissa in his grip. "She needs stitches and an IV. Warm blankets. There's a possible broken ankle, multiple lacerations. Extensive bruising and probably head trauma." Her legs dangled over the crook of his arm.

"Was she shot?" West called, running full speed along the plateau above.

"No." Blake shook his head. "Nash is dead. He's in the cave."

Blake's men continued past him to handle the crime scene.

West stopped at his side. "Marissa." He tipped his goofy sheriff's hat and smiled. "You're hard to get rid of."

She lifted a palm for a weak high five. "Like a bad rash."

"She needs medical attention," Blake complained.

"Here!" Cole raced into view, sliding through wet leaves and mud. The familiar silver stripes of a medical backpack gleamed in the waning sun. "The ski park sent an ATV to the plateau." He pointed in the direction from which he'd come. "There's an ambulance waiting just beyond that slope." He reached for Marissa, but Blake stepped away.

His eyes blurred with powerful unshed emotion. "I've got her."

And he had no intention of letting her go.

Chapter Eighteen

Marissa peeled her heavy lids open and squinted against the bright fluorescent light. The scents of bleach and Band-Aids tickled her nose. "Blake," she croaked, her throat impossibly dry.

"She's awake." Her mother's worried face swam into view.

Her mother. Marissa's frantic heart slowed by a fraction. She was safe. Nash was dead.

Blake had saved her, but where was he now?

"Thank goodness." Marissa's mother stroked her hair and kissed her cheeks. "We were terrified. You lost so much blood."

Marissa forced a smile on her tired face as she struggled for a better look at her surroundings. The simple hospital room was standard white on white with soft green accents and thick light-filtering curtains. The local news played softly on an old tube television anchored in the far corner near the ceiling. Nash's picture was wedged in the bottom corner of the screen. It was a face she longed to never see again, but knew full well he'd visit her dreams every night for years. She lifted a hand to set upon her mother's and discovered an IV line taped to her skin.

Her father levered himself out of an uncomfortable-looking chair and joined Marissa's mother at her bedside. Deep lines raced over her father's forehead. "She's got more color."

"You lost so much blood," her mother repeated.

"And Blake?" Marissa asked. "Did he go home?" Surely, he wouldn't have left without saying goodbye.

"Knock knock." A woman in a white lab coat sashayed through the door with a clipboard and a smile. "Good morning, Miss Lane. I'm glad to see you're awake."

Marissa's parents moved to the foot of her bed, eyes locked on the physician.

"I'm Dr. Starcher," the woman said. "I've been looking after you since your arrival last night."

"Thank you." Marissa choked.

The doctor poured a plastic cup of water from a bedside pitcher and handed it to her. "You had us all a little worried. I'm not sure how much your parents have had time to tell you, but you fractured your ankle. You have a mild concussion and were treated for hypothermia, multiple lacerations, extensive bruising and were given quite a few stitches for the cut on your leg."

Marissa blinked long and slow as the list of ailments and injuries settled in. She sipped the water and waited for her clogged throat to open again.

"You're one tough cookie," the doctor continued, "but I'll bet you've heard that a time or two." She cast a warm smile at Marissa's anxious parents before turning her attention to the pages on her clipboard. "After speaking to the agent and local sheriff about the week you've had, I'd say it's a miracle you're in as good of shape as you are." She tucked the board under one arm and gazed at the machinery near Marissa's bed. "All things considered, I guess dating a federal agent comes in handy at times like these."

"Agent Garrett?" Marissa guessed. Finally, someone who might tell her where he went.

Sadly, she and Blake weren't dating, but after all that they'd been through, she wished they were so much more. He was passionate and kind. Confident and funny. Blake had kept her safe but given her the space to be strong on her own. He trusted her choices, but always had her back. And that kiss. She smiled at the rising memory.

Blake was the one who set her soul on fire.

The doctor tipped her head toward the door. "That man hasn't left since we moved you in here. He set up shop right outside and personally monitored every guest until dawn, my nurses included. I think he may have finally fallen asleep."

Marissa's gaze jumped to the large silhouette suddenly filling her doorway. An exhausted-looking Blake leaned one shoulder against the jamb. Thick purple crescents underlined each sharp blue eye. A mix of relief and regret played over his handsome features.

Her heart swelled with happiness. "No. He doesn't sleep." Marissa patted the bed beside her legs.

The doctor bobbed her head. "There he is. I guess you're right." She gave Marissa a wink. "Everything looks good here. We'll get you some crutches for your ankle and a prescription for the pain. The cast comes off in a few weeks, but I'll write up your release papers this afternoon. How does that sound?"

"Wonderful," her mother said. "She'll be staying with us. I've made up her old room."

Marissa would have that discussion with her mom later. At the moment, she was afraid to take her eyes off of Blake in case he might disappear.

Blake inched into the room and took position against the wall.

"That sounds lovely." The doctor waved her parents through the doorway. "Let's talk a little more about that outside." She pulled the door closed behind them.

Marissa's heart sprinted along in her chest. Blake had stayed. What did that mean?

She patted her bed again.

Regret won the fight over relief on Blake's features. "I shouldn't. I'm big, and that bed is small, and you're covered in bruises. I don't want to hurt you."

Her gaze fell to her bare arms, visible in the ugly hospital gown. A rainbow of shades from brown to gold splayed over her pale skin. "Get over here."

His cheek twitched, and he obeyed, slowly. Blake stopped at her bedside and drifted his gaze over her face, neck and arms. "I'm so sorry."

She grabbed his wrist and tugged him down to her. "Sit with me." She wiggled to make room and winced at the sudden pain in her ankle.

"You fractured your ankle," he said. "And that little scratch you told me about needed thirty-two stitches."

She shook her head. She'd heard all that already. "When do you have to leave?" she asked, needing to get the worst part of her day over with. How long did she have to enjoy the fantasy of a life with Blake in it? How long until she had to say goodbye?

Blake lowered himself onto the edge of her bed with a frown. "What do you mean? I'm not going anywhere."

He flicked his attention to the door. "Unless you want me to."

She grabbed his hand and tugged him closer. "The case is over. You don't live here." She shot him with her best no-nonsense look. "Seems like the government would notice if it lost an agent."

"Right." Blake rubbed a heavy palm against his face. "I'm the guy who always has to leave." He peeked remorse-filled eyes at her. "I'm sorry."

"No." Marissa tugged his hand away from his face. "I meant how long will you be here? You must have to get back. You have a life in Louisville."

The worry lines slowly faded from Blake's brow. He searched her face with eager, curious eyes. "I'd like to have a life here."

Heat ran over Marissa's face, towing a wide smile behind it. "Yeah?"

"Yeah. It'll take some time to get the details in order," he said sheepishly, "and I'd have to commute an hour to work, but I love Shadow Point. I've got roots here, friends, family..." he lifted Marissa's hand to his lips. "Maybe even a girl."

"A woman," she corrected. "Absolutely."

Blake leaned closer, a moan rumbling in his chest. "Please tell me you feel well enough for a kiss."

"I do." Marissa's smiling lips met his, and she found everything she'd hoped for waiting there.

CHRISTMAS EVE ARRIVED with a foot of snow. Her ankle had finally healed, but it would be spring before she dared climb another mountain or anything more dangerous than a flight of stairs.

She poised her camera against one cheek and captured another image of Kara on horseback outside their parents' home. Large picturesque flakes made a magical backdrop to the photo. The shot would make a perfect gift for Kara's upcoming birthday.

"Merry Christmas," a familiar tenor called from behind her, setting her heart to sprint.

Marissa spun in anticipation of the only thing she'd prayed for this Christmas. Her smile fell slightly before she managed to recover. "Hi, West. Mr. Garrett. Merry Christmas." She shook Blake's brother's and father's hands. "What are you doing here?"

Marissa had nearly forgotten how similar West's voice was to Blake's. She'd spent plenty of time with the Garrett family after being released from the hospital, but she hadn't seen any of them since Blake was reassigned to a new case three weeks ago.

Their whirlwind romance had come to a screeching halt, along with Blake's house hunt in Shadow Point and their nightly phone calls. Though, she never fell asleep without receiving at least one email or text message letting her know he loved her. The notes were nice, but she dearly missed Blake's voice and the feel of his arms around her. So much so, that she almost understood how the other women in his past must have felt. It was harder than she'd expected to say goodbye, and she worried about him every day until she got that little note to say he was safe.

Mr. Garrett raised a telltale gift bag meant for wine. "I brought you a little something." He lifted a palm. "Don't open it just yet."

Marissa accepted the gift with a smile. "Thank you. I'll try to contain myself." She laughed and hooked her arm in his. "Let's go inside. Mom's made enough food to feed the town."

West waved them on. "I'll wait for Kara."

Marissa cast a curious look at West as he headed in Kara's direction.

Mr. Garrett patted her arm, drawing her attention back to him. "You know I took your dad shooting the other day. Beat him like a drum."

"Uh-huh." She nodded. "That wasn't how I heard it."

"Because he lies."

Marissa laughed as they rounded the side of her parents' home. A new line of cars filled the driveway. "What on earth?"

"Looks like there was a reason for all the food," Mr. Garrett mused.

"I guess so." They climbed the wide front steps to a porch lined in greenery and twinkle lights. A trio of women from her mother's book club waited at the door with cookie trays. "Hello," Marissa greeted them. "I didn't know you were coming, but I'm so glad you're here."

"We can't stay long," one woman said.

The front door swung open, and her mother motioned everyone inside. "Marissa, really. Why didn't you let them in?"

Marissa raised her palms.

Mr. Garrett dropped her arm and headed for the kitchen. He took her bottle of wine with him.

"Help take coats," her mother instructed.

"Sure." Marissa marveled at the house full of family and friends. Christmas music and warm apple cider wafted through the air. Every bough on the family tree hung low with white lights and handcrafted ornaments.

Proof that two tragically untalented crafters had grown up there. "Why didn't you tell me so many people were coming?"

"Why did you think I started cooking yesterday?" She gave her daughter an encouraging smile. "You've been sad lately. I know you miss him. And who doesn't like a party?"

"I'm not sad," Marissa said.

She didn't have to ask who her mother had meant by *him*. There was only one him who set fire to Marissa's world. "I'm happy. I swear it. But I do miss him."

"I know." Her mom took the coats from Marissa and nudged her toward the guests. "On second thought, I can do this. You watch the door and mingle."

Marissa opened the front door ten times in the next hour, hugging and welcoming cousins and neighbors she hadn't seen in far too long. If she couldn't be with Blake today, this was definitely the next best thing.

The bell rang again, and she spun toward it with the same puff of anticipation that came with each knock. Though Blake had told her he couldn't make it for Christmas, she couldn't resist the hope he'd be the next person through the door.

Cole and his mother stood outside.

"Come in." She kissed their cheeks and pulled them inside. "Merry Christmas."

She couldn't stop herself from stealing a peek beyond them at Cole's empty car. Unfortunately, there were no federal agents waiting to surprise her on Christmas. A twinge of sadness tugged her heart.

She took their coats and offered them a drink, then went to collapse on the couch.

"Marissa?" Kara called from the porch. She knocked

on the window and pressed her nose to the glass, mittens cupped around her face to peer inside.

Marissa laughed. "What are you doing?" She headed for the door shaking her head. Kara had done the same thing all her life, mostly when she was in trouble and needed Marissa's help to sneak past their parents. Considering Kara was now twenty-one and resided under her own roof, Marissa couldn't imagine what Kara was up to. "Goof." She opened the front door and stumbled back one big step.

Blake stood at the threshold, a small blue box in his hand. "Merry Christmas." He looked taller and broader and more handsome than she remembered. Three weeks had been far too long. His brown leather coat and jeans were speckled with melting snow, and the smile on his lips just begged for a kiss.

Kara bobbed into view. "Should we sneak him upstairs like the other boys? For old times' sake?"

Blake shot Kara a look. "I'm going to need a list of those boys' names."

"Me, too," Mr. Lane called from behind Marissa.

She twisted to find the crowded home had fallen silent. All eyes were on her and the man before her. She turned back in a flash, grabbing Blake's hands and towing him out of the cold. "I can't believe you're here."

"It's Christmas. Where else would I be?" Blake watched her silently with an expression she couldn't name.

Kara and West followed him inside and closed the door.

Marissa couldn't fight the smile on her lips. "You said you couldn't make it home for Christmas."

Blake's cheeks darkened. "I can't. Technically. I have to be somewhere first thing in the morning."

"You came all the way back for one night?" Marissa blushed at the thoughts of what they could accomplish in those precious few hours, and she wished more than ever that the nosy crowd would go back to minding its own business instead of hanging on her every word. "You didn't have to do that." It was just too much. "You don't need to zigzag the country to keep me happy." She'd known exactly what she was getting into when she'd fallen in love with Federal Agent Blake Garrett.

"I know. I'm here because I couldn't stay away." He took her left hand in his right. "I had to fly home tonight because I couldn't go another day without asking you something."

A hush rolled through the room as Blake lowered onto his knee and lifted the tiny blue box in Marissa's direction.

She startled. "Yes." Was this a proposal? "Yes."

"Wait." Blake chuckled. "I'm not finished."

"Hurry." Her eyes filled with tears and she covered her mouth to laugh.

The room giggled softly beside her.

Blake pinned her with glossy blue eyes. "I know this probably seems soon, and I haven't been around as much as I'd like to," he began. "I wish I could tell you that second part will change, but I can't. What I can tell you is that I've never loved or admired anyone the way I do you. You astound and impress me every day with your strength, your bravery and your heart for this world and everything in it. I can't promise to be here as much as other husbands, but if you'll let me, I will vow to love, honor and protect you every day of your life. I'll rock climb, parasail, scuba dive, or any other crazy thing you want. As long as I can do it with you."

Marissa's heart caught on that blessed word, *husband*. Blake Garrett wanted her to be his wife. She lowered to her knees and wrapped her arms around the man she loved more than all the things on Earth combined.

"Marry me?" he asked.

She pulled back enough to press her lips to his and was instantly folded into his arms. He deepened the kiss and she doubled his efforts.

Kara cleared her throat obnoxiously. "Excuse me."

A round of giggles pulled Marissa from another perfect kiss. The only sort Blake seemed to deliver.

He pressed his forehead to hers, creating a private space for them.

"We're waiting for an answer," someone called. "We came for the answer."

Marissa's jaw dropped, and the massive impromptu party suddenly made much more sense. "You planned this?"

"Yeah." Blake's forehead rocked against hers. "How'd I do?"

"Amazing," she whispered.

"Marry me?" he asked again, snaking his arms tighter around her waist and dragging her impossibly closer. "Don't make me beg in front of all these people."

"Yes." She nodded and smiled, then moved her mouth to his ear. "I will never resent you for your absence in my days or your dedication to this job. I love that you want to save the world, and I can't wait to explore it at your side."

"Yes?" Blake asked.

"Yes," she repeated. "Yes, to all of it. Except scuba diving. No more of that. Ever."

Somewhere nearby, a champagne cork popped, and Blake's dad cheered.

The crowd broke into applause as Blake lifted a fist in victory and kissed her once more. Exactly as he would for as long as they both should live.

* * * * *

LET'S TALK
Romance

For exclusive extracts, competitions
and special offers, find us online:

facebook.com/millsandboon

@millsandboonuk

@millsandboon

Or get in touch on 0844 844 1351*

For all the latest titles coming soon, visit
millsandboon.co.uk/nextmonth